My family advised me that the more you must explain an idea, the less masterfully it was orchestrated. Following this wisdom, I have attempted to introduce this text in only 666 words.

After a journey of iterations, I decided to call this novel '*Within a Diminishing Caricature*'. Why? Besides James Joyce's *Ulysses* (and Homer's *The Odyssey*), this novel was modeled mostly after Joyce's *A Portrait of the Artist as a Young Man* and Oscar Wilde's *The Picture of Dorian Gray*. Both titles begin with an art-form and end with a subject. This text lacks a set subject, and thus the protagonist (He, Him, and His) should be considered representational. More importantly, the art is at the <u>end</u> of the title. This is the first signal of devolution in the text. The etymologies of these four words is worth noting:

Within – used here as a direction – comes from the Old English word *wiðinnan*, which translates to "against the inside."

A – used here as an indefinite article – is a 14th century variation from the Old English '*an*', which indicates singularity.

Diminishing – used here as a descriptive – comes from the fusion of two obsolete verbs, *minish* "lessen" and *diminue* "speak disparagingly".

Caricature – used here as the art form – comes from the Italian word *caricature*, which translates to 'an overloading' from the word *caricare*, which itself is rooted in the Vulgar Latin word *carricare*, which means 'to load a car'.

Etymologically, this novel is: 'Against the insides of a lone, lessening overload' (though let us not forget that car!). This describes the novel more holistically than *Within a Diminishing Caricature*, but doesn't quite roll off the tongue. Speaking of which, the words 'Within a Diminishing' are assonant – producing euphonious vowel repetitions. Then that dissonant word 'Caricature' sounds, and you find yourself suddenly with a mouth full of rocks. It is as if the caricature does not belong…

…I began this book when components of myself were redefined to the extent in which I wondered – with a growing sense of panic – who I was and what I was supposed to be like. I had just graduated college, was published through a new internship as a journalist, gained self-collapsing knowledge of the biological parents who abandoned me, was 5,640 miles from my old friends and my ex-girlfriend who had dumped me, spoke and ate and traveled differently, breathed different air, and so on. When I returned to New York, this scission manifested into a growing desperation, depression, and distancing from everyone. Though I never went through attempting suicide, these were times where I couldn't help notice the opportunities all around me... the third rail gleaming, watching earth from towering altitudes, speeding vehicles, pills everywhere...

And then I wrote the words 'how much is a life's worth' on the first page of F. Scott Fitzgerald's psychological romance, *Tender is the Night*...

Thus, this novel began as a solitary cry for help, and has ended as an intricate but solvable puzzle of meanings. In this way, it is much like life itself.

This is ultimately <u>not</u> an autobiography (or even a biography, for that matter). This is a NECROGRAPHY (story of one's death), an UNCOMING OF AGE STORY (story of one's fragmentation), and a PSYCHO-SOCIAL ADVENTURE BOOK through the ghosts of depression. To understand this book best, you must be either 1.) A psychoanalyst evaluating the events that pass by Him and how they produce significant associations and meanings, 2.) A detective investigating sixty-five scenes to uncover the piling clues that clarify why a suicide occurred, OR 3.) Both.

I hope you enjoy reading the 93,893 words of this story (11,088 of which are unique), the hundreds of literary allusions, the dozens of psychological and sociological theories, the multitude of writing styles (text messages, 8-word streams-of-consciousness, stage-play, screen-play, poetic forms, psychiatric-catechism hybrid, epistolary, etcetera), the 11,111-word mind of the suicide note, the body of the 65 vignettes, and the 7,777-word soul of the wind.

I wish for my last words to be thank you.

The mind is like an iceberg, it floats with one-seventh of its bulk above water.
— **Sigmund S. Freud**

As social beings we live with our eyes upon our reflection, but have no assurance of the tranquility of the waters in which we see it.
— **Charles H. Cooley**

The meeting of two personalities is like the contact of two chemical substances: if there is any reaction, both are transformed.
— **Carl G. Jung**

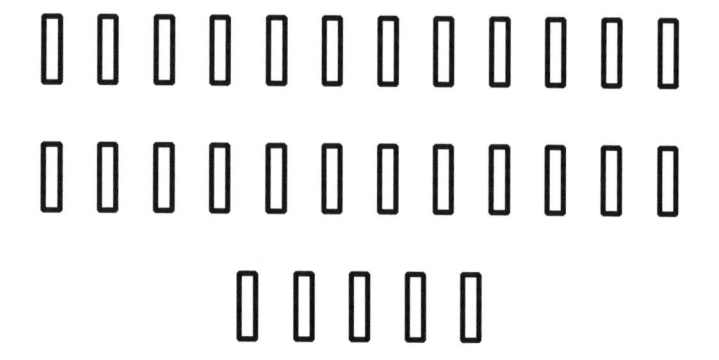

WITHIN A DIMINISHING CARICATURE

PROLOGUE

July 27th 2011 11:11 AM
I wish I had something more than words to make you understand all of this, but...
Dear father, mother, brother, Dustin, Art, Mandy, Selene, Danika, Dr. Heidelberg, and anyone else whose eyes pass over this note,
Last week - Tuesday, July 19th, 2011 - I sat on a street corner in Manhattan and tried to answer a seemingly simple question: Why should I not end my life? I found an avenue near Penn Station that was peopled enough to render me anonymous, sat down on the curb, slowed time down with Chet Baker's trumpeting in my headphones, and watched the passing figures in hopes to discover a reason to continue living.
The 800 micrograms of Lysergic Acid Diethylamide in my system morphed the human carousel around me each second. One man looked just like me, until he smiled. One woman's breasts inflated to the size of the whole city block, and I grew alarmed that I would be forced to submit to their allure. Then she passed, and again my little corner of the world glowed with welcoming daylight.
Needless to say, there were answers coruscating in every crevice of every transmuting face that strolled by, but none were answers to my question. So I changed it. As the sun blazed a burning parabola across the darkening horizon, I altered the question 65 times, concluding my journey when I came across two questions simultaneously that I could at least begin to answer. Two, impersonal queries: How much is a life's worth? What is the true cost of a human's life?
Both now and then, these questions plunge me into a lucid reverie where I imagine two, largely juxtaposed concepts:
First, my mind imagines a dim hospital room at 3 AM where a lone individual sits, unable to sleep. He is always 20 - my age - but a fatal disease has aged him gravely. He sits on his cold hospital bed with extreme discomfort;

but his head, arms, and fingers are too heavy to lift; and he is far too weak to whisper for a nurse. His reluctant visitors have left him hours ago, and, as usual, their words of false-confidence die the moment they are uttered. Feigning belief in their words is a tiring charade that weighs him down with humiliation, but he does not dare express the moribund reality of his situation. Despite his masking optimism, every word he struggles to breathe is still misconstrued by them as unappreciative, and he hasn't the energy to justify his betraying thoughts to them. Now, he is alone in the darkness, breathing in with tremendous difficulty and breathing out with tremendous difficulty. His heart monitor slows down, as if the silence of death is gradually conquering the sounds of life. A sinking feeling begins to envelop him as he feels the delicacy of the thread of life for the first time, and feels everything from fear to nostalgia to loneliness as he notices the thread irrevocably slipping away.

   The second image that follows greatly contrasts the first. It is an elderly man of a concluding age, sitting on an old wooden rocking chair on a near-desolate beach. Next to him, holding his hand and rocking at a similar pace is an old lady, whom I presume to be his wife. In many ways she resembles him, and in many ways he resembles the beach. His skin is slightly tan and wrinkled to the extent in which he appears almost to be made of sediments. His eyes are both light blue like the sky and dark blue like the ocean. The waves rock in and out of the beach, leaving tan shapes across the white sand which fade slightly until a new wave streams over. This moment I imagine is rather a moment I feel: As I envision him watching the water, he contemplates how the current of the water parallels him. He sees the waves and tide and knows they are just like his emotions, and his wife's emotions, and the emotions of all humanity. He delves far deeper into the metaphor than I can explore, but I know I am experiencing a piece of his epiphany each time. Most importantly, I know that he looks back over the course of his concluding life with complete satisfaction over the questions he has asked and the answers he has been given.

Eight days ago I couldn't figure out why it was these two images that came to mind, but I suspected that somewhere in between them I have found exactly how much a life is worth, exactly the cost of a human's life. Now, as I write this letter, I realize that this life through which we all struggle is all about harmony, about whom we are around and how we fit in. We are an amalgamation of the others in our lives. Whether we go against or go along with their words and thoughts and behaviors, we are still reacting to everyone else; and it is through the reflections of these others where we begin to understand who we truly are.

We are then each a mosaic of responses to our world. We are each a collection of scattered mirrors. We simply are our lovers, we are our family, and we are our friends. And perhaps we most resemble our friends, for we cannot choose our family, we have only partial say in whom we love (for lust and temptation challenge 'free will'), but friends... Yes, despite the inherited genetics from our family and the sexual intimacy of our lovers, friends are the most authentic mirrors we possess. Once upon a time, I had two close...

January 24th 2010

"If it weren't for you, I'd probably hate being me," He said to Selene Acerbi as she rested her head on His lap.

They sat together on the snow-frosted field of His backyard, with their legs pointing to the figure-8-pool. A wintry sun illuminated the salmon-brick-color of His family's two-story house, which stood atop the hill in the southeast corner of Old Rookvale. Chet Baker's acoustic *Blue Room* was playing on the outdoor speakers, beginning with, *'We will thrive on – keep alive on – nothing but kisses…'*

Selene was scanning back and forth down a page from a poetry book by Walt Whitman, but at the sound of His statement she moved the book away, leaned backwards and turned upwards to face Him. Her eyes – a cerulean deepened by the paleness of her softly angular face, the darkness of her wavy hair, and the liquid black frame of her long eyelashes – stared at Him, large and curious.

"Why do you say that?" she whispered.

He turned His head to the speakers jutting out from the house as Chet Baker continued chantings. He leaned His head back. His eyes - bright green with yellow streaks - illuminated in the winter sun. He looked down at her and met her concerned face. He shrugged, smiling. She rolled her eyes and turned back to her book.

Chet Baker's voice faded. He turned towards His house and saw the reflection of Himself and Selene in the sliding glass doors that divided the backyard from the TV room. He turned away from her mirror image and looked down to the brunette waves at the back of her head. He reached around towards her face, clasped her bottom lip with His fingers, tugged gently and stopped. He tugged, stopped, tugged again a bit rougher and held the bottom lip down, and felt the muscles of her lips smile, and then He smiled too. He let go and her lips made a popping noise as they snapped together.

He scanned around the backyard, stopping only to focus on several blades of grass sticking out from the snow. He plucked out a single blade, and chewed it scientifically.

"Baby," He spoke.

"Yes?"

"Say you love me."

A smile flickered across her lips.

"I love you."

He released the frost-tipped blade and watched it twirl downwards. A moment passed as He stared at the blade among snow-tipped blades.

A wind passed through the trees – the green sound of its hush rose over the choirs of birds and murmuring snow-blowers on His block – and turned the page of Selene's book. She smiled and her dark eyelashes lifted as her eyes continued forward to the top of the next page, as if the page needed to be turned anyway.

"Baaaby," He repeated in the manner of a child.

"What?"

"Say you hate me."

She turned up from His lap.

"Why?"

"Just do it," He said, holding another blade of grass at shoulder height.

"I don't though. I don't think I could ever hate you."

She turned back to her book, and after a moment underlined the words, *'through you I drain the pent-up rivers of myself'*.

An asphalt cloud passed over the sun, and the backyard dimmed. A car roared by in the distance.

"Just say the words," He beckoned, shivering slightly. "You don't *have* to mean them."

"Fine," she huffed. "I hate you."

He dropped the second blade, watched it twirl, and then stared blankly as it landed on the snow.

"Hmm."

Selene closed the book with a snap and nuzzled the side of her face onto His thighs.

"Finished already?"

"Taking a break," she responded. "Exhausting stuff."

Another breeze passed by, making music of the trees.

"But," He began, "it's going to be heavy tomorrow or whenever you read it next."

"I know but it's cumulatively exhausting. I require a cognitive exhalation." She exhaled, fluttering the dark curls of His hair with a puff of condensation.

"Let's say you didn't stop, and continued," He spoke, tracing her cream-colored cheek with His hand. "What would happen?"

"I'd lose focus no matter what. My mind is decidedly off."

He squinted towards the snow-topped branches as the cloud drifted away from the sun, and the scene before Him was bright again. Another gust breeze by, dusting sun-glimmering snow off the branches in a powdery iridescence.

"Your mind can relax too, if you ever permit it to."

"Mmmhmmm." He nodded. "Do you wanna go inside?"

"No. It's a warm, *warm* winter day."
"It *is* warm. I'm fine if you're fine."
"You're *always fine*, bello," she mumbled as her eyes opened.

She reached for her book and turned to the last page, which, like the last page of many other books, was blank.

"You wanna write?" She held the empty page to His face.

He took the book, and received the pen from her. Her eyes rested first on His big nose, big jaw, big butt-chin, and dark messy hair. She closed her eyes with a satisfied yawn.

"I don't know what to write," He contemplated aloud.

"Write about the wind."
"The wind?"
"Yeah." Selene yawned again. "A wind with no pride. There's too much of your ego in your writing."

"Oh." A frown hung across His lips.

"No 'me', no 'I', and nothing that George Herbert Mead would call the 'self'. No 'willed reactions', no associations, no beliefs. I'd like to read a story where it is that wind that watches."

"I'll call it, at least for now, Along a Passing Wind."
She giggled somnolently.

"'Passing wind'… means… farting… you… English-maj…uu…r…"

Her breathing became deep and automatic, and her muscles relaxed against Him as she fell into slumber. He began writing:

ALONG A WANDERING WIND

…WSHHH sounds from somewhere or perhaps from nowhere, as a wind begins to drift across the coast of Queens, swirling about the many moving people, noticing and understanding but not judging – a bit more intricate than your average gust (for, contrary to general belief, winds vary much in their intricacy). It was merely spectating. In fact,

that's what this wind is in its most approximate definition: A specter. It brushes across Steinway, Queens on a Wednesday morning, emerging from a polychromatic twilight and charging Long Island-bound towards the eastern sunrise. Zigzagging between cubic houses in a way only winds can, it notices beyond its own omnipresent gust the sounds of conversations, and slows down. It slows and slows and slows, until it is an andante pace. It follows a tall boy in a multicolored windbreaker with messy dark hair, and a smaller girl with chestnut hair and a plaid coat. They turn suddenly, as if tapped on their shoulders. His eyes are contemplative and mildly searching as he scans the scene behind them. Her eyes are blue and precious, and contemplative in a far deeper sense. They turn back around in a swing, not unwrapping their fingers from each other, and continue their early morning walk. She laughs, saying out loud: "Chemistry!"

"The essential study of change within the elements," the boy replies quickly.

"No!" she laughs again and squeezes the boy's hand. He squeezes back. "Define chemistry in its romantic context."

The wind plunges down into the boy's thoughts as he shuffles through his memories. Among the rippling ocean of interconnected images – scenes glistening and overlapping like sun-glinting waves – one picture radiates into focus: A ruby-crested wristwatch glistening as her hand wrapped around his for the first time; an amber candle flame casting dancing shadows of their fingers across the scarlet-linen dinner table on their first real date. The memory pulses and echoes a hint of that night's harmony into the present.

"How fast time goes when you're with someone," he responds finally. "That's what chemistry is."

"Hmmm," she hums between a cool smile. The wind gazes into the waves of her mind, and is pleased to find that she is recalling the same evening and same moment, but her memory focuses specifically on the way his eyes watched her with a vacuuming adoration as she cupped his hand.

An unusual aura catches the wind's attention. A peculiar resonation pulses from two figures in an apartment several buildings down the avenue.

The wind races eastward, climbs up along the pale-pink chipped-brick walls of a dilapidated apartment, and seeps through an open window on the west-facing wall. A young man holds the hand of an older woman in a small, disheveled room. Their blood is comprised of similar material, but hers circulates poorly. The wind senses that something is keeping her heart from pulsing properly. The man looking down at her has sincere brown eyes, a mane of reddish-brown hair, and altogether resembles a concerned hawk. His mind is neatly divided between physical chemistry and finance, his wife and his dying mother, his job and his education, the country he is from and the country he is now in. His mind fades into memories of Istanbul only a few years ago, when life was difficult but far, far less complex. He refocuses, and becomes re-aware of the open organic chemistry, biology and pharmaceutical therapy textbooks cluttering the narrow apartment.

The woman looks up at her son through a teary lens. The wind recognizes a trace of the old humility she felt when he first began injecting the soft cleavage of her breasts with morphine. Now, the wind knows, she is not only used to these injections, but she has found a vast comfort whenever she looks up at her son's aquiline face and focuses on his thoughtful eyes. It is here where she feels a new type of humility: The humility that one feels when someone else's love embraces them more than their own feeling of worth.

She inhales. She exhales. She does not inhale again.

Floating against a sudden flood of grave thoughts, he swears to himself that he has prolonged her life, that he has improved the quality of her life...

The wind slips beneath the door, fluttering the cinnabar hair strands on both of their heads, and spirals throughout the dusty, maroon hallway and out through a corridor window, continuing eastwards as always...

PART I – GRACE
July 26th 2008 – July 27th 2009

...friends: Dustin Enterline and Artyom Lavian.

Let's start with you, Dusty. You're a lazy, xenophobic hypocrite with immeasurable charm that almost always redeems you. Don't think that you win people over with your effusive eyes, or with your half-German side (they are NOT the master race you misguided psychopath, stop rejecting your mother's Italian genetics), or with the breathtaking genius you claim to possess. You are sharp, but without any discipline or determination, and thus are a needle in zero gravity, Dustin – incapable of penetrating anything. Anything, except your on-and-off waste of time girlfriend. Sara has absolutely nothing to offer you besides her curvatures and her ability to satisfy only the symptoms of your maladies, which, as I contemplate now, is probably why you've so eagerly engraved her into your life. Why do we so eagerly destroy ourselves, Dustin? You've asked me the question months ago when I ached over Selene and you cried over Sara. Ask yourself instead why YOU lie to yourself so often. Your dishonesty has become so compulsive that it has developed a truthful grace. I suspect you might translate that into a compliment. You're entitled and selfish beyond any metaphor that I can possibly conjure. Beneath your amalgamations of veils and masks, I see that you are just a trembling child gripping an oversized shield ornamented with millions of prevaricating stratagems to not be truthfully exposed. Sometimes when I looked at you, when I was not entirely apathetic to your increasingly baneful existence in my life, I pictured tears slipping down the backs of your eyes into the pools of consciousness where you don't dare swim. I forgive you for all your lies as long as you can honestly forgive yourself. I know that many of your flaws result from losing your father when you were only three years old. But goddamned it, think of his problems and how you've needlessly inherited them. Think of heroin, Dustin. Think of cocaine. Think of what you could be if you tried for once. Tried for something other than a rush like cocaine or Sara's forgiveness. A part of me genuinely wishes that you weren't in jail right now, though another part of me recognizes that extremes only speak faint whispers to you.

Artyom Lavian, my hardest-working and most grounded friend. I believe that your entirety of existence can be both defined and limited to the word 'goodness'. You are good-looking and you have a good amount of responsibility, patience, intelligence, and determination. You have good muscles, good brown eyes, a good heart, and a good amount of good friends. In life – of which you will certainly live a good amount – you will have a good amount of good times. To others, though, you are often considered as plain. Rest assured that this is only your surface layer. Because you tiptoe across the avenues of life with caution, safeness, and with no room for the logic-less stirring of furious passions, you appear standard, predictable, imitable, formulaic and simple to those who pass by you in the cameos of your life. I know that you are two years older than I, and thus perhaps two years wiser, but I am certain that you haven't yet comprehended that the bad problem with being purely good is the fact that one earns the greatness of inimitability from experiencing mistakes. Mistakes require risks, Art, and risks require a semblance of recklessness. Be reckless for once. Make mistakes. Fuck someone whom you do not love. Treat an enemy endearingly out of the blue. Take LSD and talk to someone whose judgments you fear. Be dangerous. Shake off yourself and see what new side of you appears. Without a semblance of recklessness you won't ever stir a girl's fear of loss enough for her to pulse with rapacious love for you – the particular love in which I know you wish to be held. You wish to be the first bright thought in a girl's head when she wakes up. You wish for a girl to lust for you. But you are too safe, too good, and too nice. Your choice of a Physician's Assistant in cardiology only makes too much sense in the context of your life that we share. It's a safe, responsible, good job with good pay. I love you, and am mordantly repentant for pushing you so far away. You know I've broken all the things in my life that made me a good boy. It's only obvious that I would shatter my most reliable model of decency. Like Dustin, your innate qualities have been infinitely altered by your father's passing, though your father's demise was from heart disease when you were five years old. Unlike Dustin, you have responded to your paternal loss by developing an array of strengths that would make any father tearfully proud. You've certainly earned far more respect from my father than I ever could. If I were more jealous than envious, I might have even mislabeled you a usurper. Please be aware of your foibles as you continue your ambulation as a straight line moving upwards, slowly, gently, patiently, timidly, and sagaciously in life.

My closest friends... my closest mirrors. Art, you view Dustin as an arrogant mess; Dustin, you view Art as an agonizing drone.

There is also, of course, Oliver Scoffinan, whose tralfamadorian cartoonishness introduced me to the liquid intensity of hallucinogens and unearthed my sudden addiction to writing; Alexander Teisėjakaitis, whose furious logic attempted to slap sense into me during my self-destructive duet with Danika; and Hunter Douglas Quillan Wilcox-Himmler II, whose mechanisms have taught me lessons far too late.

Why analyze any of you in this farewell note? It is both my goodbye to you all, a prerequisite to defining myself before I vanish, and perhaps the beginning of the justification of why I am doing what I am doing in the first place. But who is to say I can make such criticisms about you all? Given my moribund state and less-than-ideal plight, do I really have an authority to psychoanalyze anyone?

Yes. I am not particularly wise, nor am I logical. But I am intelligent. (Reader, whoever you end up being, don't let pedants fool you with their prolix pontifications of intelligence. Forget Gardner, Spearman, Thurstone, and Sternberg's definitions; they miss the point in entirety. They all divide intelligence by needless classifications, but fail to simply and accurately identify what this seemingly slippery word means. Intelligence is merely the quality and quantity of the questions one asks, and the quality and quantity of answers one receives. Turning a page of a novel is a series of questions: What is here? Why this sentence? How does this paragraph develop the protagonist?).

My greatest intelligence was not the art of writing I fruitlessly pursued, but rather the art of people. Howard Gardner's 'Interpersonal Intelligence': Grasping the orbits of human behaviors, and knowing what to say to gravitate an individual in desired motions. My studies in psychology, the hallucinogens, the writing – it was all to understand why we do the strange things we do, to better read people, and yes, even to manipulate.

I became a manipulator the moment that I knew my mother was sick...

I wasn't aware of how actively I manipulated behaviors until a conversation with Hunter. And now a revelation unfolds before me as I write this... that same conversation lead me to meeting Mandy Rusche. And Mandy Rusche was how I met Danika Rusche... Oh there's clearly meaning somewhere in here...

But how did Hunter perceive this manipulating quality in me? Because of sex. Lots of sex.

It's fascinating when such a diminutive word contains such power. Is sex not the cause of so much pleasure, pain, guilt, jealousy, love, and heartbreak? Right, Freud? Yes! And that Fever-Fuck 'ORGASM' word even sounds like a pleasurable spasm! The eutony! The sheer mellifluousness! And yes! That moment after an orgasm is surreal, isn't it? It is as if, for a brief moment, you are suspended in honey-like space and time, and you are convinced that all of the heavy stress of your day was just a dream, and this new somnambular happiness was the waking reality all along. Yes – oh it really is beautiful.

The first time I was exposed to sex was when I was only fourteen. It was the night prior to New Year's Eve in 2004 entering into 2005. Art and his family invited me to this annual, three-day New Year's festival that took place in a hotel in Philadelphia. There were 200 or so people there, primarily Armenians. My father was in Los Angeles, my brother was in Boston and my mother was home, I believe.

An eighteen-year-old Persian-Armenian brunette named May – upon whom I had a heart-wrenching crush – was with me in an emergency staircase. I remember that she wanted to see my penis because she had the idea that it was large, based on us dancing the evening prior.

She kissed me in that stairwell, and I was completely aroused. 'Okay, I'm ready to see it now!' was all she said, so I dropped my puppy-print pajamas. She gazed down, and after a moment asked, 'Why do you have to be fourteen?' to which I replied, 'I'm not that large!' with rogue suaveness. She started playing with my erect penis, and then, with some difficulty, tucked it back into my pajamas.

She took my hand and we left the stairwell. We walked across the carpeted corridor of the eighth floor. It was after 3 AM on the morning of December 31st, 2004, so I assume most of the guests were resting up for the New Year's Eve celebrations. I felt myself blush as I passed by a security guard with a rock-hard erection jutting two-and-a-half Doberman's forward. She paid him no mind as she led me throughout the corridor until finally we reached room 8008.

She opened the door, and I immediately heard feminine conversations hush, followed by a stir of susurrus gossiping. She brought me to the bedroom where there were two queen beds side-by-side. The bed to my left had four girls; the one to the right had two. The girl all the way on the right had long black hair that curled down to her pink sweat pants, and I found her to be immediately attractive but not as beautiful as May, and I didn't know anything about her so she was only seductive mysteries.

'Well' the girl in the pink rasped, 'He definitely is cute.' And then May urged me to 'show them it.' I turned to her and she nodded at my pajamas. I shrugged and pulled them down. What happened afterwards was a bit confusing as it also included my first few vodka shots, but I know I didn't have sexual intercourse. I remember playing with it for them, feeling like the cynosure of seduction. I also remember them all showing me their breasts, and asking me whose were the best. I picked May, retaining some sense of inebriated fidelity. May said to exclude her in the decision, so I picked the girl in pink. Her breasts weren't the best out of them, but her breathy voice was becoming increasingly sexual-sounding and I couldn't help my pulsing finger from pointing to her. The night ended with me asleep on the carpet beside the right bed with a tower of pillows around me, and two c-cup bras on my face. My balls ached until the late afternoon.

It's funny that not even Art knows this story. I began telling my brother once, but he grew alarmed when I mentioned the age disparity, so I truncated the story to a PG-13 punch line.

I lost my actual virginity three years later at the age of 17 to a licentious girl by the name of Mandy Rusche. I've had three girlfriends – Mandy, Selene, and Danika (to whom I've been monogamously faithful) – for a collective year and a half. I've slept with exactly 72 women in the three years since losing my virginity.

Is 72 a lot for three years? Probably. But, I am certain that my insatiable desire for sex is one of the several reasons I have sunken into this mess. One winter night in Manhattan, after visiting my mom in the hospital, I stepped outside into the niveous air, shivering and being wracked with conflicting emotions. I crossed the snow-filled avenue and was about to head towards the subway, when I noticed something from the second story window. Two, pulchritudinous brown-eyed girls were watching me, and their eyes fixated on me with that smoldering look that suggests unhindered misbehavior. Promiscuity hurricaned from the looks they gave me, and I was in the blessed center. It's the type of look that feels like the true beginning of sex: Before the satiated collapse, before the trembling orgasm, before the warm-rushed movements, before the clothes slide off the bodies with that flesh-feeling-fabric sound, before that luscious moment when both parties make their hints direct, before the scattered and searching flirtations across a byzantine world, and before walking over. There's that look. And I saw it, powerfully from both of them... and I passed by the building, and didn't say anything, and I didn't learn what their bodies felt like under their clothes, and didn't enjoy the pleasure of sex with them, and I went home feeling an emptiness akin to heartbreak and a loneliness so unparalleled that I briefly forgot about my mother. And it WAS NOT regret that agonized me in such a febrile delirium. It was closer to mourning than regret, and I am still haunted by their blazing eyes today.

Why? Perhaps, I'm simply fucked up and addicted to philandering. Or perhaps the painstaking truth is that I assess half my worth in the amount of female glances I receive, and – even worse – assess the remaining half in the amount of females whom receive me.

I was at a café nine days ago, and two young women and a single man were sitting at a table diagonally across the room. I was penning some flaccid poem near the corner window. One woman was talkative, wearing all black and what I judged to be too much eyeliner. The woman and man were rambling about their respective boyfriends and analyzing them via zodiacs, astrology, chakras and other apophenic phenomena. The other girl seemed unfit for the trite dialogue. She had black wavy hair that spilled down her shoulders, and she sat near-silently, daydreaming, and twirling the green straw of her iced tea. She wore jade-colored capris and a gray-tank-top with a faded white heart. For some reason, she sparked the lucidity of my imagination. Immediately after engaging in apodyopsis, I began to wonder what I initially liked about this stranger. What spurred this magnetism? What caused this chemical reaction in me with symptoms like shallow breathing, anxiety, racing thoughts, inability to focus, a heat rush, goosebumps, and a heightened awareness of the blood flowing throughout my body? What was it? Was it the faint musculature of her intermittently flexing calf-muscles as she swayed her crossed legs? Was it the idle counter-clock-wise rotation of her right-sandaled foot? Was it the preceding red-flush swirling in her cheeks prior to the smiling of her thick pink-padded lips? Or was it the punctilious way she bit her straw the moment I first laid eyes upon her? What moments and associations in my life gave any of these qualities meaning? Was the attraction entirely physical, or are these little details uncovering something greater about her and that rawer abstraction is what I am actually drawn to? Am I seeing traces of her in these little physical manifestations, and somewhere my mind can follow these traces back to that exquisite pulsing light of her true self? Are these all semblances of a 'natural self' quaquaversally translated into endless visible details – suggesting who she really is.

Who she really is. She is only what I see. Who am I? What am I even seeing? I am seeing only what I am seeing, and never what she sees.

I think the LSD has kicked in. I think I'm plunging into the wrong waters. I can't tell if my hands are sweating or if this pen is melting. No. Focus. My mind has never been so clear. I am making the right decision.

Where was I? Sex. Out of all...

July 26th 2008
...good time it was... Hunter is desiring something...

"I want to be able to get girls," Hunter Douglas Quillan Wilcox-Himmler II spoke, his 17-year-old ocean-blue eyes reflecting the early morning sunshine pouring in through The Rising Star Café and Bookseller window. Hunter's watch had just struck 8:00.

A saturating haze gleamed within the quaint café situated in the near center of Old Rookvale, Long Island. His high school graduation was two weeks ago, and many of His classmates were meandering around the town with early-summertime laziness in their strides. The murmurs of several conversations in the warmly-lit coffee shop rose and fell as He waited, staring at Hunter.

"Okay?" He shrugged, swaying to the conclusion of Chet Baker's instrumental *Blues for a Reason*. "Then have a good time, Hunter. Play. Just don't make it sound like you're collecting them. 'Get girls' sounds a bit ridiculous."

"You're telling me you don't have a technique for picking up girls? You overanalyze everything and you've hooked up with half my grade. Don't lie to me. I thought we were friends."

"I don't know what you want me to say."

"Tell me, oh muse, of your ingenious knowledge."

"I just did. Have a good time. I promise that's all you need to do. And pay attention as you're having a good time."

"Give me one of your psychological philosophies."

The sound of a teenage girl's laughter rose throughout the oak-colored room. He looked over Hunter's shoulder towards a table where several high school sophomores and junior girls sat. There: A tan, lightly-freckled, and angular face with eyes gleaming like the first burst of a sunrise. Her eyes blazed back and forth between her friends, altering shape and size effusively. She pushed away a strand of her wavy dirty-blond hair from her lips.

"The gold-skinned girl at the table behind you... I think her name is Mandy Rusche?" He asked Hunter.

"Yeah. That sounds like her laugh."

He turned to Hunter.

"Tell me something about her."

"She's Latina. She's on the swim team with me. She has an even hotter younger sister, but they look nothing ali-"

"How well do you know Mandy?"

"She's in my grade. I have, like, four classes with her," Hunter's responded, his right arm scratching his left shoulder.

He smiled.

"Oh no," Hunter wined. "What are you about to do?"

"Do you want to make a bet that I can have Mandy come here, turn around and flaunt her ass to try and impress us?"

"Yes. No-" Hunter paused. "Yes. Definitely."

"Hey, Mandy," He called out. She turned. "Can you come here for a second?" He waved her forward.

She stood up and walked towards them; her friends watched her as if pulled by her walk.

/17/

"Just don't involve me," Hunter whispered when she was still too far to hear them.

"You just identified your biggest problem," He whispered back.

"What's up?" she greeted with a voice raspy and confident. Her hands rested on her demined hips.

"Hunter just told me you're Latina. That's not true is it?"

"It is true." Her eyes burned towards Hunter, and blazed back quickly towards Him.

His eyebrows lowered, as if considering.

"Oh. Alright. Thanks."

"Why?" She giggled suddenly, exposing the white mirrors of her teeth.

He smiled.

"Isn't one of the Latina stereotypes having a big butt?" He asked, tilting His grinning face.

"I do too have a big butt!" Mandy laughed, turning to the side and showing the angle of her ass, which jutted out roundly from her tight, dark-jeaned legs.

"No way. Don't worry about it." He held His hand out, which she took into her own.

"Are you blind?" she argued as she turned with His momentum. "It's humong-o!"

She turned in a full circle – Hunter's mouth parting as she was halfway – and finishing with a bounce. She ran her thumbs through her belt loops.

"You have no idea how many chairs I've knocked over with this thing!" She flashed a glance to Hunter, swaying her hips side to side idly.

"Are you actually fully Latina?" He looked up at her.

"I'm half Columbian."

"Ah. The upper half, I bet."

"HA!" She beamed another grin. "Not funny, mister."

"I tried my very best." He shrugged. "That's all. Solamente un pregunto."

"*Una pregunta*," Mandy corrected. "Au revoir, monsieur. Ciao, Hunter." Mandy curtsied, and swayed the

[18]

curves of her slim figure back towards her seat. He gazed at the sun tattoo on the back of her neck. The sides of her cheeks were moving as if she were mouthing something to her friends. They looked to her, to Him, and then to her.

"I feel like I should pay you." Hunter laughed.

"Feel differently." His eyes remained to the back of Mandy's wavy hair.

"You do know that I've had a crush on her since like sixth grade. Her younger sister is hot too, but even crazier-"

Mandy sat down beside her friends. Her body turned towards them, but her eyes watched Him.

"...sister's name is Danika," Hunter continued. "Now, Dani..."

Their eyes remained connected, as if tangled in a gaze. A single sandaled foot twirled in small semi-circles.

"...even crazier than Mandy, if that's possible. So tell me, friend-" Hunter slapped the top of His hand.

"What?" His eyes darted back to him. "Tell you what?"

"How did you do that?"

He shook His head.

"I had fun."

Hunter waited.

"I had a little fun by getting her to have a little fun."

"Okay then what did you observe. Please, man. Nothing general. I need specifics. Give it to me."

"I just feel like this is going to feel redundant. You were here for it. You saw the whole thing."

"Please? Pretend I wasn't here."

"I called her over, as you just witnessed. We sat comfortably while she remained standing, which probably gave her this feeling that she is performing for us, which made all of this feel like an exciting challenge for her. I asked her a question about herself, which made it seem even more like she was performing for us, which also displayed to her that I might have an interest in her. But the question I asked could also be perceived as a test: My interest depends on her answer. Okay? Then she spoke about herself to us, which makes her vulnerable to our judgments. Then I teased her, joking around – nothing mean – which created a playful atmosphere. Her eyes dilated because she was attracted to the moment. I teased her about something she is proud of, which challenged her ego a bit, but also – since it is something she is proud of – encouraged her to flaunt it to us, a performance that, perhaps subconsciously, she understood as pleasing us. Thus, she associated an importance *to us*. Basic, classical, Pavlovian conditioning. Associations are almost always the answer to why we do things that seem bizarre in the present moment. After her performance, I smiled because we're both having fun and we're both playing the game of impressions and affections. Your smile is a reward for her action. That's Skinner's operant conditioning - another form of association. A treat for a treat. But, you can't be too impressed though, or else they'll feel as if you're too easy to impress, and what kind of exciting and intelligent person is easy to impress?"

He waited. Hunter blinked and nodded.

"When I took her hand, I pushed her away a little, playfully, and that made her naturally pull towards me. This natural pulling back also gives her the feeling that she is attracted. And then we end on a quick note, which suggests that there's plenty more. More mystery, and mystery evokes heightened sensations no matter the situation. In this situation the sensations are interest and desire, and preserving mystery heightens those two."

"Mystery evokes..." Hunter repeated leaning forward.

"Mystery evokes a heightened sensation," He repeated, "or a greater reaction. Mystery evokes a greater reaction. For example: If you buy your hypothetical girlfriend a rose on her birthday, she reacts with adoration. But, she expects this gift on her birthday. It's not a mystery, and thus the gift loses some of its value. The reasons are walls of defenses. She thinks: He *had* to get me something, he could have gotten me something *more*, how does this compare to other gifts, and so on. Now if you buy her a rose just because it's Tuesday - and she knows you didn't fuck up or anything – there are no defenses. It becomes a mystery, and she receives your gift more purely and reacts with a greater adoration."

"Another example. Hold on though." Hunter got up, passed quickly by Mandy and her friends with his body shrinking into itself, grabbed white napkins from the corner of the café, and returned back to the seat. He pulled a pen out of his pocket and looked up at Him. "Another please."

"Well-" His eyes bounced leftwards then rightwards, "-if you see a strange bump develop on your shoulder your reaction is fear because it's an abnormality. If you have no idea what it is, you have a large amount of fear, because it can be anything. Now, if your uncle and grandfather both developed tumors in the same area - even if they weren't benign tumors - your fear is greatly allayed because you have these walls of understanding. You can answer generally what the problem is, how to fix it, and so on."

Hunter nodded.

"A physical example would be war. It's a great metaphor. The best attack is the attack that results in the most damage. The attack that does the most damage is a surprise attack because physical defenses cannot be created. This rule applies to all."

Hunter finished writing and looked up with a knowing grin.

"Keeping girls guessing, and not being nice to them?"

"That's not what I said at all, Hunter, and this applies to everyone. Not just girls. Listen - you're nice to the girls you like not because you enjoy being nice in that moment, but because you want something in return. That's not the right way to behave. Be nice only when you enjoy being nice. Be nice when a girl does something you like. That's what I mean by have a good time. Any other time you're rewarding her for doing something that you don't want, which will encourage her to continue doing it. Do you understand?"

A silence enveloped them.

"So you ARE calculating all of this." Hunter nodded. "That's what I need to do."

His eyebrows lowered.

"I'm just enjoying myself and observing, Hunter," He spoke quietly. "If you want to learn more study haptics... or ethology... or neurolinguistic programming... or the social cognitive theory... or just Pavlov and Skinner." Hunter shook his head in disagreement. "You know exactly what you're doing, Dr. NoName." Hunter grinned.

July 27th 2008
...perfect sunny colors... how high ... ...

Fit, healthful Artyom Lavian arrived at His house at 8:00 in the morning, entered through the unlocked front door, ascended the staircase towards His room, egressed through the east-facing window, and met Him on the rooftop.

For nearly five hours, He and Art were sprawled out in their bathing suits on the rooftop of His house, smoking joints and watching the clouds laze about the blue sky. The sun smoldered directly above them, and reflected golden streaks of light on the beads of sweat atop their tan foreheads. Art inhaled their third joint - the tip reddened and then faded as gray-green smoke wound up into the air in fading spirals. A near-empty lime-colored Gatorade bottle was between them. Around the bottle were yellow drops, sizzling on the black rooftop.

"This is... the third time... I've ever... like... actually been stoned," Art spoke hoarsely.

He smiled and waited. Art sighed.

"And?" He turned to him.

"And-" Art paused, as if recalling a thought, "-and I'm... really stoned... I guess." Art chuckled. "Have you... figured out what... like... you're going to do with your life, yet?" Art asked Him, blowing out the last bit of the joint. With his eyes shut he extended the roach to Him, mumbling, "What do I do with this thing?"

"Doing with my life..." He echoed, grabbing the joint from him, and tossing it into the bottle. "In short, no."

Art – his eyes still closed – shook his head disapprovingly.

"In long..." He continued, "...no."

Art boomed a 3-syllable laugh.

"I mean, I figure psychology is the place to start. We'll find out soon enough."

"If you had... patience... you'd succeed in anything." Art yawned loudly. "I can't tell if this has been a long or short summer, but... I just can't believe it's half over, bro." A moment passed as Art yawned again – louder and longer than the last. "And you'll be... off to Boston soon." Art yawned a third time.

He closed His eyes, and time drifted forward as they slept. A wind passed in a gentle aria. The jingle of children's laughter twittered from up the block and ricocheted down the sunlit street.

A drawn-out car horn sounded. His eyes snapped open, red from marijuana and sunlight. He stood up and peered around the spire of the roof. Dustin's sapphire Jeep was in the driveway with the engine running.

He turned and looked down at Art, who was snoring quietly. He stepped into His room through the rooftop window, navigated through His bedroom, went down the flights of stairs – all the time squinting as if adjusting to the lack of sunlight. He walked through the dining room to the front door, stepped outside, and approached the vehicle. He waved to Dustin, but his gaze remained to his phone as he texted. Dustin mouthed what seemed to be profanities, nodded, and then hurled his phone onto the dashboard as if disgusted by its presence. Dustin looked upwards to the spire of the roof where He once was, and slammed the horn again.

"I'm right next to you, you insane FUCK!" He shouted, pounding His fist against the driver's seat window.

Dustin jumped, turned quickly to face Him, and slowly an enormous grin built across his large face. He opened the door, and immediately four water bottles – each filled with tobacco dip spittle - a toy Joker doll, a grape dutch, two empty beer cans, half of a Led Zeppelin CD case, a crumpled traffic ticket, an empty carton of Marlboro reds, two tins of tobacco dip (one regular, one cherry), and an American flag lighter spilled out of the car onto His driveway. An odorous hybrid of humid cherry and scrambled eggs filled the air. A frying pan rested on the passenger seat, glistening with grease.

 Dustin stumbled out. Multicolored stains coated his American flag pajama pants and white collared shirt.

 "Sup, sonnnn?" Dustin squinted, cocking his head up arrogantly.

 "You smell like a dead animal, Dusty."

 "He-he-he-huu-" Dustin laughed in mock-psychosis, rubbing his belly, and shimmying himself. "You ready?"

 "For?"

 "We're getting breakfast, son. Haven't eaten in minutes."

 "What? It's four o'clock. No."

 "Sonnnn," Dustin wined. "What are you doing now?"

 "Just blazed with Art. We're chilling on the roof."

 "Sounds hot."

 "Sure."

 "I'm gonna join you guys." Dustin stepped forward.

 He shook His head warningly. "No-no-no. You *hate* Art, and Art thinks you're a self-detonating nutcase."

 Dustin looked up to the roof with a small smile, and nodded back to Him.

 "You'd rather hang out with Art-" Dustin paused, placing a pudgy hand on his chest, "-than your *best* friend."

 He squinted.

 "The way you process information is astounding."

 "Dude, c'mon!" Dustin pleaded. "I need your advice on getting Sara back."

 "What happened now?"

 "I think this is it." Dustin threw his arms up and shook his head as if surrendering. "I think she meant it this time."

 "What did you do?"

 "Well-" Dustin grinned as he put his hands together imitating a golfer pre-swing, "-I was drinking-"

"You? Drinking? Can't be."
Dustin looked up from the imaginary golf ball in front of him and nodded approvingly. "And," he continued, "apparently... reportedly... *allegedly*... I called her mother a Muslim terrorist and her father a shylock." He swung a thin bar of nothing through the air. "Then I guess I might have told her I'd love her more if she'd be honest with herself and realize these truths." He squinted in the distance – following the trace of an imaginary golf-ball as it blasted over the neighborhood houses, above the clouds, and above the daytime moon in the blue sky – with a satisfied smile building slowly on his lips. "But I'll get her back, son. We just need to brainstorm on how to get it done quickly."

August 4th 2008
...what makes their different definition of 'love' so...

He was trotting northwards up Plandome Road in Old Rookvale as blazing clouds blasted colors about the sunrise. The Rising Star Café and Bookseller came into sight several blocks ahead. He was just passing the newly-built gazebo in town when a figure inside the structure caught His eye: Two white tennis sneakers, and from them two toned legs attached to jean shorts, and resting on the hips of the jean shorts was an SAT book, and facing the SAT book was a tan girl with black sunglasses above her high cheekbones.

"Stop studying so much, Señorita Rusche."

She looked up, her eyebrows burrowed under her sunglasses and then darted upwards as an extraordinary grin beamed from her golden face.

"Are you fucking kidding?" She shuffled the pages impatiently. "My little ass is getting fucked on these practice tests." She reached for her iced coffee and took the final sip, leaving only dark-tinted ice cubes. She bit the straw gently, and let it out from her parting lips.

He leaned on the white banisters that divided the gazebo from outside. A sun was reflected in each of the black windows of her glasses.

"Does your little ass need help?"

"Would you?" She took off her sunglasses and placed them on her head, and, it appeared for a moment as if she only removed the blackness of her sunglasses, as her eyes retained their heliacal hues. "Would you help my little ass?"

"Of course I would. Math or English? I can definitely help with the verbal section."

"Wow…" her voice softened. She crossed her legs, and swayed a single sneaker leftwards and rightwards.

"Wow, what?"

"I have a sexy tutor, now?" Mandy asked. He nodded, smiling. She slapped her textbook histrionically, "Well, let's get started quick!"

"'Quickly', not 'quick'. You're modifying a verb."

"Let's do it *quickly* then."

He looked down at her lips and then to her eyes.

"My mom thinks you're hot, by the way," she whispered. "I wasn't supposed to tell you that."

"Excellent. My great-great grandfather says he'd totally ravage you."

Mandy laughed and placed her SAT book down beside her.

"Really? That's kinda gross. How old is he?"

"No! That's a joke, Mandy. I don't even have regular grandparents. How has momma Rusche even seen my face?"

"In the year book. She's on the committee."

"And what does poppa Rusche say about her daughter's future instructor?"

"I dunno." She shrugged. Her arms lifted as if they were to cross, but instead dropped at her sides. "He's kinda kicked out of our house right now, the asshole."

"Oh." A small gray mark on the otherwise perfectly white gazebo caught His eye. "I'm sorry."

She bit her lip. "It's a shame you'll be in college next semester while I'll still be stuck in boring Old Rookvale as a baby High School Senior."

He looked up to her.

"Well – college doesn't start until mid-September. That gives us the end of the summer."

She uncrossed her legs, stood up, and leaned forward towards Him. She rested her tan elbows on the gazebo's banister.

"The end of summer for what?"

Her hand slipped between the gaps of the banister and brushed idly against His chest. He looked down at her bronze-colored arm.

"For education, of course."

August 8th 2008
...they surround Dustin because he's entertaining... Is Mandy...

The twilight rippled in the reflection of Alexander's pool in Old Rookvale, where high school students and recent graduates were swimming around, drinking, exhaling fumes into the sky, and eating what meats were left on the plate by the barbeque. Every now and then, the small crowd around Dustin erupted with laughter. Mandy appeared, entering through the picket fence by the driveway, wearing a blue-and-white pin-striped bathing suit. Hunter Douglas Quillan Wilcox-Himmler II ran in between the beer-guzzling crowd, across the grass, and hugged her. She wrapped a single arm around him, patting his back amiably - her narrow, amber eyes sinking down leftwards. Her gaze beamed up to Him. He nodded as she politely untangled from Hunter's embrace. He watched as Hunter's body moved in quick jerks as he spoke. Mandy nodded - first slowly, once; then again, quickly, as her foot began tapping. Her lips responded in curt movements.

"Yo, Hunter!" a voice called out from a car in the driveway.

Hunter showed Mandy his palms and race-walked towards the vehicle. She began walking in His direction.

"Hello, mister tutor," she spoke through a white grin. He removed the sunglasses from the top of her head and placed them on His face. "I heard from an anonymous source," Mandy continued, squinting with the sunlight illuminating her chatoyant eyes, "that you hooked up with like half the people in my grade."

"You know, I heard the same rumor," He replied. "The female half, though. Right?"

From across the pool, Dustin and Alex watched Him and Mandy. Dustin whispered to Alex. He turned to them and watched as the two mimicked sexual intercourse – Dustin on the receiving end of Alexander's merciless thrusts. He rolled His eyes. The two laughed and high-fived.

He looked down at the pool water. A single green beer bottle was at the bottom of the shallow end. He watched the silver letters shimmer, disconnect and reconnect. At one point the letters read 'Heineken', at another they read 'sign', and at another they formed nothing.

"What is distracting you from me?" Mandy asked, running her fingers through her hair.

His eyes flashed from her golden-brown hair and then to her lips.

"It seems Hunter really likes you. I wouldn't want to-"

"Don't bother," Mandy cut in. "He's *too nice*." Mandy gazed over His shoulder and grimaced. "Eughh! It's psycho Jack."

He looked across the pool at the tall, shaggy-haired bulk of Jack Ricaricare sucking a cigarette furiously.

"What's wrong with psycho Jack?"

"Besides the fact that he's a college dropout and a fucking psycho?"

"Yes, besides that. You can be crazy as long as you're photogenic. Look at Lizzie Manibasse."

"First of all, Lizzie Manibasse is God. Jack is just-" She gagged again. "He's the biggest creep ever. He has so many issues and throws tantrums every time a sensible girl rejects his crazy ass. He came over the other day – our families are friends, unfortunately – and was sitting on my bed waiting for me when I came out of the shower."

"Maybe he needed advice on bed linens?"

"Or maybe he's a bully who projects his sexual inferiority onto physically vulnerable girls."

"Hey Mandy!" Jack bellowed from across the pool. "You gonna sleep with Him, too?"

Mandy's eyes enflamed, widened, and then relaxed. She turned to Jack with a foxlike smile.

"Maybe. How's *your* sex life, Jack?"

Conversations muted as heads turned towards Jack, and then returned as if sensing no trouble.

"So, sexy future tutor of mine," Mandy continued, "you were just saying how you find me ravish-"

"My sex life is FUCKING GREAT!" Jack blasted as he ran around the pool towards Mandy. The partygoers exploded in various directions; larger bodies leapt in front of Jack like defensive linemen, while smaller figures suctioned to the perimeter of the backyard to clear the path. He watched Jack being restrained with wonder, and turned to see three girls hurried a trembling Mandy towards the entry gate.

"Give her space," He spoke, approaching the group around Mandy. "Do you want to get away from here?" He asked.

Her friends turned to Him, and then to her. Mandy nodded and crushed a tear on her cheek with her palm. They stepped outside through the white fence. He stopped her and hugged her immediately. Her panting slowed, and her sniffling subsided.

"I'm sorry. That was my fault."

"That had nothing to do with you," her voice vibrated into His chest. "It would have been any guy I spoke to."

"To whom I spoke," He corrected.

"Fuck you." Mandy laughed, poking her head out from His arms. He turned to His car, and then glanced down at the polychromatic flames of her eyes.

"Do you want me to drive you home?"

"No! I definitely don't want to go home right now."

"Thennn-" He swayed left and right with her, "-do you wanna go for a drive?"

She nodded. He let go of her body. She took His arm as they began walking.

"Nice car," were the only words she spoke during their commute from Alex's house, west on Northern Boulevard, then north on Plandome Road - passing Vane's

Diner, the gleaming white gazebo, the Rising Star Cafe, Hamilton's bar - and then west-bound towards the small beach beside Artyom's house. They stepped out and walked to the gated entrance, where a lock kept the doors closed. He spun the dial to 0-0-1, and the device clicked open.

"How safe," Mandy quipped snifflingly as they walked through the entrance and met the salty breeze.

In the distant midday waters, an elderly couple held hands on a sailboat. On the left side of the beach were three swing sets. Mandy sat down on the seat closest to the water. A wind blew. He shivered as He approached her. The sun lowered and the clouds began to redden as if a conflagration was growing in the distant seascape. She smiled as He leaned down, wrapped His hands around the swing, and pulled her close.

"I knew you didn't care," she hissed through opening lips, "about Hunt-"

He kissed Mandy Rusche. A small, victorious smirk spread across her face when their lips separated.

"That's not-"

She leaned upward and kissed Him before He could finish. He pulled her closer, running a hand through her hair, down her cheek, and bouncing off her pouting lips. He lifted her up from the swing. She wrapped her legs around His hips. Their lips smashed together passionately as they stumbled across the sand towards His car. He reached out a free hand and opened the car door. She jumped down from His arms and pulled Him inside.

August 10th 2008
...ginger waitress cute... Mandy text I wanna see ...

"I think I've jerked off so much in the past month that my balls have just sucked up into my body," Dustin meditated, stirring an early morning coffee with his finger at Vane's Diner in Old Rookvale.

Several elderly men and women turned to them, mouths ajar.

"What?" Dustin turned to them and then back to Him. "What? They won't come back down. I think they're stuck. It's because of Sara – that cunt."

He rolled His eyes. A red-haired waitress appeared, her teal eyes focusing on the elderly couple with concern.

Dustin sucked the coffee from his finger. "I gotta start washing my hands."

"Ugh," He gagged "Can you just tell me what you did to get her back this time?"

"Why do I have to tell everyone what I'm up to with Sara?"

"Fine." He stirred, as if getting up. "I don't think you and Sara are going to last, anyway."

Dustin's eyes widened.

"Wha- no – sonn - take that back…take that back, please."

"I dunno." He crossed His arms. "Next time-"

"Okay – stop –fuck – please – take that back and I'll tell you."

"Dustin," He began, "I think you and Sara Dara are going to last *forever*."

"Alright." Dustin nodded, reached down towards his watermelon-colored plaid shorts, and rolled a sleeve to reveal a tattoo of a heart with the cursive letters 'SD' wrapped around his inner thigh. "The Persian in her loved how superficial it is, and the Jewess in her appreciated how much it cost."

An Indian man in a maroon shirt and mauve turban walked into the diner. Dustin's eyes followed the man. His hand reached quickly into his pocket and extracted his inhaler. He sucked in, coughed, wheezed, and exhaled.

"So, you two are back together now because of a tattoo?" He asked. "You tattooed her initials on your fat, pale inner thigh… Now when she blows you she has something to stare at and feel good about."

"Look!" Dustin pointed.

He turned, observed the young man, and turned back, sighing.

"What is it, Dustin?"

"Do you think he has a bomb?"

"What?" He snapped. "Why the fuck would he?"

"I don't know. His *Chakras* aren't aligned." Dustin fidgeted. "We should go."

"You're terrified of a random stranger!"

"I don't know who he is! He could be a cannibal for all we know."

"So can anyone else in here," He hissed. "You're a sick kid, you know that? Like, you have a *real* problem. I can't wait to tell Alex."

Dustin stood up from the table.

"You got this one. I gotta go. I gotta go... meet Sara."

"I'm sure." He shook His head.

"I swear to god."

"Swear on Sara."

"I swear on…" Dustin's voice rose, his blue eyes sinking down-rightwards.

"Just sit down. You know you can't lie to me. You've got to stop this stupid shit. How are you supposed to function in free society when you're panicking all the time? Not everyone who isn't a WASP is a terrorist."

Dustin inhaled his inhaler, wheezed, reached across the table for the sugar packets, tore two Splendas open, and then poured the powder on top of the table.

"D'yever wanna just *do* cocaine?" Dustin asked, arranging the white powder into three lines.

"Not at all." He nodded disapprovingly. "It floods your brain with dopamine and stops the brain from recycling it. That's why soulless people feel like 'the man' when they're on it, and then feel like shit when they crash. It's a completely masturbatory substance."

"Ugggh-" Dustin rolled his eyes upwards. "I wanna try it. I wanna fucking baaathe in it."

"That is the last thing you need, Dustin. You have enough addictions to jerk yourself for a lifetime."

"Meh!" Dustin threw a single packet at Him. It bounced off of His shoulder and landed on the ground. "What do you know?"

"Far more than you do about the matter."

"Speaking of addictions," Dustin began, smirking, "you're plowing Mandy Rusche, now?"

"We're dating."

"Same thing."

"That's funny coming from a virgin."

"I'm not a FUCKING VIRGIN!" Dustin shouted, pounding his fat fist onto the table and scattering the white powder.

The redheaded waitress glanced at them, and moved towards the kitchen.

"My dick has been inside Sara. I just can't get it all in, and every time I try she says it hurts and just blows me instead. That's all. Plus, fuck you. You lost yours to the biggest whore in Old Rookvale."

He looked down at Dustin's fist.

"Do you ever go down on Sara?"

"No. I don't...I-"

"Then you don't love her," He interrupted. "You can't say you love someone and not want to pleasure them. I would build a shelter on the coastline of Mandy's vagina and camp there for years."

Dustin gazed down at the table. "I have to now, don't I?"

"Good boy."

"So-" Dustin gazed up at Him, "-Mandy Rusche. Why?"

"Because I find her attractive and attracting, and she's far more intelligent than you think," He offered. "Why do you ask?"

"Are you not at all concerned about contracting HIV-AIDS?"

He squinted.

"Okay maybe not AIDS," Dustin hesitated. "But seriously, son. Are you not at all worried about her being the whore of our high school?"

"I actually have no reason to believe any of the rumors about her. People call me a whore, too."

"But you *are* a whore!" Dustin laughed, pointing to Him condescendingly. "You're a filthy, filthy woman!"

Dustin watched as He wiped the scattered sugar off the table onto a napkin, and crushed the napkin into thirds.

"So are you going to continue dating Mandy even when you go to the Boston School, and she stays here whoring into her high school senior year?"

"I don't know, Dusty. I don't think about it. Are *you* going to continue dating Sara when you go to Noughfolk in Boston and she goes wherever she goes?"

Dustin stared at Him.

"Yes. Of course. That's half the reason why I'm going to that shitty community college. It's the best school I could get into and be near her and you."

"Wait – where is Sara going?"

"Massachusetts Fashion University in Cummington. MassFuc. Cummington. You love that, don't you?"

"Isn't that hours away from Boston?"

"135 miles. So? She loves me. She'll make the drive."

Dustin nodded to himself, scratched his thigh, and then reached for the crushed napkin.

August 24th 2008
… dating Mandy?... maybe… Boston… Her mom likes me…

The door of the massive Rusche house opened, revealing a young blonde in an American flag bathing suit. She smiled, displaying fourteen-year-old round cheeks and a wide gap in her teeth, which, combined with an adventurous expression in her enormous azure eyes gave her a puppy-like appearance.

"Whoa," she whispered in a more Long-Island rendition of Mandy's voice. "Who are *youu*?" She looked Him up and down.

"I'm Mandy's friend," He spoke, scanning the interior behind her. "What's your name?"

"Danika!" she breathed as she tapped her feet left and right on the welcome mat, kicking sand. Her eyes gazed over His shoulder. "Is that your carrrr?" she asked, running her hands through her blond hair.

"Yes."

"You *must* be rich."

He considered.

"My family is alright."

"You must be spoiled."

"Appreciative," He corrected. "Not spoiled."

She stepped closer to Him.

"Dani!" Mandy's voice called from inside.

Mandy Rusche hurried down the stairs in jean shorts and a tie-dye tank top. "Leave Him alone."

A dog barked.

"Lizzy!" Danika shouted, chasing a caramel-colored pit bull into the kitchen.

Mandy leaned on her tippy-toes and kissed Him. They drove to His house, went straight to His cabana by the pool and got naked in the shower. Before the water even hit them, she was already grabbing His penis as He kissed across her small breasts.

"Wait-" He begged.

"No," Mandy objected as she squeezed, causing His knees to buckle.

"Wait-" He laughed, "-ah-hold on."

Mandy released Him. He grabbed a yellow bucket near the shampoos, pushed her so her tan body pressed against the white-tiled walls and dodged the falling water. He turned the shower dial. The steam thickened. He filled the bucket.

"You'll enjoy this," He whispered behind her ear.

He leaned forward, pressing Himself against her bubble-shaped behind, and poured the steaming water on her head and down her neck, directly atop her sun tattoo. The peach fuzz on her neck stood up. She turned to Him, her narrow eyes smoldering amber, and pushed Him against the wall. She knelt down and filled her mouth with His penis. Her quick hand worked expertly, and within the minute His body trembled in an enormous orgasm.

Mandy laughed, reached around His body and spanked Him loudly. She opened the shower door, and stepped out into the cabana with a wave of steam following her. He splashed a bucket full of water on Himself and exhaled, displacing clouds of steam into scattering tides. He turned the shower off, snapped His bathing suit back on, and then wobbled out of the cabana. Mandy had already put her bathing suit on, and was doing laps in the pool.

    He yawned and moved towards the lounge chairs circumventing the pool. He angled one so that He would better face the sun, and collapsed back-first on the yellow netting. His eyes closed. Mandy splashed about. She sneezed loudly and He chuckled. The splashing stopped. His breathing deepened and His posture assumed somnolence. The sound of water dripping down Mandy's skin and hair onto the gray stone-and-brick floor could be heard.

    A cottony pressure weighed down on Him, and then a slightly greater pressure. His eyes half-opened. Mandy was throwing towels on His body. His eyes reclosed. A footstep, followed by another, and then a series of quickened paces. His eyes reopened as Mandy soared midair – her wet hair stretched out in Medusan angles, her face glowing with mischief – and landed with a recoiling bounce atop the pile of towels on His body. She pressed His shoulders down with her hands, kissed Him roughly, pulled away, and stared sharply into His eyes.

    "You know," she hissed through a menacing grin, "you're really not *THAT* good looking."

    "Wow," He spoke, staring wide-eyed up at her. "I'm pretty sure I just came."

    The fierceness in Mandy's vulpine grin melted away and a playful smile blossomed.

    "Why?"

    "Not sure yet. Still living it." He leaned upward and pulled her tighter against Him. "The idea of throwing towels on top of me and using them as a landing pad. Something free-spirited, creative, and physics-based about it. It's hot. The idea. Being lovely to me in the process of your own adventures."

"Are your parents home?" Mandy turned to His house, biting her lower lip.

"My parents are never home. You know that."

"Let's fuck again!" She pressed her pelvis down on Him.

"You just blew me."

"C'monnnn." She reached down under the pile of towels into His bathing suit, and wrapped her fingers around His growing penis. "We haven't fucked in like a whole day."

"I know, but you literally just blew me."

"So-" her hand stopped moving, "-I have to wait?"

"We have to."

"Okay fine." She nuzzled her face onto His shoulder. "Wake me up when its playtime."

He scanned down the sun tattoo of her neck, the musculature of her back, and the tan bubble of her ass branching out into her long, skinny legs. His eyes roved down her hamstrings, the backs of her knees, her tight calves, her achilles, and the paleness of the bottom of her feet. His eyes continued down to the pool.

"We," He whispered.

August 30th 2008

…*kissmandylipsbreastsloveperfectfearfearcoolcoldsinkcrossroad smotherfeelbetterrunningcall…*

His eyes snapped open. Quickly, He scanned the silver-outlined shadows in His room. Skeletal branches waved outside. Vibrations. His cellphone was vibrating. MOM was written on the display. He sighed, accepted the call, and pressed the phone to His ear.

"Hello?" He mumbled.

"Yes, hi, this is Officer Ledger. Am I calling from your mother's phone?"

"You are."

"We found her outside Ainsworth's. It doesn't open until 9 AM. She was making a lot of noise and the neighbors called us over. We tried your father, but apparently he's in Nova Scotia right now?"

He gulped hard.

"I see."

"She says she walked here from your home. Is there someone with a vehicle who can pick her up?"

"Yeah," His voice cracked. "Yes, sir. I'll be right there."

He wiped His eyes and headed towards the stairs. He took two steps downstairs towards the front door, walked back up, and entered His parents' room. His father was on a two-week business trip, His brother was finishing his senior year at college, and His mother was loitering three blocks away, outside of a high-end Italian restaurant that wouldn't open for another six hours. He reached through the darkness and placed His hands on His mother and father's pillows, and waited. He sniffled, smoothed the pillows, and left the room. He descended the moonlit stairs, grabbed His keys and opened the front door.

"Oh man." He sighed miserably as the cold of the night raced towards Him.

He got into His car, turned on the ignition and drove down His driveway. A sliver of moon beamed faint silver outlines onto the streets. He approached the parking lot. His mother stood outside Ainsworth's in a maroon dress, talking to a stone-faced officer. The man turned to the direction of His car, and together, he and His mother walked towards Him.

"You're the one I spoke to?" the officer inquired. The name 'Ledger' was written on his badge.

"Yes, sir."

The officer opened the passenger door for His mother.

"Have a good night, ma'am." The officer looked at Him and frowned.

His mother stepped inside the car; the ashy scent of cigarette smoke filled the air. The officer closed the door and took several paces backward, watching His eyes. He turned the engine on, and drove back towards His house. His mother breathed slowly and loudly, sitting motionless. The clock read 3:59 AM. The streetlights reflected in the curvature of her dark, vacuous eyes. Neither of them spoke a word. His eyes were low, tired, and glistening.

They approached His driveway. The clock read 4:00 AM. He yawned mutely.

"Do you think they're opened yet?" His mother spoke monotonously.

September 3rd 2008
...drunken happiness!... think Mandy... pops jetlagged... be strong...

An empty bottle of Pinot Noir stood on the table between Him and His father in the dim corner of Ainsworth's in Old Rookvale. His father had half a glass, and He finished the remainder. His eyes glazed radiantly as He rocked slowly from side to side.

"Your mother," His father continued, "is sick, son. Consider what you're like when you catch the flu. You're not yourself. There's no question. You become tired, your head becomes heavy, and as a result you can't think straight or do things properly. It's a temporary malady. Mom has a malady that's both permanent and temporary. It's controllable but needs to be maintained, and sometimes, because of the changing nature of her sickness, she may display her symptoms until we help her equalize again."

"Her depression is a cycle, though," He whispered dryly as He swirled the drop of wine in His glass and watched the maroon dregs spiraling within. "She gets down, and when I suggest she get together with one of her girlfriends, she says she doesn't feel like it. The next day I see loneliness in her eyes." His father watched the knuckles of His hand whiten as He gripped the glass tighter. "And it's so obvious that this cycle has become a habit. Loneliness is a habit. The habit is a cycle, and the cycle is a wheel that spins her backwards quicker and quicker, and I fucking hate how obvious it is, dad. Habits require change to cease being habits. I know the psychology, and I know how depression works," His voice trembled. "Why can't she just listen to me? Does she have any idea how much I've learned?" He sniffled. "I hate her when she's like this. It's just like when I was twelve."

A tear soaked into the cotton table.

His father reached for a napkin and handed it to Him. He wiped His eye. His father took a deep breath.

"You know I love you and your brother very much. And I love your mother very much, too. I love you and try to be here when I can—"

"—But you have millions of people to help," He interrupted. "I know, dad."

"Hundreds of millions of people to help. This is a sick, fat country. But ten times that amount wouldn't equal to one of you, one of your brother, or one of your mother. I can, however, see you and mom when I'm home and your brother when I'm in Boston to make sure everything is okay. If you would like to talk to someone other than me – which I would understand – I can have you meet with the best psychiatrist in Manhattan during your winter break. Would you like that?"

"Sure."

"Who knows?" His father shrugged. "Dr. Heidelberg might end up inspiring you. He asks the right questions."

"Right."

"Listen, son." His father paused, contemplating. "I know I can be demanding of you and your brother, and that I don't always have the right to be, considering that I'm not here often and all. But remember always that I love you both so much, and that I am *always* here for you to help with anything, to be someone you can talk to, to give you guidance, to make sure you're on the right path and you don't stray off course."

"I know, dad."

"You do have to understand, though, son that your mother has been... nervous in the face of her old friends after what is happening right now, especially after going through it twice before. It's not her fault that she has this sickness."

"I know... dad."

"And we are taking her to the hospital next week. She'll be getting her ECTs like last time, and everything will be normal again. Okay?"

"Right."

"Whether you need anything, or are even worried or concerned or just want to talk, call me. No matter where I am, I'll be there for you."

"Okay." He sniffled.

"You have so many talents, son. You're social – perhaps too social sometimes from what I hear about your girls. You're articulate, and you're damned smart. I didn't have half the intelligence you have when I was turning 18. I barely knew English at 18!" His father laughed. "With the right mindset you are going to be a superstar in psychology, or a superstar in whatever you seriously pursue, no question about it. As long as you have patience. Even half of Art's patience will do."

His face turned red, and an appreciative smile flickered.

"Thanks, dad."

September 5th 2008
...Not really together... why did I even stay...

His hair was still wet as He rested on the pool float, which lazed around the near-motionless water. He stared at the pool's cement bottom. His phone vibrated atop the head of the float. Chet Baker's *When Sunny Gets Blue* was playing on the house's outdoor speakers. As the float turned from the near idle current of the pool, His eyes lifted to see Alexander standing by the pool stairs, gazing at Him with his arms crossed.

"You've been motionless for ten minutes." Alex frowned, adjusted his spectacles, and shook his head." What in the blazes is going on in that crazy head of yours, man?"

"Sup 'Lex?" He mumbled into the plastic bed.

"So..." Alex began, uncrossing his arms and kicking a small pebble into the pool. "You're not actually *with* Mandy are you?"

"I don't know," He mumbled, gazing away.

Alex spotted a basketball by the edge of the pool. He tiptoed towards it, picked it up, pulled back, and launched it towards His ass. The ball slapped Him with a loud SMACK, and bounced into the water.

"What the fuck, Alex?" He yelled, rubbing His right butt-cheek.

"I'm trying to talk to you and you're just moping around," Alex shouted. "Apparently Mandy was visiting her friend this weekend at Tower University and banged some ginger college senior surfer bro named Guy Boyland. I'm being a good friend and telling you now before you get too attached to her."

"I don't care," He muttered, staring at the water with His hand still on His ass.

"Are you sure? She's a psychopathic, Old Rookvale whore. Seems about your type."

"No. I don't care. And I'm trying to take a nap. You should let me know when you're coming over so I'm not half-asleep. Can you go?"

"First of all, man, check your phone. I texted you twice. Second of all, are you kicking me out right now?" Alex smiled, half-turning. "You realize, of course, I'm just trying to express to you the illogic of growing attached to that whorish fiend." Alex chuckled on his penultimate word. "Or perhaps fiendish whore?"

"I'm just not in the mood to talk." He sighed. "We'll go to Hamilton's later and I'll get the first drink. I just want to sleep right now. Okay?"

"Alright, man." Alex shrugged, turned and walked towards the breezeway. He called out halfway around the turn: "You're leaving for school in one week. Forget about her. It's the logical thing to do."

When Alex had disappeared around the curve of His side-yard. He reached down for His phone below His dry stomach. He opened it and viewed Alex's texts.

Alex: Paging Captain fagboy? U home? We need to talk about something... (2:26)

Alex: Where r u, u big gay animal?? I've been at ur front door for 5 mins (2:31)

He scrolled down and re-opened Mandy's texts.

Muschey: I didn't mean to hurt u! (2:01)
Me: I feel like I've made a mistake knowing you. (2:12)
Muschey: I'm sorry, but it's not like we were ever really together. (2:25)

He gazed up towards the breezeway, then to the trees ahead, and then to the sky. His cell phone slipped through His hands and fell into the water. His eyes followed as it sank lower towards the pale blue surface below.

October 1st 2008
...*LSD sounds interesting*... *Mom is*... *My Birthday*... *Mandy*...

Oliver Scoffman, His roommate at BS, placed his pale hands on His shoulders and smiled as they stood together in the center of their dorm room. A blotter tab rested on His exposed tongue. On it was an image of a black pyramid with a green eye in the center. On Oliver's tongue was a larger tab of a purple baboon strumming an orange guitar with its tail.

"Upon the 1st of October in the 2008th year of our Lord, Christ Jesus," Ollie began histrionically, "the Nameless Boy celebrates His 18th birthday by experimenting with the hallucinogen colloquially abbreviated as 'LSD' – or 'drippity drops' – with His surreally handsome guitar legend roommate, Doctor Oliver Scoffman. The reason, my good sir?"

A moment passed in silence as they stared at one another. Oliver's parabolic smile grew.

"Oh-" He stirred. "My reathon, uh, tho eckth'ore my thelw through a new angul. Tho obserb the peop' aroun me an' how we connecth. Tho thee if I realithe a realer thelf."

"How Freudian," Ollie chirped.
"Thath more Eee Uwuhew Winnico', akthua'ee."
Ollie released his hands from His shoulders,
"Let's go."
    They changed into the outfits that Ollie chose, stepped out of their dorm room, walked across the tan corridors of the eighth floor at Boston School's West Campus and headed towards the elevator. Ollie pressed the down button and the elevator door opened. They entered – Ollie first, then He – and descended.
    "Did you know that two scientists gave a dolphin LSD in an attempt to teach him English?" Ollie spoke watching Him as He watched His tongue. "It didn't work out because the dolphin wanted to have sex with the scientist. You can swallow the tab now, by the way."
    The elevator door opened. Oliver and He walked through the lobby of West Campus, and stepped outside into the snowy Boston air. Oliver wore a Santa hat, a yellow scarf with blue Hebrew letters, a lime shirt and yellow pajama pants. He wore an orange camouflage hunter's beanie hat on His head, a black knit scarf, a pink pinstriped button-down, and plaid turquoise pajamas. Their figures brushed bright colors through the omnipresent whiteness as they walked along the brick path with their dormitory building on their right and the snow-packed soccer stadium to their left.
    "I know that girl!" Oliver shouted, pointing forward, and leaping - causing the white fluff-ball on his Santa hat to bounce. "That's Stephanie."
    "The blond Columbian girl?" He squinted through the flurrying snow and viewed a silhouette of two girls – one with a mane of golden locks outlined in white phosphorescence, and the other shadowed in a black winter coat.
    Oliver nodded. A trail of smoke snaked out of the latter girl's hood. The blonde tapped her on the shoulder. She looked upwards as the other leaned towards her side, as if whispering to her. She pulled down her hood, revealing a wave of dark hair. Two large grins became visible through the falling snow.

"Hey Oliver! Happy birthd-" Stephanie greeted them.

"My name's not Oliver anymore!" Oliver protested. "I hereby declare, to you, my dear sweet Columbian Madame of brobdingnagian pulchritude, that I am Rabbi Bobert Goldberg and He is now Doctor Collie McBudwick, Calypigianologist."

"Oh." Stephanie tilted her head. "Well, happy birthday to you, Collie McBudwick. Congrats on having a name. What are you two doing tonight?"

"Ooooh nothing," Oliver smiled, staring wide-eyed at them, his pupils expanding.

"Pardon Stephanie's unpardonable curtness." He took the other girl's hand in His own. "Your name?"

"Justine," she spoke through a sharp-toothed grin. "Yours? Not 'Collie'. Your *real* name?"

"He doesn't have one," Stephanie answered quickly. "By the wayyy-" Stephanie paused, turned to her friend who nodded in confirmation, and then turned back to Him, "-do you guys have any coke?"

His smile fell.

"I told you before, we don't do evil drugs like coke or pills," Rabbi Bobert Goldberg declared. "We only do happy drugs like mushrooms and acid... and DMT... and weed. Nothing addictive, dear ladies." The hallucinating rabbi turned to Collie McBudwick "What was that Harvard dream study you were talking about – showing how cocaine addicts can't internalize new information at the same-"

"Do you really do coke?" Collie McBudwick asked Stephanie.

"Nooooo." She grinned mischievously. "But if you do have some..." Her hand hovered towards His pelvis.

"That's fucking disgusting," He yelled.

Her mouth parted, not yet fully losing the curves of her smile.

"I have no idea why I thought you were better than that."

He turned and walked passed them. Oliver followed Him, caught up to Him, and stared at His face as they crunched through the snow in silence.

"So-" Ollie hesitated, "-is Collie McBudwick going to be, like, angry all night, now?"

He shook His head.

"When I'm wicked pissed I repeat the phrase 'squabbling squabblers' in a manly voice. Try it out."

"I can't tell if it's the LSD, Rabbi Goldberg, but I feel awful after that shit. I never told you about Ma-"

"Don't worry, man," Oliver interrupted. "It's not the acid. Yours won't kick in for another fifteen minutes."

"Right."

A moment passed in near-silence, clocked by soft-crunching snow.

"There's plenty of other Columbians on campus, dude," Ollie spoke. "You'll bang the next fifty."

He laughed loudly as they continued walking. The gleaming lights of BS East Campus came into view through the whiteness. A high-pitch laugh screeched ahead, coming from a vibrating figure on a bench.

"Who is that?" He asked.

The light behind the shadowy figure produced a trembling profile outlined in gold. She turned, and the overhead lights adorned the contours of her face.

"That's Wrubs!" Oliver announced.

"Wrubby?" He shouted to her.

"I-ah…haha…cahan't…ahaha…stahop…" she cried to them as they approached.

There was nothing immediately alarming about her. Her pale face was flushed with laughter, as if trapped in an inside joke. Her teal eyes were wide, glistening worriedly, but a delirious smile hindered its seriousness.

"What's wrong with her?" He asked.

"I gave her acid before – the same amount you took." Oliver joined Wrubby in laughter. "I guess she took it."

"Where…ah-ah-ahahuha…is…huuuh-huuuhaha…Nic…uuhahauhhu…ole?" Wrubby gasped.

He looked at them: First Wrubby, and then Oliver whose pupils were now completely dilated.
"Oliver," He began, and then paused as if reflecting. "Ah-lee-vur. All-Eve-Her. Ahhhhhhhhhhh-leave-her alone. Alone. A loan. All own. No-no. Oliver, don't." He shook His head. "Ollie. What's in a name, Ollie? Mihi nomen est... what the fuck is in a name? Only a concept is in a name. An ever-redefining concept is what we each truly are. A name isn't needed. It's just a sound-frame. A pointless perimeter." He pointed to Oliver's nose. "Your face looks like a pale-peach circle with a triangle in the center. That's your nose. That's it. Right there. I discovered it."

An eruption of combined laughter pounded through the cold, white-flaked air. Among the increasingly heavy snowfall around them, dark-colored figures turned towards them and whispered before vanishing back into the white-fading distance. Through the increasing opacity, Nicole emerged with four of massive-jacket-bundled friends.

"Jesus fucking Christ, Wrubby!" Nicole shook her head and then squinted towards Oliver. "How much acid did you give her?"

"I'muhh...uhhhhahuhh...going...uh-uh-uh...to...throw uhuh-up..."

Oliver crossed his arms.

"First of all, her name is Wrubby or Wrubs, or perhaps even Wrubenstie-" Oliver paused. "Wrbubrbbuwrb," he shook his lips and ended with a laugh-note. "Secondly," Oliver continued, "my name is Rabbi Bobert Goldberg. Thirdly, uhh, I gave her the same amount I gave Collie McBudwick."

"Collie who?"

"I'm Collie, now." He smiled, tipping His orange camouflage beanie to show His rose-cold cheeks.

"Congratulations on finally having a name, Collie. And happy birthday, by the way!" Nicole crossed her arms and shivered. "Now can we all go somewhere and fucking smoke?"

"Sure!" Oliver and He responded simultaneously. The two turned towards each other and giggled.

"Jesus – did you *all* drop acid?" Nicole squinted at them.

"What did you say Collie's real name was?" asked a shivering girl next to Nicole.

"Oh – this is Jenna. And Collie… doesn't really have–"

"The problem is-" Collie's laughter ceased abruptly as He stepped towards the girl, leaning His face inches away from hers, "-I actually have no name. This makes sense to you, considering I'm only a semi-solidifying slice of sentience shaped by the Grand Author in the sky." He looked outward, and then glanced back down at Jenna. "You are all just eventual tangents of my own consciousness, uniformly maintaining not only my thoughts, but *myself*, collectively depositing your voices into my totality. Be happy and enjoy so I can be happy and enjoy."

"What?" A puff of condensation fogged out from her hood.

"Consider yourself an amiable character in another's dream. A most delightful cameo. An eventual part of me, minimized, filtered and interwoven with other parts of me. A character from whom I can learn. But in the end, I'm learning from myself – or rather what I deciphered from you as part of my self. No matter what you say, it's me who is truly saying it to myself. It is I who thinks about it and absorbs it. The same goes for each of us. As for your original question, you can call me 'He' or 'Him'. Just don't call me 'Her'. That's my imaginary sister. People get us jumbled frequently."

Quietude lingered. Wrubby's laughter ceased. Jenna nodded slowly and unsurely. A heavy gust pushed the snow in an eastern torrent.

"Your sentences make me want to sink my teeth into a hamburger in front of a family of cows," Oliver announced.

"I haven't spoken a word," He said, turning to Oliver and winking.

"You two are a basket of mind-fucks aren't you?" Jenna laughed, her wind-swept face poked out from her hood.

"We isn't," He responded.

A blur of bubbling colors, twisting smoke, dancing geometries, and the ubiquitous falling of polychromatic snowflakes dominated the inebriated group... and several hours later – after Oliver accurately predicted the very minute the snowfall would cease – He found Himself in His dorm room alone with Oliver, talking to one of the two mirrors in their room.

"Wipe that stupid look off your face you fucking moron!" He demanded to Himself.

"But this is how I always look!" He responded to Himself in a petulant whine.

"You'll never make it with that fucking mug of yours," Himself said back to He.

"I'll make it with your momma's mug."

"Dude. That's messed up. That's our mom."

"Sorry."

"I forgive you."

"What are you doing?" Oliver asked, sitting on the bed and fiddling with his rosewood-guitar.

He and His reflection turned towards Oliver.

"Don't worry Ollie-Ollie-Oxen-field, boxing seals beside a fox in heels. He and I are most undividedly chums, now."

He snapped back towards His reflection. His face assumed seriousness. His eyes focused. He spoke:

"And now I'm feeling a desire I cannot explain. Expansion. Being in two places at once. Unstuck from time. One part of me is here - the shell, bones, the cardiovascular system, the blood, bones, and the mother fucking *bones*. And another part of me, a fragment of my brain the size of my thumbnail, is hanging tightly on the cliff of another place. It is wedged, WEDGED! Hanging from an ocean-side ledge. And as it hangs it is just able to peep over the edge. And what it sees is pure knowledge and information, god-like things that together resemble gusts of liquid autumn leaves, zipping around in blurs. And occasionally one of them passes by and little windy threads of information hook onto that piece of me. They wrap around it and bring to it knowledge that can't be found here. WEDGED! Yet-"

"What are you even saying?" Ollie laughed.
"What I'm saying is what I've said." He glared towards Ollie and then back to the mirror.
"Why are... you... saying... what you're saying?" Oliver struggled. "Why are you saying it?" Oliver summarized.
The muscles of His face softened.
"Oliver, dear. I am saying it for the viewers. They won't know what I'm thinking until I say it. They can't get into Our heads. They can only spectate and deduce. That was all vocalized cognition, and this particular paragraph of explanatory dialogue is vocalized metacognition, obviously. And thinking about why I'm thinking about the thoughts I'm thinking about is meta-metacognition."
"So... uhh..."
"I am saying what I think I'm thinking, so they will know what's going on in my mind right now."
"Oh... *they*." Oliver nodded, strumming. "Of course, dude. Did you know that dildos were invented 15,000 years before the wheel? I guess we didn't care about moving around too much, as long as we were being pleasured."
He snapped back to His mirror. His jaw flexing, a wild crimson swirling up the sides of His cheeks, His face vibrating, the veins on His forehead and neck protruding. Lines across His face deepened and His eyes took the shape of rage.
"There are already so many parts of Me. There's also You," He growled to His reflection. "You in the mirror, who knows more than I."
"You talk to the mirror too much," Oliver observed, reaching for his lime-colored pick
"It's my better half, the fellas say," reasoned a voice reminiscent of a 1950s Caucasian father figure on a family-friendly sitcom.
"You know they say you're not supposed to look in the mirror when you're on a hallucinogen," Ollie proclaimed, strumming a tranquil arpeggio.
"That's because you become insecure," His voice normalized. "You see your face in a different way, and that

strangles your ego because it confirms that you can see yourself as you *aren't*. It says that what you see, even if it isn't you, can actually be you."

"If I wasn't on LSD also, I might not have understood any of what you just said."

"We are in accordance then, Oliver."

"Accordions..." Ollie mumbled to his guitar, and then looked up. "Let's put on some music." Oliver whispered.

"Something in between indigo and turquoise, lavender and aquamarine. Bluish-purple. I'm feeling synesthetic and if I don't feel a synchronization of senses soon..." His voice trailed. His lips parted as He stared into His eyes. "We need more colors or I'll simply fragment, Oliver," He concluded calmly.

"I feel like I live off music, too," Ollie mumbled. "Bittersweet Symphony?"

"Yes!" He clapped, and stared at His hands with alarm. He opened and closed His palms. "Perrfeccctt."

He began speaking, very slowly, and timed as if rolling within the violin notes:

"He felt, in the center of His palms, little geysers misting misty mists outwards which would then curvilinearly fall back, splashhh, triiiickling, tickling, between the sands of His hands and feeling like cool, cold water droplets." He looked down. "Secreting secrets. He looked down at His hands and saw purple and yellow, like bruises; and around the maze of veins, He saw red and blue and green and orange, and they reminded Him of those polychromatic topographical maps from His high school just six short months ago. Six short months ago You were a different human male, weren't You? You were deeply inside Mandy, weren't you? Wasn't I? Wasn't Me? Yes. No. Was it this I? We all were, in a sensual sense. Variations of an unconfirmable past. All of the experiences in my life are just electricity and chemicals stored in brain cells." He looked away from His palms and faced Himself in the mirror. "He faced Himself in the mirror and watched Himself age into a successful man, and then youthen, and then age to a different man, and then youthen to another boy. My heart and my penis and the numbing blood that runs in-between-us." He leaned in conspiratorially and whispered, "Who am I? When am I? Who is me? I am looking at my eyes *with* my eyes. I am always You. I – Me – I – Me – George Herbert Mead," He reflected to His fellows in the mirror, and nodded, "They understood perfectly, and they know what's going to happen soon."

He made several abstract poses in front of the mirror as Oliver – with his eyes closed - moaned quietly to the music. After several minutes, He touched the mirror, saying, "He touched the mirror, and could have sworn He watched it ripple. He touched it again, if not a bit harder, and watched Himself ripple a second time, though greater – testing His frame. He touched it a third time-" He slapped the mirror and jumped backwards as it fell halfway behind the drawer.

Oliver opened his eyes. He looked down first at the unbroken mirror, then to Oliver, and then looked behind His shoulder to face the other mirror – the mirror on Ollie's side of their dorm room. He caught eyes with Himself and beamed.

"Oliver is in the future, and I'm a neon hawk-puppy with a limitless grin."

October 31st 2008
…WE EACH WEAR THE BORROWED COSTUMES OF OTHERS…

Zombies, ghosts, and miscellaneous prostitutes paraded westwards across Commonwealth Avenue in Boston, passing Him as He walked eastwards. He turned southwards on Babcock Street, eastwards again on Freeman Street, and southwards on Amory Street, heading towards Dustin's dorm on Beacon Street near Noughfolk Community College.

Turning eastwards on Beacon Street, He immediately found Dustin sitting on a bench with the Amory Park behind him. The lamp overhead shimmered gold upon the darkness, and illuminated Dustin's eyes to a blue that matched his polo sweater. He sat down beside Dustin. Together they faced Beacon Street silently, watching the costumed people pass. Dustin pulled out his inhaler, sucked, and wheezed, and then placed the device back in his pocket. From this same pocket, Dustin extracted a cigarette, lit it, and inhaled. His sad face looked Him up and down.

"Happy Halloween, son. What the fuck are you supposed to be?" Dustin asked, staring at His usual attire of jeans, a button-down and a black winter coat.

"I thought we were both homosexuals," He responded, watching as a boy dressed as a torn condom laughed beside a woman who was pregnant or costumed as pregnant.

"Riiight." Dustin nodded. "Who's bottom?"

"We both are." He turned to Dustin. "We're flexible."

"Simultaneous penetration. Wow. Can that happen? Do you think it's ever happened? Two dudes penetrating each other?"

He paused and shook His head.

"No. Obviously not."

"What?! Picture two three-foot-donged nigger Mandingos hammering away at each other's buttholes."

"That your fantasy, you racist hog?"

"Maybe." Dustin shimmied flamboyantly. "Speaking of three-foot-dongs, Sara and I broke up."

"Good." He rested an arm on Dustin's shoulder. "Now, what about your *actual* girlfriend? This Boston girl you're seeing?"

"Kat? We're doing alright, I guess. I don't know. She's not like us Long Islanders. Different class. More like Art." Dustin paused. "She's also a bitch."

"And so are you. Perfect match. Are you never going to have actual penetrative sex with her as well?"

Dustin smiled and flicked his cigarette forward. His eyes followed the cigarette's long parabola as it passed over two stumbling girls, one a bumblebee the other a ladybug.

"Look at that distance, dude," Dustin whispered, squinting toward the fading embers several meters away. He turned to Him. "By the way, dude – I went to the doctor. Wanna know what he said?"

"That you're clinically insane, jerk off too much, and have Münchausen Syndrome?"

"No. That's all old news, son. He said I have the lungs of a forty-nine-year-old!" Dustin howled with laughter that shrieked across the costumed streets. He waited as Dustin slapped his knee and wiped a tear from his eye.

"I'm considering leaving Boston, and going back to New York."

"What?" Dustin's expression became accusatory. "What the fuck? You're leaving *me*?"

"I'd be leaving all of Boston, not just you, you narcissistic fuck."

"And," Dustin argued, exhaling smoke, his eyes roving left downwards, and then up to meet His, "by extension, you're leaving me with these *wicked smaht Bostonians.*"

He nodded.

"Why? Is it something with your mom? You know that now I'm gonna have to leave Boston, too."

"That's not true. You have Kat here. And you have Sara who drives two hours from MassFuc to blow you."

Dustin's head hung low, and vacillated as if weighing options. He stopped, and squinted up at Him.

"Why the fuck are you leaving?"

"Because I haven't gone to a psych class in two weeks."

"What?" Dustin shrieked again, frightening a passing ghost. "You're becoming like me."

He shivered and stood up.

"Let's go for a walk."

"Where?"

He looked down Beacon Street, facing eastwards at the intermittently red-yellow-green and white haze.

"Kenmore?" He suggested.

"Too far. Me lungs, mate."

He sat back down.

"Why haven't you gone to a psych class?" Dustin asked, his eyes darting towards an exhausted mother ambling along three children in vampire outfits. He watched Dustin, whom, after a moment turned to Him. "What? Are you gonna tell me or not?"

"Four weeks ago-" He inhaled His cigarette, "-I was sitting down in this crowded lecture hall with about three-hundred students. Our professor – this obese blonde with a permanent smile – waddled up to the podium and gave us a four-hour lecture on the most basic psychological principles. She was telling us about Pavlov's salivating dogs. You know that-"

"Yeah – Old Rookvale High School AP Psych, son. Bells ringing and saliva. I tried to do the same with Sara, but with blow-"

"Yeah," He interrupted. "So, she finishes the lecture saying – just to give you an example of how dumbly she treats us – she says, and I quote, 'dogs are animals, and dogs can be conditioned. And humans are animals, so humans can be conditioned too!' and I swear to fucking God she just looked at us smiling, and this Asian kid next to me was writing every single word and looking up like this was the most amazing revelation in his fucking life."

"God I fucking hate Asians. Most awkward people in the world." Dustin grimaced. "No wonder they watch tentacle porn, and don't know how to drive. Driving is a fucking social ac-"

"And I just shouted to this kid, 'are you fucking kidding me?' and I stood up in the middle of the lecture hall and asked our professor why we are paying fifty grand a year to hear things we learned in high school-"

"Your doctor pop is paying for it," Dustin whispered.

"-And I just collected my shit and left the classroom."

"Love it." Dustin clapped and pulled out two cigarettes, put one in his mouth and handed the other to Him. He lit his own first and then handed Him the lighter.

He put the cigarette to His face and held the lighter in His hand.

"I feel like I was cut in half in that class. I don't know if it's an ego thing or an impatience thing, or I just realized that my motivation to master behavioral psychology since I was twelve has served no purpose at all for that lecture hall."

He lit the cigarette. A trail of smoke poured out from His lips and moved upwards into the air, illuminating with an increasing gold as it twisted towards the overhead lamp. Dustin nodded.

"I'm going to give it one more semester here, and then I'll decide. Classes start on January 26th and they end on May 6th. If I'm not challenged, I am going back to Long Island."

"I guess those psych classes were cutting into your epic Acid-head phase, too, huh?"

He pulled the cigarette away from His lips.

"That's fucking hilarious, Dustin."

Dustin slapped his knee.

"Are you going to deny that all of a sudden you do acid?"

"No. I'm not going to deny anything. You just know nothing about it, and you're talking about it like you do – jerking yourself off to comforting illusions – just like you do with everything."

"LOSERS DO ACID, MAN," Dustin screamed. "Just stick to weed, son." He paused, and considered. "Or do acid one more time and let me film you. I'd like to see that. I could get you in a cage and have people buy tickets to see you."

"When you speak to me right now – do I seem different?" He asked Dustin.

"No. Besides defending acid like a psychopath."

"Well I'm on LSD right now."

Dustin squinted and cocked his head upwards arrogantly.

"You're lying."

[56]

"Unlike you, I tell the truth sometimes. Look at my pupils."

Dustin leaned in closer and saw that His otherwise green eyes were engulfed in blackness.

"You're out of your tits, son."

"I'm on lysergic acid diethylamide, it's Halloween tonight, and you just had a full conversation with me without knowing I'm on a psychomorphic substance."

"You changed, man." Dustin shook his head.

A solemn-looking man walked down the street in a police officer's uniform.

"And you're not changing, Dustin," He responded, getting up, "while everyone else is."

December 5th 2008

...watch Ollie... stop thinking about Mandy... C'mon, Ollie...

"Are you a doctor?" a girl squawked with drunken volume over the clamor of a Boston School frat party.

She clutched His arm and pulled impatiently.

"No," He spoke, watching His roommate from across the inebriated carousel of college bodies.

"Your white button down looks doctorrrish," she stated, biting her lip.

He nodded, focusing on Oliver.

"You'd be a *hot* doctor," her voice sounded next to Him, somewhat petulantly.

He looked down at her hand on His arm, and followed her hand to her face: Reddish hair, tan skin, and brown eyes. Round cheeks colored by alcohol, flush, and makeup. A pierced navel.

"What is your name?" He asked her.

"Eve."

I want you to watch something, Eve."

"Wait – what's your name?"

"Call me Docked-whore."

"You said you're not a-"

"Wait – here it comes!" He spoke as He curled her toward Himself, rendering them fixated in a slow-dance position. "Do you see that girl and guy?" He whispered into her ear, nodding to Ollie and the blond girl to whom Oliver was speaking.

"I know her," Eve whispered back, "her name is Whitney – she's my-"

"Her name right now is 'Bunny the Viking'."

"What – why?"

He hushed her with a squeeze, and leaned towards her. She pouted, as if anticipating a kiss. He dodged her lips, and instead put His mouth to her ear.

"That's my roommate, Oliver," He whispered, "and he is with a girl you know as 'Whitney'. And 'Whitney' has a boyfriend that treats her poorly. That is why Oliver calls her 'Bunny the Viking' - it creates a new identity for her, allowing her to detach from this world and attach to the world of Oliver and her – Oliver and Bunny. Necessary dissociation for mutually beneficial re-associations, if you will."

"Did-"

"Now, he's done everything correctly: He's against the wall so all she sees is him, and his hands are on her hips but pushing away – making her pull to sustain equilibrium. The body rippling meanings to the mind. Now, he's going to look at her lips and say something like 'I'm not going to kiss you, and then-"

Oliver smiled as he spoke. Bunny's head tilted inquisitively and a sea of gold hair splashed over her shoulder. He ran his pale hand through his short brunette hair. Bunny ran a pale hand through her long blond hair.

"Echotaxia," He whispered to Eve. "Thoughts through the echoed body."

"Yeaahh, duuude?" Ollie spoke louder, squinting down at Bunny the Viking challengingly.

"Yeah, dude!" Bunny the Viking's voice responded.

"Echolalia," He hissed softer. "Thoughts through the echoed lips."

Oliver wrapped his pointer fingers in the belt loops of her jeans, and pulled her close as he turned his neck so they were cheek to cheek – somewhat resembling He and Eve watching them from across the crowded, drunken room. Oliver lowered and angled his face towards her neck, and his eyes darted up toward Him. Oliver winked to Him, and lowered closer and closer to her neck.

"Watch her reaction."

Oliver opened his mouth, and pressed his lips against her jugular, and slowly sunk teeth into the spot he kissed. Bunny the Viking's long legs straightened as she stood up on her tippy-toes. Her hand found its way to his hair, pulling him closer, tighter.

"Cool, quick currents of electricity and a breath of appreciative chemicals..." He whispered.

"Did you tell him to do that?" Eve asked Him.

He pushed her away and crossed His arms.

"I may have adamantly *suggested* it." He smiled, gazing over Eve's shoulder at the collegians moving about.

"You're man-*ipulative*."

"Maybe," He began, scanning down to her face, "but so are you. So is everyone in here. So is her boyfriend who treats her like dirt because it makes her feel like she's not good enough. Making her associate her worth to his validation. You just don't like that I'm aware that I am manipulating. Look at this room. Look at the high heels and makeup. We're inside a frat party right now. Is this not all manipulation? Unnatural behaviors used to control others. And you, Eve. Based on too many things to count right now, you're not attracted to me anymore – out of warning, perhaps; out of the loss of suspense. You fully suspect that I am up to something, instead of only half-suspecting it like everyone else here. My intentions are diaphanous." He turned to Ollie who was still kissing Bunny the Viking. "I just want to help everyone. We develop remarkably elaborate habits of denying what we truly want."

Eve waited, her eyes considering.

"Not everyone follows those standards. We're all unique-" Eve grinned, "-like snowflakes!"

"And all snowflakes are frozen water which travel down to earth from clouds, following the pattern of precipitation and condensation. They may each be unique but they follow the same rules."

"But humans have free will!"

"I don't agree, dearest. But, even though I do not believe in free will, look at Bunny and tell me what free will she is being denied? She is only being blessed with the opportunity to perceive Ollie as something other than the bland reduction of 'nice guy'. Benevolent knowledge. She will ultimately decide whether she will perpetuate this sudden courtship."

"You're going to have to repeat this when I'm sober." She put her hand on His shoulder.

"Would you sleep with me right now?" He grazed her wrist.

"What?"

"Would you?"

A second passed.

"Nooooo."

"A moment ago you would have."

"How do you know that?"

He smiled.

December 13th 2008

...inhale... inhale... PLEASE!... NO!... relax... stay calm... patience...

"No, *inhale*," He repeated, releasing an exasperated groan which echoed in His mother's room in the medical wing at the NYS Hospital on the east side of midtown Manhattan. "You have to inhale the tube. Not exhale."

His mother blew harder into the blue tube, her face reddening. He placed His hands atop hers, and gently pulled the plastic device away from her. His mother watched as He placed it on the hospital bed, beside the white-blanketed hill of her leg.

"I can't do it," His mother whimpered, avoiding His eyes as if ashamed. "I'm trying, honey bun. I am."

"You have to listen, mom." He waited for her to look up at Him, but her eyes remained on the device. He picked it up and brought it towards Him. Her eyes followed. "This thing-" He shook the plastic, "-is to clear your lungs. But you have to *inhale*, not exhale. You have to breathe in, not breathe out. Like this-" He placed the blue tube in His mouth and sucked in slowly.

The yellow marker in the center chamber floated upwards to the 2500 ml mark. His mother observed, and nodded with a glimmer of recognition in her eyes.

He wiped the nozzle of the tube, and passed her the device. She placed the tube in her mouth, kept her eyes on the yellow beacon, and exhaled with such strength that her head trembled. His eyes watered immediately.

"Inhale, pleeeeease," He repeated as she again exhaled.

His phone vibrated on the radiator. He reached for it and studied the groupchat screen.

Pop: How is she son? It's critical we get her to use the breathing device (7:52)
Bro: Use ur psychology bro (7:53)

He began texting back.

Me: I've been trying for almost two hours, now. I'm modeling it for her as I explain it so she can learn it in different manners. I just asked the nurse to bring another device so that I can do it with her. But I'm not sure if it will work. It's like talking to an infant. (7:55)

"I'm so thirsty," His mother spoke, her black bangs sticking to the beads of sweat atop her forehead.

He reached for the hospital remote, tapped the water button, and then leaned in over His mother and planted a kiss on top of her brunette skull. He hugged her tightly for a moment before sitting back down.

"Hola, señora!" chirped the Brazilian attendant with a Styrofoam cup of water and a straw. "¿Qué tal?"

"Ah, mas o menos." His mother gave the okay symbol with her hands, leaning close and squinting at the name tag. "Esperanza. That's right. ¿Y usted?"

The assistant smiled as she placed the cup on the portable tray beside them. Esperanza peered down at Him.

"Eh-she your mother?" she asked, showing the small gap in her white teeth.

"Yes."

"Everyone love her here. Eh-she's so sweet. And pretty!" She turned to His mother, grinning. His mother smiled. "If you need anything, just push the button, bella."

Both He and His mother watched as Esperanza left the room.

"She's gorgeous," His mother spoke. "If you don't get her number your brother will."

She bit down and wrapped her lips around the straw, and sipped. He watched as the water funneled up. His pupils dilated. She put the cup down. The straw floated in a counter-clockwise semicircle.

"Hey, mom," He spoke, watching the straw, "can you do me a favor and have another sip?"

His mother stared at Him blankly, and then gazed at the cup. She reached for it and squeezed the straw towards her mouth. He reached for the breathing device, and held it close. His mother's cheeks tightened as she sipped.

"Okay, great. Now, can I hold on to this for one second?" He took the cup from her, and placed the blue tube of the oxygen device in her hand. "Take this, and pretend that you're sipping water. Sip the water through this blue tube."

His mother squinted, clouds of confusion moving across her face. She shrugged, put the tube between her lips, and sucked in. The yellow meter jumped upwards.

"Oh my god," He whispered as tears fell from down His cheeks. His chest rose and fell in quick heaves. "You're doing it. Oh my god. Oh my god. Oh my god. You're amazing. Oh my god. Keep going!"

She watched as the meter moved from 0 to 250 to 500 to 1500 ml, and then floated back down. His mother,

with a face of puzzlement, removed the tube from her mouth. "There was no water?"
He fumbled for His phone.

**Me: WE DID IT!!!!!!!! (7:59)
Me: She got above 1500ml! (7:59)
Me: Im so fuxking relieved (7:59)**

He tossed His phone on the bed, laughed, and threw His arms around His mother. She smiled radiantly.

"Ladies and gentleman, it is now 8:00," a man announced on the speaker beside the bed. "Visiting hours are now over."

"I'm so proud of you, mom," He whispered to her.

His cellphone vibrated continuously on the bed. He let go of His mother, reached for His phone, and examined the groupchat responses.

**Pop: That's great news son! Now we have to figure out how to reproduce these results, and then get her do the breathing exercises on her own
Bro: Little bro with the buzzerbeater! How the hell did you pull that off? (8:01)
Bro: I can't believe it bro. Right as they're about to kick you out (8:02)
Pop: The second I get out of this meeting, we are having a conference call. Once mom's lung clots are gone, she can begin the ECTs. Great work son. Now get some sleep (8:02)**

"Hey, mom," He began, "can you try using the breathing device again?"

His mother looked down at the plastic device. She reached for the blue tube, placed it in her mouth, bit down gently on the end, and exhaled.

The yellow marker remained stagnant. His smile vanished and His face sunk. She turned to Him with an inquisitive glance.

December 18th 2008
...hopeful... Hx means 'history' and Dx means 'diagnosed'...

He and His mother sat side-by-side, holding hands, and reading in her room in the psychiatry wing at the NYS Hospital. Nadège, the third of the 24-hour attendees, sat watching them from the corner of the room. Her beaming smile flattened every time they let go of their hands to turn a page, and widened as their hands found each other again.

His mother was rereading the incipient pages of the book He had purchased for her the day before – Albert Camus's *L'Étranger* – in French. He was examining His mother's two-paged Neuropsychology Consultation Report, delivered fifteen minutes ago by the head nurse. Prior to receiving the document, He was reading Albert Camus's *The Stranger* in English.

After reading the entire document thrice, His eyes lingered on the first two lines of the REFERRAL section, which read:

...is a 62-year-old, right-handed, Caucasian, female with Hx of Bipolar disorder Dx at age 54. She was hospitalized on 09/10/08 with psychotic features and insomnia sx, and parkinsonian sx (believed related to recent treatment with...

"Can you tell me the treatment one more time, please?" His mother repeated again, lowering her book with a sigh, "I still don't understand what I'm supposed to do for tomorrow."

He gazed into His mother's eyes, which were pleading and innocent, with eyebrows perched anxiously. The massive window across the door depicted the falling snow onto a construction site outside.

"One part of me wants to repeat it to for the sixth time just to make you temporarily happy, mom. But the more logical part of me wants you to just relax, since that's all you really have to do. You've done ECTs before, and they were tremendously successful."

"He is right," Nadège spoke, her Haitian accent twisting and melting the words.

His mother stared at her blankly, and then turned to her son.

"Please? Just one last time. I promise I'll remember."

"Mom, do you recognize why you're anxious?"

His mother turned to Nadège, as if seeking a clue. Nadège gave an impatient nod to her. His mother turned back to Him.

"You just told me? One of the medications was lowered?"

"It's been lowering since last week. Today you're completely off of it."

"What? Why?"

"Because, though it's good for aiding bipolarity, it has anti-seizure qualities, which will complicate your ECTs."

"Electro..." His mother waited.

"Electroconvulsive therapy. You did it five years ago and it was a huge success. They intentionally cause very brief seizures with small currents of electricity, which is done under anesthesia so you'll be snoozing throughout the short procedure. The drug you were on would not do well with the ECTs. It's kind of like a contraindication."

"How do you know all of this?" His mother asked.

He laughed, sniffled, and kissed the top of her head. "Because it's important to me."

"So-" His mother sighed, "-can you explain to me what I have to do one more time?"

"Mom," He groaned, "I-"

"C'est ton plus jeune ou plus vieux fils?" Nadège interrupted.

Both He and His mother turned to her. She nodded expectantly at His mother.

"Plus jeune," His mother responded. "Mon fils le plus âgé était ici ce matin."

"Ah." Nadège flashed her white teeth. "Tu m'as jamais dit qu'il était aussi mignon! Ces yeux sont magnifiques."

"C'est mon fils," His mother responded, winking slyly. "À quoi vous attendiez-vous?"

Nadège laughed loudly, covering her mouth.

"What did you two just say?" He asked, smiling and examining them.

"She say you a good boy," Nadège answered, winking back at His mother.

"Ladies and gentleman, it is now 8:00," a female announced on the speaker beside the bed. "Visiting hours are now over."

"I really want to be out of this place," His mother complained. "I really don't know what to do."

"What do you mean 'this place'?"

"This hospital, this wing, this room."

"This room is larger than my dorm room at BS."

"Fine, but your roommates aren't crazy."

"You'd be surprised, mom."

His mother smiled.

"You know, your dad has canceled His trips for the last month."

"I know."

His mother gazed out of the window.

"The first place I want to go is Ainsworth's. Their branzino is spectacular."

"I know, mom. You should go there when they're open this time."

"Yeah." His mother laughed, watching the window. "You know that was where your father took me on our first date."

"Yeah, I know." Now both watched the window as the snowfall flaked across midtown Manhattan. "And when you get out, we will eat there as a family. And we will wipe out their branzino reserve."

He leaned in, gave His mother a hug, and kissed the top of her head.

"Love you," He spoke, walking towards the door. "I'll see you tomorrow." He turned to Nadège. "Three to four and then six-thirty to eight on Fridays, right? They don't count as the weekends?"

Nadège nodded in her typical serene fashion.

"Love you, too," His mother responded, sighing.

He closed the door of her room, leaving the two alone together.

"Tu ne devrais pas douter qu'il t'aime," the assistant's voice sounded, smooth and comforting. He stopped by the door and listened to the sounds coming from the room. "Tes traitements te font perdre la mémoire. Il a été là tous les jours. Il t'aime. Il t'aime."

He left the psychiatry wing, descended the elevator from the tenth floor, trotted through the hospital lobby, and stepped outside into the bitter, snowy evening. He winced immediately as the moisture below His eyes froze. He slushed His boots across the curb, and slowly paced across the powder of First Avenue. He turned southwards, with the hospital now to His left and residential buildings to His right.

It was the productions of shadows framed in an illuminated patch on the snow that caught His eye. He followed the light, squinting through the falling snow, and saw two figures moving in an amber-lit window on the second floor. There were two teenage girls – less than twenty feet away – dancing in their underwear. They were moving, drifting, playing, and watching Him with their large, brown eyes.

He stood, fixated. His face was an intermixture of crestfallenness, confusion, and fascination as the girls swayed their bodies in the amber light. Their hips rocked back and forth, their fingers traced across each other's bodies and tussled through each other's hair. On occasion, one would lower her lips down to the other's neck, and – batting a conspiratorial glance towards Him – kiss across the neck, throat, shoulder, arms, hands, and the finger tips – all while watching Him. They blew kisses, curled their pointer fingers in a 'come over here' gesture, and laughed.

After eight minutes, He took one snow-crunching step towards the building, and then shivered. "What the fuck is wrong with me?" He whispered as tears froze in the crevices of His cheeks. He pulled His boot out from the snow, and turned to walk away.

January 3rd 2009
...would Mandy think?... Ollie and I... our alchemy...

They were parked in Alexander's car near the off-white gazebo in Old Rookvale. Alex was in the driver's seat, He was in the passenger seat, and Dustin sat in the back. Dense plumes of marijuana smoke swirled inside, fogging up the view of the perpetual snowfall all around.

"You ready to hear what He and His drugged-out roommate made for us?" Alex asked, rubbing his hands together.

"Yes! Just play the song already," Dustin complained.

Alex slapped Him sharply on the shoulder.

"You ready to be judged, my man?" Alex bounced his head up and down, as if bobbing to a pre-melody.

"Probably not, but let's hear it."

A bassline produced a slap-groove with heavy delay. A Latin-Acoustic guitar joined alternating from D Minor to A Minor with an R&B flare.

His voice inhaled:
Staring at the skylight, the twilight,
as I fight this loveless seductress before me.
I should hide as I try and run away but she pulls me left
as I stepped the other way.
I say no, but she tries to tempt me with her charm,
and with the force of her arm she gets me.
Her bust 's full, she's lustful – I can't escape.
She can detect the sweat on a panicked face.
One minute, I think I'm in it to stay, given her grace,
but I guess her every breath is a riddle at bay.

The vocals of the first verse ended and the acoustic guitar riffed in the D minor pentatonic scale. The notes rolled over one another with patterns that fluctuated and diverged with every measure.

Oliver's voice sang the chorus deeply – a sense of regret building in his tone:
Why did I go with her?
Why did I stay?
Why did I hold her hand,
when I could've just walked away?
Now I'm sitting here.
Why did I stay?
Now I'm all alone.
Why did I stay?

His voice began:
I should've known that she would've flown
with any other mother lover she would condone
as a target
to break a heart quick.
I should've known don't grow attached.
She's filled with evil – now my soul is snatched.
Who would try to stare bare in Medusa's eyes?
Do you realize it's suicide?
She's a venomous specimen with the deadliest elements –
any gentleman is no relevance.
For ever-ever she's devilish... and I wish-
I could redeem myself from what lust does,
but I can't seem to remember who I once was.

Oliver's voice sang the chorus a second time, now with greater fervor; fleeting hope and growing panic trembled in his voice. The car began shaking. He turned and saw Dustin swaying his head back and forth, smiling and spitting tobacco dip into a Gatorade bottle with his eyes closed.

His voice spoke:
Now I'm in a soulless zone where no one could walk through,

> *alone in a cold zone with no one to talk to.*
> *It's never light there; I can't see or think who*
> *I once was as I sink to this new dim hue.*
> *It's like I'm stuck in a four-door room,*
> *with four of the four doors leading towards sure doom.*
> *Misery, as I try and ask me*
> *who was the past me that passed me so rashly.*
> *And that leaves - who am I today?*
> *Miles away from that twilight-skylight smiling day.*
> *I'm in pain, as I try and hide my shame while my mind replays*
> *the question: Why'd I stay?*

Oliver's voice now cried the chorus; unearthly and somber with an increasingly distant delay – sounding more and more like fragmented wails. He turned away from Dustin and faced Alexander who also bobbed his head with closed eyes.

The four words of the last line 'why did I stay' repeated over and over, jumbling atop one another until the words fused to become a single sorrowful noise sounding like 'wished'. The melody sunk into an eerie, dark, and sexual tone. A guitar solo blasted quick repeating staccato lines. The wandering sforzando vibrated throughout the car, until the solo decrescendoed and all of the music faded into nothingness.

Alex turned to Him with intensity.

"That's the type of shit I want to hear from you every fucking day, man!" Alex announced, and then turning to Dustin in the back. "Dusty?"

"The fact that that was *actually you* was the only reason I'm laughing," Dustin spoke. "Oliver might be a drugged out junkie-loser, but he can definitely play."

His eyes glistened from an increasingly red face. His cheeks flexed as if fighting an eager grin.

"How about that, man?" Alex slapped Him hard on the shoulder and shook Him. "Thumbs up all around."

"Did you actually write that?" Dustin asked.

"Yeah. Who else would write that?"

"Yeah – it would be hard to believe that Ollie can even read, let alone write."

"That's hilarious coming from you, Dusty. When's the last time you read a book?"

"I read the instructions to my inhaler, like, thirty times, sonnn."

"You're an idiot." He shook His head.

"Which of your Boston whores were you thinking of when you wrote it?" Alex asked as they pulled towards His house.

"Honestly, I wrote it for Mandy."

Alex parked the car in His driveway.

"Ha!" Dustin laughed. "You're calling me an idiot? You're out of your tits, son."

"You really need to stop thinking of that cunt," Alex groaned.

"Haven't you plowed through enough of your fellow freshman at BS yet?" Dustin spoke. "How many cunts is it going to take to forget Mandy's?"

January 8th 2009

Dr. Henry Hallward Heidelberg: *Are we doing good works?*
Him: Still getting used to college life, which, I guess, is expected from someone halfway into freshman year. My dorm-mate is great, and the girls have been lovely. Classes have been slow, but maybe they'll pick up. I mean, yeah, that was only our first semester and it has to be introductory and everything, but… but I'm not… feeling sure about psychology. I feel kind of disenchanted. I just… I just don't know if I am really learning anything new… and I don't like being in a lecture hall with three-hundred students. I'm not sure… if it's all a waste of time…

Well, what do you think you or your teacher can do differently to motivate you to continue your pursuit of psychology?
I think that the first semester concluding without a single mention of Cooley… Winnicott, Deutsch, Kohut, Durkheim, Adler, Allport, Asch, Bandura, Turner or anyone else interesting is a horrible sign. It makes me anxious, especially

when the other students don't seem to mind. We were on Pavlov, and then I skipped class for two or three weeks, and came back to find we were only on Skinner. In four months, we've covered those two, some Freud and Jung, and a little bit of Piaget and Vygotsky. That's kind of pathetic. How do you not mention Winnicott when talking about façades, or Turner when talking about depersonalization? What kind of school does that? Did your college do that?

I graduated from the very college that you are currently in and from the very program that you're in, as you've already noticed from some of the certificates behind me; but tell me, how do YOU believe we as human beings develop?
Two processes: The 'Original Self' and the 'Reflective Self'.

How does the Original Self operate?
Well, all of our influences are housed in one place. The frame of this house is our Original Self. It is this receptacle where we collect all of our experiences, and its structure is comprised of an interdependent mixture of genetics and one's intrinsic temperament in the face of basic mechanisms like survival, procreation, hunger, rest, shelter, and the like. Every day that passes, the natural self becomes less powerful – only because of the ever-increasing views collected by the Reflective Self as we continue living. That's the Self we absorb from other people.

What causes this Reflective Self?
The cause or reason for the Reflective Self is our heartfelt need to acclimate and communicate. It's the drive that causes us to analyze those living around us, to discover how they can be positive motivators in our lives. We watch and absorb our surroundings to react to, defend against, become, and harmonize with our surroundings.

And what exactly are 'positive motivators'?
Forces that perpetuate one's existence comfortably, honestly, and harmoniously. 'Mother can bring me milk' becomes: 'Mother can help me survive'. 'Father can teach me lessons'

becomes: 'If I listen to father, then I can become smarter'.
These extrinsic forces all provide positive motivation.

What then do you suppose are the forces that comprise you?
I could name ten off of the top of my head that I would say
command my behavior.

First, always, is the Original Self - the collective nexus
through which all of the reflected forces interact. Perhaps
there isn't much of a 'natural self' or 'true self' as Winnicott
suggests there is, but rather this receptacle. It is an evolving
angle viewing and learning from the effervescent stories
breezing by.

The second force is my mother. She's why I began pursuing
psychology... back when she was first sick. I wanted to
know... how to help her. I wish I could describe to you how
I still see so much strength glimmering in her, but I really
can't put into words what she's given me.

The third force, I guess, would be my father, even though
he's never home, and we speak only once a week or so... or
less... He is more of a juggernaut than anything. My mom
might have gotten me to pursue psychology, but my father is
why I pursue learning.

Fourth is my brother. He's six years older than me, and
represents all of the things I don't care about – sports, pop-
music, finance, business and the like – yet, we still get along.
Even though he's lived in Boston for the last few years, he
reminds me of what family is supposed to be.

The fifth force is Ollie, my roommate at BS. He introduced
me to the mind-expanding essence of hallucinogenic
substances like Dimethyltryptamine, Lysergic acid
diethylamide, and Psilocybin. I now know far more about
these substances than he, and the reason why is lucidly
traceable. It's the same reason why he calls mushrooms
'rocket-boosters' while I call them 'psilocybin'. Ollie doesn't

know his father, but his mother is a hippie and an accomplished painter of abstract art. My father is a chemist and the CEO of an immense pharmaceutical company. His interest in the knowledge of pharmaceuticals extends only to a basic curiosity in things that reject or invert logic in an artistic manner, like synesthesia and the alteration of moods in association with different substances. My interest is far more chemical.

Sixth is Mandy – my first girlfriend, the girl I lost my virginity to, and I guess my first love. We dated for only a few months in the summer and broke up in early September this year before I left for BS – only a few months ago… Looking back now, I realize most of our relationship consisted of either sex or the manic lust that anticipates sex. She was always in the mood for sex… even right after sex. Eventually, she cheated on me and expressed that she didn't ever feel like we were really together, and that kind of messed me up. 'How could we be on such different pages?' I thought to myself. Months of panicked metacognition made it clear to me that her… 'adultery' – let us call it – birthed in me a tremendous sex drive. Both a coping and compensational mechanism. A vice, really. Perhaps augmented by my eagerness to read people and command their movements. Sex was validation: The desired result of a sequence of stratagems. Who knows - it could have been for Mandy, as well. Maybe someone she loved or lost her virginity to cheated on her, and maybe someday I'll date a girl and devirginize her and fuck her up, and the miserable pattern will ripple throughout time… Since breaking up with Mandy three months ago, I've slept with sixteen girls. So, it's pretty clear that some part of me believes maybe I can… I don't know… fuck my way back to her. Or at least fuck my way back to not feeling fucked by her.

My friend Artyom is number seven. He may not be the most exhilarating or interesting person, but he knows a thing or two about doing things the right way. He's humble, hard-working and ordered. Art is the ideal influence…the perfect positive motivator when it comes to being an all-around good person. He's in his last year of PA school and already has a potential job lined up through one of my father's connections in the interventional cardiology department at some big hospital in Long Island.

Eight is Dustin. He's a chronic masturbator in the literal and metaphoric sense, seems to be greatly empathetic, but incapable of sympathizing. One part of me sees Dustin and thinks of Helene Deutsch's 'As-if' personalities because he doesn't actually connect with anyone deeply, but instead goes through the motions with everyone pretending 'as if' he has relating feelings with people. Another part of me believes Dustin's arrogance is too unchanging to fit that paradigm. Dustin is simply a manifestation of everything he loudly criticizes – addicts, sloths, liars... A part of me believes he wouldn't be so loud in his criticisms if he didn't feel the presence of these qualities in himself... Projections and such... but who knows? He's a xenophobic white-supremacist, yet his domineering girlfriend is Persian-Jewish... and his best friend Alexander is Lithuanian-Jewish. You know, he *must* be aware of his flaws. He's always thinking of himself. It's as if a part of him is stuck in Piaget's preoperational stage – like a three year old with social knowledge, but plagued by egocentricity and zero understanding of conservation... Chaos. That is Dustin.

And the last that I can think of is Hunter – this surfer-swimmer 'bro' I was friends with in high school. I thought we were close, but I'm not really sure anymore since we don't talk anymore. He liked a girl I dated – that Mandy girl I mentioned before – but I didn't realize really how much until after she and I began dating. He stopped talking to me immediately after, and apparently he despises me. Something about how he set us up, and I never gave him proper thanks. Last I heard he got into drugs – the bad ones, not the Ollie ones... it kind of shows you what jealousy does to someone...

That's nine, by the way, but in any case, how could you even begin to possibly divide and organize all of these contradicting forces you just mentioned?

I guess I don't divide the people as much as I divide their individualistic attributes – what of them is a positive motivator and what of them is a negative inhibitor. Dustin is always making people laugh, and it's good to make people laugh. It exhibits wit, charm, social acuity, interpersonal intelligence and a desire to please others. Dustin's social sharpness is refreshing and kind of reminds me of F. Scott Fitzgerald, but his self-deleterious nature and poor choice of a love interest is heart-wrenching… and also reminds me of Fitzgerald now that I think of it…

January 24th 2009
…ELEMENT OF SURPRISE MODIFIER… OLLIE NOT LAUGHING WHY?...

    Their voices echoed throughout the old confection stand in the basement beneath the soccer stadium at the Boston School. The blunt in His left hand and a cigarette in His right breathed out green and blue-gray smoke. As He moved His hands in gestures, the smoke rose in spiraling double helixes toward the dim light hanging from the ceiling. Ollie reached up and pushed the bulb so it swung back and forth, causing the shadows of he, Him, Nicole, Jenna, Wrubby, and three others - Kenshu, Dan, and Shawn – to sway, expand, and compress along the walls.
    "Talk about your version of God," Oliver requested.
    He looked around the room. Nicole's light brown eyes were smiling.
    "Nicole is God."
    A faint blush rose in Nicole's tan cheeks.
    "Be serious!" Nicole demanded dramatically. "This ought to be interesting," she leveled her voice.
    "Well, in conjunction with the aforementioned dialogue-" He passed the blunt to Ollie, "-all things maintain a constant equilibrium. The same way that each of our one-hundred-trillion cells knows what every other cell is doing via

electrical and chemical signaling, everything in the universe is connecting and communicating and reacting to one another. I believe that god is a dynamic equilibrium, specifically the homeostasis of all homeostases. The connection between our heartbeat, the earth's resonant frequency, and the sun's energy, and where the sun receives its energy. Ontogeny recapitulating phylogeny. Cancer being a miscommunication among cells that causes the total body to die, as miscommunications in any relationship or play or story causes destruction of the total. Prayers, sacrifices, and whims – I believe – are of no purpose other than the consolation of selves. I do not believe a God listens to anyone's prayers. I do, however, believe that if a billion people are suffering, that that very suffering is felt by that equilibrium, which responds accordingly. The response can be seen as cruel, heroic, or gracious, but it is still a response. The same way our bodies respond to aberrant entities."

"Titties," Ollie echoed.

"How does our body respond t–" Dan began.

"Very handsome question, Daniel. It depends on the aberrant entity. Heart disease, cancer, and heroin are all responded to in vastly different manners. Let's just say the response doesn't have to be fair."

"I can be on board with that." Ollie nodded. "Did you know your heartbeat mimics the music you're listening to?"

"How are you two even awake right now?" Kenshu mumbled.

Ollie and He turned to each other. He shrugged. Ollie turned back to Kenshu.

"Whatever do you mean, Master Kenshu?" Ollie inquired.

"Your eyes are lower than mine, and I'm Asian. And you-" he nodded to Him "-you usually have huge eyes."

He smiled at the sound of this. Nicole scanned the eyes of Kenshu, Dan, Shawn, Wrubby, Ollie, and Him, and then Ollie's again.

"You two began drinking at nine AM-" Nicole began, shaking her head.

"My idea!" Ollie laughed. "I threw a bottle of 151 at His face to wake Him up. Told Him we're starting this Saturday right."

"I don't..." Nicole began, stopped and shook her head again. "You guys dropped acid, and then blazed with me before breakfast."

"Then smoked with us directly after breakfast," Kenshu added, "and I'm still stupid high."

"Wait-" He interrupted, cutting the air with His cigarette, a Z of smoke swirling towards the light bulb, "-am I not making sense?"

"What?"

"Am I not speaking properly? Do I sound dumb?"

Silence.

"Like," Kenshu began, "your opinion of God and stuff?" Kenshu asked.

"Mmhmm," He mumbled through inhaling lips.

They all turned to one other and shrugged.

"You're speaking normally, and you don't sound dumb at all," Kenshu responded, receiving the blunt. "It made sense. But what does that have to do with anything?" he inquired.

"Nothing. Nothing at all," He responded.

"Aren't you thirsty?" Nicole asked, receiving the blunt from Kenshu. Everyone turned to Him. "You told me you dropped Molly with Thijs, too."

"You took molly?" Ollie turned to Him, sadness weighing down his voice. "After lecturing me that I shouldn't do it anymore?"

He inhaled slowly – watching as the blunt moved from Ollie to Nicole – and exhaled.

"You expressed... that you..." He turned to the others, then back to Ollie, "...that you were feeling less happy and more depressed. We both know MDMA resembles the molecular construct of serotonin. The rule-of-thumb is that the more a drug resembles a natural chemical in our body, the stronger it impacts us. If your serotonergic neurons release excessive serotonin each time you take MDMA – and you took MDMA a dozen times two weeks

ago, might I remind you – then your body maintains its equilibrium by producing less and less serotonin, naturally. *Less serotonin.* Think about what that means, Ollie."
"I know," Ollie mumbled. "Fine, dude. You're right."
"No. *We* are right, Ollie. You not doing MDMA was *your* decision, and it makes perfect sense. This is only my second time taking it. The first time was with you. So far, molly is the only thing that makes me forget about Mandy."
"I'm just surprised you're taking it after how destructive you made it out to be."
"Is anyone else wondering what the fuck serotonin is?" Jenna asked, exhaling blunt smoke. "And how do you even know this shit, dude?"
"Question number two: My parents, but for different reasons than you think. Question number one: Serotonin is a neurotransmitter that regulates sleep-" He nodded to Kenshu, "-regulates sex-" His eyes locked onto Nicole, "-and appetite and mood." He nodded to Ollie. "What else is there in life besides sleep, sex, appetite and mood?"
A concordant chuckle vibrated through the dim room. The cigarette went out. He dropped it on the floor and crushed it with His sneaker. Ollie passed Him the blunt. He took it in His hand and placed it in His mouth. The tip reddened and illuminated.
"Sleep, sex… sex…" He chuckled, glancing at Nicole for a moment, as if facing a stranger, and then collapsed.
…He opened His eyes. Ollie and Nicole were touching His hands. The others stood over. He stared over Ollie and Nicole's shoulders at Kenshu's tired face.
"One. Erryone. Everyone. What? What-" He blinked. "What just happened?" He asked.
"You fainted," Nicole whispered, squeezing His hand gently. He squeezed Ollie's hand back. "I think you're dehydrated."
"Am I hurt?" He asked, turning to Ollie.

"I don't know dude. I wouldn't be one to know," Ollie responded. "Are you?"

He waited, fixating on the extinguished blunt roach resting on the ground. He let go of Nicole's hand and grabbed His chin.

"My chin hurts," He whimpered. "Am I bleeding?"

"There's a cut," Nicole spoke softly, her chestnut eyes scanning slowly across His face. "Maybe it's from Ollie throwing one-fifty-one at you this morning."

"I think my chin broke my fall."

He smiled shyly, guiltily, and then chuckled. Smiles broke across the concerned faces. Then Ollie laughed, and then He chuckled, and then they were all laughing. Still on the ground, He reached for the roach.

February 9th 2009
...Heidelberg... hope this semester is better... where's professor?...

Three-hundred students sat in the maroon-cushioned seats of the Boston School auditorium in Central Campus. The falling snow could be seen through the circular windows on the left and ride side of the lecture hall. He sat in the middle of the sea of students, yawning quietly just as the professor – an ever-pleasant, plump blonde – waddled up to the podium. She opened her laptop. The projector automatically flashed the first slide of her presentation: A picture of Earth hanging in space. In white-lettered words an excerpt read:

There is no coming to consciousness without pain. People will do anything, no matter how absurd, in order to avoid facing their own Soul. One does not become enlightened by imagining figures of light, but by making the darkness conscious. – Carl Gustav Jung

"Dr. Jung declared that his first conversation with Sigmund Freud lasted over eleven hours…" the professor began.

His eyes dilated to their full capacity – a well of gazing blackness reflected the mirrored words - and then normalized. He drifted to sleep. His eyes moved rapidly behind closed eyelids. Three seconds had passed when His eyes snapped open. He reached quickly for a pen and turned His notebook to the back cover, and began writing furiously:

I am you and you are Me.
What is it you seek, nameless boy? A lesson in psychology? Is that why you are sitting here? What do you think SHE can teach you? Wouldn't you rather know what generates the sudden manifestations of vast, living, intricate thoughts that suddenly appear in your mind? Thoughts like ME.
Freefall through your waking dreamscape, and I will reveal that which you seek:
Occupying much of what humanity believes to be vacant spaces are actually diminutive spheres – 'Dream Machines', if you will – containing the pulsing alchemy of enormous concepts. These orbs are certainly real, yet even the deepest of waking dreamers will only dimly ponder the source of the grand flash of an idea which suddenly illuminates their mind – ideas that are pre-defined in their tremendous intricacy: The instantaneous imagination of bustling cities, undiscovered equations, detailed faces anchored to ghosts, echoes of perfect melodies that musicians find themselves humming. Some called us 'muses'.
The orbs have passed through your mind before, and they will pass again.
Perception, the conscious, and the subconscious. You must comprehend that the mind is a vast, wavering ocean of interlapping images upon which each human gazes down from a particular altitude. The sea possesses all that one has experienced, encoded, and stored. These are thoughts. When a figure floats above the surface, it is a

conscious thought that one can see. Below the surface – floating in the immeasurably massive depths – are the thoughts of your subconscious. When you humans labor to remember a thought, you are reeling the figure upwards from the aphotic nadirs. As the figure rises, you begin to see its outline becoming increasingly defined in the water, until it is barely a mystery. If the thought remains just below the surface, one experiences 'lethologica' (or tip-of-the-tongue syndrome [you can almost feel the surface tension]). If one succeeds in reeling the figure out so it emerges from the deep and floats upon the surface, one has succeeded in remembering the thought. This is the process of cognition and recall.

    Now, you understand that these interwoven images – 'thoughts' – can either float up to our consciousness or sink down into our subconsciousness. But what of perception or awareness? Our perception is not our thoughts, but rather the angle in which we view our thoughts. Our awareness – to put it as simply as possible – is an unblinking Eye that hovers above this ocean gazing downwards at the waves. It should be known that the Eye is closest to the water during the naiveté of youth and the senility of senescence. It is quite easy to comprehend that the closer the Eye is to the waves, the fewer thoughts the Eye can view at one time. The fewer thoughts the Eye can view, the less one can perceive the interconnectivity of thoughts, engage in hypothetical reasoning, and conceive 'the bigger picture'. I should also mention that this Eye of awareness is actually born deep inside the ocean depths – floating in a world of glimmering subconscious abstractions – and only emerges and detaches from the waters during the 22nd week of gestation. Furthermore, when one passes into the deathscape, the Eye sinks back down into the rippling, coruscating ciphers. This is why those with near-death-experiences envision such ineffable wonders.

    Stress causes the waves to move and splash over one another too quickly to focus on a single wave or thought. Sleep – beginning at Stage 1 and occurring up to Stage 5 or REM – typically stagnates the waters enough for the Eye to focus on both the subconscious thoughts and conscious thoughts simultaneously. Meditation slows these waves almost to match the tranquility of sleep.

Now, these aforementioned orbs fly far above the Eye – the vantage point from which humans gaze down at their respective oceans. On fortuitous occasions, these Dream Machines blaze down below your Eye, and blast across the ocean with immeasurable velocity. During this seldom occurrence, a human might notice the sudden ripple of the ocean waves, and may – ever so faintly – suspect something magnificent having passed by. They may suspect something immaculate having flashed.

By the time you write this, the single orb that brought me will be ineffably distant from you. But you saw me, so now I linger within You. What exactly I am has no words in your language, though CONCEPT is the closest approximation. I am a concept, and within me is a concept; within you is a concept and a concept's concept.

Remember, though, that an idea only truly exists only when you allow it to be expressed. A genius who pledges silence to his brilliance is indistinguishable from the dim commoner. It takes one expression to limn a chiaroscuro of creation upon the world. Prepare to write.

In an office located in the southwest corner of Manhattan, a troubled 12-year-old boy named Samuel will sit across from an equally troubled psychiatrists, Dr. Markus. Neither he nor Samuel will admit their own problems to themselves enough for either to begin understanding how to articulate them to each other. Some time ago, however, the orbs discovered that Samuel's vantage point is higher than others' – even higher than the typical dreamer. Nurturing by their nature, the intrigued orbs allowed the boy the sublime privilege of witnessing them, and eventually allowing them to commandeer their movements. They only requested that he did so through the effable medium of art.

In the psychiatrists' office, five minutes after the hour-long timeframe of their first session, Samuel will express art, and the trusting orbs will take flight and construct the otherwise intangible before the unassuming

psychiatrist's very eyes. The actuality of the office will be engulfed by the orbs' pre-creation; and here, Samuel and Dr. Markus will venture through their magic. Together, and with an increasing mutual trust – the two (artist and psychiatrist) will travel from dreamscape to dreamscape – making real the ciphers of their problems and uncovering the ponderous solutions to their unspoken troubles.
I am You and You are Me.

    Class had ended fifteen minutes before He finished writing. He looked up at the empty auditorium, back down at what He had scribbled, grabbed a few clean pages of loose-leaf in the back of His binder, and rewrote it in His own, clean handwriting. After He finished, He packed His things and left the room. He drifted through the red-and-gray corridors of the psychology department at BS, and exited out into the niveous Boston air.
    He walked down Commonwealth Avenue towards West Campus. A full moon was above, glowing behind the late-afternoon clouds. After the mile-long ambulation through the snow and the eight-floor elevator rise, He entered His empty dorm, dropped His backpack by His bed, and fell asleep moments after His body collapsed face-first onto His mattress…
    …Rustling pages awoke Him. He turned over, and focused on Oliver standing above Him, holding the last page of what He had written.
    "Dude-" Oliver gazed down at Him, "-did you write this?"
    He rubbed His eyes and yawned.
    "Yeah."
    "Is it an introduction? Where's the rest? Is it for a psych class?"
    "I don't know what it is, Ollie." He yawned again. "It was just a thought that popped into my head."
    "This is wicked awesome. You have to continue it, dude. Have you read Borges? The guy condenses entire worlds into three or four pages." Ollie re-examined the pages. "How do you know all this stuff? Who is Samuel?"

"I don't know. And I don't know who Borges is."

"Then where did this come from? Were you on rocket-boosters? Drippity-drops?"

"No psilocybin, no LSD. I told you, I don't know. I don't think I even know what some of the words mean."

"What do you mean, dude?" Ollie sat down at the foot of His bed. "This looks like the start of something wicked amazing. You have to continue, *Collie*. No more lighting up any wicked *McBudwick* for you until you promise to write more of it," Ollie demanded.

"Okay." He nodded, contemplating. "But can we blaze now first? For creative insight or whatnot."

Ollie smiled and extracted two joints from his pocket.

"Stop manipulating me." Ollie winked.

March 1st 2009
…*Mandy… sliding down some penis… forget… Lola… boyfriend…*

It was the third night of continuous rainfall. From His dormitory window He watched the storm pour over the soccer field. The field lights glowed through the wet air with an orange haze. Kneeling on His bed was the shaded figure of Lola unbuttoning her white shirt. Her hands hovered over her belt, as if they themselves contemplated taking her jeans off.

"Hey," she cooed, looking up at Him. "Come here."

He turned away from the window. His eyes fixed first on the small white tablets of her grin, and then to her eyes, which were bright enough to beam blueness through the orange-hued darkness. Juan Luis Borges's *Labyrinths* stood face up on the desk by the mirror, opened on a chapter titled *The Library of Babel*.

"How old is your boyfriend?" He whispered.

"Twenty-eight." Her hands drifted away from her belt. "Why?"

"And you say he's a self-made millionaire?"

"Yup. Since he was twenty-five. You've met him briefly at Nicole's party." She paused. "He really is a *nice* guy." His eyes lifted from her bra, and met her face.

"Then what are you doing wasting your time with me?"

Now it was she who turned to the window.

A week prior, He had eaten her out through her black panties. She expressed to Him that she wanted to feel a modicum of loyalty to her boyfriend, so she kept her privates concealed, but as her panties tasted less and less like dry fabric to Him, and more and more like her own sweet fluids, and as her moans loudened from regulated feminine *hmmms* to involuntary *oooohs*, He placed a finger under her underwear, and pulled it to the side while His tongue pressed her up and down. That was the closest He had ever came to having sex with her.

She gazed towards the pluvial field. The orange haze of the field projected the rain falling down the window onto Lola, making it appear as if streams of tears were trailing down her body – each drop beginning with the sudden appearance of a dark orb, and then descending her flexuous body. Finally, she turned to Him.

"You know what… out of all the things you could have possibly said right now-ugh-" she reached for her shirt, "-I don't know. This is a fucking mistake."

She began buttoning her shirt and rose from His bed. He watched as she walked to the door and stopped.

"And you're not even going to try to stop me?" Lola glared back at Him.

"You haven't answered my question, Lo."

"Really?" she shook her head. "Why do you have to know? Do you really need to have a reason? Is your ego that deprived? Do you really need that validation? Are you that narcissistic?"

He stared silently.

"You should probably ask yourself why it's so important to you, instead of just enjoying the fucking moment."

Lola opened the door – suffusing every corner of His room with the phosphorescence of the eighth floor corridor – and slammed it closed, leaving Him alone in the orange-hued darkness.

The draft from outside caused a quiet rustle in the pages.

April 4th 2009
…MANDY… ANXIETY… HOW'S MOM? … euneirophrenia… WHAT WAS THAT?

He walked down Commonwealth Avenue. A church was ahead, the cross at the spire gleaming in the Boston moonlight. Hairs stood on His arm as He gazed at the crucifix. He walked forward, clutching His chest and breathing with a sudden deliberation. Moving shadows in front of the church steps caught His eye.

The homeless. Dozens partially wrapped in black garbage bags, their feet sticking out of porous cardboard boxes. Their uncomfortable groans writhed quietly from one end of the long avenue to the other. A woman wept.

Footsteps from behind. The noise approached. A passing breeze carried forward red hair strands in front of Him, to His right. He sidled leftwards – closer to the church – providing the rushing figure more room on the sidewalk. The passing body turned to Him, her emerald-eyed smile flashing in the church lights. A fuchsia-and-gold-sequined masquerade mask sparkled across her face.

Woman: Sorry about that.

His hand let go of His chest as He nodded. The woman slowed her walk. He smiled.

Him: Why is there such a disproportionate amount of homeless people outside of that church?

The woman looked behind her shoulder, turned to Him, and slowed further to parallel His pace.

Woman: There's a sign outside the church under the crucifix that reads, *'The Lord is refuge for the oppressed, a stronghold in times of trouble'*. The church takes care of them during the day. I guess they're waiting for it to open.

Him: Oh. I didn't notice the sign.

Woman: That's because you were gazing at the cross the way a vampire would.

Him: Right.

Woman: Are you new to Boston?

Him: Five months. Not sure if that constitutes 'new' anymore.

Woman: That's true. It's different from person to person. LSD or Mushrooms?

Him: I'm sorry?

Woman: Which of the two are you on, LSD or Mushrooms? Or maybe some other hallucinogen. Your pretty-shaped eyes are all pupil right now, and it's not just the nighttime.

He hesitated.

Him: Mushrooms.

Woman: What's the difference between them, anyway?

Him: Chemically? One h-

Woman: Experientially.

A moment passed in silence.

Him: LSD manipulates your world. Mushrooms manipulates you. Both put your thoughts in capital letters.

Woman: Are we not our world?

Him: We are a floating mirror passing through a world of different floating mirrors.

Woman: Ha! Sounds like an Escherian funhouse. Our hands being drawn drawing the hands of others… So, what is it like? What are you seeing?

Him: Saturated colors. Burning reds. Burning blues. A near-emptiness and a false conception that everything is unified. Chrystal-clear memories of the homeless, a recognition that they are all components of my collective being, now.

Woman: Is that why you were looking at the cross like that?

Him: I was looking at the cross because it stirs fear deep within me.

Woman: I fear lower-case t's and busy crossroads. What's your excuse for fearing the crucifix?
Him: Associations with my mother.
Woman: Oh boy. Dark conversation?
Him: Yeah.
Woman: Okay, next conversation. What do you see when you look at me?
Him: An attractive, inquisitive twenty-year-old Irish redheaded girl from New York, visiting Boston, who has eyes sunlight through a piece of sea-glass, hair that seems important, and whose eye-mask sparkles look like exploding fireworks.
Woman: Well that's all wonderful and such, but I'm actually an 800-pound Samoan man.
Him: I was hoping I'd be attracted to men one day.
Woman: Ha! So you're attracted to me, now?
Him: The world is attracted to you right now.
A cellphone rang in her purse.
Him: See? The universe calls for your attention.
She extracted her phone from her purse, looked at the name on the screen, and placed it back into her purse.
Woman: Whatever that mirror has to say isn't as important as this conversation.
Him: I don't know if 'important' is the right word?
Woman: Right. Only my hair is important.
Him: Right.
Woman: This conversation is important in my head. Why mushrooms and not LSD? I'm assuming you've done both.
Him: Because Mushrooms are poisonous, and I wanted to be poisoned.
Woman: And why on earth would a lovely person like you want to be poisoned?
Him: Because I'm hurting and I'm feeling bad for myself
Woman: You just passed by a collection of human beings sinking in the inebriation of poverty, decaying into ash before your very eyes, and you still feel bad for yourself?

Him: The misfortunate plight of others doesn't remind me of my fortune – a quality of *schadenfreude* – but rather makes me sad for others along with sad for myself. My sadness isn't externally-caused.

Woman: Do you have depression?

Him: The probability is high.

Woman: Your mother?

Him: My mother.

Woman: Well, what pulls you up from the ocean floor?

Him: Nothing. Fucking keeps me afloat for a while.

Woman: Fucking it is, then!

He laughed, and then she laughed.

Him: What do you do?

Woman: I'm the most famous celebrity in the world, currently on tour, and right now I am avoiding the crowds and pretending to be common with my masquerade mask. Today I'm a journalist by trade, and a playwright by play. And you are a student studying the arts?

Him: I'm a student studying behavioral psychology.

Woman: Oh? I would have guessed you're a writer.

Him: That's probably the mushrooms.

Woman: I don't know. I doubt the mushrooms control what words you choose. You have a writer's mind. Has anyone told you that?

Him: One person. Recently.

Woman: Who?

Him: My roommate.

Woman: He must be smart, too. What's he studying?

Him: Music theory and anthropology.

Woman: Is he a musician?

Him: Yes.

Woman: Then he should stick to anthro.

He laughed.

Woman: I'm fucking serious, man. You think the best writers studied rhetoric? None of The Beatles could read music. It's just not necessary. Is your roommate good-looking, by the way?

Him: Very.
Woman: As good-looking as you?
Him: Significantly better-looking than I.
Woman: Then he has everything he needs. Where is this Adonis, by the way?
Him: He had a bad trip. Started when he pressed an elevator up button. He started making whale noises until his girlfriend showed up.
Woman: And his girlfriend took in your beluga friend?
Him: Yeah. She's great. He looked like he saw an angel when the elevator door opened and Bunny stepped out. Hey, I'm not keeping you from anything, right? I don't want you to think I'm following you. My dorm room is another mile down this road.
Woman: How do you know I'm not following you, handsome?
Him: That's a good point, sir. You're a wise Samoan.
Woman: I'm staying two blocks away. Not too far from the Boston School where I suppose you're headed. We'll separate soon.
Him: Okay.
Woman: You're very likeable. Did you know that?
Him: I didn't.
Woman: While we have this remaining time, can I ask you a favor?
Him: Sure.
Woman: Can you tell me what you were thinking about *before* you saw that church and its malevolent crucifix?
Him: I was thinking about people. I'm always thinking about people.
Woman: Please, be less specific.
He chuckled.
Him: Okay. I was considering that there are twelve or so presets or templates of humans based on animals. Each animal comes with a set of characteristics.
Woman: Physical or psychological?

Him: Both. The physical and psychological are often interrelated.
Woman: Can you give me an example?
Him: Okay. The moose: A naturally large and athletic human who is statistics-oriented, though not necessarily skilled in mathematics. They are drawn to figures and record-keeping, which makes them enjoy following sports and gambling. This physical-rooted admiration of athletic stats parallels their mentally-rooted admiration of financial stats, or 'wealth'. This disposition, coupled with their skills and their size, leads them to areas of power. If they do not become athletes, they become CEOs, Wall Street execs, salesman, and the like.
Woman: And who is the closest moose in your life?
Him: My brother.
Woman: Ah. You two aren't very close, are you?
Him: Not on purpose.
Woman: Give me another animal.
Him: Okay. The puppy: Attractive in its playfulness, adores being the center of attention and cannot stand being left alone. Social creature with fantastic interpersonal intelligence. Loyal, but impulsive and adventurous. Requires the smallest amount of genuine appreciation to feel wonderful, and the smallest amount of criticism to become crestfallen.
Woman: Another.
Him: The hawk: The animal at the zenith of the hierarchy. Large eyes, large nose, large head. Able to see things from far away. Sharp, innately critical, highly-productive, and quick-learning. Biggest flaws are its tendency to see too far ahead of the other animals, an outrageous temper, and the fact that it is the rarest archetype. There aren't many hawks, and talking to a human born from a different preset is always tough. The lack of communication is why it has a temper. Darwin and Steve Jobs are hawks.
Woman: What animal am I?
Him: The pup.
Woman: And what animal are you?

Him: I don't know. I haven't really gotten to me yet, but the last thought I had before your high-heeled footsteps created indigo music in my mind was that I am not worthy of the presets. That I am just air. Or dirt.

Woman: You know, it's nice to occasionally see yourself through other people's eyes. You're definitely not dirt. I don't know if I agree with the whole animal-preset conception, but you strike me as a pup, too. Maybe raised by hawks, but you're closest to a pup. I'm not just saying that so we make puppy love. You're very, very likeable. When I suggested we fuck – however so playfully – I like that it didn't affect you much. You're a refreshing human, you're really cute, and you should remember that I think you're awesome. And you should start writing.

Him: Okay.

Woman: Dare I call you hot air?

Him: Why are you flirting with me?

Woman: Well - why does one flirt with anyone?

Him: Intentions of procreation?

Woman: Yes! I want millions of your babies!

The young woman laughed loudly.

Woman: What's your name? I'd like to see you on the top-seller shelves one day.

Him: I don't have one.

Woman: What a mushroomy thing to say. Have you forgotten your name?

Him: I've never had a name.

Woman: Well, that's a bit strange. What on earth do I call you?

Him: I guess you can call me You, but with a capital Y, if you want.

Woman: Why?

Him: Yes.

Woman: No, why don't you have a name? That seems rather cruel.

Him: I just don't.

The woman slowed down by a large, white door.

Woman: This is my home. I'm going to kiss you now, and we aren't going to see each other again. Not in the flesh, at least. You'll see my worst side on the television and hear me on the radio, whether you want to or not.

Him: How do-

Her lips pressed against His, as she – with her freehand – reached behind, and opened the door with a key. She stepped back.

Woman: I'll look for a book with no author. Until then, be brilliant and resilient.

She entered through the door, and closed it without looking back.

May 24th 2009
...pops here... always moving... impress him... write more...

"Son," His father began, tucking a folder into his suitcase, "why did you leave BS? You should be in the top of your class. Dr. Heidelberg was blown away by your breadth of knowledge." His father paused. "It's drugs, isn't it?"

"No, dad." He sighed, watching His father move about the study of their house. "I simply didn't like BS anymore. The classes were too large, and nothing felt personal."

His dad examined his 9:30 PM boarding ticket to Basel-Stadt, Switzerland, and then his watch which read 6:12.

"I didn't feel motivated to stand out. How could anyone when there's that many students? The best thing about BS was discovering that I want to write."

"Writing what, though?" His father put the ticket in his coat pocket, zipped the suitcase, and looked at his son. "Stories? Movie scripts? Novels? Songs? Without having a proper course of action you will fail in any writing you pursue, son."

"I guess short-stories and novels."

"I guess?" His father echoed, shaking his head. He put on his blazer coat and grabbed his suitcase. "What will you do until then?"

"What do you mean?"

"Well, before you have a piece of work that you can publish and therefore begin financing yourself, writing is just a masturbatory hobby. So, what are you doing?"

"I... well-"

"You dropped out of BS," His father recounted, turning towards the door and motioning for Him to follow, "which mom and I were very lenient about." The rolling wheels scraped over the wooden floor as His father walked and He followed. "Perhaps *too lenient*. You're eighteen years old, you aren't in school, and you don't have a job. You don't have any producible work to send out. So the question remains – what are you doing?"

"I – I know I made a mistake, but..." His voice trailed.

"The greatest consolation to making mistakes is that you can learn from them. What are you doing about it?" His father asked, opening the front door.

"I – I don't know." He looked down.

His father stepped outside and turned around.

"You don't know?"

"I send out my stories to a bunch of writing contests. It's just-" He hesitated, "-I'm trying. I sent my resume to a bunch of publishing houses..."

"Do you even know what 'trying' is?" His father raised his voice.

"I do. I try every day. I've sent resumes to at least a hundreds of publishers. Entry-level stuff."

"And?"

"And no one will hire a college dropout."

"And?"

"And I don't know." He sighed. "What do you want me to say?"

"I want you to show yourself results. I want you to stop thinking about what job or school you think you deserve and accept what job or school you can get. You dropped out of BS. You haven't finished a final draft of anything you've started writing. So the reality is – you are bullshitting. You are bullshitting yourself and you are bullshitting me, and spending the money I've worked my ass off to make."

"I *am* trying," He whispered hoarsely.

"Do you want to know what trying is, son? I left Istanbul and came to this country not knowing a word of English. I was seventeen and taking care of my own mother in a small apartment in Steinway until heart disease ended her life. I commuted two hours back and forth to school by bus, and earned enough respect from *just one* of my professors to eventually work for him." At this point, a taxi crunched up the driveway. "I worked at a gas station, helped teach, learned English, and still had enough time to inject morphine into my mother to blunt her pain until her very last breath. Trying – *really trying* – is when you look back and know with certitude that you couldn't have done a thing more. Can you honestly say you've done that?"

"I-"

"No, son. You can't. Don't bullshit me." His father eyed Him closely. "You're going to the Queens School. You have a week to apply." His father turned and walked towards the cab. "I'll be back late July, son."

PART II – REDEMPTION
July 27th 2009 – July 27th 2010

...the times that I've had sex, the best were not the unhinged, feral, hair-pulling, lip-biting, ass-slapping rough fucking that popstars like Lizzie Manibasse and smut books like 22-Hues of Blue drone about. No.
It's the looks. It's the electric glances. It's when, no matter what angles your bodies fold into, every flash of their eyes upon yours fills you to the brim with basorexia – the overwhelming desire to kiss. Those captivating looks – the looks of love – are what pulse the pleasures with infinite radiance.
 There's something truly edenic about lying beside the person you love. It is an ephemeral return to innocence. For a moment, the intricate bubble of your adult life shrinks back to the smallness of your childhood – when most of the space was occupied by loving and being loved... but what an inebriated illusion that is.
 And that is what love is. Love IS drunkenness: A highly emotional state where peripheral details are blurred and the illusion of general satisfaction leaves one's judgements ungrounded.
 Three loves had me: Mandy, Selene, Danika. I can remember the moment I fell in love with each of you, for each time it hit me so deeply, instantly and inextricably.
 Mandy: You had given me the pleasures of seduction and satisfaction in the cabana, freedom when you alone swam while I rested, comfort with a kiss, and a challenge to my ego with an insult - all done within an hour. Each action – individually and collectively – revealed that you were thinking of me. Even months after you cheated, I continued to contemplate your hypersexual adoration whenever I needed a boost in confidence. Whenever I needed a reminder of my worth.
 Selene: When you woke up in front of me, and the previous night's fucking was still pillowing us, and the morning sunlight rays fell across your radiant and tired eyes,

and you disclosed to me in early morning whispers the secrets of your burdened upbringing, I wanted to hold on to you and protect you forever – because you trusted ME with your darkly glimmering secrets.

  Danika: When you were waiting at the Old Rookvale train station for me, and you thought that I wasn't there, and you sighed with a defeated sadness, I felt an overwhelming wave of love for you because I could see in the shadow of your gloom the illuminated truth that you once relied on me. You were disappointed that I was not there. Though I was! Right behind you! It was a joke on you. How beautiful that the tables have turned and now I sigh at what feels like an empty parking lot when everyone else had just returned to their loved ones before my eyes. The joke is now on me. Ah! And how you would laugh too loudly and too dopily at something I'd say, and I just couldn't help falling in love with you over and over again the second that the tragedy returned in your expression.

  I guess I can say this now: I wrote for you, Selene. There's of course so much more to say, but even now, I cannot begin to express it. Ollie might have introduced me to literature, but you introduced me to art. You opened up a whole new universe of words and worlds to admire. It was sight at first love. Yes, I wrote for you, Selene. And I fucked for Mandy. And for Danika, I know not what I've done, but it simply cannot be something good. I wrote for you, Selene. Even before I met you it was for you. And I read the books that I saw you had read to stir awake the ghost of you in me, to find you and to bring you back. How funny it is that when you, Selene, left me, my desire to write skyrocketed while my ability to actually do so plummeted. Scripturient agraphia isn't a healthy state. Look at all these words I learned for you!

  Why do we try so desperately to re-fill our voids with that which created our voids in the first place?

  Dustin, what qualities of yours did I inherit when you were imprisoned last week? What changed in me when you, Dani, drove away for good?

Love surely is drunkenness. Just as reflecting on memories of being drunk causes one to feel a stir of inebriation, the memory of these loves in my mind still instills within me a slight spinning sensation.

I'm surely getting hectic with my thoughts. We all know nostalgia plays tricks with memories. Nostalgia denies today's blessings. Why is it that memories - even the ones we recognize as horrible and sad and miserable - can be saturated with the most forgiving colors, the most desirable hues, and the most loving perspectives as they tick towards the past? It's as if there is a light far away in our early lives, and as each event blazes beyond the present and becomes a memory, it moves closer to that light, increasingly illuminating with lovely non-clarity until it's just a romantic, imaginative haze. Why this retrospective optimism? Is it solely to make today seem relatively monochromatic? To render today's gleaming sun just a lurid ball of smoldering ash? Nostalgia is a most toxic illusion that strangles today by its endorphins.

Or perhaps the good moments become visible emotions in our minds and the bad moments slowly evolve into lessons - lessons through which we have the confident assurance of having survived. The good remains a photo archive of exuberance; the bad becomes a chalkboard of 'thou shalt not' do ever again. If only we always listened to the chalkboard. If only I glanced at it more often. I might have even circumvented the virulent allure of you, Dani...

When you love someone you have chosen to relinquish a part of yourself in order to inherit a part of them, and what perpetuates that love is the feeling of confident appreciation for such a potentially debilitating trade. That's why heartbreak feels like a sudden void. Appreciation is so much of it. Insanity, specifically insanity that is not hereditarily-induced, can be entirely conjured by the unending feeling of un-appreciation, or more specifically, a lack of proper appreciation. That is why the psychologically impaired often create magnificent alter egos or additional personalities where many sought-out dreams become 'realities'. I do wonder though, about that systemically amnestic process that creates the fading mist of logic and stimuli which engulfs previous experiences into nothingness. How much did my mother lose during her treatments? How much appreciation does she feel for what I've done?

Appreciation, another thing I have lost. For myself, for everyone, for everything. Everyone has something for which they want to be most appreciated. For me it was writing, I think. Crafted revelation. Writing was my key to understanding this world. This sounds vain because writing is a vain act. Even now, these parting words should instead be egoless like the parting words of Seneca before he was sentenced to end his own life. But I am incapable of thwarting my ego.

Many times I have written, drunken off my imagination, then read what I've written, marveled at the glow of a corpuscular idea amid tangled and tenebrous sentences, and have gotten drunk all over again. It's wondrous to consider that symbols of ink - when arranged properly - have the power to activate the soul, illuminate the stage of the mind's eye, and tug at the currents of one's emotions. Symbols, shapes, spaces, and patterns. 'Wrote note. Took pills. Now... wait' - that's a full story in six words that I've read somewhere. How fitting it is today.

When I couldn't write and the artist in me was ignored for too long - or for what felt like too long - something poisonous would happen to me: The unused creativity built, and then turned its back on me. It poured fragments of imaginative nonsense into my consciousness, and I was forced into seeing scenes of me that were disagreeable and deflating and depressing, and eventually, as I was swarmed with these subduing hallucinations, I would begin to forget who I really am... and the world swirled by, and then - in that precise moment when my mind can suddenly refocus on the details of the world around me - I would feel tricked, arriving late to a joke that involved me, and everyone else would be booming with laughter. It feels like I am heavily intoxicated, barely standing in the center of a merry-go-round, watching the familiar shapes go by. And I am the wobbly fool within a diminishing caricature.

And every day that passed where I felt as if no one appreciated me sunk me further and further down into this inescapable sadness. This would have been far less dreary if I felt the Grand Equilibrium at work - for me to feel satisfied the next day, to be at some point higher tomorrow than yesterday's low. But, no; I was ever-downwards. Thus, I was forced to witness the mortality of my situation, for how deep can one submerge until the lungs sob for air?

Let it be known, reader, that I was once breathing, dreaming, moving, screaming, drinking, perhaps even smiling (notice that smiling is subsequent to drinking) before the end of this day. I am a real person, reader. I swear of it. And I will be gone before your eyes trace over these sentences.

Yes, the greatest thing in this life is to feel appreciated. More so, to be appreciated precisely for what one truly wants to be appreciated. That feeling - that feeling that Danika, Selene, and Mandy intermittently gave me - it releases the highest amount of love... a love which pours out to the world, out to the person who has appreciated you, and into yourself. That form of appreciation causes this ecstatic confirmation that you weren't wrong all along - that you always had a special gift, that someone else found it in you, too. That you were worth something.

LSD. It courses thickly in my blood right now. I can feel every vein and valve bubbling.

Focus, now: There are two suicide pills being cradled in my left hand as I write these words. What a peculiar idea I think now as these two black Death-capsules roll across my palm. 'Take two of these and the pain goes away, the tears go away, the eyes go away. Take two of these and you go away'.

One has a red dot on it, the other green. The way in which these lovely pills will end my life is worth explaining:

The first pill is actually a 500mg PDE5-Inhibitor (like Viagra and other drugs for Erectile Dysfunction). PDE5 stands for Phosphodiesterase Type 5. Inhibiting the PDE5 enzyme results in vasodilation (blood-vessel widening) in the penis – increasing its blood flow. Inopportunely for most, this PDE5 enzyme that is inhibited is not only found in the penis, but also in the smooth muscle cells of the arterial walls of the pulmonary system. Taking this red-dotted pill relaxes the arterial walls along the lungs' vasculature and reduces one's overall blood pressure.

The second pill is a potent, non-FDA approved Nitrate. Now, for anyone who isn't my father or Artyom, mixing a PDE5-Inhibitor with a Nitrate is a big no-no. They are contraindicated with one another (as they both result in lowering one's blood pressure). The effect of taking this second pill in conjunction with the first is critical hypotension – the fatal drop of blood pressure.

If I take this first pill and do not take the second pill, the symptoms don't extend much beyond dyspepsia, kidney pain, and vertigo – all of which I experience diurnally. I was also warned about the miniscule chance of sudden hearing loss – which had me intrigued and pondering over whether the silence would rid me of my perpetual migraine.

Upon ingesting the second pill, I have only a few minutes to vomit the life-ending interaction. In less than thirty minutes, I will drift away into the ethereal dreamscape of the nonliving.

Two suicide pills were in my left hand. Now only one is in my left hand...

The taste begins with the expected chalkiness of most medicines, but ends with a curious hint of sour cherry that tastes almost sweet. Two hours left to take the second pill. Two hours left to write. The LSD tells me that the glowing time on my car's dashboard says S:OS, when I know it is 5:05.

But why am I committing suicide? Have I even come close to answering my two questions? How much is a life's worth? What is the cost of a human's life? Probably not.

I wish I could blame this circumscription on my ADHD, but I took my focus pills this morning. Focus pills...

death pills... health pills, cock pills, lung pills... My mom's pills used to turn her into a ghost...

I've taken concentration medication since I was seven years old, but have changed prescriptions three times. The first one - I don't remember the name of it - had some adverse effects on me when I was twelve. First, it was merely bouts of insomnia, infrequent mood swings, and vivid daydreams that were difficult to snap out of. The most bizarre symptom was what seemed to be a perceptible increase in the loudness of my imagination. I recall on one sleepless evening, I was staring at the ceiling without the slightest sense of somnolence. A couple minutes passed 3:30 AM, my meandering contemplations imagined an elementary school friend of mine saying the word 'He'. I then quite audibly heard him whisper 'He' somewhere in the furthest corner of my bedroom. Slightly alarmed but very much intrigued, I imagined him saying it again and again, hearing 'He' each time. Then something rather unsettling occurred: I entirely lost control of the voice. It detached from me and began shouting 'he - he! - He! - HE! - HE!!' louder and louder until it was roaring stentorian blasts throughout the whole world. I leapt out of bed covering my ears, ran shrieking to my parents' room, woke them up and told them between panicked sobs what was happening.

Mother was understandably alarmed. Father was immediately pharmaceutical. 18-year-old brother was home from college that day and was quick to say that I was 'faking it' for attention. Despite his ultracrepidarian cynicism, I was off the medication the next day, and switched on to another more suitable collection of chemicals...

Mother, father, older brother. What a family you comprise.

I guess we should talk, finally. Let's begin with you, mother.

Anyone who knows your redeeming qualities squints distantly towards your excellence as a translator and a church Sunday school teacher nearly a decade ago, mother. You speak English, French, Italian, Spanish, Greek, Armenian, Turkish and Arabic fluently; though you pretend to not know how to speak them anymore. A silent polyglottic translator - the irony defines you. You learned Armenian, Greek, Turkish and Arabic through Artyom's mother. I wish you had the humble courage to still speak to her. Don't be so embarrassed that she saw you at your absolute worst... The ghosts who once called you a friend are still closely familiar with your multitudinous charms. Others might not suspect your linguistic erudition. The Old Rookvale police, for example, know you very differently... Eight years ago, when I was twelve years old, a chemical misbalance occurred in your mind and your then-regulated bipolarity spiraled out of control. One evening you'd be manically chain-smoking cigarettes outside of Ainsworth's at 3AM, and the next day you would be hibernating in your bedroom and thinking lowly of yourself. I'm beyond grateful that the chemical imbalance that caused your aberrant behavior was normalized. I'm at least mature enough to think of psychological maladies in the same way people see physical problems - like a broken leg - and that your healing was at least synonymous to the mending of bones, muscles, and tendons. Too many people disregard psychological problems as 'being crazy' which is reductive, and lazy... and fucking wrong. Despite being your regularly-balanced self after a single vicissitudinous year, by the time I was 13 you were a completely redefined individual in my mind, and I relinquished your right to be my authority. You had infuriated me to the point where I blacked out with rage. At first, before anyone understood how bad it would get, father was almost never there (always on his intercontinental trips) and brother was a freshman in Boston. It was just 12-year-old me laboring through puberty, and you. Though, one day, when dad was indeed home, and you were wearing that crucifix, you said something infandous to me, something unredeemable... Despite it all, I forgive you for the malady that cursed you when I was 12 and again when I was 17. But there is something that I cannot forgive: You tried to resume being my mother. Though I continued loving you, I had already mourned your maternal death. Every time you attempted to exercise parental authority over me, the result was clearly fury on my end. I would not serve as your son again. When you were sick, you listened to me when we were in the hospital room together, and it helped you. If, when you got out of the hospital and were feeling better, you took my advice ever, our lives would be colored quite differently. You'd have reached out to Artyom's mother, instead of hiding from her. You wouldn't have pushed all of your friends away... I guess in this regard you and I are similar... I should say, though, that it was in that earthquake of my 12th year when my lucid daydreams began – perhaps engendered from a desire to escape. So, I guess, I have you to thank for this feral imagination of mine.

'Father, father, where are you going? O do not walk so fast. Listen father, listen to your little boy, or else I should be lost.' William Blake put it best. I will never become you or become half of what you want me to become. Your superior son might be able to, but not I. How am I supposed to compete with the poor immigrant who personally administered morphine shots into his dying mother when he was only 17 and already on his way to earn a PhD in Physical Chemistry, and who made himself into the renowned chemist-turned-businessman that discovered Kavum? Yes! The creator of Kavum - the near-curer of the number one cause of death in America. Let us inform our reader the facts, father. You'd like that. Heart disease kills roughly 600,000 Americans per year - 1/4 of the total deaths in America. It only makes perfect sense that you would be obligated to ceaselessly travel for your lectures, investment meetings, and pharmaceutical-business deals. I did get the privilege of seeing you once or twice a month. And when you would visit, for some reason, things did appear to be agreeable. And then you yourself got heart disease. I still can't believe it's only been 3 months since your triple-bypass surgery. It's ghastly that you would have the same heart problem as your mother, and would need surgery at the same age she was when she passed away. I guess we all really are slaves to our genetics... Everything I did – except for writing – seemed to be the momentum of a movement you have pushed. I idolized you and still do, which is awful because I've conceded to your beliefs over mine too often. (Read Winnicott, father. It's your turn to read.) Now, I view your consistently logical advice as attempts to extend your control over me further, you totalitarian ghost. My world couldn't be controlled, and my imagination could not be regulated. It's barely mine to begin with. The calculating human in me knows that besides the police, you will be the first person to read these words, father. As you hold this letter and woefully wonder why I am mordantly slumped in this car, I want you to ask yourself the questions: How often have you seen me within these last three years? Do you know my dreams? What my Along a Wandering Wind story was about? No, because none of it was profitable. I think a stranger reading this note would know more about me than you do before these pages are in your possession. Even when you're a distant object floating about in your own multimillion-dollar endeavors, you have the potency to pull me into a most uncomfortable disharmony with myself. You should have either decided to really leave me alone or really have been there. You and mother should have separated from me and not each other.

   And you, my successful investment banker brother. We can communicate sincerely for once: I know that you have never liked me. Never. When I asked you for the smallest of favors, the simplest of advice, or even the slightest respect, it would be too much. There's no way around it. Just like our parents, you are blithely ignorant of the destruction you've casually inflicted within me. Think about the reason why I haven't spoken to you since early May. Like mom, you still text and call with a familiar expectancy – as if everything is alright. Well, ever since that day where you told me to go fuck myself - when you vocalized what I've always known - I can confidently and sincerely say I finally fucking hate you back. I fucking furiously hate your taste, style, words, and all of it. Why do you blast Lizzie Manibasse and all the teen-pop-music singers in the car when you know I loathe them? What makes you think you can commandeer my hours and writing? Every time you imperatively yell at the television about something an athlete does or should have done I want to run up to you and slam my clenched fist into your face and shatter your jaw into a million pieces. I fucking hate how people like you find such joy and belonging and fraternal camaraderie in a putt of golf, or a three-pointer, or a touchdown. I fucking hate it and I fucking hate all of them. And I fucking hate that the eyes of a stranger reading this might widen here with a 'woah' and then relax with an equalizing thought that I am overreacting. It is quite the opposite: There isn't a word to properly portray my exothermic rage at seeing such inhumanely depersonalizing behavior.

There you have it: Psychologically-unstable polylingual wife, American-dream-attaining genius immigrant husband, and financially savvy white-collar grand-consumer son. Mother, father, brother: You...

     July 27th 2009
     ...financial discussions as always... wait... colors... I wrote...

     His father, mother, older brother and He were sitting down at the dinner table. His father had just returned from Basel-Stadt, Switzerland, and would be home for two days before a trip to San Francisco, California. His older brother had taken the train home from Boston for the occasion.
     His father continued summarizing a how-to business book that associated workers with hat colors based on their qualitative skills and weaknesses, concluding with: "The ideal work environment in any office has an equilibrium of colors."
     "I wrote something like this at the Boston School!" He announced.
     "Ha!" His brother snorted.
     Immediately, He looked down at the salmon on His plate. His father turned to His Brother.
     "Don't laugh at Him. He knows all about this psychology stuff. Give him credit. He might teach us something. Tell us, son."

"It wasn't colors or hats," He began lamely, still staring at the dead fish on His plate. "It was animals, and… and… yeah… It's not really important. Never mind."

Silence. His mother took another gulp of the red wine in front of her.

"When did this get published, dad?" His brother asked.

His father waited, lingering on his younger son. "The book? Last November."

"Can I be excused?" He spoke, still staring at the meatless salmon skin-and-bones on His plate.

"What's wrong?" His mother spoke.

"Nothing." His eyes remained low. "I'm finished… and want to continue reading."

His father looked at His brother accusingly, then at Him and His empty plate, and finally at His mother who poured herself another glass of wine.

"Okay."

He got up, took His plate to the sink in the kitchen, and walked through the living room towards the study - looking out of the sliding glass doors to the pool – and continued to the den. He sat down at the desk, reached for Oscar Wilde's *The Picture of Dorian Gray*, and turned midway into chapter two.

Only minutes had passed before His brother crept into the room.

"Hey, bro," His brother spoke.

He nodded, and grabbed a pen from the desk.

"I didn't mean any of that back there that to be insulting. No one questions that you know how to write, or that you write well. Or that you know your psychology stuff. It's just, you know, it's a *business* book. You hate business and finance and that sorta stuff. You told me yourself. I wasn't questioning your ability in anything. If you want to tell me about that idea you were writing, I'd love to hear it."

"Right," He responded after a moment, making a movement like He was underlining passages. In reality, His pen had crossed out several of Basil's words.

August 5th 2009
...reread Borges... why is brother so loud?... sports...

  He was in the study, and through the glass window that divided it from the living room was His brother, sitting on the couch and watching a basketball game.
  "YEAH BABY!" His brother shouted, jumping up and swinging an arm through the air. He clapped loudly as he sat back down.
  He shook His head and looked down at the pages on the desk.

'The Muse of the Sixty-fifth Minute', or, 'Among the Dream Machines'

  Dr. Markus sat atop the edge of a tree stump which stood miles and miles high, his feet dangling in the air, his eyes smiling at the pristine colors and shapes he had created all around. He hadn't scratched his hands for some time now. He jumped off the ledge, and floated above the bucolic landscape. He orchestrated another sunrise to illuminate the curvature of this pastoral world. Like everything else he had learned to create, it was exactly what he had imagined it to be. Soon, he knew, he would have to delve into the source of his problems and face them in a way he had never imagined: Making the psychological physical. In the distance, the figure of Samuel soared nearer, waving warmly...

-

  A high pitched tone, specifically the sound silence makes when overstretched, rang in the psychiatrist's ears as he gazed at the vacant space between himself and Samuel sitting in the chair across his office. Ten minutes had dragged by in their second appointment, with both patient and doctor laboring to keep the inevitable unmentioned. Dr. Markus cleared his throat.
  "I'm going to level with you, Sam," the doctor began, and then paused. He suddenly felt too large for his black leather seat, too big for his office. Movement seemed

perilous. He considered claustrophobia and micropsia, and then turned to the mirror on the right wall. The shine of the sun through the closed window illuminated the sweat atop his forehead. The stubble across his tan cheek was too dark, he could see. The psychiatrist cuffed his hands together, and with the fingers of each opposite hand, he scratched his palms until Samuel's green-eyed gaze again pierced his peripherals. He turned back to face the troubled teenager.

"I'm surprised you came back," the psychiatrist continued, "even though I called you in and asked you..." his voice trailed, "to... come back."

"I know," the boy mumbled, nodding slowly.

The psychiatrist laughed anxiously.

"Are you nervous, too?"

"No." the boy sighed. "Rueful, perhaps."

The psychiatrist reflexively reached for his pen to write on the unwritten journal, but his mind descended into nothingness when his fingers coiled around its shaft. He let go of the pen, which rolled loudly across the desk and onto the carpet. He laughed again – louder and more anxious-sounding than the first – and threw his hands into the air.

"Now I'm starting to think there's something wrong with me," he choked.

A cool wind blew through the office. The windows were all closed. The fan was off. He looked up from the ebony desk and towards Samuel.

"About our last meeting..." He squirmed, stopped and sighed. He scratched his palms.

*

A week back in their first appointment, Samuel sat in the same fuzzy white chair that slouched too deeply inward and had armrests too high for a regular-sized human to sit comfortably. Across from him, the psychiatrist sat in the same large black revolving seat. There were five minutes remaining in Samuel's one-hour introductory session. Within their hour-long session, Dr. Markus listened with increasing interest as Samuel spoke of his melancholy childhood: A step-father who was always traveling, a mother who was diagnosed with manic-depression and committed suicide when he was twelve, and being an only child. He spoke of intelligence, creativity, emotions, and moments in his life where he felt especially alone. He showed the psychiatrist detailed pictures he had drawn and poems that he wrote with them; all of which, Samuel kept reminding the doctor, were expressions of his past. Dr. Markus decided against reminding Samuel that all the art we create are expressions of our past, and more often than not, indications of our future.

Samuel handed Dr. Markus a defined sketch of a woman who was Samuel's mother. In the picture she stood outside what looked like an empty diner. A crescent moon coruscated among a tapestry of stars. A large, glowing orb floated above her right hand, which seemed to pour out images of twisting clocks and faded-faced figures in the café behind them. There was something paradoxical about her welcoming smile and her challenging eyes, yet it was all eerily human.

Nearly five minutes had passed beyond their appointment. The psychiatrist had five pages filled with his reflections of the boy. Aside from brief notations of anxiety, repression, and possible ADHD, several of the pages were crammed with nothing but lauding analyses of the boy's mind. On the fifth page he was finishing a sentence with '...and quite moving' when he noticed the time. Samuel looked down at his feet.

"Doctor - I know there is so much wrong with me, and I trust you and everything, but I don't know how to explain without..." The boy's voice trailed.

The psychiatrist smiled. He heard similar worries uttered countless times by countless voices, all with similar tones of distraught. Though this phrase was one he had grown accustomed to - perhaps even jaded to - he could not help but consider that Samuel seemed the most composed of his patients.

"You've said that three times," he began in that particular tone between encouragement, authority, and tenderness that great psychiatrists master, "and when I ask you for clarification, you tell me we need to change the subject. You have a ten-"

"Did my step-dad tell you why I'm here?" Samuel interrupted.

He pulled back in surprise.

"Well, his exact words were that I needed your exact words."

Samuel studied him closely. Behind the psychiatrist's spectacles were sincerely good, brown eyes. Samuel closed his eyes and inhaled deeply.

"Doctor-"

"Yes?"

"I didn't really write those poems or draw those pictures."

Dr. Markus waited, knowing that silence typically continues an incomplete revelation, but Samuel remained still.

"Pardon?" Markus finally asked. "What do-"

"Not by myself at least."

A cloud passed in front of the sun; the room dimmed.

"I didn't write any of them alone," Samuel repeated, breathing heavily. "I'm afraid to show you, but that's why I'm here, isn't it? To show you."

The pen atop the desk rolled across the ebony surface toward Samuel. It fell from the desk onto the off-blue carpet and rolled across the carpet to Samuel's feet.

"Take a deep breath. You can-"

"You will see," Samuel interrupted, his voice echoing a deeper sound.

Silence. A high pitched noise. And then, the doctor felt a downward tug on his heart, like the quick pull of a dangling switch from an antique lamp. He grabbed the wooden desk quickly with two hands, as if he were about to fall. His body tensed inwards, and then relaxed. He took a hurried breath. Something brushed against his face. Something was there. It felt like a cool mist. A white orb appeared, glowing and hovering across the center of the office. The doctor felt his heart beating slow, heavy pounds. Samuel leaned forward and whispered:

> "Our lives: the paths we take
> across Life – the vast oceans.
> Our Time: Oarsmen who navigate
> through wakes of others' passed motions."

The orb flashed above them as the maroon walls dripped downward and the hues of nighttime oozed through where the walls once stood. Darkness was all around. The desk, Samuel's chair, and the doctor's seat conjoined into a small wooden boat, rocking across a pitch-black sea. Behind Samuel's right shoulder, the doctor gazed upon a tremendously detailed pale-yellow moon. Below, the flat ocean reflected the moon perfectly, creating a sense of a mirror below them. Trillions of sparkling stars stretched about on all sides of the horizon, curving down the black dome of the skies and reflecting again in the seascape.

Another frosted wind gusted by as Samuel continued:

> "Each day a wave of different hues
> with great twists and vicissitudes"

The doctor's hands gripped tightly on the sides of the rocking boat as he leaned starboard and peered down at the ocean. The water produced a mirror-image of his face – astonishment – and behind, the scintillating nebulae above him. He reached downward into the water and watched his fingers disappear beneath its surface. Cold electricity tingled up his arms. He ruminated over somatic hallucinations. Water droplets splashed over the reflected moon as he lifted his hand from the water. The doctor watched as thousands of pale-yellow particles of the reflection scattered about like lightning bugs. Slowly, they came together to recreate its fullness as the water regained smooth tranquility.

The salty aroma of the ocean poured into the doctor's lungs as he inhaled. Trails of twisting lights swirled by overhead like illuminated winds. A distant splash sounded to his right. The doctor turned his head and froze. Two boats, each of which containing a single shadowed oarsmen, approached from the distant darkness, drifting several feet apart from one another, moving parallel to one another. Both had Samuel's face, though one grinned manically while the other glared despondently. They passed by Samuel and the doctor – their expressions unchanging portraits – and faded into the other side of the nights shade.

> "Waves of sorrow and rage
> May borrow our days,
> While waves smooth and flat
> Permit us to relax."

The stars began fading. Samuel's voice whispered in the darkness. A gentle splash. The silhouettes of another pair of Samuels appeared in the distance from where the previous two had approached.

> "We must always see the sea,
> and embrace what we reap
> if we are to keep our seat
> moving all ways upon the face of the deep."

The weight pulling the doctors heart downward let go. He felt it slowly rise in his chest, beating hard but regularly-timed on the way up. He adjusted his glasses and stared at Samuel as four massive planks of wood emerged from the black water around him – displacing tremendous dark waves in all directions. The planks rose in the form of burgundy walls and met a lowering ceiling, where at the center a wooden fan sprouted. A bookcase leaned against the wall. The boat snapped loudly into three drifting sections. Two-thirds of the boat transformed into Samuel and the psychiatrists' respective chair, and the third piece in between them swelled to an ebony desk. A carpet bloomed

from the ground as the ocean water drained away. Fourteen framed psychiatric certificates reappeared on the far wall, behind Samuel's shoulder.
    Silence.
    A bird calling out in the distant sun-setting sky of Manhattan.
    Silence.
    The ring of the clock dial.
    The psychiatrist examined his hand, which was still cold from the ocean water. A sigh filled the room and sank into the growing pit of silence. A minute passed, as did another – both lost in a fragmented dance of logic and illogic, chaos and order in the psychiatrist's mind; thoughts combining all around him, leaving him slow, cautious, confounded – like a metamorphed-caterpillar suddenly cognizant to the enormousness of the world beyond the garden. At some point, perhaps hours after Samuel had shuffled awkwardly out of the office, the doctor heard a high-pitch tone.

*

    A cool wind blew through the office. The windows were all closed.
    "About our last meeting..." He squirmed, stopped and sighed. He scratched his palms.
    "Yeah," Samuel responded, eyeing the carpet with a melancholy gaze.
    The psychiatrist waited for Samuel to say something else, but he did not. Samuel looked up. The psychiatrist removed his spectacles and eyed Samuel sincerely.
    "Do it again," the psychiatrist spoke.
    A faint smile bloomed on Samuel's face as books pulled away from the shelf and hovered towards them.
    "We have so much to work on if you're going to really help me, doctor. Let's start by meeting my mother. Brace yourself. Seriously."

After writing the words 'seriously', He got up from the study and walked towards the TV room where His brother sat.

"Hey, do you have a sec?"

"For what?" His brother responded, keeping his eye on the television.

"Can you take a look at this and tell me what you-"

"THADDA BABY!" His brother jumped up, clapping as the Knicks scored another three-pointer. "LET'S GO NEW YORK!" His brother pounded his chest loudly.

The television went to a commercial break. His brother turned to Him.

"Let me see that." He grabbed the paper and the pen from His hand and immediately began crossing out words.

A commercial for the US Army appeared. His brother looked up and watched as soldiers ran through fields carrying firearms, throwing artillery at one another, high-fiving one another, slapping each other's bottoms, huddling together, smiling together and working together. The next commercial appeared, advertising a jazz trumpeter's upcoming New York performance. He turned back to the paper, and continued crossing words out.

A few minutes later the television returned to the game.

"Here," His brother said, quickly pushing the paper and pen out towards Him. "Get rid of all of the adverbs. You don't need them."

He returned to the study, His eyebrows lowered. He sat down at the desk and examined the edited story. All of the adverbs were crossed out.

"There's no way he read anything," He said aloud. "Adverbs: They describe *how* an action happens. I am editing. I am editing *poorly*. I am editing *lazily*. I am editing *quickly*."

After reading the edited document twice, He spotted the adjective 'melancholy' crossed out. He gritted His teeth, His chest lifted and fell quickly, and the veins on His forehead prostrated.

"I am editing *cuntily*. I am editing *assholeishly*. I am editing *fuckingselfish-moronically*. I am editing *dickheaded-bovine-piece-of-shittishly*. I am…"

"Yeah baby!" His brother jumped from his seat.

August 13th 2009
…my stupid writing… mom upset…hope it's not…

"Come home!" His mother snapped over the receiver.

"I'm reading something over right now. I'm at The Rising Star. Is it an emergency?" He asked.

"Well," His mother began, "yes. If you can take a break from your busy writing schedule-"

"Ugh," He groaned as He hung up the phone. He crumpled up *The Muse of the 65th Minute or Among the Dream Machines*, got up from His seat, and threw the paper into the trash. "Busy writing schedule," He echoed, staring at the garbage bin.

He headed to His car, got in, and drove the ten minute Old Rookvale drive to His house. He opened the front door, and immediately faced His mother. She watched Him with her arms crossed.

"By the way," He began, "Art called me this morning and said his mom was trying to reach you for like the eighth time this week."

She waited silently as He closed the front door.

"Look!" She pointed to the wooden piano by the staircase, where a full bottle of water sat atop. "See anything wrong with this picture?"

"Yeah. I guess I left a water bottle on top of the piano."

"You know not to leave things on top of the piano. It damages the wood. Do you have any idea how much dad spent on the piano? Do you want me to call your father and tell him?"

"Jeez, relax. This is the first time it's happened."

"No, *you* relax. You have no responsibility. Where are you even going all the time? Why are you never home?"

"Okay," He raised His voice. "You care so much about the price of this piano and the damage the water does. Why did you leave the bottle there?"

"To prove a point. You wouldn't believe you did it if I moved it."

"What? So you'd rather further the water damage on the piano just to prove a point, and you're upset at me for leaving it there? Can you see the flaw in that logic? What mistake have I made that you haven't mirrored?"

"You're always making mistakes. It's time to act your age. You're going to be nineteen in two months. Start acting your age."

"I accidentally forgot it, once. ONCE! ONCE!" He screamed, slapping the piano top loudly, "-for the first time in eighteen years, and you left it there purposely to make a point. Time is the destructive property here. I was ignorant to it, where you extended it cognizantly. *That's* why that was illogical."

"So, I'm illogical, now?"

"No. That is NOT what I said. I said that that *action* was illogical. Not that *you* were illogical. What is wrong with you?"

"What is wrong with *you*?"

"And then you just repeat back what I say. Do you have any idea how immature that is?"

"I guess I'm immature."

"No. Again, I'm pointing out the specific..." His voice trailed. "You know what - never mind. You're absolutely too broken-minded. Call Art's mom. Occupy your time with something positive."

"I'll call her when I want to."

"It's been two weeks!" He shouted. "She's your only friend left!"

"Why does this concern you? Is it any of your business?"

"It is COMPLETELY MY BUSINESS!" He roared, punching the wall and denting the plaster. "YOU'RE MY FAMILY AND THAT'S MY BEST FRIEND'S MOTHER! FUCKING CALL HER, NOW! WHAT DID SHE EVER

DO TO YOU? Are you upset with her? Are you being LAZY?"

"You're calling *me* lazy? Isn't that a bit like the pot calling the kettle black?" She challenged, crossing her arms.

"What am I doing that's lazy? I'm writing every single day and trying to... figure everything out."

"You just drop out of schools and keep doing whatever you want."

"God you're so-" He clenched His jaw, breathed heavily and shook His head, "-*miserable*."

He turned to the door.

"What did you call me?" His mother asked as He stepped halfway through the door.

"MISERABLE!" He screamed as He slammed the door, shaking the whole house.

September 8th 2009
...slight breeze... there she is!... soft and slight...

He had learned the mysterious girl's movements between her classes by the 2nd week of His first semester at the Queens School. On Tuesdays and Thursdays, the dark-haired girl with the celeste-hued eyes would walk out of the newly constructed three-story Dollymount Arts and Sciences Center – which had vast glass windows, a glistening grand piano, and tremendous paintings of artists with saturnine expressions – climb down the tan-stone steps towards the terrace, and head into the palatial café of the Holy Redeemer Library. She would order a black hazelnut iced coffee in the café wing.

Through His cautious and strategic steps, He and she saw each other with greater frequency - enough for her to wave to Him, then for Him to high-five her while pretending to rush along. One time, He offered her a histrionic fist-bump to which she obliged laughingly. Then came slower-passing handshakes, and then secret handshakes with skin-sliding-against-skin in multitudinous angles with wordless giggles. Finally, one day, as they clutched hands and their gazes entangled, He smiled and asked her who she was, to which she responded, 'Selene Acerbi'.

Now, they were in the QS Holy Redeemer Library together, sitting on a couch on the top floor. In front of them was a coffee table, and a few feet ahead was a large window that faced the QS Great Lawn. In between watching especially alluring figures pass, He told her that He was an English major – a sophomore transfer from BS. She revealed that she too was a sophomore English major. He mentioned that He was from Old Rookvale, and she revealed that she was from Syosset – several town east in Long Island. He asked if she would read a poem He was working on for one of His classes.

"Promise me you won't laugh," He begged as she moved closer to Him. "This is just a bricolage... I know too little about poetry, and I'm trying to learn how to feel its dynamics, what the words can really do, what-"

"Bah!" she groaned through an opening grin. "Just read it, already!"

He lifted the paper up, angling it so she could read alongside, lightly grazing her arm with His arm, which she did not move away, and took a deep breath.

<u>Helio's Luna</u>
The eve of night would breathe a cool, slight breeze.
With all the calm it seemed like a light dream
to the graceful angel who faced forward
atop a skyscraper and gazed toward
the size of the wide, beautiful city
with eyes squinting hinted hues of pity.
They shone blue and gold. Truth be told, they looked
like the sun and the ocean fused their souls.
And such eyes blazed with a dazed amazement
For no trains made ways, no cars raced pavements,
and not a knock atop the cobblestone;
So it was through a lonely hollow tone
that came the breath of Helio who stepped.
"Was this the city that never slept?" "Yes."
This demon's eyes were brown and green:

> *A dark fountain stream down a mountain's gleam.*
> *Though they had been apart for centuries*
> *and distant were there living memories*
> *back when warring wills had divorced their lives,*
> *their briefly won peace of love crossed their minds:*
> *(Luna's Reverie)*
> *Heat Rush; cheeks blushed like rose swirls. And her hair:*
> *Tossed. Back arched, her toes curled in the warm air.*
> *While kissing her he softly whispered words:*
> *Sights she envisioned as her vision blurred.*

Selene looked at the blankness below the paper.

"So, what happens to them?" she asked.

"I'm not sure yet. They're immortal and the breathing world is ending. A comet is descending towards Earth – which is a pre-Christian story about Satan. I want the angel and demon to examine the behavior of humans who know they're lives will end soon. The demon will speak of the goodness and the angel will speak of the badness. I want their dialogue to subtly express the psychological mechanisms they possessed as humans."

Her head bobbed slowly.

"And, yeah, that's the direction I am going."

"Well, I admire the leveraging of assonance and internal rhyme, and the imagery isn't bad, and the concept is intriguing; but it's a little bit…"

"Purple?" He offered, half-folding the paper away and moving it towards Himself. "Overly descriptive? Stupidly-rhymed? Naïve? Over-reaching?"

She laughed loudly and covered her mouth as people gazed up from their textbooks.

"Effeminate!" she shouted into her palm. "It sounds very feminine."

He looked at her small wrinkling nose and her smile-squinting eyes, and then down at His paper.

"Ouch," He whimpered, red-faced and grimacing, "my ego."

"I'm sorry!" She moved her hand away and pressed her arm against His. "In coincidental news: 'Luna' is 'moon' as you know, and my nickname in high school was 'Moon-Butt'."

He nodded, staring at His fully-folded paper.

She pulled His arm closer.

"Moon-Butt wants to see the remainder of this poem by next week, mister."

September 13th 2009
…Cheer brother up… use his language… assets… investments…

He gazed intently at His brother as he stepped out of the taxicab, collected his luggage, paid the driver, and waved the cab off.

"Greetings, sir." He extended His hand to His brother formally.

"What's up, bro?" His brother greeted Him with a nod.

His brother saw His hand still extended. He chuckled, placed his bags on the ground, and shook His hand in a mock-formal manner.

"How was dad's guest-lecture?" He asked.

"Great, bro. The entire MIT business school and medical staff was there. It was pretty intense."

"So you enjoyed it?"

"Yeah," His brother mumbled.

"You're still upset?" He asked.

"A little. Yeah."

A wind passed, hushing the area to a silence. A cloud swept over the sun; their shadows vanished, and they themselves became shades.

"Why?" He asked His brother. "Tell me."

"You know why, bro." His brother pulled his hand away. "Cali broke up with me."

"And you're feeling a bit lost and empty… and maybe nauseous."

"In so many words, yeah."

"A part of you became a part of her, and now that she's gone that part of you is vacant. You are left with a part of her which feels out of place. It all feels like a bizarre transaction. Maybe even a lost gamble."

"Right." His brother nodded slowly.

"But, you also know that she's not the right one for you. You've been with girls in the past and will be with girls in the future that are more attractive and better for you. What you feel now is rejection, and that hurts because you're smart, and a smart person tries to identify faults in himself when something goes wrong. It's a survival mechanism, maybe even an excelling mechanism – you want to be better than yesterday, so you search for flaws in yourself when something goes wrong. But you should consider that the fault is not yours."

"Bu-"

"Many people will simply not see your great qualities," He interrupted, "or they only see a select few of them. They may even see many of them at first, and then you'll develop differently and they will lose sight of them – even if you are indeed gaining more and more great qualities. That's just the business of human nature. That doesn't mean there aren't thousands of great assets there. Don't ever consider her leaving you a flaw of your own. You're a six-foot-six, strong, big-hearted athlete with intelligence, great looks, perfect health, and an extremely high-paying occupation. This feeling of heartbreak is a short-term loss. Your great qualities are a long-term investment."

His brother nodded. The sun peeked down the perimeter of the passing cloud.

"You'll be fucking super models like Lizzie Manibasse in no time, bro."

His brother boomed a laugh into the reappearing sunshine.

"Thanks."

He grabbed His brother's bags, and, with His free hand, opened the front door.

"Every time you think of her and are feeling down, find me and I will annoy you with my highbrow sophistry until you associate thinking of her with being bored out of your fucking mind. It's better to feel harangued than heartbroken."

"Thank you, bro." His brother patted Him on the shoulder. "I mean it."

"Anytime, bro." He smiled. "Now let's go enjoy some of your bad music taste and cheer for sports teams as they run back and forth and toss their balls around."

"Ha!" His brother snorted.

October 1st 2009
...that smile is the best birthday present I'll...

The lights of Selene's black 1991 Mazda blasted eastwards down Jericho Turnpike at 7:59 PM. He sat in the passenger seat and watched as she shifted into 5th gear, and the numbers on the LED speedometer screen jumbled atop one-another – from 59 to 79. She turned the car and dodged a motorcyclist in the left lane.

"Vaffancullo! Cretino!" she snapped.

His knuckles were turning white as He gripped the sides of the seat. He turned suddenly.

"Wait – that's the bar! Metastrada – on the right!"

Selene swerved the car into the right-most lane, and slammed the brakes. He fell forward, His face moving close to the speedometer's cascading numbers. She switched the car in reverse and slammed the gas. The seat belt pulled His neck as He moved further towards the speedometer. The car sped backward on the highway. She slammed the shift into forward and turned into the exit ramp, accelerating towards the parking lot of the bar, entered and drifted sharply into a vacant space.

"Perfecto!" she clapped.

"You drive the way my mind thinks." He laughed, rubbing the red seat-belt mark on His neck.

"Poetically? Mmm, birthday bello?" she asked, nudging Him with her arm.

"Sure. We'll go with that."

Her phone – which was on the panel between them – vibrated. The name 'MIKE' flashed on the display, covering the eyes of a man in an army uniform. They both looked down at the gleaming phone.

"It appears as if your boy-*friend* is calling you."

"I don't care." She pressed the ignore button, lifted the phone and punched it into her purse. "I told you, we aren't really together anymore. I just don't know how to break it off. I can't stand him. We're nothing alike, and only growing more distant. He's this army-rat, and is always obsessed with guns and shooting and war and competing… and that kind of stuff. He's like the complete opposite of me. Plus," she continued as the two got out of the car and walked across the parking lot towards the bar, "when you cheat on someone – even if it's only once…"

…An hour swung by with three beers for Him and a single mixed vodka drink for her, and circuitous conversations about where ideas come from, William Shakespeare, William Wordsworth, William Blake, Allen Ginsburg, Homosexuality, and politics. Their dialogue spiraled around the billiards table during their three games, all of which Selene won. In the ultimate match, She made only two balls in the pockets when He scratched on His last ball again, causing her to win a third time.

"Ugh!" He groaned. "You're so much better than meeee."

"Yeah right. You let me win again!" She waved the stick at Him like a spear. "I'm on to you, mister."

He put His coat on, and grabbed hers off the hook.

"Do you wanna get out of here?" He asked her.

"Sure," she replied, slipping into her jacket.

They stepped outside. He held out His arm and she wrapped hers around it. They walked slowly, silently. When they approached the parking lot He turned towards her.

"I'm sorry if you don't want to hear this—" He placed His hands gently around her hips, and altered between pushing her away and pulling her closer, "—but you have no idea how much I like you."

"I like you, too." She leaned her face towards Him.

"But-" He began.

"I have to pee!" she interrupted.

"So? Go pee."

"Where?"

He pointed to a large, round shrub at the corner of a driveway a short ways down the shadowed road.

"There. That's the spot."

"What?! Are you crazy! No!" She laughed. "I can run back inside."

He took her hand, turned and walked with her towards the foliage.

"C'mon. I have to pee, too. You go behind the shrub and I'll look out."

A moment passed, filled with their footsteps across the asphalt.

"I can't believe I am doing this," she spoke finally. "It's just because it's your birthday."

"Urination is my birthday present?" He laughed.

"Consenting to that which I wouldn't otherwise do, bello."

He stopped in front of the shrub as she bounced around it. He pulled out His penis – which wasn't entirely flaccid - and immediately began peeing. A second shyer sibilant stream sounded subsequently from across the shrub.

"No peaking!" she shouted.

He turned and looked up at the waxing gibbous moon, and then faced the empty road they had just traversed. A boy in a navy blue windbreaker was whimpering loudly into his cell phone. "Why would you say that to me, baby? You know that makes me feel awful…" the boy's voice trembled across the cool evening. A wind passed. Dead leaves – dim orange – scraped across the asphalt.

He shook His penis and placed it back inside His jeans. Selene appeared next to Him, smiling in the moonlight and shaking her head.

"I can't believe I actually just did that, and in front of you on our first night out. I never do this. I never do these kinds of things."

"Do what?" He whispered, leaning forward and kissing the cream-colored softness of her left cheek.

She looked up at Him, her teal-colored eyes moving as if searching His gaze.

"Any of this. Peeing in bushes." Selene laughed. "I've only been with one guy, and I'm still kind of with him, even though I don't want to be. And-"

"It's your life," He interrupted, putting His hands on her hips and pulling her forward to be embraced. "You decide if you're going to be happy or upset. No one else does. You're the main character. If everyone in your life dies except for you, the pages keep going in your book, right? The same for me. The same for anyone. Life is just our personal collection of good and bad experiences which create good and bad associations. I hope that when you remember this moment – the sibilant sound of piss, the pine air, the glowing and fading lights of cars passing in the night, triumphing over my billiards skills, the near-full moon and the irony with your nickname, and everything else in this sublunary moment – that this was a good experience for you and-"

Her lips closed warmly around His.

October 4th 2009
...moonbutt... Petrichor! – post-rainfall scent... she loves these words...

It was midnight, and Selene and He were by the newly-repainted-blue gazebo near the train station. The air was soaked with a dense fog which hung over Old Rookvale, converting the avenues into mists of orange-pink from the coruscating street lanterns, with intermittent red-yellow-green sprays from the traffic lights, and with a full moon casting a wide halo of light through the bubbling haze above them.

An old Nikon Camera bobbed from Selene's neck as she gamboled about the small park. From where He stood, the mist converted her figure into wet blurs. He knelt down by a long series of interconnected benches, and, with His cell phone, took a photo of her taking a photograph of the gazebo. He looked at the image on the screen. Even in the dim haze, one could make out a large denim butt jutting out of a dancer's figure.

"Let's go to Art's beach?" He called out.
She snapped another photo, examined the shot, turned, and then walked in His direction. The electricity of her eyes pierced the fog first, then slowly she regained detail.
"Mwahahah! Everything is so sepulchral and sublime!" She removed her camera from her neck and turned it to face Him. "What do you think?" she asked, displaying a photo of the gazebo. She looked at Him as if awaiting a response, her eyes darting back and forth from the camera. "The angle is just as important as the content, if not more. What word comes to mind when you look at it?"
"Entrance." He scrutinized the photo – the railings were at eye level and a chip was in focus with the yellow haze bubbling in the background – and then gazed down at her lips. Her smile widened, as it often did when they stared silently at one another, and her eyes moved back and forth across His as if she were reading a poem. She leaned in and kissed Him.
"Can I ask you a stupid question?" He began as they pulled away.
"Stupid questions are my favorite. Inquire away, bello."
"Are we dating?" He shuffled. "Like – are we together?"
Selene put her camera down and placed her body against His, lifting her gaze up to Him.
"Yes," she whispered. "We're definitely dating, and I'm glad we're alone together."
"Me too."
She kissed Him and then turned towards the gazebo.
"I love how this thing is all fragmented and hurt-looking."
"You love it?"
"Yeah." She turned towards it and nodded towards a loose piece of wood. Even in the tenebrous mist one could see where the original white paint had chipped away, revealing creases under the blue coating. The luminous dew on the splintering wood gave the gazebo a cerulean aura.

"Beach?" she reminded. "Shall we resume our vespertine tryst at Artyom's estuary?"

"Yeah."

They got in the Mercedes together. *Any Colour You Like* by Pink Floyd was playing on the radio as they sped north - passed Vanes Diner and passed The Rising Star Café and Bookseller – towards Port Washington. The lyrics ceased, the notes faded and the song descended into its unearthly soundscape.

They pulled into Art's beach and stepped out of the car. He kept the engine and lights on. Selene immediately aimed her camera at the full moon which stood between two hand-like clouds, creating the impression of two hands reaching for a clouded pearl.

Selene turned to Him. He watched the third swing – closest to the water – as it swung idly along a passing breeze.

"What are you thinking about?" Selene asked, reaching for His hand and squeezing it gently.

"You." He squeezed her hand back. "I was thinking about how happy I am when you hold my hand. And that I'm by the water and there's a view of the full moon, and I'm speaking to you, and couldn't be better."

"Mmm," Selene cooed. "Nice and lame. Just the way I like it."

"Hey, check this out," He spoke, walking towards the shining headlights.

"What are you doing?" she whispered.

"Come." He knelt down.

She crouched down next to Him so her face was also only a meter away from the shining lights. She turned towards the car beams and her glowing mouth dropped at the sight of trillions of scintillating spectrums scattered everywhere before her. The fog through the light created a panorama of erratically-swirling bubbles, each of them silver-lined and possessing a glowing spectrum. "Whoa," she gasped, her exhale forming a shadowy serpent which snaked through the spheres before vanishing into their iridescence. "The orbs you wrote about... the preternatural dream-machines," her voice trailed, her aquamarine-glowing eyes narrowed. "You shouldn't have thrown that story out." She turned, and observed Him across the sea of sparkling colors occupying the air. "I'm sure your brother didn't hate it as much as you think."

His pupils were needle-sized as rainbow pixels drifted across his green-glistening eyes. "Maybe it wasn't animals," He mumbled to the light. "Maybe it *was* colors all along."

"What's in that crammed head of yours?" Selene reached across the polychromatic light-beams and touched His shoulder.

"You." He looked down at her hands – at the glowing hues and shadowed hills of her little veins – and then back at her. "I am thinking of you, and me, and us; and how everything suddenly seems connected."

October 17th 2009
...sports, business, and shitty music... pissing me off...

*"Dance – Dance – Dance – Dance – Dance – Dance
Everywhere we'll dance. Everything will dance."*

Lizzie Manibasse crooned from the car radio over an electro-house beat with blaring synths. His brother was driving and singing - mostly circumventing the appropriate C note in which she sang - while He stared out of the window with His jaw clenching tightly. His brother lowered the volume.

"What's wrong bro?" His brother nudged Him. "Not in the mood for a duet?"

"Explain to me," He spoke, His forehead pressed against the window, "how by now you still can't tell that I fucking detest this discordant garbage?"

"Whoa!" His brother laughed. "No need to get bent out of shape, bro." His brother lowered the music to silence. Rain pitter-pattered on the windshield. "So," he continued, "besides being a music snob, how've you been?"

"I'm not a music snob. Noting balsamic vinegar isn't suitable wine doesn't make one a sommelier. Your pop music is garbage and I hate it and I never want to fucking hear it, and you know that quite well and you play it anyway every single fucking time I'm in a car with you because you're inconsiderate, and it makes me hate you."

His brother laughed again.

"Well, I'm pretty sure nine out of ten people you meet will say that getting bent out of shape over a single song makes you a music snob." His brother turned to Him and smiled. "I'm telling you. Trust me on that one. It's a ten-minute car ride. Then the car is yours. I think you'll live. Let me do me, bro. If I'm not getting too embarrassed about my brother dropping out of BS, refusing to find a job, and going to a much lower school - than I think you can try to be fine about me enjoying a song you don't deem worthy."

He turned and looked out of the window at the passing gazebo. A stain of vomit trailed over the bottom few of the circling steps.

"So how's-" His brother paused, "-Sabrina?" he attempted.

"Selene," He corrected. "She's well."

"Good. You two getting serious?"

"I don't know what that means."

"Are you two seriously dating?"

"Yes."

"Alright, good. Cali and I are back together and everything is fine." His brother sighed and drummed the steering wheel with his fingers. "So, how's the writing?"

"Going."

"I wanted to tell you: One of dad's business friends – Dr. Sanjeev Lovejoy - is related to the COO of some huge publishing house. Like the fourth or fifth largest one in America or something. I think it would be a good idea to contact him."

"Contact him then." He stared out of the window.

"Do you know what a COO is?"

"Clitoral-Orgasm Operator?"

His brother turned to Him and shook his head.

"Chief Operating Officer, close enough. You know, you're going to have to know this stuff eventually, bro."

"I promise you I won't."

"Alright. What are you going to do then? Instead of reaching out to this unbelievably strong contact – you're going to... what? Write for hours in bars and cafés and waste dad's money more? You're in school to write, and that's fine, but - unless I'm missing something - you haven't connected with a single one of your teachers on the steps to get published. You just write. It's a hobby until you make money off of it, bro. I would reach out to him-"

"-And what the fuck would I say to him? 'Hey – I'm writing this novelette about how art has the ability to illuminate people's minds, and that I believe there are pre-living ideas that search around for us, and that only certain people have it? Oh, by the way, my brother read it and thought it was awful.' How's that?"

"I didn't think it was awful at all, bro. I don't know where you got that idea." His brother shook his head. "And I'd work on that elevator pitch a bit. Look - you know you're a good writer, so I don't know why you have this defeatist attitude about it. You can get it done. If I were you, I would get the guy's contact information from dad, and email him saying, 'Hi – I'm related to so-and-so, and I'm writing this novel, and, while I know you must get these requests every day, I would be honored to have some of your guidance on it. From the little I know about the business, it doesn't seem to fit in any particular genre I know of, but I would like to see it move in the right direction. If you have any free time at all, I would love to treat you to coffee or lunch or whatever and get your feedback'. That's it. It's simple. He has no reason to say no to you, and if he does, so what? You at least gave it a shot."

"I'll be just a cunty nineteen-year-old nobody demanding his time."

"It's not demanding his time. And that's not how it works."

"Can we talk about something else?"
His brother sighed.
"I'm just trying to help you out, bro."

"Pardon my breviloquence, but I don't want your help. Now can we talk about literally anything else besides sports, occupations, and business?"

"Like?"

"I don't know." He turned and looked out of the window at the passing people. "Physics, science, psychology, sociology, metempsychosis, philandering, pharmaceuticals, the phenomenon of 'noctilucent clouds', the paradoxical attraction to asses you and I seem to share, alcohol, art - REAL fucking art and not that garbage music – literature, whether or not 'cunt' can be an endearing term in the United States, semiotics, etcetera. Anything but sports and business for once. Can you do that?"

"I read a fiction novel kinda recently," His brother declared.

"Really?" He turned suddenly. "Did you like it? What was it? Do tell."

"Well-" His brother hesitated, "-it's actually Cali's book. I didn't buy it-"

"Okay. You read a book your girlfriend bought. What book? Have I heard of it? Was it good?"

His brother shrugged. "*22 Hues of Blue.*"

"Ugh!" He spat against the window.

November 2nd 2009

...Glad Selene loves Chet Baker now... adore me...

Chet Baker's *Blue Moon* was playing – beginning with, *'Blue moon, you saw me standing alone, without a dream in my heart...'* – as He drove northbound with Selene towards the beach by Art's house.

"He really *is* awesome," Selene declared, watching the variegated leaves on the passing trees above. "Keep showing me this guy. He has the sweetest voice. Every song sounds like he's chantepleuring."

"And that means?"

"To cry while singing, bello."

The song faded as Chet Baker scatted an indebted decrescendo over a lulling piano. He pulled into the sandy driveway of Art's beach, parked, turned the car off and stepped out of the car. Selene followed, buttoning up her wool coat and smiling her turquoise eyes to Him.

They walked hand-in-hand across the beach and towards the pier. The November sun had just fallen below the Long Island Sound's seascape, and the sky was a darkening duet of orange and purple. Two seagulls soared above, and their gray-and-white flecks matched the white-and-gray wooden boards below their feet. The seagulls called out. The wooden planks creaked. The waves lapped tranquilly below them.

"Who do you think I'll like more?" Selene asked Him. "Dustin or Art?"

"I'm afraid I'll influence your natural opinion if I even begin to contemplate that."

At the end of the pier was a small portico made from the same wood as the boardwalk, and at its farthest end was a balustrade that looked over the sea. When they reached it, Selene rested her elbows on the wooden balcony and looked out.

"You don't strike me as someone who throws in with the idea of natural opinions," Selene opined.

"I love the fact that you know me so well," He said, wrapping His arms around her hips and kissing the top of her head.

She grabbed His hand from her waist, lifted it to her lips, and kissed His palm.

"I think Dustin sounds the most interesting," she began, "but Art definitely sounds the sweetest."

A wind blew through her hair, which lifted and glimmered in the setting sun.

"Probably Dustin. The fact that he's opinionated interests me. The opinionated are often the most inimitable."

"Dustin's opinions are based on almost nothing, though."

"Well, he reads."

"Only sappy love stories like *The Notebook*, sports books about athletes he lionizes, and tirades by insanely radical republicans."

"*The Notebook* was actually a great book. Never let the crowd ruin your judgment of the spectacle, bello. That's a mistake I make too often. Sometimes you have to look out at the world and ask what the fuck 'normal' is anyway."

"Okay, maybe not *The Notebook*. But the little that Dustin reads is mostly nonsense. It's not stimulating or different or intriguing. It's the most inactive reading can be."

"Oh! I want to show you something!" Selene turned around and reached into her purse. "Speaking of ridiculous spectacles-" she spoke as she pulled out a book. The words *22-Hues of Blue* appeared on its many-blued cover.

"Why do you have that?" He stepped back. Selene turned. The lights of the pavilion turned on, illuminating her eyes to a celadon hue. The sun was now halfway below the horizon, still blasting aureate colors into the dimming sky.

"I figure if I am going to hate something I should know a good amount about it. I started reading it yesterday, and it's delightfully abhorrent. Apparently the biggest gimmick in the book – besides the gratuitous sex – is the fact that the girl's love interest's eyes change to be twenty-two hues of the color blue. It's the worst thing I've ever read. It's like a twelve year old learned about a girl's holes." Selene laughed. "Look, I highlighted pages that I thought you'd enjoy." She opened the book towards Him and then pulled it away. "Remember! People are taking this book seriously. This is from page eleven."

I never knew pleasuring someone could be so pleasurable, watching him wildly writhe with untamed lust. My spirit nymph is doing the flamenco with some disco moves.

"Wait – wait-" Selene laughed, grabbing the book and flipping forward further, "-this is from page eighty-eight."

Lizzie Manibasse is singing in my headphones about not belonging. The song used to mean a lot to me; that's because I feel like I am always not belonging. I have never belonged anywhere.

"I don't even know if it's legal to put Lizzie Manibasse's name in the book." She looked at Him. "What do you think? Thumping good read, huh, bello?"

"The fact that this book sold tens of millions..." His voice trailed. "What is wrong with this world?"

"When people are busy with their boredom they're more inclined to seek cheap thrills. I think that's how it starts. Everyone is damned by dull hours at jobs they don't care about. That's why cheap gossip and drama intrigue people. When you don't have time to think, easy thrills can pass for entertainment. From there, it's probably habitual, like everything else we do."

"I'd like to see a book that fucks and uses words like 'fuck' but then explores the mind and uses words like 'sagaciously'."

"He fucking said sagaciously," Selene said sagaciously.

He tapped His fingers atop her bottom lip.

"I've never been-" He began, pulling her close to Himself, "-so sure that I'm completely in love with you."

He kissed her. She kissed Him. They kissed as many waves moved in and out of the shore below them. The sun extinguished below the horizon.

When they pulled away, Selene opened her mouth as if to speak, but her verdigris eyes darted towards the beach. He turned. Together they watched an old couple walk from the sand covered parking lot towards the swing set at the opposite end of the beach. Both were tan-colored, silver-haired and dressed in cream hues. The old man held his flimsy arm out and helped the woman as she slowly sat down on the swing closest to the water. She began swaying forward and back, keeping her tan feet on the sand. He sat on the swing next to her. Holding hands, they swung together in harmonious parabolas. Every now and then, their lips moved, and a near-silent echo could be heard where Selene and He stood watching.

"They are perfect."

"They are."

A moment passed as they watched in silence.

"If you could be anyone in this world besides yourself, who would you be?" He whispered to her, wrapping His hands around her and letting them rest on her abdomen.

"I'm not sure. I'm pretty good on this right now." She placed her hand on top of His, and ran her thumbs across the tops of His hands. "But if I had to pick someone else... a part of me would say Lizzie Manibasse."

"Umm - why her?" He questioned through a frown.

"I knew you were going to ask that!" Selene laughed, squeezing His hand. "Take a second and ignore her pop music and the people like your brother who fawn over her stupid songs on the radio, and think about the fact that she's been a movie star since she was twelve years old, speaks like ten languages, has her own fashion line, and is entirely independent."

"So you would be her because?"

"Because she can produce whatever she wants. She is a go-getter. She's free. Once in a while she comes out with a song that is pure poetry, and the radio never plays it because that's not what the people want. But she is totally free to produce it, and people like me who are looking will find it."

He nodded.

"And that's what you want? Freedom. Not being controlled or limited by anyone."

"Hmmm," Her voice vibrated. "I don't want to end up like my mom – ensnared by responsibilities I've incidentally accepted. Being totally free." She sighed. "That's exactly what I want, as long as you're being free next to me."

Art's 2001 Audi appeared, the tires crushing the sediments of the parking lot. He stepped out, wearing a cordovan thermal.

"Good day for November," Art called out, waving, and reaching into the trunk. He pulled out a red cooler and began walking towards them. "Good day for anything, really!"

"I like him already," Selene whispered. "Do I call him Art or Artyom?"

"Call him Doctor."

"Greetings, Doctor Artyooooom!" Selene called out, waving theatrically.

Art laughed and quickened his pace. He stopped in front of them and put down the cooler.

"Well, it's actually soon-to-be *Physician's Assistant* Artyom Lavian, but I'll let this one go." Art held out his hand. Selene took it eagerly.

"The name is Selene Acerbi, soon-to-be famous poetess."

"You're already pretty famous to this guy." Art nodded to Him.

"I see you brought presents with your presence," He spoke.

Art opened the cooler and handed Him a Heineken.

"Pick your poison, Selene," Art spoke, his hand hovering above the beers.

"I'll have a Heineken, too."

"A match made in Heaven's pub." Art chuckled. "Bro, you made it sound like Dustin and Sara would be here before me."

"He said he'd be here a half hour ago." He looked out as Dustin's cobalt Jeep appeared through the gates and rolled slowly to the parking lot. "And on Dustin's delayed time he should just be arriving now."

"Ah!" Art turned. "Speak of the devil."

The Jeep door opened. Shadows that resembled a sponge, a fork, a shoe, and another fork fell out onto the sand. The figures of a jacketed Dustin and Sara approached. Their whispering could be heard punctuated by Dustin spitting tobacco dip onto the sand.

"'et's see 'er 'lreadeh'!" Dustin called out, a massive horseshoe of tobacco dip rendering his speech both aphaeretic and apocopic.

Selene grabbed His hand and looked up at Him with a curious grin. He spun her. Her hair lifted, and as she finished spinning she pirouetted and her hair fell to her shoulders.

"'ell, she 'efinitely is 'ore attractive tha' you." Dustin laughed and spat.

Sara mumbled something inaudible and ran back to the car. Dustin looked back towards her and then continued towards Selene and Him. As Dustin approached, the curves and concaves of his enormous, flush face became increasingly defined in the orange hues of the boardwalk.

"He's 'efinitely a 'etter 'allerina, ih' you can ever 'queezj' His big ass indo a dutu." Dustin winked an electric blue eye to Him. "Like the good ol' days."

Selene touched His arm. He turned down to face her.

"You're going to have to do that now." She grinned up to Him. "I'm gonna squeeze your ass in a tutu."

Dustin's car door closed. The shadow of a now unjacketed Sara appeared.

"Hello?" Art spoke into his cell phone, walking towards the water away from Him. "Hi, Doctor Lovejoy-"

"I'm gonna say hi to her," Selene whispered up to Him, nodding at Sara, and pulsing His hand. He pulsed back. She nodded approvingly to Dustin, stepped passed him across the boardwalk and ambled across the beach towards the shadow of Sara.

"Ey see she' reading 'arah's 'avorite 'ook." Dustin glanced to the *22-Hues of Blue* cover resting on the balustrade.

"Ha! Not at all. We were just thumbing through it for laughs."

"Ah. She really eh' gorge'. Ih doo bad she' I'alian." Dustin nodded and looked towards Him. "Gue' what, sonn?"

He turned away from Selene to face him.

"You went down on Sara again and found a few dollars? I don't know. What?"

"I 'id it." Dustin shook, turned, hacked, and ejaculated an enormous glob of tobacco dip off the pier into the black-orange gleaming water.

"I GOT THE JOB DUDE!" Art shouted in the distance, tucking his phone into his pocket.

"Dude, that's fucking fantastic!" He called out. He turned to Dustin. "Art got a job as a Physician's Assistant in interventional cardiology. What did *you* do?"

Dustin ran his tongue across his now unoccupied bottom lip, and spat darkened saliva onto the boardwalk.

"I fucked her, son." An extraordinary smile grew on his quick-nodding face as he turned back to Him. "I finally had sex with Sara. I pumped my best six-inch semi-softy in her ten or eleven times then blasted away!" Dustin laughed. "I got excited so it was quick, but it was marvelous, son."

"Really?" He turned to the figures of Sara and Selene talking.

"Hi, mom!" Art could be heard at the gate of the beach. "Guess what?"

He could see only the back of Sara talking to Selene, whose smile opened as she laughed loudly. A small strand of seaweed had wrapped itself around Selene's left foot in the shape of a crescent moon. Suddenly, a white firework shot upwards across the sky. Sara turned to the ocean. The firework exploded and a revealing whiteness illuminated her face. He observed Sara's large and round and excited smoky eyes, her olive-colored cheek bones, her jet-black straight hair running down to the small of her back, a white-tooth grin beaming excitement, her Mediterranean hips wrapped in her long-sleeved black dress with gold trimmings that ornamented her protruding breasts, the dozen clinquant bangles on both of her wrists, the Arabic-lettered tattoo on her outer wrist, and the purple nail polish on her olive hands.

"O!" Selene and Sara called out uniformly.

The whiteness in the sky faded and Sara was again in shadow. Above, a full moon glowed.

December 2nd 2009
...waking up beside her... she's snoring how cute...

His eyelids lifted when the chirping of a bird, a whooshing wind drifting snow, and a branch snapping sounded simultaneously. He yawned, and attempted to stretch in His bed, but only lifted His right arm. He turned and faced Selene whose warm body rested on His left forearm beneath the endless blue of His bed sheets. The contours of her muscles relaxed in full slumber. A child-like smile shone across His face.

A low snore trembled from her nose. He chuckled. Her eyelids half opened. A ray of sunlight beamed through the window and streaked across her narrow eyes like a visor, illuminating the beryl hues. She smiled bashfully.

"Oh no," she mumbled as she reached for His arm, pulled it tighter against her, and rested her head on His shoulder. "What did I do?"

"You snored."

"Shaddd up." She shook her head. "I'm not a snorer. *You're* a snorer, you otorhinolaryngolic vibrator, you."

Her eyelids descended. He leaned in and kissed her lips. Her eyes opened wide. Blue faced green, and green faced blue.

"You ever notice," He began as their noses pressed against each other, "that when we're this close it looks like we only have one eye?"

"Whad dou you meang?" she asked nasally. "I've alwayj beeng a shyclopsh."

Their noses unscrunched. Selene turned to her cellphone at the foot of the bed, which was too far away for her to reach.

"What time is it?"

"12:15"

"What?!" Selene jumped up from the bed towards the window.

"Yup."

"Oh man," Selene spoke, staring out at the snow-covered trees. "This is the latest I've ever slept, bello."

"I told you my body is comfortable. It's the chest hair. My fur is a blanket."

"We slept passed breakfast," Selene whispered.

"We almost slept passed lunch," He added.

"That's not as big of a deal. I used to skip lunch all the time - but, breakfast!" she exclaimed. "That's what really starts the d-"

"Why'd you skip lunch?"

Selene paused.

"I never really ate lunch. I don't know."

"What about school? Didn't you have a lunch period?"

"My grandpa would give me three dollars a day for lunch money, and I'd just end up saving it up."

"What? Weren't you hungry?"

"Well-" she shrugged uncomfortably, "-sometimes people would offer to share, but eventually I just learned to suppress my appetite. Sometimes people were bullies about it, calling me anorexic." She laughed. "Not with this ass."

He wrapped His arms around her and kissed the top of her head.

"For what were you saving up?" He spoke as she nuzzled her head below His chin.

"My family... I-" Selene hesitated, "-I don't really want to talk about it."

"Yes, you do." He held her at arm's length. "There's no one better to speak your memories." He kissed her pale shoulder. "I adore everything I see in you. Do you really think I would like you any less from knowing how you came to be this person I adore? We can tell each other our secrets. We can share pieces of each other that few others can claim-" He hesitated, "-and there's no one I want to understand and appreciate more than you. And that requires knowing your family, your friends, your loves, and your hates. And especially your problems. Release them." He kissed her forehead. "I mean, think about it: Right now we are open books to one another, intrigued only by each other's incipient chapters. Let's learn more. Let's learn the stuff that we can't show to others."

Selene closed her eyes.

"My dad used to hurt my mom-" she sighed tremblingly, "-a lot, and it scared our whole family. I was twelve, and," Selene's voice quivered, "my sisters and my brother and I would witness our mom blaming herself. She would occasionally reprimand us for trying to help. My dad was the one who earned the money in our family. My mom was going to pursue her bachelor's degree when they came to America from Modena, but he told her it was a waste of time

because he would own a car shop, and that he was the best at taking apart and putting together cars."
"And?"
"And he *was* one of the best mechanics in Modena. But when they moved to Syosset, he learned that a mechanic isn't exactly the prestigious career that he thought it would be. And he became embittered and wouldn't let my mother work. Then she had my oldest sister Claudia, then Isabella, and then me, and then Diana and then finally Maximiliano. Of course he stops impregnating her when he has a boy." Selene chuckled sadly. "At that point, the abuse was getting nightmarish. He broke our telephone over my mom's face when I was thirteen. That weekend she kicked him out of the house, and then they began the whole divorce process. I'd have to sit down with these lawyers and psychiatrists, and was ordered to spend time with my dad. I guess… I guess I was saving money so I can get away from all of them."
"How was it when you spent time with your dad?"
"I mean… he's a dick. That's what he is. He can't help it. Everyone at the car shop asks me how I survive being his daughter, and honestly, I don't really know. Sometimes I'm not sure if all of me survives when I leave him. I can see him for one hour or one week - it doesn't matter. It's like I'm exchanging energy with a vacuum."
"And the psychiatrists?"
"All were horrible except one. She told me to write. She told me to hug trees and embrace my inner paroxysms. She told me to cry and yell and scream and smile and track why these things happen, but to do so through writing. She gave me a poetry book by Virginia Woolf, and after that I always wrote poetry."
"Why poetry?"
Selene looked at the blue sky through the window.
"After this we need to go to QS, okay? No more pre-lucubratory dormancy. You have class at two and I have to start studying for finals."
"Okay. No more pre-class naptime." He smiled proudly. "Now tell me why your one good psychiatrist recommended poetry."

"Because poetry is, by nature, reading between the lines and extracting worlds of information. I knew why I was upset, but I didn't know why I would look in the mirror and want to shatter that slave in the looking glass. I knew why I wanted to graduate so badly and why I was afraid of not earning a degree, but I didn't really understand how I felt these sensations of physical pain when I got anything less than an A. Poetry helped me be honest with the feelings that I couldn't express in regular prose. I began to fall in love with people again, even the fragmented ones, especially the intricate ones. Ones who had problems and were laboring to fix them. Everything was vicissitudinous, and I realized that I could live through all of the motions as long as I had a pen and paper to eventually ground myself."

December 29th 2009
Dr. Henry Hallward Heidelberg: *So, if you think that you're really slipping away from the positive judgments of your family, what can you do to again be received in their favor?*
Him: Ever since dropping out of BS, my family regarded me as kind of a waste. I lost their respect. It was assumed that I would excel in psychology, which I did – in all fairness – until I couldn't take the slowness anymore and stopped attending classes. But, I got into QS, have a 4.0 average my first semester, and am trying to prove myself as a writer. First, I have to establish my family's new judgment that I can write well, and then I have to exceed it. I've sent my short stories to over one-hundred writing contests. I have to get published somehow. That's what I'm doing to regain my family's positive judgments of me. Writing every day, and surrounding myself with goodness. All in all – if there were ever such a thing as 'free will' I would say I'm using it wisely. Using it to harmonize and work hard.

You don't think that we ourselves can have free will?
By no means do we have free will. We have 'willed reactions' - responses to the actions of others. The Self-Categorization Theory suggests that at the lowest level of abstraction is the self as an individual - wholly oneself and free of the

comparisons and influences of others. In my opinion, that does not exist. Take Dustin and Art - antithetical personalities who share the loss of their fathers at a pre-pubescent stage. Art lost his father to heart disease when he was five and is becoming a strait-laced and salubrious physician's assistant working in interventional cardiology and medicine. Dustin, when he was three years old, lost his father to a heroin overdose, and subsequently developed the most addictive personality I know. Now, what moves one positively and the other negatively? Art, as I've watched him mature, seems to be reacting to his father's death the same way the subconscious works in our dreams. To our current understanding, dreams are a subconscious filtration of information to decipher the day's stimuli. Art is positively learning via subconscious recapitulation, and performing all of the things he can do to not die from heart disease. Dreams help us understand what we *think* is most important. Now Dustin, in stark contrast, reacts to his father's death in the same way traumatic nightmares operate. Traumatic nightmares differ from standard dreams in that they recreate the scenario of the trauma - and while this is terrifying for the dreamer, it is, in essence, the mind's effort to help an individual *master* the trauma. And that is *exactly* what Dustin is doing. He is forcing himself into the very situation that ended his dad's life. Maybe it is to master the trauma, or maybe it is to prove something to himself - like he is less mortal than his father. Or, he may just be punishing himself for the loss in general. I mean, at such a young age, the world is so microcosmic that we tend to blame ourselves for massive occurrences that affect us. In either case, Dustin is addicted to nicotine, tobacco, alcohol, his girlfriend, heartbreak, love, being sick in his hypochondriacal fashion, masturbation, and, I can tell soon, cocaine. He tried it when I was at BS, and he can't stop raving about it. All of these things - including his girlfriend - are entirely self-deleterious. Dustin and Art are so different, yet both still ripple from a long-gone wave. So, free will? *Total* free will? No. Never. Willed reactions probably, but not free will. Even the associations we make are based on others. I do worry about Dustin, though. I once thought of the Maslow's pyramid of needs and thought that Dustin can't really develop the other needs like love and belonging properly if his hypochondriac self is always concerned about his physiological being. It's almost funny, the way he imagines he's sick all the time, and then just drugs himself excessively anyway. Kind of like a masochistic version of Münchausen syndrome. Alex claims that Dustin's doctor told him he doesn't even have asthma, and that it's all in his head. That would be something else, if it were true. It really would be.

If no mere creature has free will and is instead a 'collection of reactions to other people's influences', how do you justify your clear dissatisfaction towards your brother?
You know, let's switch 'collection of reactions' to John Turner's term 'perceiver readiness', and view humans as being comprised of past experience, present needs, and future expectations. Okay? My brother's obsession with watching sports paradigmatically represents all of the depersonalizing processes of self-stereotyping. There is such inactivity inherent in their vicarious competitiveness when watching these games. Morons dressing up in their team's uniforms and cheering and crying moronically at bar televisions everywhere. Superficially, they're showing their support, but what they are really doing is placating their insecurities of not being an actual part of 'their' team. It's a social process to conform to the social category of 'the team'. This is why they inherit their stupid rivalries. 'They're *my* team' 'it's New York' 'It's *my* city' they proclaim in their pathetic attempts at accentuation. Do you know how many people on the Yankees were actually from New York this year? In 2009? I shit you not - only 2 out of 43. And I have nothing against any of those athletes except the amount they're paid for being the best wood-swingers and ball-throwers and ball-catchers. It's the fans that nauseate me. Instead of doing something that builds the self – like creating art or building something or learning something – they become one another in the ambiguous crowd orbiting around an illusion of a team, which is actually a corporation that does not give a flying fuck about them. Inactive, non-progressive idolatry. I find that

repugnant. A complete waste of time.

Without total free-will and only 'willed reactions" what do you do to better yourself or to redeem yourself?
I don't know. I guess… I consider Bronfenbrenner's Ecological Theory, and try to surround myself with positive circles. So, surrounding myself with truly good things and good people and try to find the harmony of it all. I'm trying to be everything I'm expected to be. I went back to school. I mean, QS isn't as great as BS on the record books, but it's still a good school. And it's where I met Selene, and she's lovely. I feel like she's the one really redeeming me. There's my intrinsic motivation to be as intelligent as possible, but she's the real extrinsic motivation for me. She's the reason I continue to go to QS. Selene makes me a better person.

How does Selene make you a better person?
Foucault says that we have to create ourselves as works of art. Now, again, I don't think we have much control over our own selves, or at least far less than we imagine. But if we surround ourselves with things that give us positive motivation, we will probably see some good work come out of us. Selene is a hard worker, and she's so loving and quirky and artistic. She's like a good book I know I can get lost in. She teaches me new concepts, new figures, new authors, new words, new worlds. And she makes me think. I can be honest with her, and she helps me find the balance of it all. Pardon the cliché of it, but she enables me to be true to myself.

If there's no free will then how can you be true to yourself?
Well, again, there's willed reactions. We do have some say in what we do. It's just not absolute free will, and is almost always a reaction to something set forth in us. For example, to try and prove to you I have free will, I can pick up that copy of *22-Hues of Blue* book that you have on your bookshelf and throw it out of your window – resulting in a dramatic spike in your shelf's literary merit. But at the same time, every part of that is a reaction from so many complexes, perhaps the most simple being my desire to prove something to

someone as intelligent as you. The trick is to try to mediate everything. To ensure that the 'original self' which churns the information of others is healthy.

22-Hues of Blue is on my desk because it is part of today's popular culture and is thus a book most of my patients have read, but going back to your answer, how does one mediate everything?
D. W. Winnicott would say that there are two general selves - there's the true self and the false self. The true self is developed through spontaneous and genuine experiences. And the false self, according to Winnicott, is this defensive façade. It is essentially when you regard other people's expectations of you as more important than your own - even if they are contradicting to your true self's yearnings. It leads, he states, to one feeling empty and dead inside. In contrast, surrounding yourself with people who have appropriate expectations of you restores a sense of harmony which strengthens the churning mechanism. That churning mechanism is the mediator. When you're hurt by something, the churning mechanism becomes sloppy and you don't always mirror the things you want to. You're still absorbing your world – you just may not do it in the precise way you would like. One may perceive loss as a victory of experience or as a tragedy of time depending on the state of their true or Original Self. I know that ever since Mandy, that churning mechanism of my Original Self was damaged, and that ever since Selene, it has been recovering.

But how do you know that?
You do something enough times and it becomes habit. Heinz Kohut says that narcissists evolve this defensive shield around their damaged inner selves. Constantly thinking about themselves - outward expressions of over-confidence masking inward expressions of insecurity. I was beginning to feel like that. I was overcompensating for sex. I was overcompensating for psychology – placating my impatience in BS's learning speed by repeating to myself that I am more intelligent than my professors. I was over compensating for everything. I wasn't finding what I was looking for, and I was

becoming increasingly impatient. That's how I know. Part of my natural self - the churning me - has been irrevocably fragmented. But since Selene and writing at QS, I at least have the drive to be a good boy, a well-behaved son, and an overall hard-worker...

February 6th 2010
...a Wandering Wind impresses Selene... Write... don't drink tonight...

He and Alex were watching a movie in His living room in Old Rookvale. A knock came from outside the sliding glass doors. He got up and slid the door open, revealing a puffy-eyed Dustin standing in the dim-glistening snow.

"Whattup, son?" Dustin huffed in the darkness, his eyes wet and blue from the inside lights, the cold clinging to his round cheeks.

"I haven't seen you in a while, Dusty." He smiled. "You alright there, buddy?"

"Never better." Dustin flashed a solid-blue four-month sobriety chip and then waved a wine bottle in a brown bag in front of Him. "Sobriety's been treating me well."

Dustin stepped forward, but He stood in the way.

"Why are you so winded?"

"I ran here, dude."

"Why'd you run here?"

"I don't know," Dustin huffed, looking back over his shoulder at the footprints crunched into the snow. "There's acid-heads crawling around everywhere in your backyard."

"You don't-" He paused, squinting, "-you don't think you're having a *panic attack* do you?"

"Sonnnn," Dustin wined, reflexively grabbing his inhaler from his pocket, lifting it to his lips, sucking in, wheezing, and then coughing.

"You really shouldn't drink so much." He indicated the bag in Dustin's hands. "You're wasting your time at the AA meetings."

"And you shouldn't drop acid so much." Dustin took a swig from the wine bottle and wiped off his purpled lips. "And I stopped doing cocaine, so there. Now are you gonna let your *friend* inside?"

He rolled His eyes and stepped back.

"Haven't dropped acid since BS, baby girl."

Dustin stepped in – stomping snow powder on the wooden floor - and sat down next to Alex.

"Did I miss much?"

"Only half the movie," Alex responded, nodding to Him, "but, I'm sure your brilliance will figure it out."

A skinny, dark-haired character appeared on the screen. The camera focused on his despondent, brown-eyed gaze.

"Wow – they're really casting anyone these days."

"What do you mean?" Alex asked.

"He's hideous."

"Are you kidding? Girls literally toss their vaginas at him."

"He's too ethnic-looking." Dustin grimaced.

"You're fucking insane!" Alex shouted shaking his head.

Dustin's phone vibrated once. Twice. He lifted the screen to his face and began texting. The bright white light illuminated the round curves of a growing smile.

"Sara?" He asked Dustin.

"No. A girl I met in AA. Really hot."

"German?" Alex asked. "English?"

"No." Dustin grinned. "Irish, lad."

He watched as Dustin texted, grinning whenever the phone vibrated.

"What about Sara?" He asked finally.

"I think she's really done with me this time, dude."

Alex and He looked at each other, eyebrows raised. On the screen, a lighter-haired junkie jammed a syringe into his forearm. Dustin stared up at the screen. His pupils dilated. The screen on the television blurred. The camera zoomed out. The dilapidated blue walls morphed into stacks of large breasts with erect pink nipples. Moaning sounds rose into the

[150]

air. The screen swayed left and right. The junkie joined in the moaning, fell down on his back in slow-motion, and thrusted his pelvis in the air. The colors changed, became warmer with reds and yellows saturating the room.

"The cinematography is a-"

"I knew you were going to say something gay like that," Dustin interrupted. "Who the fuck cares about cinematography?"

He turned to Dustin.

"Yeah, you're totally right. The angle in which a story is captured doesn't matter at all."

"No. It's all about PLOT. The story. If the story is interesting."

"You're an idiot."

"You sound like one of those gay-ass QS hipster faggots! You've gotta stop hanging out with those morons," Dustin shouted at Him, "or is this Selene talking? That's definitely it!"

"You know *absolutely nothing* about film, Dustin. The way one person captures the world is ENTIRELY different from another. The capturing has meaning. The person has meaning. The person as the noun has a meaning. The action, verb, and plot has meaning! The way the action is done, the cinematography, the goddamned motherfucking *adverb* has meaning! What is shown has fucking meaning. What isn't fucking shown has fucking meaning. Wh-"

"Both of you calm your tits!" Alex held his arms out, as if stopping them from getting up. "If you two morons argue the whole fucking time, then none of us are going to fucking see the plot *or* the camera work."

When the television screen went black and the film finished, Alex nodded approvingly at the screen and Dustin stared at his cell phone. Together, the two stood up and headed towards the sliding doors to His backyard. Dustin stepped out, and Alex turned, halfway outside.

"What are you doing later?" he asked Him.

"Writing, and then meeting Selene."

"If you want to join us after, we'll be drinking at my house."

"Alright."
He closed the door as they walked out into the night. He stepped into the study, grabbed a piece of computer paper from the printer, reached for the blue fountain pen that Selene had bought Him, and began writing at His study desk.

ALONG A WANDERING WIND

...The wind passes into an apartment in Flushing Meadows, Queens, where a chubby boy sits on an auburn-hued couch with two of his friends. They are watching the television, but he is facing his cell phone. His awareness of all the world around him - friends, the television, the billiard table - fades into dim, dark blurs. He focuses only on the brightly illuminated screen glowing in his hand. This new girl is texting him. What is she to him? The wind asks, and searches in his mind for the answer - which comes immediately in a mosaic of illusions.

She is a new voice in person, new problems, new eyes, new smiles, a new voice breathed over a telephone, new compliments, a new pale naked body his eyes might gaze over for the first time in an unforgettable moment when an inevitable pale-red moon outside an inevitable window emphasized her contours, a new refresher, a new hint of love, new future memories, a new voice captured in flirtatious texts, an apologetic smooch to the ego - all now a collection of mysteries that he would grow to embellish in his subconscious where another heart lay crying, ignored.

He vibrates out of his daydreams of her.
Another text.
Another text.
"That's two!" he thinks in his mind, like a little boy discovering presents.

His memory of her face becomes even more beautiful, but it is her voice he clings to most passionately. She spoke to him of her problems, and that made him forget his own. She told him that he was intelligent, thoughtful, becoming, and deeply magnetic - everything he wanted so badly for her to see in him. Attention is the greatest gift when you're too afraid to pay it to yourself, the *wind ruminates. It drifts away from the boy holding his glowing white rectangle, and continues eastward...*

March 30th 2010

Thank you for considering us as a potential agency to represent your collection of short stories 'ALONG A WANDERING WIND'. We have reviewed the material you sent, and we regret that we will not be offering to review your work further at this time. We believe that the lack of plot and main character(s) do not match our selective requirements. We encourage you to keep writing, and we wish you every success. If you decide to put this work aside and draft a work with a more direct and traditional narrative, we would be keen to review it as well. Please forgive the brevity of this note. We receive a tremendous number of queries and are forced to focus our attention on a limited number of projects.

His eyes moved down the laptop screen. A pen scraped across paper in front of Him. He gazed over His laptop towards Selene across the table at The Rising Star Café and Bookseller. He watched as her pen formed blue lines and shapes quickly across the white page. He focused back on His monitor. The mouse hovered upwards, until it rested above MOVE. He clicked, and a dropdown menu presented the option of folders. He selected REJECTION LETTERS. The italicized 99 enclosed in a parenthesis became 100.

He sighed. Selene glanced up at Him.

"What's wrong, bello?" she asked. "Your eyes whisper defeat."

He shook his head and closed the laptop. Selene reached across the table with her free hand and placed it atop His. He looked up. A sympathetic smile lit her beryl eyes.

"Eventually you *will* get published and the world will know the brilliant charybidis of your mind."

"What are you writing?" A nod indicated the growing scribbles of ultramarine ink across Selene's notepad.

Her hand released His. She pulled the pad several inches closer to herself, frowning timidly.

"I wish I could show you-" she looked down at the words, something in between accusation and guilt forming in her frown, "-but you know I can't." Her face shone up to Him again. "I love you too much to show you my poetry."

Silence weighed between them. He watched Selene as she searched a blank spot on the increasingly blue paper.

"Can you, at the very least, confide in your boyfriend whom you read last?"

"Allen Ginsberg," she responded, her fingers tiptoeing across the table to the pen.

He nodded, stood up and walked passed the tables. Slowing as He passed Selene, He looked over her shoulder and traced over the words 'beautiful, haunting aeonian sauntering'. Selene coughed and He spun forward, as if avoiding being caught.

Café-dwellers ingressed and egressed in the early afternoon of Old Rookvale. He perused the bookshelves, stopping at what was once the third of the 'classics' section. What was originally a shelf of minimalistically-styled covers of republished classics was now a mosaic of three books: *22 Hues of Blue*, and its sequels: *22 Hues Bluer* and *22 Hues Bleed*. Below the tiles of blueness, a golden placard proclaimed that an upcoming film adaptation would leave its 'curious' fans 'blown away'.

He moved towards the second shelf of classics. Only now, there were no classics. Self-help books lined the rows. Presumptuous claims, titles in the 2nd person, 'your best self'. He laughed. A pixie-haired woman scowled at Him, punching the book titled 'Surpassing your Yesterdays' back onto the shelf.

He passed over shelves and shelves, until He found the single-shelved poetry section. His fingers traced over various spines, tapping on Green, Gunn, Gray, Guest, Graves, Giovanni, Gibran, and then – on a double tap – Ginsberg. He extracted a monochrome *Howl and other Poems*, and paced back towards Selene.

As He approached, He again looked over her shoulder, scanning the words 'temporary moon looming in sempiternal crescent eyes'. Passing her, He plopped down on His seat and opened the text to page one.

"What are you doing?" Selene's voice sounded. He lowered the page to see a squint-eyed smiling Selene, pen pointing forward.

Seconds passed. Their smiles grew. Selene laughed first. "Tell me!"

"Isn't it obvious?" Slowly, He raised the book to obfuscate their respective paths of vision to one another. "I'm chasing after your mind, *the best mind of my time*," He spoke into the opened page.

The eventual sound of scribbling halted His eyes from roving down the Whitmanian verses of *Howl*. He lowered the book enough to peek at Selene. Her cheeks were flushed. She bit her lip, writing with fervent deliberation. He lowered the book further and gazed at the words.

These were different words; right-side-up words, words He could read cleanly: *We're fucking the second we come home, bello.*

April 28th 2010
...*Selene... relax... Ginsberg... assonance... CivILLians... Selene... mILLions... lasciviousness...*

Over two-hundred bodies shuffled about on the navy seats of the QS auditorium as He climbed up the stage. Amid the shadowed figures and the bright lights in His eyes, He could still catch sight of Selene beaming in the 3rd row and 11th aisle. Her lips mouthed the words 'good luck'.

"Before I begin this poem titled 'As for SA', which I hope you all enjoy, I want to take a quick moment and tell you that it is dedicated to my conversations with my girlfriend – Selene Acerbi."

Feminine 'awwws' rippled across the audience, accompanied by masculine chuckles.

He breathed in:

"As civilians by millions live,
giving vivid colors to each other,
there are those who chose pedestals so high
to walk atop proud clouds in their sky,
afraid they may face the old and ageless,
cold pavement felt below by those who step,
grounded, down-to-Earth, spent; yet innocent.
As these dishonest, fast-flown promises
of news, hues, dos and don'ts become none but
sad, drone shadows that pass slow fading numb
like unimportant jazz-notes heard only
by lonely, drunken crowds, together drunk
less than the tragic, boney, shrunken clown
who, being a stumped fool, dumped his madness
in the high key of a trumpet's sadness
which can open doors of old remorse:
This talent appreciated solely
by the venue owner's soulless wallet
whom truly appreciates and FATTENS.
As competitive ball-chasing athletes
will sweat, will push, and will thrust hard forward
like drunken gladiators who will brawl
not for survival or honor at all,
but for grand paychecks and rings they won't wear.
All the while fans shout louder and louder
for their fake heroes whom sweat more and more
until it's over and all are gasping.
Individual athletes, uniformed,
resembling so much the coteries of
soldiers who tightly grab and cock phallic
ejaculators – shooting and shooting.
Then naked and showering together
in that frat-boy pride that is constructed
of at least five-guys, ten-fists, and high-fives.
As children look up to and envision
televised sex-stars of astronomic
superciliousness and dim knowledge,

and hope to shine and imitate their light
of enlightening lasciviousness.
Manibassean muses amusing
these children, teenagers, adults, and YOU
passing these magazines that COVER the truths
virulently, and in truth's stead they flaunt
the gaunt, emaciated mannequins,
set to design you to be paper-thin
and flat like the pages their eyes and minds
and lines and lies are barely confined to.
  As literature becomes so shallow,
swam in mostly by amateur swimmers
clutching 'no-fear' flotation devices
who've never dove the oceans of a tome –
which is becoming 'to me' and nothing
more than a bifurcated dual-letter
divorce that asked 'who reads?' with no 'I do.'
Unmarried, producing sad, dry off-spring.
So adieu, poor tome, unloved, tragic tome
that floats ashore dying, gasping, dying,
"To be or not to be" put together.
  As more and more morons scribble drivel
and their subordinates read their thin words
and <u>their</u> subordinates focus on breath
and breathing, hardly, air-sucking phrases,
promoting inkless, thoughtless, thinkless books:
Those new, novel heaps of 'literature',
those hybrids of 'Litter' and 'Amateur'
embellishing top-seller booths you see
in the vanishing book store while you walk
passed the 22 Hues of Blue faces
towards the crowded children corners where
collegians collectively contemplate
their pasts that passed so fast ungrasped, and ask,
"Can this other's self-help book self-help ME?"
  As the poor-poor people impoverished
decay into ash, so cold and alike
the As itself: Backwards, perverse, and wrong.
and the wealthy steadily lose the worth

of everything – unlike the beggar, who
when even dragged and drugged and drunken by
the inebriation of poverty
stands knowing the true value tightly gripped
in her cold, tired, shivering, empty hands.
 As we all watch love visibly evolve
to a badly backwards broken mistake
while hate burns hellish heat into falsified eyes
that have never once focused or realized
they can opt out of this distorted view
of things that blur away our world today.
 As people become popular through lies
running from their truths like politicians –
– politicians who promise to lie to us
with ideological idioms that won one's id
and make an idiot's idea logical.
 As is backwards, wrong, this world, it's endless
 WHERE it shoots fast passed those living in dreams
 WHO find time for their mind to inquire
 WHY we're not progressing forward rightly
 WHEN small boys grow to cold, full-blown monsters
 HOW assholes become dicks and pussies grow balls!
 WHAT bodies become holy apostles?
 As these backwards days sway away each day
with raucous rage roaring right behind you,
find this page, for it will always find you.
 As it bled its ink from a heart that thinks
to painfully drink: Questions and answers,
sights, nights, pains, gains, miseries, victories,
and remain to always truly love you.

   Silence, followed by the rustling of trembling pages as He folded the paper and stared at the crowd. A clap from Selene. Another clap elsewhere. A burst of cheers, laughs, snapping fingers, clapping, seats moving as people stood filled the auditorium. Selene was grinning, He could see. He nodded to her with the rare face of acknowledged appreciation. He stepped off of the stage, moved towards the applauding figures and approached Selene who stood with her arms out to Him. He sidled across the rows, hands slapping His back, and was met by her encapsulating arms as she hugged Him and kissed His shoulder.

"They both have nice asses!" a girl's voice whispered behind them.

"First of all," Selene spoke into His neck, and then pulling away to face Him, "that was amazing. I loved it. Ginsberg might have made an impression on you after all."

"Awesome," He spoke as they sat down not untangling their gazes. "It was for you. I also have something for you. It's another Along a Wandering Wind. This one is about Ollie – my roommate from BS."

He pulled out a folded piece of paper from His pocket. The crowd began to quiet.

"Second of all – you looked so hot up there."

A new speaker walked up on the stage. He had red hair, a clean-shaven face, and muscles protruding from a skin-tight V-neck which depicted the original book cover of Hemingway's *The Old Man and the Sea*.

"My name is Nunzio Esposito," the boy announced himself.

"Third," Selene continued, leaning closer to Him with her cyan eyes darkening as the lights dimmed again, "and I hope you take this the way I want you to – *lamely* – but your vocabulary has grown insanely. It's pure xenoglossy. I don't know how you did it, but it's impressive. I never imagined I would ask *you* what a word meant. I had to look up 'lasciviousness' in my phone."

"Well-"

"Euneirophrenia," the boy on the stage began, "the ineluctable modality of the sybaritic…"

Selene's eyes dilated as she turned away from Him and gazed up at the speaker.

The paper folding away in His hand read:

ALONG A WANDERING WIND

...The wind hovers over the town of Douglaston in Queens, where it immediately detects an enigmatic verve flowing out from a boy in the lobby of a copper-colored apartment building. The wind drifts towards the entrance, and observes him as he stands by an elevator in a tangerine veterinarian scrub. The boy plays with the idea that he is – and will be for the next few hours – the king of disappearing fragments. He stares wide-eyed at the elevator up button that he has just pressed. An orange ring beams around it. He still feels the honey-colored tab under his tongue, even though the chemicals have long been absorbed into his bloodstream.

His mind is the picture of an earthquake in a strange city; unusual thoughts fall like descending rubble, pieces of asymmetrical ideas drop from the sky - ideas like the homographic word 'entrance', rainbow-colored zebras, the unicorn being the mutual ancestor of the rhinoceros and the stallion, ancient aliens initiating the rapid spike of human intelligence via controlled chromosomal manipulation and occult knowledge approximately 88,000 years ago, Deuteronomy 4:19, the Igigi and the Anunnaki and Atlantis and the rise of the homosapien, the specific age of whales which he understands to be sixty-million years old, the predatorial nightmare of the megalodon shark and if it is extant considering recent findings, what a blind man envisions when inhaling dimethyltryptamine, the pineal gland of reptiles, the anatomy of an eye, and how dogs are colorblind but their sense of smell divides one odor into different quantities of varying smells, unlike humans who instead divide sight into various wavelengths as colors but can smell only collective odors. The thoughts fall and land, pulverized and bubbling and forgotten on some vaguely present psychological asphalt.

He stares at the orange-ringed up arrow, and then at the unlit down arrow. He presses the up button again, and then presses the down button out of curiosity. An orange ring illuminates around both the up and down arrows now.

The wind watches as constructs of Heaven and Hell arise and collide within him. Heaven is a cool mist, and laying in shallow Bahamian water with wavelets trickling over his body as he burrows in the soft sand. Around him are his friends and beautiful foreign women with gold skin, pouting lips, and amber-hued eyes. Hell begins with a syrupy film coating his eyes, and then sinks to reveal a burning, wolf-like claw reaching out and wrapping its long smoldering nails around his heart, grabbing it, squeezing it sharply, and then yanking it downward into a darker part of him. The snatching feeling causes his knees to click together. His throat tastes of bile. He begins sweating. The wind twists through the quickening flurry of hallucinatory thought-waves. There is a monster in him. The idea of hell isn't going away. Is he bad? Is he evil? No. NO. He certainly has improper thoughts sometimes. NOO. Tears form in his eyes. He doesn't want to die. He is a good human. A good human being being a human good. He only wanted to test the buttons. He starts to sob. Tears fell from his face as his back buckles suddenly and he slouches in a heavily depressed parabola.

  He flings himself backwards, jerks his head upwards facing the ceiling, and produces a most hellish scream. His throat burns with furious vibrations. Would this expel the monster? Maybe the whales could help! Call for the humpback!

  The elevator door opens, revealing a feminine figure draped in a garden of glimmering gold.

  "Jeez! Stop! Fuck! Stop yelling! What's wrong?"

  He stops. The face is familiar. Amethyst eyes and pale skin. Thick, ruddy lips. Blond curls. Memories swarm. Kisses and warmth. Citrus-mint scent. His girlfriend. Before she could emerge from the halo of the elevator he lunges forward and wraps his arms around her body.

  "I've been waiting for you for hours!" he sobs.

  She feels his heart pound against her jacket, her shirt, and her bra; and feels her own heartbeat accelerate.

  "But, you texted me, like, two minutes ago."

A guilty look forms across her face which now rests on his shoulder as she began patting his back.

"Oh no, you took too much," she speaks as she releases him and observes his face.

His eyes are soaked and his lips pout tremblingly. Now it is she who wraps her arms around him.

"Come upstairs. I'll make you soup and we'll listen to the Beatles, and lay down and-"

The elevator doors close on his dazed expression and her blushing face, muffling her heartfelt apologies.

The wind scratches its chin, and blasts through the window moving eastwards...

July 22nd 2010

...athenaeum... bibliophile... sesquipedalian... is Selene peeing or pooping?...

He was in Selene's family's house for the very first time, standing in her bedroom alone and gazing first at the word 'noncomedogenic' on her moisturizer atop her bookcase, and then at her literature.

"You're such a bibliophile!" He called out.

"I'm the wormiest of the bookworms!" Selene's voice giggled from the bathroom across the hall.

His eyes passed over the collectanea of Petrarch's poetry, an opuscule of Ovid, a novelette by Negri, a panoply of Poe, and incunable works of the classic Italian literati.

"Selene's colors," He murmured.

The toilet flushed across the hall. He continued perusing the spines, and then stopped at the words *22-Hues of Blue*.

"I hope you're absolutely famished, bello," Selene spoke, walking into the room. "I don't know if you can hear the tintibulation from downstairs, but it sounds like Mama Acerbi is preparing a feast for us." She rubbed His abdomen. "She's excited to meet-"

"Why is this book here?" He interrupted.

Selene turned immediately towards the book, and turned slowly back towards Him.

"It's the one I showed you at Art's beach. I bought it for my mom." Her eyes moved up-leftwards. "I'm not sure how it got in my room." She grabbed the book and tossed it aside.

He looked into her eyes.

"Tutti a tavola!" a young boy's voice called from downstairs.

"Let's go, bello."

Selene pulled Him out of the room and towards the corridor.

"I left something in your room," He spoke as they descended the stairs.

"It better be more of *Along a Wandering Wind*."

"It might be."

"Is this one of the dark ones?"

"Yes."

"Good. Tragedy is what redirects our hearts. Who in your world is the wind analyzing this time?"

"You'll see. It's on your pillow."

"Ah. My little *Truth Fairy*." Selene contemplated. "Dustin I bet. Art is too *good* to write about, huh, bello?"

He smiled as they walked downstairs and into the kitchen, where a young girl and two older girls were speaking Italian and gesticulating rapidly.

"Ciao!" Selene called, watching them and squeezing His hand. A moment passed before He squeezed her hand back, softer.

Three pairs of sea-glass-colored eyes beamed up at Him. Lips smiled. The older two turned quickly to each other, nodding approvingly.

"This is Diana, my youngest sister-" Selene started on the right side of the table, "-and this is Isabella." Selene nodded to the thicker, tanner girl. "She graduated from QS two years ago." His eyes remained on Diana – who resembled Selene with her sharp cerulean eyes and timid smile. "And my oldest-"

"-And wisest," the eldest sister interrupted as she stood up from the table. She walked towards Him. Her wedding ring scintillated as she shook His hand. "Claudia," she spoke as if reciting a well-known melody.

"Second-wisest," came a response, sotto voce, from behind them.

He turned around and saw Ms. Acerbi removing her right oven mitt. Her wizened face was a lower, tired, and grayer rendition of Selene's; rumors of a European beauty still emanated from features. A small scar crisscrossed over the left side of her temple. She extended her hand and He took it, shaking it firmly. "I'm Bellona Acerbi," she spoke warmly. "Welcome to our home, bello."

In a loud rush, a boy rollerbladed into the kitchen. With breakneck speed, Ms. Acerbi caught the boy and hugged him against her.

"And this," Ms. Acerbi spoke, turning the boy forward, "is little Maximiliano. The least wise of the Acerbi family."

"Hey!" the long-lashed, blue-eyed boy called out.

"Though," Ms. Acerbi began, ruffling the boy's messy hair, "we are all wise in our own ways."

"The girls are, at least," Claudia murmured, turning back to rejoin her sisters at the dinner table.

"So, Selene told me a few things about you," Ms. Acerbi spoke, releasing the boy, who rolled idly towards the table.

"Only the good, I hope."

"Well she's right about you being handsome," Claudia called out. Diana blushed.

"Is it true that you're trying to be a writer, like Selene?" Isabella questioned as her un-ringed fingers ran up and down the stem of her wine glass.

"Yes." His eyes flickered to Selene. "Though I'm nowhere near as well of a writer as she."

"Why don't you have a name?" Diana finally spoke, her dulciloquence suffusing the room with brightness. A wind passed. The smell of cooking fish grew more present. Branches moved outside the pastel-framed windows; shadows danced across the off-white walls and onto the wooden kitchen floor. "Isn't that strange?"

"I don't know." He shrugged. "No one ever gave me one."

Selene's siblings looked to each other and then turned in unison to their mother who nodded slowly. The oven dinged. She turned around.

"Are your parents together?" she asked, scrutinizing the orange-pink roasting branzino.

A flush rose to His face. Selene looked down at her empty plate.

"Well," He began, His voice trembling gently, "they're separated. They still love each other but-"

"Ah," Ms. Acerbi interrupted. "It happens." She reached into the oven. "When is your birthday, bello?"

"October first. Finally a question I can answer directly." He laughed.

Ms. Acerbi froze, her hand halfway into the oven. Now it was Selene's cheeks that reddened. All of the siblings looked down at their dinner plates as if imitating Selene, while Selene herself gazed slowly up towards Him, her face burning with sadness. "That's my father's birthday," Selene whispered, her voice a warning.

He turned back to Ms. Acerbi. She shook her head and pulled the branzino out. Behind her shoulder was a cartoon picture of an older woman smiling. Above her face, in red cursive, were the words: RAN INTO MY EX THE OTHER DAY – PUT THE CAR IN REVERSE AND RAN INTO HIM AGAIN!

"He was a dick," both Mrs. Acerbi and Maximiliano spoke simultaneously. She glared down at the boy.

"What? You said-" he looked desperately to his sisters, seeking aid. "He is!"

Upstairs, on Selene's pillow, a single page read:

ALONG A WANDERING WIND

...The wind drifts to Great Neck, Long Island, and finds an overweight man in his late forties leaning over the exposed hood of a pick-up truck, whose pale-yellow color matches both his jacket and the home behind him. He is the stepfather of the family inside the house. He is breathing

heavily. His thoughts parallel the engine he so meticulously tweaks: Logical, lineal, admittedly in need of slight tuning, non-creative, effective and non-affective: That goes there and only there.

  A blonde woman – his wife – watches him from the upstairs window. Their bedroom is a deep red with gold trimmings: 'To help the romance.' She wonders what he thinks as he's working, and what he thought the day before, and what he would think tomorrow; and imagines thoughts that are more similar to her own than any he would ever have. And these are only some of the thoughts waving about in her chaotic mind. Is her oldest son okay? Is her younger son a homosexual as the other parents implied? How will these siblings and a lost father impact the love life of her daughter – a middle child, after all? So impressionable. There are so many concerns, so many doubts, so many regrets – all in the form of individually definable thoughts, yet there are too many to distinguish one from another for too long. They are like words in a crowded room: Muttled, unclear, one vast, encompassing, murmurous sound. The wind notes how isolating a single thought in her current state resembles focusing on the trajectory of a single wave during an ocean thunderstorm. The woman, however, understands that the collective cognitions certainly has a monochrome to it.

  Downstairs, a chubby eleven-year-old boy is listening to music and swaying his head, occasionally stealing glances at his older brother laying across from him on the couch, snoring vociferously and smelling of whiskey and smoke. He's already confused as to why he wants to kiss the lips of boys. He also wonders – not in logical thoughts but rather in somber question marks audible only though his sighs – why he doesn't seem to have friends like his older sister or brother. He wonders, and hypothesizes if things would be different if he liked girls the way he likes boys, and considers if he could change himself for a friend. His brother's phone vibrates again.

  He begins contemplating what loneliness truly means, and if it really has anything to do with anyone else.

The wind leaps out of the window and continues eastward. It shifts a few degrees southward, soaring towards Old Rookvale along the Sunrise Highway...

July 26th 2010
...maybe her poetry got published?... heart beating quickly...

My Love: WE NEED TO TALK. RISING STAR CAFÉ IN 20. (3:32)

    A graying haze hung over the quaint café in the near center of Old Rookvale, where He sat by the window, watching the next wave of recently-graduated high schoolers meander around the town with early-summertime laziness. The café was quieter than usual. His hand occasionally massaged His chest.
    "Oh!" He gasped, as if recalling something.
    He walked towards the barista and ordered a black hazelnut iced coffee, and another black iced coffee for Himself. He collected both drinks and sat back down, waiting.
    At 4:01, Selene paced inside, her hands punched into the front pocket of her gray jumper. He started to get up, but she motioned quickly for Him to remain seated.
    "What's wrong?" He asked.
    Selene sniffled as she sat down. She watched Him for a moment, extracted Gabriel Garcia Marquez's *Love in the Time of Cholera* from the front pocket of her hoodie, and tossed it onto the table.
    "We are breaking up right now."
    "W-"
    "No," she hissed. "Don't say anything. Just read."
    She opened the book to the inside of the back cover, and slid it across the table.
    He looked down, and read:

    Aug. 24th 2008 TASKS:
    Finish reading Jung's Modern Man in Search of a Soul

> *Write out difference between Jung's concept of dreaming and Freud's*
>
> *Fuck Muschey more often*

The handwriting of the last item on the list resembled that of Mandy Rusche.

"That's from before I even met you. I didn't even know she wro-"

"No!" Selene snapped. "Do you have any idea how embarrassing this is? Do you know how many stories I hear about you? How you use and fuck girls? I know I've only been with Michael before you – but I know this can't be how it should feel."

"How it should feel? We've been dating for over a year, now. I-"

"I lent this book to my friend. She lent it to her mom. Her mom read this, knowing it was *your* book. She told my friend. She called me and-"

"But-"

"Stop," Selene snapped, turning away. "God, I can't even look at you."

"But, I didn't do anything wrong."

"No. You didn't." Selene stood up. "I did."

"Wait-" He begged softly.

"No."

"WAIT!" He hissed. Faces turned towards them. Selene shook her head and raced towards the exit. He ran after her as she stepped outside to the parking lot and paced quickly towards her car.

"Stop!" He yelled, jumping in front of her Mazda with His arms outstretched. "You're throwing this away because of rumors and a joke from two years ago! I love you and you know this. I would never cheat-"

She opened the door and stepped out in front of Him.

"Every *god damned week* I hear stories about you. My friends ask me what we are. I don't even know. It's been a year and I don't know what we are. Last week, some stranger from your town asked if I was one of your side girls."

"I have never cheated, I don't have *side girls,* and I don't know what you're talking about, Selene," He whispered, stepping towards her. "You and I are boyfriend and girlfriend."

"No." She recoiled quickly. "Just, leave me alone for a while. This is exhausting. I hate seeing your face right now."

She stepped back into her car, slammed the door and turned on the ignition. The engine roared, and – immediately after – the tires screeched as she sped out of the parking lot. The roar of the engine faded, until it was swallowed by the sound of another wind passing. Leaves and blades of grass lifted from the air and fell back slowly onto the gray asphalt.

PART III – MISERY
July 27th 2010 – July 27th 2011

...are a paradigmatic triumvirate without me. I will die here, and you all will continue living, loving, and laughing in the inter-concatenated orchestra that is this life.
Mother, father, brother... Why does my heart become a tormenting inferno when I recall your faces? Why do my eyes water with guilt as I reveal such detestable feelings? Why is it that whenever I stop thinking of you all, whenever I feel the reflective shards of your faces in my mind become more distant, it is only then when I begin to feel catharsis.
All I ever wanted to do was to grab my pen, aim myself in the right direction, and launch and blaze into the high atmosphere, gaining the momentum of learned talent and experience and knowledge, and then explode in nebulae of sentences blazed across the sky for individuals lost in crowds to point at and admire and see new and encouraging and scintillating reflections of themselves. Yes, THAT is what I wanted.
Sometimes, I would become so angry at you all just for the fact that none of you could participate in the struggling conversations I would have with myself, and could never understand that if I was ever going to make you proud it would solely be through my independent writing. Father, you're too business-oriented to lucidly see my illogical reasoning. Mother, you're too simple to begin reading anything I wrote. And brother... you simply wouldn't help me.
You know it's true, brother. Remember the first time that you were heartbroken by Calliope? I orbited closely around you as much as I could, struggling to deign my words to your language to radiate the world around you. When I was heartbroken about Selene - shortly after you were back with Calliope, if you remember - you lazily told me to use my own words of wisdom to feel better, and then left me. If only you had the social insight or selflessness to

understand that heartbreak - though a universal human emotion - is an individualized injury. One can mend another only through personal and caring explorations and understandings of the victim. But, don't worry about it, brother. Just practice selfless consideration after I am gone. I will conclude my own life as mind-broken, soul-broken, and heart-broken 20 year old. I will die as a person whose access to pleasures has run far too thin, and whose sensitivities to life's miseries has become far too severe.

Last night, however, was perhaps different. Shortly after saying goodbye to Dani, leaving her a bitter-sweet present, imbibing too much whiskey, and then penning a potentially penultimate scene of Along a Wandering Wind back in the study, I decided to treat myself to a departing ambulation. I reminded myself that that very night – Tuesday July 26th, 2011 – would be the last evening that my living eyes would watch the world. When you're about to depart this existence, it's amazing how tender the nocturnal wind feels when it grazes your lips, cheeks, eyes, arms... It's incredible the whole animate pulse of everything... It's marvelous, the whole life of everything...

During my nighttime peregrination, I passed by The Rising Star Café, and saw that there were tables outside. It's actually quite funny; that's the first time they've ever done that. As I passed by the faces of the diners enjoying their late-night summertime community, I hypothesized that if there had been outdoor seating the day I met Mandy three years ago, would it have changed anything? Would I be in this car right now, inhaling and exhaling my last hours? But... what good does looking back and asking 'what if' accomplish, now?

I counted 8 tables, 24 seats, and 16 faces – all of whom ignorant to my imminent death, all of whom steadily reminding me that the world will continue living and moving after I'm gone... There were a few couples seated there, and of course those were the ones that my eyes lingered on most. Crestfallen faces, ecstatic faces, indifferent faces, captivated faces. A grinning face made beautiful by the amber-colored evening lighting. A fraternal laugh. A flirtatious giggle.

Illuminated windows. Straws being sipped. Cigarette smoke absconding into the midnight dome above. 16 people, and a thousand Danikas, Selenes, and Mandys...

...The acid has worn off. I've sat in this car for at least six hours now. The time is 5:37. The sun is beginning to set, and so am I.

...Melancholy is when happiness filters through sadness; that's why it feels so empty. Sadness filtered by happiness might be hope; that's why it often feels ungrounded...

Are people supposed to feel the way I've felt this last year, or have I always had a psychological disorder and this is its final manifestation? Disorder. Are emotions supposed to be this intensely dominating over one's logic? Logic and emotions... they're brothers - related, and they fight often. But my emotions, my damned emotions, they are the worst part of me. They come in such overpowering waves, like swarms of specters, like demons, like preternatural equilibrium-topplers. Happiness lifts every vein and valve with tremblingly giddy smiles, and loneliness always feels like a permanently crippling abandonment. And sadness, and rage... let's not delve down deeply into those darker waters.

And I never get to choose when they appear... If only I could have controlled these tidal waves, I might have heard my logic whisper that I did have a family that cared for me, I did have friends, and I did have women whom would have loved to plague themselves by intertwining our lives.

Then why am I concluding my life? Was I spoiled with friends, love, sex, and appreciation? I had everything going for me. Everything was fine once upon a time. What caused the bouleversement?

Heartbreak has something to do with it. The thing about heartbreak is that it renders one selfish - it is such a challenge to leave your aching self and consider others except through the darkly reductive angles of jealousy, envy, and hatred. The people passing in the outside world are rendered tenebrous and distant, even when they are being thoughtful and welcoming to you. Heartbreak is a sickness somewhat akin to depression – the inability to conceive a positive future while drowning in the present – and your instinct when sick is to cure yourself, but the usual medicine of your benevolent memories has expired and has actually become your very poison. And that is exactly how nostalgia operates.

Heartbreak's most intrinsic element is nostalgia, and nostalgia evokes the most incapacitating synesthesia: All experiences filter through a lens of morbidity. There's surely a color to a smile and a melody to a compliment – but it all becomes pale, dull, and flat through a depressed lens. And everything that is negative increases in volume, until even the abstract blurs of dissatisfying moments swell into heart-wrenching tragedies. You become so sensitive that even an iota of dissatisfaction magnifies into a deleterious leviathan of misery.

Two weeks ago, for example, while I was sitting on the overly air-conditioned Long Island Rail Road, I noticed an illusively familiar 40-something old woman eating sushi rolls from a plastic container. She ate slowly and looked like she was lost in a deep thought. No matter how much my stare attempted to reel in her gaze, her eyes never glanced towards me or anywhere in the animate world in front of her, so I continued watching her. Under the luridly pale fluorescent lights, she would take a small bite of her sushi, pause momentarily as if proposing to herself a melancholy question, and then took another small bite. I could confidently swear that she was hurting from unrequited love. She checked her phone several times, and it was clear that she did not see what she was waiting for. And then, perhaps the dozenth time she checked her phone, lines of disappointment creviced across her beautiful face and she released a defeated sigh – a sigh that I know all too well – and immediately my eyes teared and I was forced to rush out of the train one stop early.

I waited, sniffling and vicariously heartbroken as I watched the train snake away from the platform moving eastwards in the dark distance towards Old Rookvale. And in that moment, standing on that platform, I again had that

strange feeling... that feeling where I completely forget who I am. I'll feel a vague possession of my arms, hands, and my fingers, and will commandeer them in awkward movements. I'll catch sight of my reflection, and I'll see my unsmiling green eyes searching, and suddenly I'll recall the departures of the many people that once held me together.
 Yes...
 I've answered the question finally. I am committing suicide because I am no longer me. A life's worth nothing when all harmony is gone. I've ruined the friendships and family and loves that made me who I once was. There's nothing left to destroy except for the empty receptacle that I've become. That is why I am ending my life... I think. But who knows why we really do anything? Who knows why we do what we do when we do it? Why your local barista greeted you with a curt 'hi' instead of her usual, mellifluous-sounding 'hello' has a trillion justifications. So, why someone decides to commit suicide might take a while to explain, and a lifetime to begin comprehending.
 Why do we learn the things we learn? Why do we think the things we think? Why do we feel the things we feel? Why did the pianist in my story's story need to be masked? An homage to that mysterious Boston girl? An allusion to my father's absence or my mother's many faces? I hope that in this mess of elements, I've presented the alchemy suitable for proposing some answers.
 I know at least that I've perpetuated the inevitability of my self-destruction by thrice allowing myself to be heartbroken. Mandy proved that I could be deeply fractured, and Selene taught me that I could be shattered to pieces. And, while in pieces, I was foolish enough to offer my fragmented self to another who crushed the pieces to dust before the experience of life and medicine of time could piece me back together. How senseless of me to find a broken girl to mend my own breakages. This is one objectively clear indication of my immaturity - the arrogant desire to 'fix' a girl. Was I really delusional enough to consider myself stable enough to mend someone else? Was Danika more or less whole than I? Broken shapes rarely fit

together... Dear women everywhere – when a man swears to you that he wants to save you and his every intention is to revive you, understand please that it is most likely he who needs to be saved, he who requires revival.

Almost two months ago, I trudged into a near-empty library and, despite being alongside Alexander, I felt a most redundant loneliness. It almost felt as if the world were bidding me good-bye. And, of course, Selene walked in looking enchanting as always. She stabbed me with a quick piercing gaze, and continued walking, ignoring me. Yes, I was still with Danika (though already growing desperate to free her of me), but it was still a thunderstorm to me, and my thoughts further drowned beneath the maddening waves.

Why is it that only on those singular nights, where - by chance of a peripheral glance in a mirror - you deem yourself abnormally good-looking, do you end up strutting into a perplexingly vacant world? Why is that on those nights where all you want is to be seen, are there no people to see you? Conversely, why is it those nights where all you wish is to be alone, do you end up in a vortex of terribly familiar glares?

After seeing Selene pass by me almost two months ago, it became clear that this burden of misery will never go away. I've tried so many times to remind myself how to be happy; now I don't even know what that concept feels like. It's as simple as that. It's not just heartbreak; it's a breakage of everything... Of myself.

Life is intimately lonely when you yourself have become no one. When the sun falls below the horizon, and I'm at some inane social gathering, morbid thoughts wrestle me down. At first I can maintain the illusion of my former self for everyone, but then slowly that mirage fades, and I'll watch from the corner of a room as everyone swarms about in their conversations and all I can do is drink my inevitable drink, and think that everybody is here but me...

Me: A hopeless nullifidian nearing the cenotaph of nullibicity. Me: College dropout. Family reject. Friendless. Aimless. Hopeless. Loveless. The writer who can't ever finish writing anything, even though skipping one day of writing fills him with anxiety, forgetfulness, and convolution. 'I must write' I shout – an arrogant and solipsistic spectacle to anyone with seeing eyes. Then why haven't I finished writing ALONG A WANDERING WIND? Why do I treat it as an intermittent luxury and nothing else? Why do I wait for it to write itself in dark moments, instead of crafting it like a true artsmith? My father has asked me a dozen times why I haven't finished yet, and I give the half-truth that relaying a proper story is a Sisyphean labor. But I've been writing that story since Selene inspired me exactly one and a half years ago.

Drinking and smoking and writing and lust and love and sex no longer provide me the illusion of happiness. No more nepenthes. Dustin is in jail, I've coerced Artyom and Alexander into hating me, my family into loathing me, and everyone I once loved into forgetting any of my goodness.

Every day since Danika and I broke up the first time, thoughts of suicide passed through my mind more and more frequently. When my father called me a prick, when Alex called me a psycho... each time I knew it was going to happen soon. The world without me. Me without the world. What a wondrous wonder. I'm not good enough for this world.

Poor bratty child. Getting the silver spoon so early, and then sobbing when it's taken away. I would have hung myself but I'm too afraid of the pain... and of the inevitable erection... and of allowing the seemingly too-apparent theme of my feet 'not touching the ground' for all of those people who knew me only as a dreamer.

People. There's so many of them in this world. In my world.

Friends: Artyom, Dustin,
Family: Mom, Dad, Brother
Fascinations: Mandy, Selene, Danika
Familiars: Dr. Henry Hallward Heidelberg, Alexander Teisėjakaitis, Oliver Scoffman, Hunter Clarence Quillan Wilcox Himmler II,

When I look at these names, dim hues of our shared memories swim through the darkening ocean of my mind's eye. Though, of course, there is no such thing as shared memories, but only shared moments. You are all the main characters in my life, and I hope I was something good in yours, if at least once, somehow. Because once is enough, since everything is temporary anyway. Everything. Friends - temporary. Family - temporary. That triumphant feeling of seeing a new naked girl in front of me - temporary. Everything is fleeting, yet, even in its evanescence, everything is also redundant. Friends - redundant. Family - redundant. Sinking away when I realize she's not as great as the illusion I've pedestalled her up to, and that I'm not as great as the self-image I've flaunted to her - definitely redundant. Everything is redundant and fleeting. Except life and death. We only have one of those. And yet even life and death exist as patterns like everything in this world. Sometimes, the patterns seem obvious - almost preordained by a sardonic, unskilled god. Sometimes the patterns hide behind a single note of a repeating laugh throughout time. Borges proposes the pattern that each of us is everyone else. I am the Walt Whitman that Selene once read; I am Selene, and Selene is Walt Whitman. Good-bye, Selene, Walt Whitman, and I. I've fucked two of us then. Sorry, Walt.

  I'm sure I have gone mad, yet things have never seemed clearer. I know I will not find happiness. I know I will not find joy. I know I will...

August 22nd 2010
 ...what if Selene calls back and I'm stoned?...

  "It's been a month, son. Just shut the fuck up about Selene, and smoke some weed!" Dustin urged, pushing the black-and-turquoise pipe towards Him. From below his turned-up American-flag hoodie, a chubby smile gleamed in the evening mist. "It will make you feel better, I promise."

  "Thinking about her won't help you, man," Alex added, dipping his foot into His backyard pool.

  "But I might talk to her later," He responded, wrapping His hands around the neck.

"You said you wouldn't try to talk to her!" Alex snapped.

"I know." He nodded, pulling the bowl towards Himself. He lit the phallic-shaped pipe, and tapped on and off the carburetor while inhaling. A smoky smile peaked on the sides of His lips.

"Better, man?" Alex nodded.

He exhaled the smoke, and shrugged.

"Told you," Dustin and Alex spoke simultaneously.

A dozen puffs and a half hour later they were lumbering down His driveway, down the massive hill where His house was atop. A glimmering fog drifted about Old Rookvale. The grass sparkled in hues of green and silver, and the earth smelled of petrichor.

"Why are you twenty miles ahead of us?" Dustin shouted.

"Stop being antisocial!" Alex called out.

He was indeed ahead of them, texting. His phone vibrated. He examined the screen.

Me: Do you sincerely question my capacity to make you feel better? (11:43)

My Love: I don't understand. I question everyone's ability to make me feel better. It's impossible. (12:12)

Me: Well, I understand that you get the final say in what makes you feel better, but I also think there are particular people more capable at draining the pent-up rivers of yourself. (12:13)

He nodded at His cell phone, and dropped it in His pocket. As He did so, the phone rang. He pulled the phone back out of His pocket and squinted at the words MY LOVE flashing across His blood-shot eyes. He smiled, frowned, and then assumed a face of stern punctiliousness as He tapped the ACCEPT button.

"Why do you say that?" Selene spoke through the receiver, a distant gloom hanging in her voice.

He stared down Village Road, which stretched out and shimmered through the darkness.

"I was reflecting on what our relationship was, and how you are different from any other girl I've been with… asking myself to prove how you were actually someone I ever loved, and not just a glorified booty call-"

"Glorified booty call?" Selene chuckled.

"-and," He continued, "it all had to do with communication. Do you remember when we first started talking on the phone?"

"Yeah," Selene responded after a moment's pause.

"Do you remember how often I asked you to guess how long we were speaking? You'd guess fifteen minutes, and in reality we had been speaking for over an hour. You'd guess an hour and it would be three. That's what chemistry is – how fast time goes when you're with someone. You're the one who allowed me to experience that truth…"

Their conversation continued as He turned around and saw Alexander and Dustin in the darkness – a tall skinny figure and a short fat figure – both waving impatiently. He looked at them and sliced the air furiously with His hand. They looked at one another and turned the other direction.

"Talk to me about your day," He spoke in the receiver as the shapes of Dustin and Alex shrunk in the distance.

He turned back around and continued walking through the Old Rookvale backstreets, all the while listening to the increasingly vocal Selene, and responding tenderly. Over a half hour passed as Selene spoke of the plausibility of dropping out of QS, how last weekend she tried marijuana for the third time and did not enjoy it, and how Chet Baker has become her favorite artist.

"…I miss you too," she spoke through her second yawn of their conversation. "I guess we can get coffee tomorrow."

"Good. Friday, August 23rd we get coffee."

"Okay."

"Wait—"

"What?"

"How long have we been on the phone?"
"I don't know," Selene responded, a smile rounding her voice. "20 minutes?"
He grinned.
"Check when we hang up. Ciao, Moon-butt."
"Ciao, bello."
He hung up the phone. The call time read 53:08.

August 24th 2010
… I want to be alone… with Selene… that's all…

He was in the Hamilton's Tavern bathroom, staring in the mirror and focusing intently at the illumination of His green eyes in the gold lighting. He rechecked His phone.

Me: Yesterday was awesome. I'm glad it happened. I'll see you tonight. (12:20)
My Love: Hamilton's at 6:30. Got it. (4:39)
Me: Perfect. (6:16)

He stepped out of the bathroom, entered the main room of Hamilton's Tavern, and plopped down on the barstool. Above, a clock read 6:31. A salt-water scent filled the air. He looked around. A single woman at the farthest corner of the bar ate her final piece of boxed sushi. He watched her as she sighed with an air of defeat, cracked her neck, lifted from her seat, trudged passed Him, and headed towards the back exit to the parking lot.

A glacial hand pressed down on His shoulder. He turned and saw the oceanic eyes of Hunter Douglas Quillan Wilcox-Himmler II glimmering down at Him. "Look who it is!" Hunter bellowed.

"Hey," He spoke, nodding. His eyes brightened as He spotted a female figure walk in through the snowy entrance. As she approached the bar area, the light illuminated her, revealing a Mediterranean-featured older woman. She joined a group of ladies her age at the corner of the bar. Her heavily made-up eyes found His as she took her seat.

"What's going on, my man?" Hunter yelled, rubbing His shoulder.

He turned to Hunter's face and then down to a trident-shaped scar running down from his knuckles to the cuff of his wrist.

"What happened to your hands?"

"It's nothing." Hunter moved his hand away quickly and sat down next to Him. "Tell me - who are you fucking these days?"

His phone vibrated. He fumbled it out quickly – nearly tossing it onto the bar – and examined the screen.

My Love: Hamilton's at 6:30. Got it. (4:39)
Me: Perfect. (6:16)
My Love: I am so sorry. I know it's strange and soon... but I'm kind of seeing someone else now. I've known him for a while. His name is Nunzio... and I kind of like him. I don't know what else to say. I am so confused about everything. I was in my car for 10 minutes and even drove half way to Hamilton's to meet you, and then turned back around. I don't think it's a good idea for you and me to see each other right now. It's too soon. I don't hate you. You are nice, but I can't seem to think of you in a great light anymore. I'm sorry. I'm staying home. (6:40)

"Myself," He spoke dryly, trembling as He tucked the phone back into His pocket.

"Nice," Hunter yelled. "Guess who I'm fucking?"

As Hunter spoke, His eyes were pulled towards the glistening green gaze of the woman across the tavern. Crow's feet adorned her eyes. Her skin was hazelnut colored, her mascara was thick, and her hair was black. She shot Him an amorous glance and began mouthing words to Him. His phone vibrated twice. He pulled His phone out, and observed the new texts.

Art: We still on for Vane's Diner next-next Friday? September 5th? I get out at 6:00 pm. Tell me how it all goes with selene tonight bro. Be patient. (6:42)

    Alexander: Dustin and I are getting drinks at Hamilton's Friday night. Theres some show playing and if I am informed correctly there will be bountiful hoes in attendance. If ur not feeling like a heartbroken homo come join us man. (6:42)

    "...psychotic, but fucks like a goddess, and her ass is stellar," Hunter continued. "So, the equation equals out, right?"

    "Right," He echoed.

    The waitress walked up to Him.

    "Hey, Vera." Hunter winked.

    She rolled her eyes, and scrutinized Him.

    "What will it be, hun?"

    He looked at His phone, and then up to her. His hand reached into the denim of His pocket, and His thumb wrapped around His car keys. Chet Baker's *Born to Blue* began playing, commencing with, *'Some folks are meant to live in clover, but they are such a chosen few...'*

    "I'll take a triple shot of Jack."

    "If you want some of me all you have to do is ask, baby boy," the voice of Jack Ricaricare boomed as he slapped Him hard on the back.

    He recoiled, and watched as Jack's massive frame passed by. Wrapped tightly on his arm was a younger girl, about a third his size. Her sun-burned skinny legs motioned dizzily forward with Jack.

    "That guy's a creep, huh?" Hunter laughed as he watched them exit. "Look how he has to try to keep the girl tightly towards him. Total beta, right?" Hunter looked back at Him, searching.

    "He's supporting her," He spoke to His approaching glass.

    "Maybe, yeah." Hunter nodded. "Maybe."

    He put the empty glass back down on the table. A new glass appeared in front of Him. He looked up at the bartender with an inquisitive glance.

"From the MILF in the corner, hun," the bartender cooed. "You know she's been eye-fucking you since she sat down right?"

"Does *He* know?" Hunter shook his head with disbelief. The bartender rolled her eyes, and frowned towards a group of underage boys entering. "She doesn't know you the way I do," Hunter whispered.

He turned and glanced across the bar. The woman raised her drink to Him and winked.

"I would totally plow her if I were you. Then I'd *really* be a motherfucker!" Hunter laughed.

He looked at His phone, and then up to the bartender who was walking away.

"Pardon me," He called out.

She turned and approached Him.

"Yes, hun?"

"Can I have a piece of paper?"

"Is a receipt okay?"

"Sure."

The bartender turned towards the register.

"Hi cuntmuffin," Hunter spoke into his phone. "Yeah – no. I don't have any... But – but no, wait, listen. I can get..." Hunter paused, his eyes dancing about the room. "Now? Okay. See you in a few."

Hunter got up and slapped a hand on His shoulder as the waitress placed receipt paper and a pen in front of Him.

"I gotta go see a girl about a horse-cock!" Hunter laughed loudly.

"May you and your equestrienne friend enjoy," He mumbled, staring down at the blank paper.

Hunter shook His shoulder cordially, turned away, and raced towards the exit. He watched Hunter's figure move through the closing door out into the night. He caught eyes with the older woman again. An increasing crowd of faces and bodies and patterns of movements and glasses filled the room. He chuckled sadly, looked down at the blankness, and began writing:

ALONG A WANDERING WIND

...The wind drifts towards the sea-foam façade of a tavern in Commack, Long Island. It presses its face against the green-tinted glass windows, and observes five women of similar ages – three of them married mothers – drinking and chattering to one another. Occasionally, they steal glances at the two young men who sat down at the opposite side of the bar just a moment ago. The youngest of the women has a birthday card that has the number 44 written on it. She tangles glances with one of the boys across the bar. They are both perhaps half her age. He smiles rakishly at her. He has wet-green eyes, she notices. An arousal heats within her. She already imagines him naked, sweat dripping down his sharply-cut abs flexing as he conducts rough sexual acts on her, all perfected by her imagination.

The wind sees her thoughts of his penis as it enters her, his hands around her throat, his eyes setting her soul aflame. Yet, something undesired bubbles beneath this viridian imagination. Hazed memories of drunkenly driving after another young boy she met at the same bar a year ago flashes dimly in her again drunken mind: When she made it clear that she desired the intimacy of some sort of conversation – too much commitment for the drunken dance before sex – his impatient desires focused away from her. The wind comprehends that the source of her desire to sleep with this new boy across the bar is mostly validation. Will the acceptance of this boy with the long lashes and liquid green eyes compensate for the previous green-eyed boy's rejection? This isn't a concrete thought she thinks, but rather fragments she ignores.

Nonetheless, this new boy's attention in front of her – his every smile, his every glance up from his glass – hints the confirmation that she – a forty-four-year-old woman – is still fuckable, and that is all she wishes for on her forty-fourth birthday.

The wind drifts away from the window and breezes eastward. As it soars in the encroaching twilight, it notices a rushed change of sentiments in a luxurious building up ahead in the town of Hauppauge. A window is open on the third floor. The wind squeezes inside, fluttering the gossamer curtains. It immediately catches sight of a twenty-four-year-old girl whose thoughts repeatedly remind herself how divine she must look in her new, expensive olive-hued cock-tail dress as the boy she dated for four years approaches her.

Anger stirs within her when she notices his cool, radiant-eyed smile. That salesman.

"How've you been?" he asks her.

Alarm. He bypassed the basic salutations and inquired about her plight. Her husband left the room only a few minutes ago. She tries to focus that man. Words and images of their three years force upwards through the waves of her thoughts: Marriage, envious glances down the aisle, satisfied parents, luxurious dresses, the happy rustle of more cash she's ever seen in a single wallet, a large house with high ceilings and O that chandelier is lovely, big rooms but not too lonely, maybe a little white fluffy puppy soon (he promised!) squeezes through the panic-rippling ocean of her mind, his penis...

"Look at my wedding ring!" she demands as she force-grins that extraordinary smile that turns crowds.

He understands one or two of the hundred interweaving reasons why she is thrusting her emerald-encrusted wedding ring in his face. He cannot begin to understand how this is yet another of her hints that it is they whom should have gotten married, that this is both a proposal and a rejection and a question and an answer twisted in a pride-panicked pantomime.

"Nice," he says.

She wants so badly for him to say more, to move more, to react more, to be effected more, to be affected more goddamn it. He turns slightly, as if about to leave the conversation. As she sees this, the dark light of loss shines gray shadows of sex in her mind, and she gently panics because again she can't ignore her extant love for him. The wind notes how his very presence in her mind becomes more outlined the second she considers that he is going away. The wind notes the connection between recognizing

potential loss and comprehending worth. A thought... a desire appears... panic... warmth throughout her body... The ocean waves sink and are overlapped entirely by new waves, waves of him and her...
  He was the one who used to fuck her and didn't treat her well, and she loved it because everyone else treated her well; and he fucked her anally and she loved that too because it was another thing she would never ever sacrifice but did anyway for him; and he never gave her the mutualizing pleasure of a heartfelt thanks so she learned to be better at it; and now, whenever any of the eleven boys she's had anatomical relationships ever grazed her anus – by means of sensual hand slaps, inebriated cunnilingus, or an overly-zealous and misguided penis – just subsequent to that pleasurable sacral tightening, a bursting bubbling image of this boy's face appeared before her mind's eye.
  "Nice," she echoes him automatically. A part of her immediately punishes herself for this demeaning behavior.
  "I've gotta go," she lies quickly, but he is already turning away.
  The wind notes that those who are self-centered often require the company of one even more selfish in order to consider acting selflessly. One's own qualities are never more magnified than when they appear within someone desired.
  The wind floats forward, dodging the wealth of bodies bustling in the ballroom, and locates a window on the eastern corner. It drifts in between the fluttering curtains, and continues eastward...

August 26th 2010
Dear Selene,
  It's only fair for me to show you what I've experienced over the last few days, at least to clarify everything through a just lens.
  Thursday night: I was outside by my pool, right where you inspired me to begin writing Along a Wandering Wind seven months and one day ago. Alex and Dustin convinced me to get high, and somewhere in my illusive self-

assurance I decided to text you what I was thinking. When you responded... I felt myself return to me. I knew it was drizzling before, but it wasn't until I saw your name on my phone that I felt the cool mist on my skin, the scents of petrichor and wet asphalt filling my lungs, the crystalline green shimmers of the arboreal backstreets of Old Rookvale. When you called me, I felt me become me again. And when we spoke, it was clear why you called. It's the very same reason why I picked up. We are still in love. That's why we agreed to meet the next day.

Friday morning: Cast the spotlight of your mind on three mornings ago, and ask yourself what brightly lit memories shimmer in the byzantine ocean of your thoughts. My Friday was watching you sit down in front of me with every muscle suggesting imminent departure. We were, after all, just meeting for coffee and a more complete closure. But that's not what happened, now was it? Time did that thing again, allowing its minutes to devour hours. We both know chemistry closely controls clocks. My Friday was the sight of your timid smiles, the sound of your mellifluously dopey laughs, and the experience of you surreptitiously doodling a hawk-faced puppy on my notebook. Your wrath and my despair – such imposters – vanished under the reality of us being us. We blasted forward through time, laughing so hard we held our ribs. You even said your cheeks hurt as tears filled your eyes, which made me wonder when you had last laughed. We kissed again, we held hands again, we walked silently again, and we were alone together again...

Solemn, saturnine Saturday: I waited at Hamilton's for you, longing for the return of our vespertine trysts. My mind imagined you walking in, blue-eyed beautifully. We would have a drink, and then continue the nyctophilial gallivanting that both began and defined our love. I waited, feeling my manic joy sip down grain by grain as 6:30 dragged its heels into 6:32. I tried to imagine what Selene you were in that moment: The heavenly Selene pulling at my currents and illuminating the world? The enslaved solivagant Selene shackled to a treadmill? Were you upset with your overbearing mother, raucous father, and the ceaseless chatter of your omnipresent siblings? I received your jealousy-inspiring rejection with remorse. However, even in the panicked midst of heart-wrenching thoughts, I refrained from texting you back, at least to prove to you I possess a modicum of patience.

<u>Sunday</u>: Silence. I texted you asking how you were, because I could not equate both Friday's exultation and Saturday's apprehension to the same human body. Silence. I was left reverberating your last utterance – that you were seeing another boy. 48 hours prior we were everything ecstatic. Yet in that moment we were nothing. That's a charybdis of pain, misery, sadness, fear, and jealousy – all excruciated by the suspense, by the mystery. I called you three times throughout the day, desperately seeking the anxiolytic of your voice. On the third call, I hear you talking and laughing to some man with a familiar voice.

You say you're confused, Selene. You say you're confused... I am drowning in conflicting currents. I have no idea what has happened, what is happening, and what will happen. You say you feel trapped in your life, yet you don't consider that I was one of the few freedoms in our life. I was there to unbuckle what strained your mind whenever you needed. Do you not recall these moments? You were insecure and never had the courage to confirm that I was only yours, and I was insecure and never had the courage to tell you that everything in me was yours. It still is yours. It's not who I am to be hiding the extent of my love, but it is in who I am to be afraid. You should understand this. You kept me away from so much. I didn't know what your friends were like, you barely showed me your writing, and you never let me meet your father... The most I knew from you was your smiles and frowns, laughs and cries, and the upside-down words of the poetry you wrote but were too timid to show me.

Despite all of the tenebrous negativity, when we were together on Friday, we coruscated brilliantly. Through crepuscular sensations of confusion, sadness, and hopelessness, we could still find ourselves radiating together through the time machine of harmony. I've made mistakes

in the past, but for us to not be together anymore... think of how much we both lose.
Don't let the breathing gift in our alchemy vanish. To aeonian amorous ambulations, sempiternal selenian sauntering, and snoring in Aeolian symphonies, - The foggy photographer, the effeminate poetess to your masculine poet, the Boy with No Name.

Post-scriptum: Attached is a moment that I wish I revealed to you long ago, back when you asked why I fear the crucifix...

ALONG A WANDERING WIND

...the wind finds a house at the east-most point of Old Rookvale, and seeps in through an open window to face a living room. A twelve-year-old boy ascends the stairs of his basement, ambles over the blue carpets, and enters the kitchen where his parents wait. Video game pause music jingles from the basement.

The boy replays his father's aberrant tone on the intercom beckoning him upstairs. The wind watches as he paces to his parents.

His mother sits on a steel chair wearing all black save for a large cross ornamented with tanzanite stones. There is a peculiar blankness in her dark eyes. Standing behind her, with one hand on her shoulder, is his father, smiling in a navy button-down.

The wind detects abnormalities in both of their minds. The father's mind is too confident, and has thus leapt over his own logic. More noticeable, the glaring woman's mind glows with a carousel of sinister hallucinations and a misanthropic distrust.

"Well, honey," the father speaks through his grin, "tell Joshua what you just told me."

The woman's unblinking eyes continue to burn towards the boy, who is now staring down at his feet.

"I want to kill your dad," she declares. "I want him gone."

A shattering noise sounds inside the boy's mind. His heart pumps blood to his muscles with rapidly accelerating pounds, as if preparing against a massive attack. His vision blurs and refocuses. He looks up at his father, who waits with unrestrained anticipation. His father believes that his son will understand that this is indomitable proof that the woman before him is not his mother. Not now, at least. The woman who raised him would never utter those words. No question about it.

"Okay," the boy responds, nodding towards his father, feigning understanding. His father nods back, confident that his expectations were met.

He turns around, concentrating with trembling difficulty on his breathing – which suddenly seems manual – and heads back to the basement. Her eyes, the cross – the details of this thought are massive as they crash into the ocean, displacing waves in all directions, crushing previous thoughts. He returns to the couch, grabs the video game controller, unpauses the game, and continues losing the battle against a four-armed monster.

The ocean of the boy's thoughts are maddening. A waterfall of horrid emotions begins to fill him. This stew of rage rises from his toes, to his chest – which still endures a crashing heart – to his face – which causes his eyes to glaze – and then to his crown as perspiration glistens on his forehead. The video game controller drops to the ground. The boy buries his burning face into his hands. The screen goes dark. The four-armed villain trots towards his character – a blue ninja – and tears his head off, laughing demonically.

WHY ME?! The thought blasts in a shriek so powerful that it catapults the wind out from the boy's mind. A bolt of fury rips across the air as tears burst from his eyes, trickling between his fingers. The wind struggles to regain footing through the violent maelstrom emanating from the boy. As the last of the most turbulent waves pass, the wind begins to stabilize. Upon normalizing, it gazes again into the storm of the boy's mind, and is shocked to find much of the ocean of memories have been erased. What little remains of the sea ripples furiously.

The wind understands: A major portion of the young boy's mind has just died with the formation of this new memory. So this is what trauma is, the wind ponders, accessing the word from somewhere in the boy's budding knowledge of the subject. The event was too much to encode and store for the ocean of his mind. The wind considers how trauma is – in essence – just a memory that violates previous memories too barbarically, an event that devastatingly conflicts against everything else one knows.

Now, bits of this traumatic memory are scattered everywhere, too disconnected to fully retrieve consciously. The wind wonders if the boy has willingly killed this part of himself out of furious anger, or if some survival mechanism has done so out of the fear of having loved something that can cause such hurt. In either case, the wind knows with certainty, the boy will never be the same.

The wind sighs and tip-toes out of the house, eastward as always...

September 1st 2010
...call... no... text... no... fucking LOVE me again...

"-and it's His birthday soon!" His father announced with enthusiasm, lifting a glass towards Him. His brother and His mother lifted their drinks. The amber lights of the quaint Italian restaurant shone through their glasses, producing three bubbling shadows across the white-linen table just beside the single lit candle at the center.

He looked up from His seat. They were all standing now. His father had a few sips of wine. His mother had a full glass. His brother ordered a light beer.

"That's right," His brother added as He continued staring at them silently. "Turning twenty in one month. How does it feel?"

He cleared His throat, and coiled His hands around the whiskey glass. The ice floated about as He lifted it off the table.

"Well, I'm just happy that dad is home for the weekend and able to relax even though he's leaving for

Switzerland tomorrow morning, that mom is happy and not donning her garish crucifix, that my older brother is happy and mutually enamored with the girl who broke up with him, and that this liquor will depress my central nervous system – ultimately inhibiting the cortisol levels being produced in the zona fasticulata of my adrenal cortex." He stood up, raised His glass, and clinked it sharply against their glasses in a trinote. "So cheers, everyone. Carpe diem, carpe noctem, et carpe omnia. Sic transit gloria mundi. Excelsior!"

He tossed the liquor down His throat as He plopped back into His seat.

His father opened his mouth, but a telephonic ringing punctured the quietude hovering over their table. "Hi, Sanjeev - let me call you back in a half hour. Yes. That's fine." His father shoved his cell phone back into his pocket, as His mother finished translating the Latin phrases to His brother.

"You know-" His brother leaned closer to Him, "next year when you're turning 21, you and I are going to rip a hole in Manhattan, right?" His brother shook His shoulder playfully.

"At least make it wine and not beer, please." His father chuckled. "We have enough overweight people in this country."

"Wine has more calories than beer," He spoke.

"What? That can't be." His father shook his head.

"Don't second-guess me."

His mother and His brother turned to His father. His hawk-like eyes shaded under lowered eyebrows. His face reddened.

"24 calories in an ounce of your average wine for every 13 calories of your average beer," He lectured. "If you want, pop, there's enough time until your next flight for us to argue about it."

"I understand you're upset about Selene," His father began, taking a deep breath. "But don't let it impact your judgements, boy." Again, His father's cell phone rang. Two, three, four, and five rings as he watched Him. He stood up, extracted the phone from his coat pocket, and stepped outside.

He looked down at His own cell phone – which He hid beneath the table – and began typing across the bright screen:

> **Me (unsent draft):** Selene, I don't want to be dramatic, but I wish you knew how I feel r

Then He deleted the words, and began typing:

> **Me (unsent draft):** "I wish-"

He deleted the words as the hairs of His arms rose and the candle in the center of the table went out. He looked up and watched as a wisp of smoke twisted towards the chandelier above, fading into wisps. He sighed and looked down at the phone between His thighs.

> **Me:** Just wanted to say happy birthday to your sister. I remembered Diana's is today, almost exactly one month before mine. Hope all is well with everyone. (8:44)

His father returned – glistening from the drizzling world outside – just as the grouper was served. By 9:39, they had finished eating, the receipt had been returned, and they were on their way outside.
"I'm sorry," He murmured to His father. "Good night. Have a safe trip. Love you."
His father smiled sadly as he hugged his sons and their mother. Their parents took separate cars home. His mother drove the Mercedes SUV Long-Island-bound, while a car service picked up His father and drove JFK-bound. His brother waved them off as both cars headed eastward down the misting avenue. When the cars were distant bulbs of light, he turned to Him.
"What's wrong?" he asked. "And where are you headed?"
"Nothing, and Penn Station. Back to Old Rookvale," He responded. "You?"

"Flying back to Boston, but later." His brother paused and stared down the avenue. The cars separated. "Why didn't you drive back with mom?"

"Because being in a car alone with mom for a half hour sounds nauseating right now."

His brother shook his head. "Walk with me to the subway?" he beckoned.

The two of them trudged the two blocks south towards the 123 Train on 103rd street and Broadway. The descending mist thickened into rain drops pit-pattering down onto the city streets.

"Why do you insist on being alone and miserable so often these days, bro?" His brother spoke, his squinting face glistening in the salmon-orange street lights. "You know we care for you, right?"

"I don't insist on anything."

His brother sighed.

"Are you alright, then?"

"Yeah. I'm fine."

"Listen, I understand about Selene. Listen to the words you told me back when Calliope and I weren't doing well."

Before He could respond, a leggy blonde with lips painted crimson passed between them. First He then His brother turned and watched her tightly-squeezed bottom bounce in her tessellated leggings. His brother laughed and reached out his hand to Him. He looked at him and then at his hand. He shook it quickly and pulled to move away, but His brother gripped it tightly.

"Call me if you need anything, bro. Anything."

"Okay."

His brother lingered.

"You sure you're fine? You don't want to talk?"

"No, no." He shook His head quickly. "I'm alright."

His brother lingered, scrutinizing Him contemplatively, and then nodded, turned and descended the subway steps. At ground level, where He remained, the rain fell louder. The street became reflective and shone the lights of the trafficking city, dripping with moving hues. Charcoal clouds lumbered across a bruised-orange sky. He walked southbound down Central Park West, keeping close to the building facades. Umbrellas – mostly black – rushed and twirled by Him with individuals squinting beneath. Occasionally, a couple would pass, together squeezed underneath, murmuring affectionately. The rain descended heavier and heavier. A fork of lightning flashed across the sky. Now, the roar of rainfall drowned out the perpetual hum of vehicular engines.

    His suit was drenched and His short hair stuck to His forehead in damp clumps. He had walked forty-two blocks through the rain. He turned and faced a bar with a Jack of Hearts logo glowing on the façade. He descended a staircase into the maroon-lit pub, and plopped down on the bar seat. Minutes passed as His gaze drifted back and forth between the wine and beer menus. Every moment or so, a bartender with half her head shaved gravitated away from a fraternity of baseball-cap-wearing young adults, and regarded His soaked jacket. He looked up from the menu and caught her glance. She looked away immediately, and then turned back to Him.

    He opened His mouth, but a light beamed from His pants. He got up and walked towards the bathroom with the phone to His ear.

    "Hey—" He mustered, the closing door muting the bar's din.

    "I need you," Selene's voice scraped through static, "to just *leave me alone!*"

    Tears framed His eyelids. He locked the bathroom door behind Him.

    "W-what?"

    "I don't want you mentioning my family. I don't want you harassing me. Leave me alone!"

    "I—" He sniffed, "—wish…"

    He hung up the phone and began trembling downwards towards the sink. After a moment's struggle, He lifted Himself up and stared in the mirror, heaving desperately. His eyes were bloodshot and fiercely green, and

His long eyelashes were darkened. He swiped out paper towels from the wall-mounted dispenser, and blew His nose. He lifted His hand and traced the outline of his reflection, starting with His short wet hair, the beads of water along His forehead, the stubble running down His sharp face, the wine-shades of His lips and cheeks, His chin cleft, His chest-hair exposed from the now soaked and diaphanous open white-button down, and the outline of His muscle from the tightness of His drenched jacket. He opened His mouth widely and forced His jaw to manipulate a furious grin. He stopped, sniffled, and shook His head like a dog. Water sprayed on the mirror.

"What does He see?" His pupils dilated. "What does He feel?" A quick, contemplating glance away and back. "More unfixable breakages and the void growing." He looked at His hand, His eyebrows lowering as He glared again into His eyes. "We do *not* like what is happening," He growled. "All the colors are changing-" He wound up and punched the mirror.

The looking glass cracked in the center, not precisely shattering, but forming a triptych of warped reflections divided by a splintering V. He faced three varied angles of Himself. Blood dripped from the center of the fracture and dripped down the crevices.

He took a deep breath, shoved His bleeding hand into His pocket, turned around, unlocked the door and swung it open. At once, music returned with the voice of Lizzie Manibasse and a pounding bass:
Dance – Dance – Dance – Dance – Dance – Dance
Everywhere we'll dance. Everything will dance.

He hurried back towards the bar, avoiding eye-contact with the frowning barista as He stepped outside.

The rain had concluded, though the sleepless avenues still shimmered. He glanced up at the towering buildings. A light like the morning sun glowed from the building in front of Him. He crossed over the avenue and entered the lobby. A red-coated woman stood at the counter. 'ELEN D.' was engraved across her golden nametag.

[196]

"Hello again." He nodded as He passed her for the first time in His life. She looked up from her book. His eyes passed over the cover of *22-Hues of Blue* in her hands. "Lovely weather we're having."

He entered the elevator from the lobby and pressed the button marked PH. The elevator ascended slowly up sixty-five floors. The doors opened. He stepped out into the corridor and gazed in both directions. He ambled towards a staircase indicating ROOFTOP, opened the door to the terrace steps, climbed up to the rooftop and walked towards the ledge. The rain resumed, thundering down furiously. He stood at the edge of the roof, with His shoes half-off of the building. He stared down at the street below. The thousands of passing cars trundled around the blocks like glistening ants marching. Tiny, slower-moving umbrellas encircled the avenues. He watched the machinery of night as it droned on. Occasionally a miniscule pair of legs could be seen kicking forward underneath an umbrella.

His face twisted with agony as He grabbed His chest. He stood, wobbling forward and backward over the ledge. He sat down and extended His legs so they dangled in the air. The rain fell in thick sheets. He let His hand sway over the cliff and watched as the rain fused with the blood on His knuckles into a translucent red, which dripped down to the umbrellas below.

Before eventually leaning backwards over the rooftop and allowing consciousness to slip out of Him, He wrote on a piece of blank paper. Blood and rain soaked into the words, but did not entirely remove the ink.

ALONG A WANDERING WIND

...The wind soars above a locomotive as it trundles slower and slower towards the town of Greenvale. Inside are exactly sixty-five bodies.

All of the passengers have cell phones. Most are listening to music. Few are reading. None are conscious to the fact that they are attempting to switch the background of their distractions with the foreground of reality – yet they are all successful to some degree. The distractions do their job;

the wind senses no epiphanous ruminations. Here and there are intriguing thoughts, but they are too entangled with blasting melodies, indistinct lyrics, rushing sentences, and shapes on screens to link to other thoughts and develop deeply.

The wind senses two readers: A young man and young woman catch each other's gaze. He has his finger tucked into the earlier half of James Joyce's A Portrait of the Artist as a Young Man, and she has Oscar Wilde's The Picture of Dorian Gray open midway. She gives him a look that asks 'are we the only real-live humans on this small chugging world?' He squints into the distance, as if their temporary connection was accidental, and turns back into Joyce. She watches him, laboring to reel back his attention.

Another man watches her. He was reading from an E-reader 22-Hues of Blue – just to see what all the hype is about, or so he told those circling about his life – barely aware that everything he has ever read was to assess some hype of some sort. He watches as she watches the other man, and tells himself for the hundredth time that the world is unfair, that it does not cater to his special kind.

A vociferous screech announces the train's ingression into the Greenvale station. The wind notes the sudden and uniform enervated celebrations glowing from many of the bodies inside the train – the bodies that are collecting their things, heading towards the train doors, and imagining supper.

A singular pang of despair looming ahead on the train platform distracts the wind.

Up ahead on the station platform stands a blond-haired brown-eyed girl in an indigo dress who has just shouted a name - 'Christopher!' – as she spotted a tall boy with high cheekbones. The boy turns to the sound of his name and sees her. As she runs across the platform and her skirt flutters above her knees, all of the somber and heartbroken feelings tormenting the boy begin to dissipate. By the time she wraps her arms around him, he has even forgotten that he is heartbroken.

The wind sees that their arms squeeze around each other tightly, and that her perfume in the air awakens in him the long-lost sense of intimacy. He closes his damp eyes and hugs her as tightly as the memories he held only a moment ago.

Three seconds pass before she presses a hand ever-so-gently on his skinny chest, and reflexively applies a pushing force. As she does so, all of the warm-hued happiness in the boy's mind shatters and explodes into piercingly cold shards of half-asked-half-answered questions. The wind listens closely to the ripples of the waves, and hears: 'Why Britta pushing me away? - I'm ugly desperate' 'Have I lost old me? - I'm visibly broken' - 'What does Britta see me as? Pathetic unwanted' echoing quickly. The wind turns and peers inside the girl's mind. Deep down in abstract waiver-trails – deep, deep, deep, deep, deep, deep, deep down beyond her own understanding of her thoughts - the wind sees a near aphotic figure of large, dirty-callused hands of an uncle who used to touch her when she was too young to comprehend why she really didn't want to be touched. The memory, like all trauma, has poured threads of meaning into the multitude of thoughts comprising the vast waters above.

She is beaming now at the boy that has been her friend since, like, forever, and notices that he is skinnier, definitely cuter, that his hair is all messy, and that the almond-colored eyes regarding her from those infinite eyelashes seem brighter... glistening even...

She simpers – feeling as if she has flirted graciously – and decides conclusively that she wants to see him again as soon as possible.

Though he smiles back, he watches her with the dull blade of misery hammering down on his chest. The subtle push of her hand has filled him with rejection. She has rejected him, just like the girl he loved has rejected him; now he wishes he could reject himself. The boy is heartbroken all over again, even though she isn't a girl to whom he ever gave his heart.

Neither boy nor girl suspects a fraction of what the other is thinking. The eastward current pulls the wind away, and their thoughts begin to slip from the wind. She mutters something sweet-sounding as she steps towards the train. The boy makes some sort of excuse to stay on the platform. The wind senses a lie being sought out in his desperate mind, one about waiting for the local line. Bitter relief ripples across the waves of his agony. She nods and boards the train while He remains standing on the platform. The wind, moving eastward inevitably, feels the figures shrink smaller in the distance. The last experience it senses is the heat rising to his cheeks, and the blush rising to hers.

The wind ruminates, with a sense of vicarious heartbreak, how both the boy and the girl are gripping tightly to their perceived illusions. Both are beginning to plan their alterations in behavior for their next encounter, so that their next actions properly fit their illusions. Both -unknowingly - are laboring to actualize their illusions. The girl is moving too far westward for the wind to sense individually among the other spiraling thoughts enclosed in the Queens-bound locomotive. The boy remains on the platform, drowning under a force greater than his previous despair. A trick of the mind slingshots a joke - 'maybe I love her' - across his thoughts, and he laughs at the ludicrousness as the tears begin slipping out.

The wind continues eastward...

September 5th 2010

...What's happening to the lights?... Hallucinations? No... colors...

POP! The neon sign outside Vane's Diner burnt out as the red-headed waitress stepped out from the kitchen holding His and Artyom's plates. The baked salmon produced thick tufts of stream which traced behind the plates like white-hued comet tails.

"Anything else?" she asked, smiling at Art and lowering the plates down on the table.

"No, thank you," He responded.

The waitress turned and walked passed the crowded booths and stepped into the kitchen where white figures moved about. The door swung closed.

"She likes you," He informed Art.

"Meh." Art bit the translucent-white straw and sipped his water. "Maybe."

"Trust me, she does. You should do something about it."

"Why?"

He turned back to look at the silver kitchen doors. A red figure passed left and right.

"Because you're attracted to her." He turned back to Art, His smile fading. "You think she's pretty, do you not?"

The waitress reappeared with two plates in her hands and one balancing on her left forearm. Her pixie-styled red hair strands bounced and flopped as she approached an old couple seated by the entrance.

"I mean," Art struggled, "yeah. She is. Very. But I don't wanna bother her."

He sighed and stuck a knife into His salmon.

"Just say something pleasant to her. You clearly are attracted to her. Just remind her that she's appreciated on this Friday evening where no one is noticing her. You don't know how much she might need to hear it, how much it will brighten her evening."

"I don't know," Art responded, watching her as she raced back into the kitchen. "She's pretty busy. I don't want to bother her."

"It's not bothering her."

"If you feel so strong about it, why don't you tell her?"

"THAT'S-" His voice rose, and normalized, "-not the point. That is not the point, Art. This isn't a risk, nor is it something you should be worried about."

The waitress reappeared, walking in their direction. He took a huge bite from His salmon and swallowed.

"Excuse me," He called out. She stopped and turned to Him, gray-green eyes waiting. "So – I know you're busy running back and forth tonight, but I just want you to know that my friend and I were just commenting on how cinematic you look with your awesome hair. Pardon the forwardness. I just thought you should know."

"Thank you. That's so sweet." She stared at Him, and a small smile built across her lips. "Wait – can I ask you a very odd question?"

"I guess."

"This is going to sound strange, but, aren't you friends with the kid who never washed his hands-" she saw Art's smile, and confidence solidified in her voice, "-and couldn't stop... masturbating?"

"Sounds like Dustin to me," Art spoke through a flexing smile.

"Well," He began, "I-"

"Justine!" a gruff voice grumbled from the kitchen. The waitress turned to the kitchen and gravitated automatically towards the doors.

"That's very... *nice* of you," she spoke over her shoulder before vanishing again.

Artyom laughed into his palms. "That's why I don't do these things!"

He turned away from the kitchen and glared at Art.

"What the fuck is that supposed to mean?"

"No, no." Art chuckled, putting his palms forward. "I'm just saying... I'm not like you. I don't find any reason for flirting with strangers to make them feel... appreciated."

"You not finding a reason to be social is why people see you as plain."

"But I'm not plain, bro," Art's smile faded. "Last week I jumped out of an airplane for the third time. I deal with the insides of patients' hearts for a living. I'm not simple or boring or anything that these people say. I just don't destroy myself like you and Dustin. And I don't care about what other people think the way you do."

"I don't believe you. I think you want to reach out to people more than anything. I know, at least, with complete certainty that you want a girl to be in love with you. That much is obvious in everything I see."

"Well, yeah. Who doesn't?"

"Homosexuals, that's who!" He shouted, smiling.
"But really," Art pursued, shaking his head. "Who doesn't want to be loved?"
"That's not the point, again. You want something and you don't even try to entertain getting it by reaching out and talking to people. And it's ridiculous that you would d-"
"Listen, bro. If this is about Selene breaking up with y-"
He got up from the table, slapped a twenty by His unfinished fish, and headed towards the door.
"Save it, Art."
He stepped out quickly into the cool Old Rookvale evening. He pulled out a cigarette and trotted towards His car, which was parked beside the gray-chipped, dilapidated gazebo. Laughter sounded in the distance, echoing out of Hamilton's down the street. He walked passed His car, walked down the street, and peered through the tavern windows. Between underage bodies, blond hair, and dim-colored sports caps, He saw Dustin's red face frowning heavily and Alex shouting down to him. He stepped inside.
Lights and music burst around Him as He navigated through the bustling tavern. A live band was jamming in the back. Bottles and glasses clinked and clanked on the oak-colored bar table.
"THAT'S NOT THE FUCKING POINT!" Alex's voice pounded into the busy room, barely camouflaging into the clamor.
Dustin raised a chubby hand and ran it through his slicked-back hair, and massaged the back of his neck.
"But, that is MY point, Alex," Dustin groaned. His blue eyes darted towards Him as He approached. "Look at this handsome man walking in."
He forced His way between the seated Dustin and standing Alex, turned, and leaned against the bar to face them.
"Your chronic masturbation cost me a phone nu-"
"TELL ME THIS," Alex interrupted Him, pushing a heavy hand down on His shoulder. "Dustin just stopped me from protecting a girl from being RAPED."

"That is literally NOT what happened at-"
"SHUT THE FUCK UP, YOU SLEEZEBALL!" Alex screamed.

He looked back and forth between the low-eyed Dustin and the fierce-eyed Alex.

"Let's not be pugnacious drunkards. Tell me your side, Dusty."

"Jack Ricaricare – that crazy kid, like, four grades above us – was talking to some girl and-"

"SHE'S 17! JACK IS FUCKING 24!"

"That's not-"

"I saved her and you're defending a PEDOPHILE, you PIECE OF SHIT!"

"I'm not! How do you not see this? You budded into their conversation – which she was completely into, by the way – and Jack was looking at you like he was about to punch you in the face."

"GOOD!" Alex leaned over Dustin "You think I care about being punched in the face?!"

"Yes, I do," Dustin spoke softly.

"You're a fucking dirtball. Go fuck yourself!" Alex snapped, turning towards the bathroom and disappearing into the crowd.

Dustin's head hung low, swaying left and right, as if in melancholy disagreement with himself. He caught eyes with Him.

"D'ya wanna have a cigarette, dude?" Dustin asked.

A nod and a stir through the rumbling tavern brought them to the back of Hamilton's where a group of a dozen boys and girls were smoking by the brick half-wall that encircled the back-entrance.

"Who are *you*?" a blonde with three marks on her hands asked Him as they stepped outside.

"Nobody." He shook His head, avoiding her glistening eyes.

"What the fuck? Was that Ma-" the blonde spoke to a friend as they walked inside the tavern.

Dustin tucked a cigarette into His hand, pulled another out and placed it in his lips, lit it, and inhaled. He breathed out ash hues, wheezed, and plopped down with his back against the brick wall. Immediately, Dustin extracted his white inhaler, sucked in, exhaled, and wheezed again.

"Alex really is an angry drunk," He spoke, kneeling down beside him.

"The worst," Dustin whispered between a flurry of coughs. He looked up at Him with glistening eyes. "You have no idea."

"Why is he always so argumentative?"

"His parents are both divorce lawyers, and they're divorced. Probably has something to do with it."

The back door blasted open and Alex appeared.

"ERRRRM!" Alex swung his arms, stretching.

"Irony," He whispered to Dustin.

"Hey fags!" a voice called out. A figure stumbled from the shadows of the parking lot, gaining light until the figure of Hunter Douglas Quillan Wilcox-Himmler II appeared in the form of wet eyes, ivory skin, and a bathing suit of a sea-chariot being pulled by Hippocampi. He stammered towards the crowd, and tripped over himself. A cigarette pack fell out of his back pocket as he regained balance. "Does anyone have a cigarette I can bum?" he pleaded to the crowd.

"Irony," He repeated to Dustin, sitting down next to him and watching Hunter move about.

"There's definitely nothing in there."

"Check, mate."

Dustin's gaze locked onto Hunter's form moving desperately from person to person right in front of them. Dustin's eyes shifted from sympathetic ovals to reproachful slits. He stood up, paced eight steps towards the shadowy parking lot, and reached down for the pack. A papery shaking sound followed by a chuckle filled the air. Dustin turned back and sat next to Him. "Would you believe me if I said there's like three or four in here?"

"You're lying."

"I never lie, sonnn." Dustin laughed, opening the dry white lips of the pack, revealing four cigarettes.

"Definitely irony."

Dustin handed Him a cigarette.

"For your troubles, dude."

"We'll need a couple dozen more nicotine barrels for that."

"What's wrong? Selene?"

"She's already with someone else, Dustin."

"What?" Dustin's voice snapped. "That dirty cunt broke up with you less than two months ago." He gazed into the darkness, the jaw muscles below his round cheeks flexed. "What's the faggot-fuck's name?"

"Nunzio Esposito."

"Italian? She chose an Italian Ginny WOP Guido fuck over you?" Dustin paused and nodded quickly. "Yeah. Good. Great, actually! That cunt deserves to be with her own Gino-meatball kind."

"I don't know if-"

"Wait-" Dustin scanned the parking lot. "Fuck. Alex left. He's my ride."

"I'll give you a ride home."

Dustin sighed.

"Can you give me a ride to Alex's instead? It's much closer, anyway."

"Why?"

"My d-" Dustin paused. "My stepdad-" Dustin paused again, his voice trembling before starting again "Mario is kinda upset with me. I drank two of his wine bottles the other night. I-I've been staying at Alex's place like four-five nights a week, lately."

A moment passed as the two were silent under the ramblings of the crowd several meters before them. Hunter's red-soaked eyes flickered towards Him before he prematurely tossed his newly-acquired cigarette, and fumbled inside.

"I hate making mistakes, Dustin," He spoke.

Dustin placed a hand on His shoulder. The two stared into each other's eyes.

"I make mistakes every day, son. In ten years this 'mistake' will be the last thing on your mind."

A high school student stepped out from the back of Hamilton's with a glass in his hands.

"Hey – what the fuck are you doing?" Dustin called out.

"Wha?" the kid slurred.

"This is a fucking establishment. Bring your beer inside."

"Fuck you, you short, fat fuck!" The boy smiled. "You look like a fat DiCaprio."

"Listen here you little piece of shit," Dustin called out. "I'm gonna bend your little ass over and give you the swine flu if you don't bring your drink inside."

"What are you looking at?" The kid turned to Him challengingly.

"I am looking at nothing," He responded.

The kid spat to the ground, surveyed the crowd of high school and college students, nodded to himself, took a final searching glance at Him, and then stomped back inside. Dustin turned to Him, shaking his head.

"I swear to god, this world is sliding straight down into the gutter."

"I know." He nodded, flicking His cigarette.

The two walked towards Vane's Diner where His SUV was parked and got in. Pink Floyd's *Hey You* – the first song of the second disk of The Wall – played as they headed south on Plandome Road, passed the closed Rising Star Café and the chipped gazebo and Vane's Diner, turned eastward on Northern Boulevard, and headed towards Alex's house.

"Why do you think he gets so angry with you?" He asked.

"I don't know. He's right, though. The principle is wrong. I technically am supporting a pedophile by taking Jack's side."

"No. That's not your point though. That's an insanely black-and-white angle to view it. Pyscho Jack is *actually* psychotic. He would have mauled, raped, and eaten Alex. He's crazier than Hunter."

"Speaking of that mouse, did you know he talks about you all the time?"

"Really? Good, bad, ugly?"

"I don't know. He's obsessed with the Rusche sisters. And you *did* fuck Mandy."

"That was two years ago." He paused. "Exactly two years ago today we broke up. It doesn't even feel like that was me, floating in the pool."

"Sara was almost a year ago and I still think of her every morning."

"Didn't Sara blow you, like, last week?"

"Yeah, but it's different. We're not dating anymore. She's done being my girlfriend." Dustin paused. "You're not going back to QS this semester are you?"

"No." He looked down. "I'm officially a dropout."

"Okay." Dustin shuffled into his pocket as they pulled onto Alex's street and approached his house. "For your other troubles." Dustin extracted a joint from his pocket and handed it to Him. "Can you… can you stay until I'm inside. He might not let me in."

"Sure, Dusty."

"Thanks, son," Dustin half-whispered as he stepped out of the car. "It's not acid, but it's really strong stuff."

He turned off the car's ignition and rolled down the window. The lights of the Mercedes SUV shut off. He lit the joint and began puffing out of the window. From the distant darkness, He watched Dustin walk across the shadow-draped stage of the street, towards the silver silhouette of Alexander's house. He wheezed, inhaled and exhaled, then knocked on the door. The next song on the album began. The golden mail slip on the door opened.

Gold Mail Slip
(Metallically)
CLIINNK

Alexander
(Furiously)
What the fuck do you want?

Radio
(Single-Voicedly)

> Is there anybody-

> Radio
> (Many-Voicedly)
> *Out there?*

> Dustin
> (Whimperingly)
> Dude, I'm sorry. I don't-

> Hunter's Car
> (Passing)
> YyyyouRrrrrrrrmmmm

> Alexander
> No – you're a fucking grime ball. You take fucking psycho Jack's side? And then tell Him I'm a fucking angry drunk?

> Dustin
> (Pleadingly)
> Those were His words!

> Alexander
> (Venomously)
> Yeah that's because He's a fucking idiot!

Dustin looked back over his shoulder, staring blue-eyed apologetically at the waiting black Mercedes SUV with its lights off parked down the dark street.

> Dustin
> (Pathetically)
> Yes. You're right. I know. Don't blame me for the shit He says.

> Radio
> (Single-Voicedly)
> Is there anybody-

Radio
(Many-Voicedly)
Out there?

Alexander
(Aggressively)
I fucking know I'm right.

Coleslaw
(Deliciously)
Chrncleev Chrncleev

Dustin
(Peeking-into-slip-inquisitively)
What are you eating, dude?

Alexander
(Informatively)
Cole slaw.

Dustin
(High-pitched-Laughingly)
Is that a fucking bucket of coleslaw?

Alexander
(Energetically)
You're god damned right it's a bucket of coleslaw

Dustin
(Comedic-Sexual-Desperately)
Lots o' mayo?

Radio
(Single-Voicedly)
Is there anybody-

Radio
(Many-Voicedly)
Out there?

Alexander
(Playful-Satisfiedly)
Sooo much mayo

Coleslaw
(Still-deliciously)
Chrncleev Chrncleev

Dustin
(Happy-desperately)
How am I supposed to beg my friend to let me in his house when he's chomping away on that bucket... and I'm outside in the cold? Cold, fat, and hungry.

Alexander
(Happy-entertainedly)
Well, man, you're gonna have to try

Dustin
(Melancholically)
Duuude. I'm your friend. I'll give you two most-wonderful stoges.

Alexander
(Happy-entertained-playful/disgusted-inquisitively)
You bought another pack, you sick fucking animal?

Dustin
(low-pitched-dialogically)
Nah – they fell out of... (high-pitched dialogically)... His pocket when He was asking people for cigarettes.(low-pitched-dialogically) I'll tell you the whole story.

Radio
(Single-Voicedly)
Is there anybody-

Radio
(Many-Voicedly)

>Out there?

Gold Mail Slip
(Metallically)
CLIINNK-iink

Door Lock
(Metallically)
NYOWNK

Door
(Woodenly)
Eihhhnn

Dustin
(Grateful-calm-down-smiledly)
Thanks, dude.

Door
(Woodenly)
Errouutnfk

Door Lock
(Metallically)
CLEENGD

HIM
(Sniffle-Changedly)
.

His car turned on, and, with its lights off, drove towards His house in darkness.

December 4th 2010
...last... verge of crying... like sickness... Dustin's father...

The somber melodies of Chet Baker's *I Fall in Love Too Easily* played in the Mercedes as He and Dustin stared through the rain tapping on the windshield, blurring the vista

of an Old Rookvale backstreet. They agreed that the road looked familiar, but neither were sure.
"I like this guy. He has a sad voice," Dustin whispered between sips of a whiskey-filled water bottle. He turned to Dustin and examined the road ahead reflected in his glazed eyes.
"He was a heroin addict," He responded in a cracked voice. "The word for what Chet Baker does is 'chantepleure'. It means to cry while singing. Even though he's not crying, you can hear the tears dripping down in his voice. It's beautiful."
Dustin nodded and took another sip.
"Did he die from heroin?"
"Do you want the whole story, Dustin?"
"Yeah."
"At around 3 AM on May 13th, 1988, Chet Baker was found dead outside of his 2nd-story hotel room in Amsterdam near Zeedijk – which was a very drugged-out part of the city. The autopsy confirmed heroin and cocaine in his body, and there was no evidence of a struggle. I think it's suggested that he was getting high by his hotel window, and somewhere during the rush he lost control and fell out of the window."
"From the second floor?" Dustin spoke after a moment of trumpeting gloom. "Couldn't he break his fall? He didn't have to die from that."
"I don't think you know what 'falling' is when you're high on coke and heroin. Such a vulnerable concept would probably be inaccessible when those fake endorphins are flooding your synapses." He turned to Dustin. "In other words, I don't think he even tried to break his fall. He would have been feeling too relieved."
"How the fuck do you know that?" Dustin demanded.
He remained silent. Dustin sighed as a tear rolled down his face. He wiped it with his shoulder as He turned to face him, "It makes me wonder about…" Dustin's voice trailed. "What was this Chet guy like before he…" Dustin's

whisper thinned to silence. He inhaled tremblingly. "Was this song before or after he started doing it?"

"Not sure. He was an addict to the point where he'd sell his instruments – his true love, pleasure, and skill – for more of it."

The song changed to Chet Baker's instrumental *Alone Together.*

"I'm sorry if I can't cheer you up about Selene, son," Dustin whispered. "It's not easy when I'm alone and miserable too."

"No – it's much easier. We're speaking in the same language. Our worlds would be un-relatable if one was happy and the other depressed."

The piano and trumpet swayed together in a melancholic slow-dance.

"I've never seen it that way." Dustin lifted the plastic bottle to his lips and paused. "I guess you're right." He downed the rest of the whiskey. "I'd hate you if you were bubbly right now."

"Through mutual misery, we see similarly. A moment captured through the lens of family, the context of heartbreak, the angle of appreciation are all vastly different. Remember that, Dustin, you sympathy-void." He sighed. "I guess my belletristic bordereau didn't make a difference to Selene."

"Your ballyhoo?" Dustin turned.

"My… letter to her."

"Listen," Dustin began, "I'm sorry about lying about Hunter's pack of cigarettes and telling Alex that they were yours. And for calling you an idiot. We both know you're an intelligent, independent woman."

"It's alright."

"I just needed to make him laugh. You know, so he'd be agreeable and let me sleep there. He's a horrible drunk. You know?"

"I know."

"And, you know, Mario won't let me in the house sometimes… and I needed to make Alex laugh. You're not an idiot. I love you as much as I hate almost everyone else, son."

"I understand." He sighed, looking out of the window. "Dusty... do you ever have thoughts of killing yourself?"

"Pretty much every day, son." Dustin shrilled a double-note cackle. "Are you kidding? I absolutely *loathe* my life. I'm sure your psychoanalytical ass could have read that in me by now. My life has been pure misery."

"But, why?"

"Seriously? What I told you isn't enough? I got nothing, son. I just told you that my Italian step-dad doesn't let me in my own house. Whenever I'm given something great, it seems like I do everything I can to lose it," Dustin reflected. "I spend all my energy either pushing Sara away when I have her, or sacrificing what little I have left to get her back. I cried in front of her when she said she hated me, and she threw her arms around me and said she loved me, and immediately I couldn't help but laugh. I just couldn't hold it in. I don't know what the hell is wrong with me."

"You're testing the limits of how much she appreciates you, Dustin. I can empathize with that."

"It's so bad, though. It's all just for a quick rush. That temporary validation." Dustin sighed. "Why do we so eagerly destroy ourselves?"

The car vibrated with the gentle sound Him weeping. Dustin watched.

"No, no, no. It kills me to see you like this, son."

"I just wish... I didn't have the ability to feel *this* sad. Why must it feel this horrible? I can't-" He shook His head. "I wish-"

"Appreciate that life has given you this range of emotion. Think about how much more of life you experience when you have access to your depth."

"I'd rather be Hunter and have his little range of emo—"

"What?" Dustin's face twisted with disgust. "That gay-ass machine-like faggot? You wouldn't have half the memories. Plus, you're you. You're a good writer and you'll be ass-fucking one of your other dozen girls before next week."

"I can't stop thinking about Selene."

"Well – listen, she chose to be with someone lower than you. He's some Guinea fuck who probably goes to clubs with all of the dirty, lazy meatballs in Astoria. Understand that. Selene isn't nearly as great as you thought if that's what she's capable of – breaking up with you and choosing this retarded Gino fuck." Dustin coughed, wheezed, pulled out his inhaler, sucked in, and then wheezed again. "You believe intelligence is everything and that we are mirrors of the people around us, right? So, she chose to downgrade to some idiot grease-ball WOP as someone to identify with, rather than having someone smart and creative like you, son. It's a blessing. Trust me, son. She's clearly not as great as you thought she was. There's clearly a dark side."

"I fucking hate making mistakes, Dustin," He sighed.

"I make mistakes every day, dude."

"Like Sara with you?"

Dustin's phone vibrated.

"Alex just texted me." Dustin chuckled. "I told him you were all broken up and shit. He says... here—" He handed Him his phone. He squinted down and read:

Lex: Tell Him – 1. Hes a fucking idiot. 2. He wasnt going to marry her and that's clearly what she wanted so this was inevitable. 3. If He did marry her and have children they would be 5-foot-tall midgets with hairy arms and low IQs. Biology man. 4. If He's not in the mood it's fine, but I left my cigs in His car. 5. From what I've heard, He has an above average-sized dong. He should considering using His massive DNA blaster violently upon one of His endless squad of smuts.

"Ah. Alexander." He chuckled. "I have his logic and your chaos to help me out."

"What? What do you mean *his* logic? What about *my* logic? I just gave you *gold*, son!"

Dustin swiped the phone from His hand.

January 7th 2011
...women still fuck me... worthiness... How many cunts...

    He stumbled into Hamilton's Tavern with the smell of misery and recent sex trailing closely behind. He staggered determinedly towards the bar, until a familiar, golden-haired figure sitting alone in the corner booth caught His attention.
    Danika Rusche's tremendous downcast eyes glistened ultramarine, and her vacant smile appeared tragic across her round cheeks. A single dim light illuminated her like an actress on a decrepit stage. She wrapped her fingers around the thin red straw of her drink, bit down, sipped, and sighed. Every now and then, her eyes transitioned from a tired blue to a celestial fury seething the nothingness before her.
    He walked towards her.
    "Dah-nee-kah?" He spoke, squinting.
    "Mr. NoNaaame," she whispered. Her pupils were dilated, but one could still see that the thin ringlet around her vacuous pupils were cobalt.
    "Do you know the first thing you ever said to me?" He asked as He sat down across from her. "It was almost three years ago."
    One side of her sad smile lifted higher as her eyes roved up-rightwards.
    "Ummm – that you're hot, probably?"
    Chet Baker's rendition of *Almost Blue* began playing, and the wails of the trumpet and light piano swept despondency across the near-vacant tavern.
    "You asked me if I was rich because I drove a Benz," He spoke as the pads of her lips opened to reveal an opalescent grin, "and I said that my family is alright. Then you said, 'I bet you're spoiled.' And I, in response said that I was privileged. Being spoiled entails a sense of entitlement."
    She nodded slowly. "I remember," her voice spoke even softer now as her gaze sunk down to His drink. "What's your poison?"
    "Whiskey. You?"
    "Raspberry vodka. It's Hunter's gay drink."

"I had no idea there were drinks for gays." He smiled. "Are you two still dating? Or is Hunter actually a homose-"

"-No way," Danika snapped. "I'm not dating that faggot. He's fucking crazy."

Hunter Clarence Quillan Wilcox Himmler II, as if on cue, appeared with a drink in his hand.

"Jack Daniels for *you*," Hunter spoke to her, watching Him.

"Finally a *real* drink." She grabbed the drink from Hunter. With her free hand she gripped Hunter's pudgy stomach. "Who's got a big, fat beer-belly?"

Hunter slapped her hand away, turned, and rushed out of the bar into the snowy evening, sniffling and scratching the flesh of his hands.

The trumpet, piano, and mizzling percussion drained into the background, and Chet's voice sang, beginning with, "*Almost blue - Almost doing things we used to do…*"

"God," Danika groaned. "Hunter's doing his 'I'm too cool to sit with you' game. Gay faggot loser homo."

"I'm sorry." He began getting up. "I should-"

"Why are you sorry?"

He was silent.

"Hunter hates when I grab his fat. Now he's gone and you're here with me, so everything is delightful."

He sat back down, and their voices serenaded the tavern.

He had four double shots of Jack Daniels and two dark beers. Six of Danika's friends, Jack Ricaricare and his new girlfriend, and several other strangers surrounded them at the corner booth. He was speaking authoritatively about nothing. Danika announced that someone should kiss Him because His eyes were so green and attractive. He said He was practicing selective celibacy – no kissing, only cunnilingus and intense handholding. He had another shot. It wasn't His. Everyone was laughing. The crowd moved piece by piece away from the table, and they were alone again. His eyes became increasingly vacant, slowly matching hers…

...A drunken world... lights and laughter and music... Danika wearing His jacket... a faded moon above and stars rippling around Him and snowflakes falling to His sides... ink-like semi-frozen water, high-tide, and silver speckles simmering... golden hair... snow on a swing, snow on the sand, and then snow on a lawn... the view of His home... the pillow of His bed... tears against a pillow... vomit splashing against a midnight carpet... His hand gripping His chest over His blast-beating heart...

January 9th 2011
...Dani thinking about me? ... marks on her hands?...

"In summary, my good sir," Art recounted as they exercised in the basement gym of His house, "a CABG requires cutting open the leg and extracting the great saphenous vein from the leg – which is an ideal conduit to bypass the clogged artery. Oh - you'd like this-" Art spoke as he placed the thirty-five pound weights onto the barbell and lifted the barbell up towards the preacher curl station, "-the etymology of that vein – 'saphenous' – isn't really known. It's either from Greek meaning 'clearly seen' or from Arabic meaning 'hidden'. Total opposites."

"That *is* cool," He breathed quickly in between jumping rope.

"Yeah, so anyway," Art grunted as he lifted the seventy-pound weights up and began curling. "They CUT open the chest, and open UPPP the ribs, drill these HOOLEES near the sternuMMM to insert wires to coNNNNNNNNect the body to a HEART-lung machIIIIIIne," Art gasped in between curls. "They cut open the PERRambular sack, extracting this one VEIN from the leg and connecting THEMM to the heart to bypass the clogged arteries, and THENNNNN-NNN closing the chest, and then closing the leg." Art exhaled deeply at the zenith of his penultimate repetition, lowered the weights slowly, and then lifted them back up – his face growing red and vascular as he inhaled – and then let the weights drop on the preacher curl bench. "They sew up... the leg afterwards," Art heaved.

His cell phone vibrated on the table against the wall. He stopped jumping rope.

"What about the wires?" He asked, stepping towards the table and reaching for His phone. "The wires that bypass the clogged arteries?"

"They cut the ends of the wires, and the rest dissolves," Art responded, adding two ten pound weights to the barbell resting on the preacher curl bench. Art looked down at the weight smiling, and then turned to Him. He was beaming at His phone.

"What's her name?" Art asked knowingly. "I know that look."

"Her name is Stevennnn," He spoke back flamboyantly.

"What?" Art laughed. "Seriously, what's her name? I haven't seen that look since Selene. It's kind of scaring me."

"Her name is Danika."

"Danika? Why does that name sound familiar? Did she go to Old Rookvale High School?"

"She's-" He hesitated, "-Mandy's little sister."

"Mandy as in psycho Mandy? 'Many D' Mandy? The slutty girl you played around with in High School? The one who fucked everyone?"

He paused, looking up at Art with a flicker of anger, and then glanced down to His phone.

"Sure. That's the one. Her sister."

Art squinted, shook his head, and turned back towards the preacher bench.

"You just search for trouble don't you?"

"Eagerly."

"I'm serious." Art sat down and lifted the barbell up, inhaling. "When did you meet her?" he exhaled.

"Two years ago, actually. I was picking up Mandy one day back when we were fucking, and Dani opened the door for me. But I saw her Friday night." He looked at the weight on the preacher barbell. "You're curling forty-five on each side? When did you get so strong?"

"AND?" Art inhaled, lifting the weight up towards himself.

"And I'm not really sure what happened, but we were having a good time and then I think gave her my jacket, drove her home, and then drove myself home."

"You think?"

"I was very drunk."

Art put the weights back down on the bench, and looked up at Him.

"You were driving blacked-out? Dude, you have to stop that shit."

"I know. You're right," He spoke, clutching His chest and panting lightly.

The phone vibrated in His hands. Art stood up, his eyes focusing on His chest.

"Why are you breathing so hard? Are you okay?"

"Yeah," He spoke quickly. "I saw her two nights ago. She was in the corner of the bar with Hunter."

"Hunter Wilcox-Smyth Francis McGrath III?"

"McGraw, but yes. Him."

"Why is she with that mess?"

"They dated a year ago. Any way – so – when I met her two years ago we spoke for a little, and I could tell she had a little crush on me. So the first thing I did is bring that up to set the mood with a positive memory. And we spoke and I ordered another drink or two or three, and then before I knew it, her friends were all around us. Most of them were her age – seventeen – except for Jack Ricaricare and a few others. I'm not sure how it happened, but I brought her to my car and reclined the seats and we listened to music. And then I honestly don't remember a thing."

Art added another ten pounds to each side of the barbell, raising the weight to fifty-five pounds on each side.

"First, promise me that that's the last time you're going to drunken drive. Is that the end of the story?"

"Not really. Last night I went back to that bar, and saw her there, and she winked at me and left, touching my arm affectionately before leaving. I'm not sure what it meant, but all of a sudden, a bunch of younger guys – Old Rookvale juniors – were coming up to me and saying things like 'good job, dude' and patting me on the shoulder. I played dumb and ordered a few drinks and left."

"Drunk driving again, of course." Art shook his head.

"My few drinks is your sip."

"That's a stupid fucking thing to say to someone who's worried about you."

"That's not what-"

"Is this because of Selene?" Art asked, lifting the weight upwards.

He looked down at His cell phone quickly. It wasn't vibrating.

"I don't know. Maybe?" He looked back up to Art. "But I got home, and Facebook messaged her my number and said to text me today."

Art finished his third set of preacher curls – eight repetitions – and placed the weight down on the bench.

"And?"

"Aaaand – I don't know. Read this-" He handed Art His cellphone. "I made her name Duschey in my phone."

Duschey: Guess who... What did you need to speak to me about? (2:06)

Me: I'm guessing Dr. Duschey. (2:06)

Duschey: Good guess (2:07)

Me: Yeah. Why is there a rumor about us, Dani?? (2:10)

Duschey: Idk! I was gonna ask you the same thing... Going into your car to listen to music probably wasnt the best idea (2:11)

Me: You're right. (2:12)

Duschey: Yeah everyone was giving me shit for it last night :((2:14)

Me: I really don't want to associate you with the delinquents that were trying to high-five me over rumors. I don't care about them much. They're idiots. But I do want you to tell me that you did not contribute to the creation of this. (2:19)

Duschey: Haha I didn't add to it I don't necessarily like rumors going around that I'm a slut. Thats never fun. Didn't even tell people we kissed cause I knew Hunter would flip (2:40)

Me: Good. We didn't kiss. Do you wanna grab a drink this week? If u do, wear my jacket and make it look awesome. (3:01)

"You left out the part about you hooking up."

"We didn't hookup. That's the thing."

His phone vibrated in Art's hands. He turned it over and read.

"She says, 'we didn't? I guess I was dreaming.'"

He smiled, walked towards Art, and then stopped with His mouth parted.

"Holy shit."

"What?"

"I remember it now."

"Remember what?"

He paced in small circles, stopped, and turned to Art.

"I remember where we went. I drove her to the beach by your house. The same beach I took Mandy. I parked somewhere on the sand, she sat on the swing closest to the water, and then we walked down to the boardwalk – all the way passed the portico to the floating raft – and laid down there. I remember it now. I was lying down, looking up at the stars and they were all around me and reflecting in the water, and she was on top of me and she kissed me. Oh my God. Then I drove her home after a long, long time. I think I drove all over the lawn of her front yard."

"Jesus. You're both trouble."

"Fuck. And I haven't stopped thinking about her all morning."

"Why? Why can't you stop thinking about her? Why not any of the million girls you fuck around with?"

"I don't know. She's so sad and so happy. She has the most attractive presence."

"It's like you want to set yourself up for disasters. She's too young. And she's Mandy's sister for God's sakes." Art added another ten pounds to each side, making the barbell have sixty-five pounds on each side.

January 29th 2011
...Laughter in the Dark... I'll never be Nabokov...

He had finally convinced Danika to come over. Now, they were sitting Indian-style across from one another on the carpet in His room, and the lights were dim enough to see that He was wearing an open white button-down and plaid pajama pants. She swayed in her neon green short-shorts and tie-dyed tank-top to the sound of Chet Baker's instrumental *When Sunny Gets Blue* playing on the speakers. In between them was a skeletal watermelon they had devoured over the course of an hour. Her large sapphire eyes transitioned from dazed to focused as they passed the time laughing and whispering in the darkness.

"I need you to know something," she spoke through a fading smile. "I'm leaving Long Island soon… for a bit."

His eyes glistened in the dark.

"Where?" He asked. "Why?"

"I'm going on…" Danika hesitated and scratched the three red scars atop her hands, "…a retreat. A cleansing. For a month. Kind of like rehab."

A moment passed.

"Rehab for what?" He finally spoke.

"You know," her whisper sunk to an exhale. "Alcohol, weed, mushrooms, partying, some of the natural stuff, some of the other stuff."

He squinted.

"I just want you to know," she continued, hesitatingly, "because I like you a lot. Like a lot a lot."

Two white smiles illuminated the dark. He got up off the floor and collapsed onto the bed.

"Join me," He called out from the bouncing bed.

She rose up, and moved towards the bed. She curled down next to Him, her gold hair splashing over His shoulder.

"Is this your sex playlist?" Danika whispered. "Did you play this for Mandy, too?"

"No, love. It's Chet Baker."

He kissed her gently on her round cheek, and then on her neck.

"I can't imagine what sex with you would be like," she whispered.

He took her hand lightly in His, and rolled downward with her, using His falling momentum to lift her on top of Him. He looked up at her grinning. She ran her thumb down the stubbled cleft of His chin.

"You listen to this sexy slow bluesy loungey music, but I feel like you're a rough puppy."

"Rough puppy," He echoed.

He rolled again, pulling her down under Him. He kissed down her abdomen. When His lips reached the brim of her shorts, He bit down the brim and lowered them to her knees. She kicked off her shorts, and flung off her tie-dye tank top, revealing the musculature of her tight abdomen. He moved His lips to the neon green thong glowing between her toned legs.

"Nooooo-" she began, brushing her hands over His face.

"Yes," He whispered.

"Nnm-" she attempted, but instead ran one hand through His hair as she lifted off the bed, her bottom flexing as she peeled off her thong. He reached behind her back and snapped off her bra.

He sat up and looked down at her gleaming nakedness laying sideways on His bed. The full moon glowing by the window outlined the muscular curves of her flexuous body, adding porcelain shades and gray outlines to her toned abdomen, rounding her plumb breasts and shadowing her nipples, further volumizing the large curve of her protruding ass, and deepening the v-shaped concave of her hips which curved towards her bare mons. He smiled and slowly lowered His mouth between her legs.

February 27th 2011
...windows... Dani's voice loving... tristiloquence... we really together?...

There were perhaps fifty men and women in their late teens and early twenties, shuffling atop a roof in Chelsea, Manhattan. The bulk of the crowd gravitated around the diminishing pyramid of unopened beers. He remained by the opposite ledge, crouching by a protruding chimney duct, with Danika's voice breathing into His ear. His eyes roved out east into the pulsing lights of midtown Manhattan. He fixated first on two figures moving inside a distant window. Slowly, the square window dimmed from its illuminated orange to pitch blackness. His gaze lowered to the carousel of vehicles – all with their brake lights illuminating by the traffic light at the corner – casting faint red hazes across the distant avenues.

"Heroin – this white heroin they're calling white bull," Danika continued apologetically. "That's the real reason why I am here. I would inject it into my hands." She laughed sadly. "That's why I'm always scratching them like a monkey. That's why they have those three lines."

"Did-" He paused and looked out to the swarm of figures moving atop the belvedere, "-did Hunter introduce it to you?"

"Yeah," Danika responded. "Though I was already kinda interested before I even met him. But he and I did it a lot. Like, a lot a lot. We pretty much just surfed and swam and used. Then at some point while we were together I realized I was addicted." She sighed. "Why do you ask about Hunter?"

He opened His mouth as if to speak, but sighed instead. He scratched His shoulder.

"I'm really sorry I didn't tell you the real reason," Danika whimpered.

"You did tell me. Addiction. Whether it's one thing or another doesn't make a difference to me."

"So you're not grossed out? Being with some little, spoiled, heroin-addicted college freshman who's always scratching her hands and being held up in a crummy rehab center in the middle of nowhere?"

"I guess that's one way to see it, but it's not the way I do." A ripple of laughter stirred behind Him. He turned and witnessed the conclusion of a toast. A group of six men with beers and one woman with a water bottle clunked their drinks together before taking swigs. He leaned His back against the chimney duct, and observed the partygoers. "I see a smart but troubled girl, who – being a bit wild by nature – stumbled into something that temporarily trapped her. More importantly, she had the tremendous power and courage to get herself out."

"Like Lizzie Manibasse? She's getting out of rehab on July third."

"Sure." He shook His head. "Just like Lizzie Manibasse."

"I miss you," she whispered. "I miss you so much and I hate being in this crummy place."

"I miss you too. How long can you talk tonight?"

"I'm already over the limit. I don't know why these Nazis took away my cell phone. It's not like I'm going to score anything here. I feel like a ten-year-old girl with this stupid landline phone."

"I want to hear your voice again as soon as possible."

"You know," she began, her voice trembling, "you're the first person to call me. Before my bitch of a mom, my shitty asshole dad, my friends-" her voice softened, "-not even Mandy called to see how her baby sister is. You're the first person to call me."

He waited. More bodies appeared on the roof, their conversations loudening.

"Is that bad?" He whispered.

"No. It's perfect. The minute I come back home and settle back in, you're visiting me."

"Okay."

"I'm going to be staying in the same NYS dorm room on the Upper East Side for a bit. Everyone says I should keep away from Old Rookvale. They don't think it's a good idea for me to be around there. Bad associations."

"And school?"

A moment of silence.

"I'm going to have to redo last semester. I wasn't a very good fresh-woman. I barely remember a single class."

He and Alexander made eye contact in between the bustling figures. Alex shook his head and paced towards Him. An older woman's voice scolded distantly through the receiver.

"Booo," Danika whimpered. "The Third Reich is telling me I have to go. I really want to be out of this place. I really don't know what to do."

He sighed.

"When can I call you?" they asked simultaneously.

She laughed.

"I guess just call and ask for me," Danika spoke. "From three to four and six-thirty to eight we can receive calls."

"You know," He began. "I can hear your smile in the way you said that. There's a roundness to your words."

"I'm always smiling when I'm talking to you."

They bid good night to one another with the somnambular tone of new love. Alex was in front of Him now, standing akimbo. He placed His cellphone back inside His pocket.

"You're a romantic basket-case."

"Yup."

"Be careful, man," Alex warned, placing his hand on His shoulder.

"Why, my friend, do you say this?" He responded placing His own hand on Alex's shoulder, aping his gesture.

Alex pushed Him away, and both of their arms fell.

"Because she's INSANE, man!" Alex yelled. "Reason with yourself. Use some logic for once. She's too young for you, you fucked her sister, she's a former heroin addict and god-knows what else, and she's a fucking Rusche! That family is literally out of their tits."

"'Literally' doesn't apply there, and one's family doesn't define them."

"Alright, man. That's psycho-socially philosophical and all, but she's in rehab and from what I hear she's just like Mandy. She fucked Hunter, dude. How can you stomach that?"

"Point taken. I appreciate the concern. I always knew you loved me deep down, Alexander."

"You-"

"Wait-" He looked around. "Why isn't Dusty here?"

"Nice subject change, you manipulative fuck." Alex winked. "A man with a turban boarded the LIRR at the Woodside stop, so obviously Dustin decided it was safer to get off there and take the subway. But enough of that idiot. Do you understand that Danika will end up making you miserable? I hope you realize that. You make fun of Dustin for dating Sara just because she's attractive. Look at what you're doing. At least Sara isn't a junkie, man."

"I'm dating Dani because I like her, not just because she's attractive. I care about her."

"I will never understand why you gravitate towards such psychotic girls. They're poisonous, man."

"To test my mortality." He nodded knowingly.

Alex pointed to the remainder of beers.

"Can I interest you in a much more desirable poison?" Alex led Him into the crowd.

March 5th 2011
...she loves me... does she love me?... together?...

It was nighttime and the weather was warm. He leaned against the brick terrace of the Old Rookvale train station and gazed out west down the Long Island Railroad tracks. Behind Him was a staircase that led from the platform below to the parking lot. If one climbed the stairs, they would walk passed Him toward the parking lot, never seeing Him in the shadows of the terrace just behind the mouth of the ascending stairs. He looked down at His phone, and saw the time read 4:47. His eyes lowered to Danika's text.

Duschey: Don't be late, please, my phone is about to dieee (4:17)

  A figure outlined in red and white bulbs gleamed far in the dark distance. As it snaked forward, the train's metallic body became increasingly illuminated; depths and shades reflected the orange-pink-salmon light that glowed from the overhead lights of the station. The train slowed, slowed, and stopped.

  He exhaled the cigarette smoke and watched the gray wisps twist and vanish into the night. The train doors opened. Crowds egressed, and walked towards the steps. He turned around and watched them climb the steps in front of Him – with their backs to Him – and then continue forward to the parking lot. As expected, no one turned around and saw Him waiting in the shadows.

  Danika emerged from the stairs in a black cocktail dress that accentuated her Latin curves and contrasted the long golden plumage of her hair. She stopped at the curb of the parking lot and scanned slowly left to right. Little by little, the crowd disappeared into their sedans and SUVs and drifted out of the parking lot. Danika scratched her head and reached automatically for her phone. He quickly powered His off. She dialed His number. The parking lot was quiet enough now for Him to hear His voicemail sound from her phone.

  He stepped forward. His facial muscles were tense, as if restraining a tremulous laugh. He stepped closer. Suddenly, her proud figure curved down into a defeated arch as she sighed a "humph" that sounded like another expected disappointment.

  He froze mid-step. Tears filled His eyes. He wiped the moisture dry in two quick swipes, and moved closer until He was merely inches behind her.

  "Lovely evening, isn't it?"

  She turned quickly, facing Him with wide, tanzanite eyes.

  "That was," He began, "the most adorable noise I've ever heard."

"Damn it!" she yelled, slapping His chest. "I thought you forgot about me. And my phone is about to die, and-"

He pulled her close and kissed her. A wind passed, lifting her golden hair as she shivered.

March 27th 2011
...bitching... not used to facing her problems... I'll...

Danika stepped outside of her dormitory on the Upper East Side in Manhattan wearing sunglasses, denim shorts, tan boots, an American-flag-colored tie-dye shirt, and a crown of intertwined rosewood twigs atop her blond hair. The sun lowered onto the asphalt horizon as they traversed across the city.

"Can we eat already?" she complained, stopping. "Are we almost there?"

"You can keep asking that, Dani, but it's not going to make you any less hungry."

"We should've taken a cab."

He turned to her. Her sunglasses reflected translucent setting suns, and through them, He could see her blue eyes narrowing impatiently.

"Stop whining. We're one block away."

He took her hand, and together they crossed the street, moved towards a red awning.

"Ew! Is this a steakhouse?" she shouted. "I'm vegetarian now, remember?"

"It's not really a steakhouse. It's a really good place, though, and you can order-"

"Yuck!" she interrupted. She removed her sunglasses as a cloud passed over the sun, and faced Him with a zaffre glare. "No way, dude. I can't even be around your bloody murder-burgers."

"You didn't say that. Why didn't you say that before?"

"I didn't know you were planning on being around dead animals."

"Fine."

They walked south down Madison Avenue. Ten minutes passed as Danika rejected each place they passed by.

"I'm realllllly hungry now," she whimpered, holding her stomach.

"For fuck's sake - let's just eat somewhere then."

A bull-figured man in a sleeveless V-neck passed by. Danika turned and watched him. He observed as she eyed the passing stranger. He smiled.

"You should just grab food with him."

"Who?" Danika turned back quickly.

"That guy you were just checking out. Looks like a total vegan."

"I wasn't checking him out," Danika's voice rose. His smile faded.

"Yes. You were. I just saw you do it. Don't lie to me. That's not cool. I don't mind you eye-fucking anyone."

"I didn't check anyone out. I don't know what you're talking about."

"My stomach is about to cave in," Danika added quickly. "I would settle for your meat food right now. Can we just take a cab back?"

"You know what-" He smiled, letting go of her hand, "-you can eat whatever you want." He rushed towards an unoccupied cab down the street, opened the door and stepped inside.

"Can you take me to-" He paused. Across the street was Danika. Her eyes swollen and glistening, mouth parted, face heavy with sadness. "Take me to Madison and 59th, but first pick up that pretty girl looking this way."

The cab crept forward. Danika shoved her hands in her pockets and looked down at her feet as the taxi stopped. He opened the door. She removed her rosewood crown and got in quietly. Her eyes were wet. He pulled her close to Him, and she tucked into His body. Aside from Danika's intermittent sniffling and the faint melody of Lizzie Manibasse playing on the taxi's radio, they drove in absolute silence. Danika's eyes hung to a spot on the cab floor.

They returned to her dormitory and ordered Japanese food. Chet Baker's *Jealous Blues* grooved on her speakers while she ate boxed sushi on His lap. After she finished her last bite, she bent down, placed the empty plate on the carpet, and turned to Him with her legs wrapped around Him.

"Please," she spoke for the first time since the cab ride, her fingers scratching her palm lightly, "don't do that to me again."

"I won't. I promise. I'm sorry."

"And I'm sorry for making fun of the meat food and whining so much. It's just, I am not used to having to really deal w-"

He pressed His lips against hers. She smiled and began tying her hair up.

"I'm gonna go shower, kay?" she spoke. "You're sleeping over here, right?"

He nodded.

"Good."

She took her shirt and bra off, tossed them behind her – her bra landing atop the plastic sushi box – and leaned closer to Him, her breasts pressing against His chest. She kissed Him. He sunk His teeth down on her bottom lip and pulled away gently, until her lip was freed.

"I love when you do that," she whispered. "Join me in five minutes?"

"Sure."

Danika got up from His lap, pulled down her denim shorts and folded them neatly on His lap, around the bulge in His jeans.

"Five minutes and then playtime," she repeated as she turned slowly – poking her behind out towards Him – and swayed her voluminous figure towards the bathroom. "Don't make me wait too long."

Through the open bathroom door He watched the central star of the American flag thong on her large swaying bottom, and gazed down her toned legs. The bathroom door closed.

"Playtime..." He whispered as the shower began running.

April 2nd 2011
...breasts... grin... Mandy's seduction... sister... seventeen... I'm twenty...

He hadn't slept for three nights. He was in Danika's apartment, lying on her couch as she got out of the shower.

His eyes traced over their most recent texts:

Me: I get worried when you're not around me. (4:17)
Duschey: But I can't be with you all the time, so it doesn't really work that way. (4:20)
Me: You don't need to be with me all the time. Just know I'm here for you all the time. You making me worried that you're going to relapse is the same as me making you think I'm taking a cab home and leaving you. Same worry, same sadness, same fear of loss. (4:21)
Duschey: But you're not going to ever lose me. Huge diff. (4:21)

Danika walked by Him wearing only a towel around her head. She stepped towards her mirror and began rubbing moisturizer on her face. He stared at the bathing suit tan-line around her round bottom. She waved her butt back and forth. He looked up and saw her smiling at Him in the reflection.

"How are you feeling?" He asked her. Her smile became contemplative as her hand dabbed cream on her jaw.

"My mouth hurts," she answered, pouting. "I hate wisdom teeth. They're so unwise."

She moved towards Him and reached behind His shoulder for the bottle of Tylenol on the nightstand beside the couch. He watched as her breasts lifted and fell lightly as she plopped down on His lap. Eight pills were in her hand. She swallowed them at once.

"Ummm - isn't that way too much?"

"Not at all, Dr. Noname. Tylenol doesn't do shit for me. Hey! Did you know that the brain releases so much dopamine during orgasms, that if you took a brain scan of someone during climax, it would resemble someone on heroin?"

"No. I did not know that."

"Yeah. So, like, if we keep having sex like this you won't even have to worry about me relapsing."

He opened His mouth, but a ring blared from her laptop.

"Friends!" she shouted, hopping up towards the closet. He watched her legs flex as she reached for a robe and wrapped it around her body. She ran back to the laptop and accepted the call.

Two girls appeared.

"Hey girly!" they shouted. "We're soooo glad to see you! Look how hawt you look! You look stellar!"

She put headphone in her ears and plugged it into the laptop. He got up and walked around the couch, behind the laptop, and paced towards the shower. She grabbed His forearm. He looked down and saw her bright lapis-lazuli eyes as she puckered her lips to Him.

He ran a hand through her golden hair, kissed her, and turned towards the bathroom.

"Yup. That's Him," she spoke, grinning. She waited a moment. "Two months. Yeah, I'm surprised too…"

When He got out of the shower, she was sprawled out on the couch wearing a white tank top and American flag boxer shorts, sleeping. Her breasts pressing against her shirt rose and fell with each somnolent breath. Fresh nail marks glowed from the red raw skin below her knuckles. He saw the Tylenol bottle on the table next to the couch, next to an ashtray with a joint exhaling a dying gray-green thread. He picked up the bottle, walked into the kitchen, and looked around. His eyes found the refrigerator. He stood on His tiptoes and placed the Tylenol bottle on top of the fridge, sliding it all the way to the back.

He stretched, walked back to the couch, and slid behind Danika – assuming the big spoon. A half hour later

Danika whimpered. His eyes opened and closed. She got up, rubbed her jaw, and reached for the table where the Tylenol once stood. Her hand tapped the glass searchingly, worriedly, and then aggressively. She got up, careful not to move Him, and headed towards her kitchen. The light switched on. He turned over and gazed across the apartment at the glowing rectangle across the room where the sounds of cabinets opening and shutting could be heard. The noises ceased, followed by a long, defeated groan. The light switched off. He turned back around and closed His eyes. Her feet dragged back towards the couch, where she looked down at Him.

"Damn it, you," she mumbled as she reached for the television remote.

She forced her way back into His arms, and turned on the TV. Lizzie Manibasse's voice sang:
Dance – Dance – Dance – Dance – Dance – Dance
Everywhere we'll dance. Everything will dance."

Danika swayed her head gently side-to-side. The sound of nails scratching hands matched the melody.

May 6th 2011
...distract myself... Dani... Respond?... stupid basketball game... melancholy...

       He, Alexander, Dustin and several others were at Alex's house, sitting on the tan L-shaped couch. He was staring at a picture of Danika on His phone. She was smiling on the beach. Everyone else was watching the Knicks play against the Nets. Number three on the Knicks had just been fouled by the Nets, and was walking towards the foul line. He looked up at Dustin.

"I'll bet you ten right now that he makes both shots in."

"That homo?" Dustin laughed and spat the last glob of tobacco into a water bottle. "He's a retarded faggot."

"So you would like to bet?"

Dustin nodded.

The allegedly retarded faggot made the first shot in. An opposing teammate grabbed the rebound and bounce-

passed the ball back to him. His teammates slapped him high fives and slapped his bottom. The player again threw the ball into the air. It curved through the air and fell through the rim, swishing gracefully.
"Pay up, baby girl," He commanded.
"No," Dustin responded.
"Are you kidding?"
"I only have eighty bucks and I need it to buy some more-" a beat passed as Dustin grinned his tobacco-yellowed teeth, "-cocaine."
A fraternal laugh rippled across the couch.
"You shook on it. What's the point of betting money with you?"
"Quit being a god-damned Jew-bag. You hated sports ever since Selene told you to." The room laughed. Alexander did not. "Ten dollars means nothing to you. You're rich!"
"You're fucking disgusting."
"Alright," Dustin heaved throatily as he lifted from the couch. "I don't want to listen to this."
Dustin stepped quickly towards the kitchen.
"Does no one see a problem with this?" He asked the rest of them.
"If you are aware that Dustin is a real live degenerate asshole," Alex spoke, keeping his eyes on the television screen, "spends the money that his grandparents give him on drugs, and is altogether a lying fuck – then betting him makes how much sense?"
"I can't possibly imagine how this doesn't infuriate you."
He raced to the kitchen. Dustin was pouring himself a water-bottle's-worth of whiskey.
"Why does it matter so much to you?" Dustin asked before He opened His mouth.
"BECAUSE-" His voice raised, and then lowered. "Because I want you to stop lying. Be fucking honest to your friend. You say you're broke, and then you spend what money you get on cocaine. That's how you want to fucking live, you fucking Punchinello?"

Dustin squinted and smiled defiantly.

"Yeah. That's exactly how I want to live." He laughed. "And what the fuck is a 'Punchinello'? I need a dictionary when I talk to you. Seriously."

"What would your grandmother say about this?"

"You know what-" Dustin stopped. "Never mind."

"What?"

"No. You're going to get offended and take it personally and get bent out of shape."

"Go ahead."

"You're loaded! I'm not. If you want the ten dollars that badly, if you're that much of a shylock Jew and ten bucks really means that much to you-"

"No!" He shouted. "You don't get the point. Your fucking grandmother just hands you hundreds of dollars each week. Money she and your grandfather worked hard for. And you inhale it. You fucking inhale it, Dustin. You could be doing-"

"Shut up!" Dustin's face twisted. "What the fuck do you know? You're an idiot. Fuck you!" Dustin shook his head, spat a whiskey-with-tobacco-flaked glob on Alex's white kitchen tile, and turned to walk away. He stopped, turned back, grabbed his whiskey, shot Him a second hateful glance, and began walking back towards the living room couch.

"You're never going to get Sara back that way."

Dustin stopped. His shoulders dropped. He gesticulated as if he was going to cross his arms, but instead and let them dangle. He looked over his shoulder at Him with bloodshot eyes. "Fuck you, you acid-headed, spoiled hypocrite." He coughed, wheezed, grabbed his inhaler with his free hand, puffed, sucked, inhaled, exhaled, coughed, and wheezed again. "I wish –" his voice trailed. He faced forward, standing still and silent. A moment passed as He stared at Dustin's back, waiting. Dustin shook his head and continued to the couch.

He remained in the kitchen, His face reddening. The echo of Dustin's voice murmured incomprehensible

sentences from the TV room. Another burst of laughter sounded. He took out His phone and examined the screen.
Duschey: I get home from NepTunes tomorrow night. When and where are we meeting? And r u still upset with me? (9:06)

He began typing:

Me: Tomorrow night at the gazebo. 9:00. (9:16)

He stepped outside into the dark and headed towards His car, the figure of a cigarette moving towards His lips.

May 7th 2011
...stop scratching, Dani... don't worry... you'll be fine...

The clouds hung low in the darkening sky as He and Danika walked up the spiral staircase that led inside the gazebo. The original white paint and second coat of blue were completely gone, and wood-chips splintered in different directions as if pulling themselves from the original frame. Danika entered first. She turned, leaned back against the railing, and faced Him.
"So-" she began, throwing a single eyebrow up and presenting a broad grin, "what did I do this time?"
She extracted a pack of cigarettes from her pocket, pulled two out and ignited them together. She exhaled dual puffs of smoke as she separated one from her lips and placed it filter-first in front of Him. He leaned forward and took the cigarette between His teeth.
"I think we need to break up, Dani."
"Ummm-" her glaucous-colored eyes scanned the slow-moving traffic passing behind Him, and then returned to His eyes, "-how about we don't?"
He laughed.

"I don't want to sound like a little bitch, but I feel like I'm caring a little too much about you and that it's not reciprocated at all."

"Well, mister serious pants, how do I *reciprocate* it?" she moved closer to Him.

"I don't know. I just think you and I aren't working out. You go to these music festivals every weekend and I never see you. I don't… I just… I don't know." He shrugged. "It might sound strange to you, but I have no proof that you care about any of this."

"It's summer. It's festival season. I'm sorry I love music so much."

"No. I… worry about you, and it brings me down, you know? I mean, you did just, you know, got out of reha-"

"Does this help?" she lifted her sweater up and squeezed her plump, bare breasts upwards to Him. She grinned and jumped, rubbing them together.

"A little." He kissed her. "But, I… when we can't spend the night together I admit that I get a little upset, but when you go to week-long music festival and don't respond to a text for seven hours I feel… worried that you might…" His voice trailed.

"But I *live* off music. I told you." She frowned as she lowered her sweater over her breasts, "and I don't keep my cell phone with me. I leave it in a friend's car."

"Which friend?" He shook His head quickly and took a step backwards. "This is exactly my point. I shouldn't have to worry about this at all."

"Since when are you so jealous?" She grinned, playfully slapping the wooden banister of the decrepit gazebo. He winced.

"I don't think I have any reason to feel jealous. It's just – I've never felt so distanced from someone I'm supposedly dating. It just doesn't feel right."

"I think you're being too dramatic, and rather *uncharacteristically* insecure."

"Yes, fine. But, the very fact that I am being uncharacteristically insecure and dramatic about our relationship is proof that we don't belong together. Do you understand?"

"Ugh," Danika groaned, leaning forward and wrapping her arms around the back of His neck. "Can we just stop being so serious, and go back to the fun crazy boy I *do* like and *do* care about. We can fuck all night tonight."

She leaned upwards and kissed Him. He pulled away slightly but she pulled Him closer.

"Fine. Never mind." He sighed, pulling her closer. "I want you to read something I wrote. It's music-based so you may enjoy it."

He pulled out a folded piece paper from His pocket, and handed it to her.

"Don't read it now."

He placed the folded piece of paper in her pocket. The page read:

ALONG A WANDERING WIND

...The wind listens to a light melody trickling out from an elegant, white building in Selden, Long Island. It climbs up the wooden patio decorated with violets, and enters inside. Here, several empty pink-linen tables encircle an open dance floor. There is an adolescent boy sitting at one of these tables. He is staring over the wedding-gowned shoulder of his soon-to-be married older sister, and beyond the fuchsia-hued bride's maids at a single pianist. The musician is playing a melody that the boy doesn't know, but it is stirring the waves of ideas and feelings in his young mind. The wind peers at the sheet music, which reads F. Chopin (1810-1849) Nocturne in E-flat Major, Op. 55, No. 1.

The boy removes his new golden fountain pen and a small sealed cup of ink from his pocket – two birthday presents given to him by his father last week – and places them atop the table. The boy holds his pen over a napkin, peeks out of the window ahead where the sun is resting halfway below the horizon, and descends his pen into a confident cursive forming the words 'Zirna and the Nightsong.'

He smiles confidently, and again descends the pen over the paper. He freezes. Little-by-little, the parabola of his smile flattens.

"Hmm," he mumbles.

In his mind – racing too quickly for his pen to capture – is a story: An older gentleman wearing a mask is playing music in a crowded ballroom. A young woman will notice him, will come to speak to him, and will introduce herself as Zirna. This man will know plenty about time, dreams, and the piano. He will play music, and as he does so, the world will ripple and change. With a strange melody, he will physically transport Zirna directly back into her childhood, where she will touch and smell and see her old home. When the man finishes playing, Zirna will return back to the crowded ballroom and again be in front of him. She will ask how he brought her to her childhood, and the man will reveal that he had only played the music of nostalgia, and that she alone had decided where this feeling would take her. She will contemplate, and then ask if he could play something to make her see her deceased father again. He will warn her that this will inevitably lead to heartbreak, but she will not listen. He will relent, and take her to her father with a new emotion. She and her father will be together for a week, and then her father will behave irrationally - becoming repetitive and illogical – and it will frighten young Zirna. She will shatter this nightmare, and realize that she was always in front of the pianist. The pianist will reveal to her that she ran out of memories to reproduce his behavior, and that this is a natural tragedy of human loss. She will know that she reproduced her father the way she wanted him to be, and will admit to herself that her father was barely there in her childhood. She will say 'it almost seems like we create the ones we lose in ourselves', and then will ask the pianist if he ever recreates his own lost loves. The pianist will reveal that he does, but he alters them and alters himself so that they cannot fully recognize each other, because a fictional memory allows the infinite room of imagination whereas a real memory has limitations. The pianist will tremble and choke back a sob, as Zirna begins to recognize him. He will lift his hands from the piano, and Zirna will instantly disappear. The pianist will be maskless in an empty room with a dusty piano, upon which a scroll will read, 'The Nocturne for My Dearly Missed Daughter, Zirna'.

Thus, a disguised man will reproduce his lost one through a song, creating a story where his lost one will try to reproduce him.

The wind senses that the ripples and waves of this same thought are being wished into existence somewhere else. It rushes eagerly towards the sensation, nearing one of the very few apartment complexes in Coram, Long Island.

It peers through the bathroom window, where a naked twenty-year-old boy sits in his empty bathtub holding a pen. A pad of paper rests atop his folded knees. Angry words scream from the floor above. The boy is thinking of the fortunate moments when he could drown out the booming arguments of the highly-sexual couple above him into low bass murmurs by letting his ears sink down into the muting water of the tub. But now the tub is empty, and Chopin's Nocturne in E-flat Major, Op. 55, No. 2 lulls from the record player in his room beside a stack of music theory textbooks. The female in the floor above shrills the words 'JUST LIKE YOUR FATHER!'. Then that thing happens again to the boy... something like daydreams, but louder; more like actual dreams in the sense that an hour of imagination could fill a second of the 'real' world. He knows his racing thoughts began with the memory of his own father, who passed away when he was only twelve. His pen moves quickly across the paper:

I Overture

...*"Music,"* the masked pianist answered, keeping his silver, crescent-moon eyes on the keys, *"is how we decorate time, just as art is how we decorate space. The true beauty is that music itself is time, it is a collection of violations and justifications of time's many equations. The equation is temporarily real when the music begins, and* temporarily set when the music ends. How much do you know of the piano?"

"I used to take lessons," Zirna responded confidently.

"To what genre of instrument does the piano belong?" the man asked, a challenging smile beaming towards his quick-moving fingers.

She considered.

"Strings?" Zirna attempted. "There are strings in the piano."

"There are strings. Two-hundred-thirty strings to be exact, but you are incorrect my dear. The piano-" the sounds intensified as he pounded upon the keys with increasing force, "-belongs-" his voice raised and thundered down with each note, "to... THE... PERCUSSION!"

His fingers slid across the key in a lightly descending arpeggio.

"Like the drums. One might say the piano is a hybrid of percussion and strings. You see, when I press a key-" he held down only the double high C, "-a wooden hammer will strike one, two, or three steel wire strings. The hammer then slides back down into its appropriate place, permitting the strings to vibrate. The sound of this vibration relies on the length, weight, thickness, and tension of the strings. Then we have music, or the artistic population of time, which can inspire the mind and soul to wakingly dip their toes into cognitive dreamscapes. You know, in many ways the piano is like the mind. The visible keys – that which you see – are only the superficial. The real beauty – the complex harmonies – remain hidden to both the entertainer and the entertained. The master pianist knows the dynamics of each vibration as vaguely as the master psychologist knows his own mind. In totality, my dear, all of this is most simply," he continued whispering as a strange, lullaby-like progression of chords sounded, "a collection of vibrations and reactions"

The following melody brought forth – vividly in the mind's eye of Zirna – many sad days of rain falling, tapping against her attic window where, as a young girl, she would stand and look out to the lonely dirt road that led to her old home. It was these days where all the vibrant colors of the world were depleted to shades of gray, where the only smiles were to squeeze back her tears, and where joy was merely the temporary absence of sorrows. In the slowest movements, her heart crashed heavy pounds against her chest. Suddenly, she was a child again. She was there in her dusty, gray attic. She stood in the center of the pallid room, alone. Slowly, as if testing her own body, she stepped towards the single window. She lifted her hand, placed it flat against the glass, and felt the numbing touch of ice burn the skin of her palm. Frost appeared, circumventing her hand and slowly emanating outward across the glass. Loneliness and hopelessness swarmed within her like merciless ghosts. The frost emitted from her hand now stretched across the entire glass plane, rendering the entire window a glowing square of opaque whiteness. A rogue tear trickled down her cheek...

...Back in the ballroom, within a long vacant space between the notes of The Nocturne, a tear splashing against a piano top could be heard perfectly. The pianist looked at her, watching misery and redemption in her soft, dreamscaped eyes. Though it was inflicting upon her a nearly unbearable sorrow, one that made her heart plunge downwards with utter agony, she had found a numb comfort in the somnambular melody. She was reliving and re-experiencing. There was something infinitely ethereal and magnificent about rewinding time and witnessing the past with such precise detail; it was such a gift to be wholly present in erstwhile experiences – even those filled with heartache...

"Are you enjoying your own sadness?" the phrase breezed over the sound of the white rainfall beyond the window.

The somber grays of her reverie blurred away and all the hues of the tremendous ballroom swirled at once before her eyes. She staggered for a moment, startled and drunk with confusion. Her hand caught the piano top. A mere five seconds had passed...

II Exposition

...and after these five seconds came another five, and another, and several more. A collection of seconds streamed across the perpetual gust of time as she leaned on the piano, incognizant to the absent look in her eyes. She seemed to stare deeply into nothingness. She was, however, focusing with furious intensity, grasping tightly to an evanescent dream. But it was no use. After a series of intermittent flashes of her reverie, it was gone.

The sudden presence of silver eyes like glowing moons frightened her. Below these eyes, lips parted to form the words, 'Are you enjoying your own sadness?'...

-

The wind marvels for a moment at the beauty of this newly-learnt wonder – that thoughts are connected between people – and wonders why only one was able to create his thoughts. The wind watches the teenager and the bathtub shrink in the distance as it drifts eastwards, and begins considering the primary disparity of their minds. The boy is satisfied, and the teenager is not. The wind considers artistic intelligence, or creativity, and how dissatisfaction augments it. The wind reflects: The desire to create is inseparable from the desire to change. It is when humans are most dissatisfied when they desire change most. Creativity, then, must be somewhat rooted in dissatisfaction.

The wind turns away from the scribbling speck in the window, and navigates eastward, searching for more people from whom it can learn...

May 13th 2011
...172... pleeease... pleeese... pleeease... 170... c'mon... relax... pleeeeeeease...

He was alone in the dark hospital room with His father, four days after His father's unexpected triple bypass surgery. The clock read 3:00, and the heart monitor's BPM screen danced between 120 and 180. His dad labored to lift up from the hospital bed, first by moving the wire connected to his sternum. He was playing Chet Baker's rendition of *Blues in the Closet* from His cellphone.

"I liked that. Very relaxing," His father spoke as the melody began to fade. "Help me up? I have to urinate."

He pulled His father up gently.

"Slow breaths, pop."

His father sat up, and placed his hands on the bed to support himself.

"Wait," He whispered soothingly. "Take a few deep breaths, please."

"Okay, son." He examined a spot on the floor, bounced with a silent laugh, and glanced up at his son. "Did you ever think that you'd see your old man in this shape?"

"Please." He smiled and shook His head. "You're not an 'old man' and you just endured a surgery that traumatizes multiple parts of your body. The procedure itself is a collection of miracles. And you're dominating it."

His father nodded, rising slowly. They paced together into the bathroom. His father clutched His wrist in one hand and the rolling cardiac monitor cable in the other. He bent his knees with difficulty and plopped down onto the toilet seat.

"Okay, son," His father spoke through a sigh. "I think I'm good."

"Are you sure?"

"Yes. You can wait outside."

"Alright."

"I'll play the water running song on my phone."

"It's worked so far," His father uttered, smiling wanly.

He stepped out of the bathroom and loaded a YouTube video titled, *'WATER POURING'*. A long, streaming sound resonated from the speakers. After the sound ended He tapped replay on the screen. Midway into the third repetition, the sound of urination could be heard from behind the door. He smiled at its sound. "It's amazing what you appreciate in times like this," He muttered to Himself, staring at His cell phone screen. The stream stopped. He looked up at the wooden door.

"You done, pops?"
"I'm going to try and crap again."
"Okay. I'm right outside the door. Should I try to find an inspiring crap video?" He laughed.
"Ha-ha," His father chuckled faintly.
His phone vibrated. He looked down.

Mother: I'll be there in about 30 minutes. Sit tight. How's he feeling? (3:22)
Me: Okay, mom. He's alright. Weak, but keeping his spirits up. (3:22)
Mother: Your father knows too much. He was in bed this morning when the surgeons came in and talked about the different medications and pills he has to take, and every time they mentioned one he would go on and on about the side effects. (3:40)
Mother: I suppose that's the problem with knowing things. I'll be there in ten, honey bun. (3:41)

He smiled as His eyes passed over the last text.

Me: As long as he takes them. He can't be stubborn here, madre. He has to follow what they say. See you soon. (3:41)

Before He placed the phone back into His pocket, it vibrated again. He glanced at it.

Mother: Are you and I engaging in a loving, familial conversation for once? :) (3:41)
Me (unsent draft): Yeah, I guess we ar

"SON! SON!" His father cried out.
He turned quickly to the heart monitor which read '140', then '155', '191', '204', and then '???'. He dropped His phone, swung the door opened and saw His father, wide-eyed, panicking with his arms jerking about.
"SON-SON-SON-"
"I'm here, dad." He rushed towards him.

"The heart monitor!" His father gasped. "What does the heart monitor say?"

"It says 155. Relax, please, relax."

His father's arms moved in a flurry of spasms, the veins on his neck pulsing.

"I-I'm dying, son."

His eyes glistened as He leaned closer to His father.

"No you're not. You're okay."

"Come here," His father groaned mercifully.

He leaned down towards the toilet and hugged His father, who buried his face into His shoulder.

"Breathe with me. You're fine. Right now-" He inhaled slowly, "-just breathe with me." He exhaled deeply.

His father inhaled and exhaled.

"I'm dying, son," he wailed. "I feel so bad. I feel so bad."

"Dad-" He said, struggling to keep His voice steady, "-I promise you that you're okay."

He rubbed His dad's back in slow, clockwise circles. Together they inhaled and exhaled, inhaled and exhaled, over and over, over and over.

"Keep breathing with me."

After a fifteen minutes of Him half-squatting over His father to allow him to rest his head comfortably on His shoulder, a knock sounded.

"Is everything okay?" His mother called from behind the bathroom door.

"What does the monitor say, dear?" His father groaned.

"It's decent. 158. Is everything okay in there?"

"Yeah," He responded, still massaging His father's back. "Just a little scare." He kissed the top of His father's head.

A moment later they stood up together. He flushed the toilet, opened the door, and held His father up tightly as they waddled to the door. He opened the door and found His mother waiting.

"165," His mother spoke. "It's probably because you just got up," she added quickly.

They sidled towards the bed. His father positioned himself to sit.

"Slowly," He whispered.

"Easy," His mother encouraged.

Just as His father sat down another knock came from the door. All three turned to find a silver-haired, dark-faced man standing by the room entrance. On his white coat, beside a dangling stethoscope, was the name Dr. Iorgo Epiktetos. His mother glanced at the name, back at His father, and then again towards the doctor.

"Ti prépei na kánei o sýzygós mou gia na aisthantheíte kalýtera?" His mother spoke with a sense of deliberation. "Emeís tha ton peísei."

"O sýzygós sas tha prépei na lávei to-" the doctor paused, as if laboring to find a word, "aíma-leptótero. Aftó pou milísame prin. An po ti léxi, o sýzygós sas tha xérete ti syzitáme, kai o ánthropos tha arnitheí."

"Entáxei." His mother smiled. "Emeís tha frontísoume gia aftó. Sas efcharistó, giatré."

"Kalí týchi na ton peísei," the doctor spoke to His mother, and then turned to His father. "How are you feeling?"

"Lousy. What's my heartrate?"

His mother glanced up and then back down to him. "You're at 118. You really feel that bad? How about you take a beta-blocker? It will relax you. Would you rather get a teensy bit nauseous and fix this problem, or keep worrying about your heart-rate every two seconds? It will calm you down, no question about it."

After a moment of what appeared to be strenuous meditation, His father finally nodded. The doctor's eye brows lifted in surprise.

"Okay," He said, sidling around the doctor as He paced towards the door. "I'll get it. They've been wanting you to take it all day."

He left the room, went to a nurse, and asked for a Beta-blocker in room 1065. She nodded, typed into her computer, stood up and vanished into a backroom. He returned to the room. The doctor was gone. His mother was

massaging His father's feet. He gazed at him. His eyes were closed and his face assumed practiced serenity. The monitor read 112.
"I'm going to get some water. Mom, do you need anything?"
"I'm good honey bun. Thanks."
"You okay, pop?"
"Just a little dizzy. Thanks, son."
"Please." He shook His head. "I did nothing. It's all you."
"No." His father's eyes opened. He turned to His mother. "If He weren't here I would have been gone."
"Don't say that," His mother reprimanded him. "It was just a scare."
"I'll be right back," He mumbled, His voice hoarse.
He stepped towards the hospital hallway towards the lurid fluorescent of the main room. He squinted as He stammered dazedly through the monochromatically white walkway. He passed by a blond nurse in a white scrub who smiled to Him. Beads of sweat formed on His forehead as He began trembling. He raced towards the men's bathroom. He punched inside a closed stall. His hands shook as He fumbled for His phone and dialed Art's number.
"Give me a second, bro, I'm just signing out a patient," Art's voice sounded after the first ring. "How's your dad?"
He collapsed onto a toilet as tears poured down His face. A trickle of bile streamed down from His mouth and splashed between His legs into the toilet water.
"I'm so scared, Art," He heaved.
"Woah-woah-woah! Breathe, dude. Fuck – what the fuck happened?"
"I – I-" He shook, tears and sweat glistening across His wet face. Slowly, the color faded from His cheeks. "Cold…"
"Breathe, bro. Stop. Stop talking. Take a long, deep breath."
He inhaled slowly and exhaled slowly.

"What happened, bro. Tell me, please. Everything is going to be alright."

"My father's blood pressure rose passed 200, and then the heart monitor showed question marks, and then he kept saying…" He sniffled deeply, "…He kept saying he was going to die, Art."

"What? 200? Wait- is he okay, now?"

"Yeah. I think so. It lowered back to 120."

"What happened to lower it?"

"He was in the-" He paused, gagged mutely, and coughed. "He just rested his head on my shoulder for a while."

A moment passed.

"Your father had an arrhythmia, and His body performed a vasovagal response," Art spoke confidently.

"What?"

"A vasovagal response. You don't know what that is?"

"No. I don't fucking know." He sniffled again. "Sorry. Teach me, please."

"No, I'm sorry," Art spoke. "I thought you already knew it. It's when you're not getting enough blood to your brain. It's common after heart surgery. It's essentially a survival mechanism that forces the body to faint, so the head can be lower than the heart to allow blood to rush towards the brain. It's common. Trust me. How long did it last?"

"I don't know. I was kind of out of it too." He laughed sadly. "Maybe twenty minutes?"

"And it's back down, now? He's okay. Trust me."

"Okay."

"Now tell me you're good," Art commanded.

He wiped the sweat from His forehead, and took several deep breaths as the color returned to His face.

"Are you sure it's common?"

"I'm very sure it's very common, bro. Especially after a triple bypass surgery. Five of our patients have had vasovagal responses today, and all five are fine right now."

"Okay. I'm okay."

"You promise, bro?"

"Yes." He wiped the wetness from His cheeks. "I'm good. I'm good. Thank you so much, Art."

"Dude, call me anytime."

"I will."

"Okay. Can you do me a quick favor?"

"Sure."

"Where are you?"

"In one of the bathrooms."

"Taking a stress poop?"

He laughed.

"Good, bro. It's good to hear that laugh. Tell me three things you can identify in the room."

He looked around.

"A lack of toilet paper, a very detailed drawing of an overly-vascular, uncircumcised penis drawn on the wall of this stall, and-" He opened His legs and looked down at the bile floating in the water. It was yellow with blood-red sediments. "-And you on the phone with me."

"Good. That works."

"What was that for?"

"To make sure you don't pull a Dustin and have a panic attack." Art chuckled. "You're not the only one who knows the tricks of the mind. Identifying the things around us helps us remember that we are in control."

"You really are the best, Art. Thank you."

"No problem, bro. Now don't forget to wipe. Tell your dad that I say to keep his chin up. Literally. I'm sure by now he knows what happened."

May 15th 2011

Bro: When r u getting here? I'm still at the hospital (2:02)

Me: Hopefully soon. LIE was a parking lot around Bayside. GPS says 24 mins, but that bitch don't know my driving skills. (2:03)

Bro: Okay I need the car to take care of some things (2:08)

Me: Oh... I need the car to get back to Long Island... (2:09)
Bro: What? How long were u planning on staying? (2:09)
Me: 2-3 hours? (2:09)
Bro: Do u need the car for job hunting? (2:10)
Me: No? (2:10)
Bro: Do u need the car for applying to another school? (2:10)
Bro: Or dropping off any of your manuscripts? (2:10)
Me: No... I don't understand... (2:10)
Me: .... (2:14)
Bro: Then u can go to Penn and take the LIRR back (2:15)
Me: Why couldn't you just let me know that you needed the car before? (2:16)
Bro: I'm sorry if I cut into ur busy social schedule. Maybe u should consider the fact that our dad is in the hospital right now and that he funds ur entire life (2:22)
Me: 1. Sarcasm completely unnecessary. 2. You didn't answer my question. 3. I AM considering the fact that dad is going to want to sleep, as that is what he should be doing. 4. What does any of this have to do with you not telling me that you need to use the car? (2:29)
Bro: Dad didn't sleep until 3AM last night (2:29)
Me: Okay? How could I have possibly known that? And that only corroborates my contention that dad is going to want to sleep. (2:30)
Me: I'm here. (2:34)
Me: Where are you? I'm parked outside the hospital. (2:40)
Bro: Found a ride (2:41)
Me: ...Why didn't you tell me? (2:42)

Bro: I figured u were too busy with u social schedule (2:44)
Me: Again, (thinly-veiled) sarcasm is not necessary. Can you have the slightest amount of politeness or decency to let me know these things? I would gladly give you the car if you took the time to tell me in advanced. (2:46)
Me: Or just don't answer... (2:55)
Bro: Fuck u (2:58)
Me: Really? (2:58)
Me: Very mature. (2:58)
Me: Have I really made a mistake? (2:59)
Me (unsent draft): You're just like mom.

June 15th 2011
...Dani... no... like we're not really together... Dani...

Alexander and He were at The Rising Star Café and Bookseller in Old Rookvale. Alexander was filling out an LSAT prep book, and He was reading page 165 of Gabriel Garcia Marquez' *One Hundred Years of Solitude*, underlining the words, '*He felt scattered about, multiplied, and more solitary than ever*'.

His phone vibrated.

Duschey: Not gonna lie. Idk half these words. Somnambular? Erstwhile? You gotta dumb it down for meee (4:08)

He shook His head, and looked up at Alex who was writing in his textbook.

"How can you expect to improve on a logic-based examination when you're spending your days with Dustin?"

"Okay," Alex's voice rose as he put the book down. "How the hell does hanging out with Dustin have ANYTHING to do with my LSAT scores?"

"Relax," He calmed.

"No. I am relaxed. You can't just spout these meaningless things and not back any of it up. Support your case."

"We are sociological creatures, Alex. When you hang out with someone, you inherit their qualities and they inherit yours, or they may increase or decrease an already existing quality in you - like openness or tolerance or humility. Now, when you spend the majority of your days with the most illogical fuck that we know, who is unfocused, undetermined, lazy, and altogether an alcoholic vagrant - how could you possibly expect to get better scores? That's all. Now relax." He crossed His arms and leaned back in His chair.

"So you're telling me-" Alex cocked his head up condescendingly, "-that if I hang out with a homosexual, that I'm going to eventually become a homosexual?"

"You're too black-and-white, my friend. My answer to that question will only provoke your arrogance."

"Well, now you have to tell me."

He buried His face buried in *One Hundred Years of Solitude*.

"C'mon, writer."

"I'm going to prematurely evacuate this conversation by answering your obviously reductive question with: It depends on what you mean by 'become a homosexual'."

Alex shook his head laughing, and then stopped abruptly. Suddenly rigid, Alex gazed over His shoulder as Selene walked in, emerging from the entrance and walking towards the café counter.

"Okay," Alex began softly as Selene was just passing their table. "Now you promise *me* that you're going to relax."

"I'm alright, Lex." He turned a page and shook His head. "Maybe it's because my dad is already flying around the world again, but I'm just feeling strangely alone despite the fact that I'm sort of still with-" He looked up, His eyes finding Alex's. He followed his gaze to Selene. "With-" His eyes followed her, "w-" His voice cut out as Selene quickened her pace. "w-" He repeated, as if detached from the previous thought. "Wish-"

"Listen to me," Alex demanded. "Think of your girlfriend, Dani."
"I-" His voice vibrated through short frantic breaths. His face reddened. His body closed inwards.
"Stop!" Alex snapped.
His book dropped from His hands onto the ground. He turned to it, and then turned to Selene whose oceanic eyes drifted to and away from Him a second time. She walked passed them, focusing her eyes with what appeared to be intense concentration on her name written cursively across the coffee cup. She approached the exit. He stood up, but Alex rose quickly and placed a heavy hand on His shoulder, sitting Him back down.
"Be logical," Alex pleaded.
Tears fell on His lap.
"She doesn't even-" His voice cracked loudly as He shook His head. People turned towards Him. His face was vibrating in His hands.
"Stop. Listen to me," Alex demanded, grabbing the fallen book and placing it back on the table.
"Her memories of me are gone, Alex. I don't exist to her."
He looked up, His eyes deeply bloodshot.
"She isn't important anymore. She's - she's…" Alex struggled, "…she's… a book you've already read," he offered. "She's not important anymore."
He buried His face into the book, His spine thrusting with each sob. Alex winced as He cried quietly into the novel, quivering in the center of the crowded bookstore.
"Gone," He whispered in between sobs.

June 18th 2011
…recidivism… why did… dating… Mandy Selene Dani… windows…

He and Alexander were outside the Teisėjakaitis house, enjoying a cigarette in the outdoor lights as the navy sky dimmed. Through a window, they observed Dustin and several others drinking as they watched a basketball game.

"...And Dani left for a five-day concert this morning, Alex," He continued, "and hasn't texted me once since leaving. Yet, from what I hear, she really is serious about being with me. I no longer want to get it. How do I cut her off?" His voice cracked.

"Shut up!" Alex demanded. He put his hand on His shoulder. "Listen, just tell her simply that you don't love her anymore, and stop talking to her until you two are face-to-face. And don't be hypnotized by her massive tits, you fucking sex addict. I don't want to have to see you mope around like you did with Selene when she dumped you. Dump Danika, and move on to someone more appropriate, which is literally anyone in the world, honestly."

"I never said 'I love you' to her." He shook His head, exhaling zigzagging puffs of smoke which glowed in the outdoor light.

"Then tell her you don't *like* her anymore. Plain and simple. You are no longer interested in her – all of her, which includes her junkie-like qualities that you seem to deemphasize. Use logic for once, please! She's too young, insane, and spoiled to know how to appreciate you, and it seems like that's what you really want, man. Dump her."

"This is all a mistake," He exhaled. "I can't keep making these stupid mistakes."

"If you hate making stupid mistake, stop making them so often."

"I-"

"Nope. Dump her. You've got your answer. You're not interested in her, and frankly, *frankly*, I'm getting bored of this routine. I'm going to go inside and enjoy the game with everyone. Are you going to join us, man, or are you going to stand out here and be a lugubrious homo?"

His phone rang. Danika's grin flashed on the screen. He smiled and then frowned.

"Lugubrious homo it is," Alex muttered, shaking his head as he stepped back into his house.

He picked up the phone.

"Hey-"

"Heyy," Danika's voice sounded far from the phone. A thousand drunken conversations and thunderous music pounded in the background. A wind produced a melancholic aria through the tree branches around Him. "What's up?" her voice continued.

"What's up?" He repeated back to her. "Okay, before you say anything else, I want you to know that we are breaking up. Completely. It's over."

"What – no – why? Stop! I didn't do anything! I'm behaving!"

He stepped away from Alex's house as His voice grew louder.

"Dani – you were supposed to come over last night – and you didn't, and didn't even have the courtesy to text me."

"I was at the hospital. My friend had an asthma attack."

"Yet, you're at your concert as of this morning and haven't responded to a single text."

"My pho-"

"STOP!" He thundered, His voice cracking into a shrill cry. "JUST STOP. IT'S NOT WORKING OUT. I DON'T WANT TO DO THIS ANYMORE!" He clicked the phone off.

Before He could punch the phone into His pocket, it began vibrating with Danika's face. He pressed the ignore button, and continued walking. The phone vibrated again. He pressed ignore. The phone vibrated. He accepted the call, picked up, and shouted "NO" into the receiver. His phone vibrated repeatedly. He looked at His phone. Seven texts. He opened them.

Duschey: Oh and u can hang up on me but u get mad when I do it (11:11)
Duschey: No fairr (11:11)
Duschey: Pick uppp (11:12)
Duschey: Y r u always mad at me! (11:12)
Duschey: Please pick up (11:12)
Duschey: Talk to me. Let me explain. (11:12)

Duschey: Please pick up. I'm sorry. (11:13)

Danika was calling again. He picked up the phone. The sound of muffled crying came from the receiver.

"What do you want me to do?" she cried. "Tell me! Do I have to – to –tell you I love you? Is *that* what you need to hear?" she sobbed.

His face untightened. A hint of a smile formed. He sighed and ran a hand across His face.

"No. Don't say anything. Just–"

"I love you okay?!" she continued. "Don't say we're over. I'm your girlfriend and you're my boyfriend. Okay?"

He waited.

"Okay?" the question vibrated softly, desperately.

He looked at His phone. The time behind Danika's grinning picture read 11:57 PM.

"Text me at exactly 1:05."

"Why?" Danika sniffled.

"Just do it."

"Why?"

"Just - fucking - do - it," He spoke through gritted teeth.

"What am I texting?"

"Anything. How you're feeling. When your last period was. What you had for breakfast. What the subsequent crap after breakfast was like. Your thoughts on ontogeny recapitulating phylogeny."

"Onto-who?"

"It doesn't matter."

"Can you please tell me why 1:05?"

"Because," He began, rubbing His temples, "I want to know that you are checking your phone for me enough to track the time and be responsible."

"Okay," she responded after a moment.

"Alright. Bye."

"Wait?"

"What?"

"Are you mad at me?"

"Bye."

"Wait – we're not allowed to hang up until the conversation is over. These are *your* rules and *I* follow them."
"Okay. What is it?"
"Are you mad at me?"
"Yes. Of course I am."
He looked through the window and saw Dustin gesturing something to Alex and the crowd. They all fell back on the couch, clutching their sides and laughing. He saw Dustin smile and look down as they all laughed.
"You *were* mad at me," Danika whispered over the fading music, "but I love you, and admitted it to you – which you didn't say back, which is fine, but… are you going to be mad at me after you hang up?"
He watched as Dustin's face turned away from the others and, in a flash, twisted with anguish. Dustin turned back to Alex, laughing and slapping his knee, as if on cue.
"If I say no, will you let me hang up?" He whispered to His phone.
"Only if you mean it," Danika breathed back to Him.
"Then I will not be mad at you after we hang up."
"Okay," her voice cooed. "I miss you."
He paused.
"I miss you too. Good night."
"Night."
He hung up and paced back to Alex's house. When the clock read 1:05 He had already checked His phone sixty-five times. At 1:07 He texted her:

Me: DONE. ENJOY YOUR STUPID FUCKING SHOW. (1:07)

His phone vibrated a minute later with Danika's grin flashing. He got up slowly and left the room and stepped outside. He clicked the ACCEPT button. Music blasted from the phone's speaker.
"Wish – do-" her voice faded in and out beyond the jam-band music, "-set rules!?" she cried. "Why – be – fun?"
"Dani, I can't fucking hear you."

"You – I'm – have a good - and probably – smoke – bull –"

He looked at the phone and ended the call.

"How many cunts does it take?" He squeezed the phone tightly.

"Well, man-" Alex appeared by the back door, watching Him with his arms crossed, "-you clearly didn't listen to my advice. As your friend, I extend a very tender 'fuck you' into your night."

"I did listen!" He shouted.

"No!" Alex shouted back. "You didn't! You said, presumably-" he swayed his arm in a cynical gesticulation at the word, "-that you don't love her, *like* her, whatever. But then you picked up your god-damned phone when she called you."

He watched Alex silently.

"Not exercising logic there, man." Alex turned around and began walking back inside.

He remained in the darkness. After a moment of idle silence, He reached for His phone and began texting Art.

Me: I can't tell if I still love her, or if I just desperately want to be in love again, or if I am just trying to like myself again. (11:55)

He clutched His chest and took slow, deep breaths. By His third exhalation, His phone vibrated.

Art: You're making a mistake, and you're going to hate yourself if you don't cut her out of your life. I thought you two broke up like a month ago? You told me that you were finally done with all of her craziness. (11:56)

His phone vibrated again.

Art: By the way bro you have to meet my friend's cousin Mary. She's Greek (huge booty). She saw a picture of us and digs you (her vision is bad I

guess haha). I put in the good word. She's a photographer. Could be good medicine for you bro. (11:58)

He snorted and began texting back.

Me: If she's a good person you should keep her far from me. (11:59)

June 29th 2011
...*kill myself?... Mary... Mandy... May... how many cunts?...*

Immediately upon entering the Starbucks around the corner from the Queens School, His eyes beheld the tan girl in the white capris sitting cross-legged near the far corner, scrolling down her cellphone. He passed by the line of customers and moved towards the empty seat beside her. He pulled out His cell phone charger, reached down to the outlet, and attempted to place the charger into the socket. The plug fell out. He attempted to enter it in again, and again the plug fell out. He glanced upwards to the tan girl as she continued scrolling.
"This outlet is too loose for my charger. Can I plug into yours?" He indicated the outlet below her legs.
"Sure," she spoke to her phone.
"It may vibrate a few times, because I'm, like, really popular."
She looked down at Him.
"Is that so?" Her honey-colored eyes hinted amusement.
"I think so. It's what my mom tells me." He placed His cell phone on the seat, crouched to the outlet next to her, slipped His cord into the port just next to her long dark legs, and smiled. He turned around and moved towards the bar.
"Iced Grande Mocha Frappuccino, please," He requested, extending a five-dollar bill to the shaggy-haired barista.

"Name?" the barista asked Him, his pen hovering above the plastic cup.

"I don't have one." He shrugged.

"Ah. You. The manager told me about You. The guy with no name. I'm one of the new people they just hired." The barista pointed to his tag. "I'm Nemo. Welcome back, sir."

"Thanks." He nodded and received His change.

The girl stood up, walked towards Him, and tapped His shoulder. He turned around. His cell phone rested on the seat behind her.

"You, like, totally planned it to vibrate that much." She grinned – her tan complexion contrasting her teeth, which seemed to glow with whiteness. "Some girl named Mary just sent you like a billion texts."

"That sounds like Mary." He watched His phone vibrate on the seat.

"Mocha Frappuccino for…" the barista struggled, "…umm…Him?" he pointed.

He spun around to face the barista, and received His drink.

"That's a pretty flamboyant drink for a guy," the girl jested.

"I order it to hide how truly masculine I am," He defended.

She nibbled her straw and ran her fingers through her hair. His eyes glistened. He looked behind her grinning face and saw several construction workers staring at her ass, whispering to each other and performing sexual gesticulations.

"There's a group of good-looking men staring at your ass right behind you. We should give them a show." He took her hand softly. "Tell me which one you think is the most gorgeous."

He spun her slowly, as the construction workers laughed in excitement.

"I think the one with the man-boobs and the unibrow."

"Ah, love is abreast. Let's go talk to him."

"Nooooo!" she begged. "How do you even know I'm single?"

"You're too attractive for a guy with any sense to try to pick you up."

"Are you suggesting that you have no sense?"

"Are you suggesting that I'm trying to pick you up?" She smiled and sipped.

"Well played."

"Thank you." He smiled. "When are you heading back to QS, Lizzie?"

A moment passed.

"Do I know you? How do you know my name?"

"Your name is on your coffee cup and you have a QS bag. So where are you headed?"

"I am heading towards QS, actually. Summer classes. You?"

"Opposite direction. But because we're dating now I guess I have to walk you at least half-way." He wrapped His arm around hers. "Let's go, honey bunch."

"Do you, like, pick up every girl that you talk to at Starbucks?"

"Yup. Every single one. Guys too. I also like to diversify to Dunkin Donuts. I feel the name of that particular establishment better suits my intentions."

He looked down at the empty cup in His free hand.

"Hmm... I guess I need more coffee."

"Wow. You inhaled that. Was that even a minute?"

He shrugged, and walked back towards the register. A new barista with no nametag on his shirt stood, waiting and watching Him as He approached him. He looked at His eyes, then at Lizzie who was tapping her feet behind Him, then back at Him. He looked at the man's large, green eyes. The two stood silently for a moment, each seemingly searching the other.

Chet Baker's instrumental *Anticipated Blues* filled with its bouncing sound. He placed His hand on His heart. His phone vibrated loudly on the seat behind Him.

"Just a black iced coffee. Nothing in it," He spoke hoarsely.

"Name?" the man barked.
He opened His mouth. No sound came out.
"Name?" the man repeated impatiently. "Give me your name, so they know what's yours."
He looked at the pen in the man's hand hovering over a clear plastic cup, then at the man. A large, silver cross hung from his neck.
Lizzie's phone rang.
"Dance – Dance – Dance – Dance – Dance – Dance Everywhere we'll dance. Everything will dance."
"I-" His voice cracked. He cleared His throat as His eyes watered. "My name…"
The barista sighed and slowly scraped three gray question marks on the cup – each producing an unforgiving wine. He looked at the cup's '???', and then glanced back at Lizzie. A cloud passed over the sun. Her tan skin and honey-hued eyes had paled. His phone continued vibrating. He walked across the café and picked it up.

Mary (21 unread): Earth to Mr. Noname. Do you or do you not want to see me again? (12:08)

His phone vibrated in His hands.

Duschey: Ur confusing me :((12:09)

His phone rang. Danika's face appeared. He pressed the ignore button.
"I gotta go," He wheezed, holding His heart.
"What?" Lizzie tilted her tan head. "We like-"
"No," He spoke before sprinting quickly out of the café, gagging, covering His mouth with one hand while the other clenched His chest.

July 21st 2011
…it's all over next week… Dustin… doesn't matter…

The nighttime air shimmered with a perpetual mist, graying the soft-rippling pool water and sparkling the grass with silver patterns as He sat in the darkness of His backyard on a wet chaise. He stared at His most recent text from Alex.

Alex: DUSTIN IS IN JAIL COMING OVER NOW. (9:39)
Me (unsent draft): Good.

A wind passed. He brushed His hand over the goosebumps on His wet neck.

"Yo!" the figure of Alex called out, emerging from the outdoor breezeway to the pool area with a cup in his hand and a tobacco-bump jutting out of his lower lip.

He nodded.

"You won't believe this shit, man." Alex shook his head. "Are you ready to hear this?" Alex stopped and looked around. "Wait – why are you laying outside in the rain?"

"It feels right," He spoke, watching the outline of Alex's dark face tilt. "Are you going to tell me the story?"

"You're a strange woman, but alright." Alex lifted the hood of his jacket over his head. "Dustin went out Friday night, and apparently he was parading around the city shouting about how he was the leader of the Back to Africa movement, and hailing cabs only to stop the Arabic drivers to ask how many terrorists they were hiding. Just fucking absurd shit. But anyway-" Alex spat into his cup, "-he arrived at my house at around 4 AM, and me being a friend, I let him in. As usual, he was loud and completely obnoxious, and left the TV on with the volume up, which I've already yelled at him about."

"Why doesn't he just turn it off?"

"He doesn't like knowing he's alone, but that's not the point."

"I mean... it's your fucking home though."

"I know. He should respect that. But listen-" Alex spat into his cup again. "He wakes up at my house at around 9 AM, which is when his shift starts at Vane's Diner. But he has stains all over his shirt and doesn't want to show up like that since it's only his third week there. What the stains are from – I have not the slightest clue. A good amount of it is probably-" Alex swooshed the tobacco cup in the air, and spat again. "Anyway, he drives to his house-" the silhouette of Alex leaned in towards Him, shaking his head and lifting his arms upwards as if in defeat, "-and fucking JERKS OFF before changing!"

He stared motionlessly at the dark figure of Alex.

"I know, man. It's fucking absurd."

"The kid has a problem, Alex," He spoke finally

"One of many. Yeah. So he gets to the restaurant an hour or so late instead of ten or fifteen minutes late. It's only his third week, so, you know, they fired his ass. He tried to lie about having an asthma attack but they didn't buy it. By the way – he was wearing the same stained shirt. The idiot forgot to change."

He chuckled quietly. Distant thunder rumbled.

"Alright – so it gets so much worse. Instead of work, Dustin goes to the bar. He calls me at 11 AM, but I was asleep. I wake up a little after noon, saw the fuck's missed call, and tried to connect with him, but it went straight to voicemail."

"Where was he?"

"I don't know. But apparently he was in and out of the bar."

"Hamilton's? Do they even serve alcohol that early?"

"Apparently he charmed them. So from 11 AM to around 7 PM, Dustin was drinking."

"Hmm."

"The bartender – Vera – the tall blonde whose name you never remember. She-"

"She never remembers *my name*!" He interrupted.

"Very funny, man. You don't even have a name." Alex smiled and shook his head. "So listen and stop fucking interrupting, man. Vera told me that Dustin was in and out of the bathroom, and each time he came back he was sniffling and acting jittery, grinding his teeth like a mad man and twisting his hands."

"How can that fat fuck even afford coke at this point?"

"His grandparents. You know that. So get this: At around eight at night he hops on the LIRR to go to the city to buy coke from one of his dealers. Allegedly, he bought an obscene amount. Later, Dustin was outside of a bar and was just blowing coke on the street – on top of newspaper dispensers and shit – because he thinks he's invincible." Alex spat and made a theatrical movement with his shadowed hand. "An UNDER-fucking-COVER cop sees him, walks up to him and just asks him 'are you fucking serious?' Dustin has the coke literally in his hands and nose in public."

"Okay."

"So he gets taken in and they find like dozens of unaddressed parking tickets and a recent DUI charge that he never responded to. They call his step-dad, Mario. He hears what happened and just hangs up and doesn't tell Dustin's mom. She finds out this afternoon when they called a second time. So she tells Dustin's stepdad that she is going to bail him out, and his stepdad says if Dustin comes back home in this next year he's leaving the family."

He looked up to the black sky and looked back down to Alex.

"Alright."

"So, besides the fact that Mario's position is ridiculous as it doesn't logically help the problem, Dustin is going to be in jail for at least a year."

"Good."

"Excuse me?" Alex recoiled.

Lightning flashed above, shining the mist all around them. In the illumination, Alex's face: Concerned, eyebrows sinking below his glasses, mouth parted. His face: Calm, low-eyed, soft-smiled, accepting.

"It's good that Dustin is in jail." He shrugged. "He needs it."

Thunder cracked loudly across the skies. The mist thickened into rainfall.

"What? Why the fuck would that be a good thing?"

"Because he'll be forced to stop his destructive habits. Dustin has deserved jail for a while now. It can be his rehab, though I'm sure he'll make a few friends there."

"That-" Alex spat into his cup, "-is FUCKING insane! That's our FUCKING friend and you say it's a good fucking thing that he's in jail? What the fuck is wrong with you, you psychopath?" The shadow of Alex's figure stepped backwards. "Talk to me when you're ready to be fucking logical about this, man." He turned around and walked back towards the breezeway, towards the driveway, and towards his car.

From where He remained – now drenched in the pluvial, shadowy backyard – the engine of Alex's car could be heard revving as he sped off.

"Fuck you, too."

July 22nd 2011
...*Dani*... *fugacious gift*... *Wednesday*... *embarcadero to Elysium*... *cenotaph*...

The rainy morning skies poured forth color-seeping darkness into the crowded Rising Star Café as He sat by the window, watching the cars pass, watching the next wave of recently graduated high school trundle by hidden under their umbrellas. His phone vibrated on the table. He sighed and reached for it, picked it up and faced the home screen. In the texts screen, His eyes pass over the sixty-five character preview of each person's most recent text:

(2 unread) Bro: I didn't get those edits. Did u send them? Send them again before...
(1 unread) Art: Stop being a dick. Mary is a crazy wreck. At least talk to the po...
(5 unread) Mother: Everything alright? - ma :)
(8 unread) Mary: Yes 4 tmrw night despite ungodly hour. Now ur turn 2 answer my qu...

He looked up and saw Mandy Rusche standing over Him.

"Hey," He spoke, covering the paper.

"Did you *really* have to fuck my little sister?" Mandy hissed, her eyes a narrowing conflagration. "You do realize she *just* got out of rehab. She already has problems. She doesn't need a drop-out, drugged-out, manipulative loser like *you* to add to them."

Café-goers turned to them. Mandy caught eyes with a group of young female students.

"This kid writes notes about how to manipulate and fuck girls. He thinks he's some sort of a pick-up artist."

"Pick up… artist?" He looked around helplessly.

"Don't pretend you don't know what that is!" she shouted. "You just use people, and you're using my fucking sister and-"

"That's not true at all." He shook His head, and then grabbed His chest, wincing.

Mandy paused and smiled.

"Hunter showed us the one where you give a girl a nickname so she feels like you and her have this secret world together," Mandy lectured to the crowd. "Very clever. My name was 'Muschey'. And Dani was 'Duschey'. Very creative. You can be 'douchey'." Mandy laughed. "I really like the one where you pick a part of a girl's body and give it backwards compliments repeatedly, making her insecure without sounding mean and making her want to validate herself to you."

He shook His head, still clenching His chest.

"I don't do an-"

"How cool is this guy? He knows how to *get girls*. Pig!" Mandy glanced at the barista who was leaning forward intently. "The element of surprise… it's a bitch isn't it?"

She glared down at the paper He was covering, laughed again, and turned away. He watched the sun tattoo on her neck shrink until she vanished outside. He looked down, moved His hands from the paper, and read:

Schedule for July 28th, 2011:
  - Leave at 8:00 AM for Montauk Point. Should be there by 11:00. Should be dead by 7:00.

  - Try to answer how much a life is worth / what the cost of a human's life is
  Bring:
  - 3 Tabs (200-300 micrograms/tab.)

- *Pack of reds*
- *Tobacco-dip & spitting bottle*
- *1.75 ml bottle of Single-malt scotch-whiskey*
- *Two pens and a pad of paper*
- *One dozen water bottles*

July 23rd 2011
…dulciloquence… delitescent dalliances… why did Mary even bother…

At 11:11 PM, the pale and petite figure of Mary entered into the dimness of Hamilton's Tavern. For a moment, as the moonlight through the shutting door shone upon her curling waves of dark hair, she closely resembled Selene. Her typically crystal-blue eyes scanned grayly between the passing masses of bodies towering around her. He watched her between the coats, and smiled whenever He caught a flash of her somber face. She found Him sitting from the corner booth, and smiled back to Him. He turned down to His whiskey, lifted the glass up to His face, and poured the Jack Daniels down between grimacing lips.

Chet Baker's *Little Girl Blue* began playing, starting with, '*Sit there, count your fingers…*'

By the time He placed the glass down on the wooden table, she sat before Him.

"You lost your tan," she spoke.

"I lost all my colors," He responded quickly.

The waitress placed a new glass in front of Him. He looked down at the ice swirling around the clear amber liquid. He looked up from the glass towards her lips, which moved as if practicing words.

"Explain to me, please-" the gray discs of her low-lidded eyes remained on the glass, "-why all of a sudden you don't want to be with me."

"Do you remember when we first met, Mary?"

"Yes. Artyom's beach party. A month and three days ago."

"Right, and do you remember the first words I said to you?"

"That I reminded you of a scene from Fitzgerald's 'The Beautiful and The Damned'."

"'*The Beautiful and Damned*'," He corrected. "There's no second 'the'. The beautiful *are* damned. And you remind me of a character named Dot." He paused, His eyes scanning across the bar and then returning to Mary who was leaning towards Him. His eyes bounced from her fingers, to her eyes, to her body. "Do you remember me talking about how the book strikes a lovely balance between love's intrinsic perseverance and love's immense potential for self-annihilation?"

She nodded, a reminiscing smile glowing from her face. The music lowered. Hunter Douglas Quillan Wilcox-Himmler II appeared, stammering towards the jukebox in the corner. He grinned furiously. A wave of bodies passed by him, and he vanished in their stream.

"And then we spoke about painting," He continued, "and art, and you told me about how you don't trust or even like people, and then I told you that I just got out of a relationship with a heroin addict, and then you spoke about your parents' divorce, and how your father is a chef, and that you used to starve yourself to rebel against him, thinking that that was a way to not rely on him or be in his debt, and how that led to anorexia nervosa, and that it made you stop having your period – which you thought was great until you started getting stomach aches every day and had to have a piece of your lower intestines taken out – and now you wonder if it's the work of a derisive god who wouldn't let you enjoy not having to deal with the female burden of menstrual pains, and then we spoke about associations and sociological conditioning mechanisms. And later I relayed to you my fear that I've associated psychology – something I've loved and craved to master since my mother was first ill – with not learning anything at BS, and how that fills me with absolute dread, and makes me sincerely despise a large portion of my own development, almost as if the majority of me was rendered a cadaver."

"Yes." Mary smiled, showing her small white teeth. Her eyes still fixated on His amber glass with the diaphanous cubes. "That's exactly how it began."

"And do you remember what you felt during this?"

Mary paused.

"What do you mean?"

"It's a simple question. Can you approximate the sensation you experienced during our frescade along the estuary of Art's beach beneath the nebulae of a clear evening?"

A tender trumpet sounded somberly over a trickling piano.

"Intrigue?"

"You felt alive. You felt awakened and excited to hear a new voice teach and portray a world to you. You felt aroused and enlivened and important by the increasingly veritable prospect that your voice could teach and portray your world to someone new. You felt increasingly confident that you and I were making a connection - that the center of the Venn-diagram of our individual worlds was expanding with every articulation. You felt the way you feel when you forget there's other people around you – when the world folds away in inconspicuous patterns, and the noises of other voices become backgrounded to the sound of your quickened heartbeat. And there was that moment when you walked away from me, and sat on the swing, and waited for me to walk to you – which I did – and you pretended to examine your sandals, and then you looked up at me with that face, that alluring face. If I could have placed my ear softly against the surface of your coruscating thoughts, I could maybe even *hear* your inner nymph commanding 'kiss me'." He took another sip of His whiskey. "I knew you didn't like your friend's boyfriend – the overweight blond-haired idiot who drove the beige Cadillac sedan, blasting Lizzie Manibasse which the closed windows thankfully muffled. I could see by the diminutive squint, the lowered eyebrows, the pursed lips, the crossed arms, the tapped foot, the closed body, the re-angled frame, the sharper breathing, and your little closed fists that when he called your friend - his apparent girlfriend -

'babers' - that you did not like him. And it makes sense. None of you know that he is cheating on her, but he is, and every reason why he is cheating on her is why you hate him. Egocentricity, arrogance, presumptuousness, lack-of-depth, a sense of entitlement, a needless competitive nature, and the overall way he simply lumbered around the beach like a tranquilized alpha-bear. You and I dislike the same things, but I could see that you *really* despised him, with disgust radiating visibly off of your every follicle, just like how I can tell right now by the dilation of your unusually gray eyes, the way your finger is running up and down your water glass, the slight parting of your lips, and the vacuuming body language that you're thinking of sex with me right now even though I am just giving you a pointless amount of-"

A white-vested waitress walked by their table. The music faded mid-song.

"Will you be having another?"

"I will," He responded.

The waitress turned to Mary, and Mary shook her head. The waitress turned around and walked towards the bar.

He leaned back.

"-amount of detail," He concluded. "But what was I thinking, Mary?"

Outside, Mandy and Danika Rusche were walking down Plandome Road. A shooting star sparkled above, glittering across the humid, night-blue umbra. Mandy's smoldering eyes followed its trajectory until it extinguished above the tavern. She turned to her sister. Danika continued gazing at her feet as she trotted, a frown weighing down her round face.

"Wanna grab a drink, sis?" Mandy asked, her voice a tender invitation.

A wind passed, lifting Danika's wild, golden curls. Her blue eyes lifted and peered through the window. Immediately, Danika spotted Him sitting beside a skinny girl with dark hair. Her pupils dilated.

"No. Not tonight. Don't really feel like drinking." She scratched her palms as they ambled along.

A plane scraped across the sky, heading towards JFK. His father was among the 165 passengers inside.

Inside, Mary had answered: "I don't know. About yourself, probably. Or that I'm just another of your billion girls."

"A solipsist wouldn't have listened to your words with such attention, and we both know your latter answer is reductive." He shook His head. "If you can imagine a multitude of conflicting demands shouting in a crowded room, you'll know how I think. At that time, my thoughts were: 'Why must every girl I like sit on the third swing closest to the water at Art's beach? Is this a rebound from a rebound's rebound? Are you as seductive as Mandy, poetic as Selene, or as wild as Danika? What do your breasts look like underneath your black romper? Are they larger than Dani's or at least Selene's? Could I use your love to reconstruct my crippled identity? Why are you so readable? So artless? What would your legs around my neck feel like and am I right in thinking you a virgin?' The latter cognition being corroborated first by the aforementioned bovine blond boy when he threw his arm on my shoulder during my until-then-uninterrupted urination – an attempted gesture of dominance – and asked me if I possessed a proclivity for, and I quote, 'cherry-popping'."

Mary shuddered and crossed her arms over her chest.

"You must be proud for being right all the time," she spoke, her eyes remained fixed on His glass.

"If I was wrong about what I've said, you'd need not respond with acerbity."

"What does any of this have anything to do with you no longer wanting to be with me?"

"I already told you, Mary, in so, so many words." He moved the glass closer to Himself, disconnecting Mary's gaze. She looked up to Him with glistening eyes. "You're too good."

He tossed the liquid down His opened mouth. The glass was now empty. The waitress reappeared and placed a new glass in front of Him, smiled and walked away. Mary's gray eyes narrowed.

"I don't understand what that means."

He nodded knowingly.

"You're too innocent. Too proper. Too happy," He clarified, shaking His head. "There are not enough compliments I can give you to properly detail why you and I are incompatible."

"Then why did you have an interest in me in the first place?" Her eyes sunk down from His, and gravitated to the new glass.

"Because you're attractive, Mary. You're a very attractive girl." He rolled blood-shot eyes. "You're an incredibly desirable girl, Mary"

"But why were you so-" her eyes seemed to struggle upwards from the glass to meet His gaze as a faint blush rose to her pale cheeks, "-forward with me?"

"Forward?" He waited. She waited. He waited. She waited. A grin built across His face. "You mean how was it that you were naked in my bed on our third rendezvous?"

She flickered a smile.

"You think I'm dumb, don't you?" She asked crossing her arms.

His phone vibrated. He looked down at the text.

Art: Bro she's nice, funny, an artist like you, has those sad blueish eyes you love, and is crazy about you for some reason. What is your problem? Just give the girl a fucking chance (10:52)

His eyes lingered on 'fucking chance'.

"I don't think you're dumb at all," He spoke towards His phone, and then looked up to Mary. "I don't." He shoved His phone into His jacket pocket and leaned back. "I think you are just structured, and ordered, and expected... and too good for me."

"Boring, then?"

"No." His hand squeezed into a fist beneath the table. "Those are different words and mean different things. I genuinely believe you are too good for me"

An old, white-haired man with a gray cap sat down at the bar and looked up towards the basketball game on the television.

"Explain the difference to me."

"Great." He nodded to the white-haired man. "That man has no idea what he's doing being here. Walking in as we're speaking. How his presence is altering the whole scene."

"What?"

"No character can be in a room without sentences of meaning dripping off their actions, entirely redefining the context of everything."

"Huh?"

"Never mind. Please say 'Pardon' not 'Huh?' I've told you before it sounds plebian."

"YES!" the white-haired man shouted, swinging his fist through the air.

"It speaks!" He laughed.

Mary shook her head, shaking the jet curls around her face.

"Explain the difference between being boring and being expected."

"No," He responded through gritted teeth. "It's not important."

"Why?"

"Oh my GOD, MARY!" He groaned. Faces turned, glances beheld them, and a white-vested waitress whispered wildly to another white-vested waitress. The old man looked over his shoulder at them, and then turned back to the basketball game. "Why are you interrogating me for pardoning you from a world of tenebrous morbidity? Why?"

"Why are you so negative about yourself? You're smart, you speak well… you might have more hate than love right now, but you're really a nice g-"

"Okay!" He stopped her. "I – do – not – want-" He paused, staring at her, unblinking, nodding slowly, "-to – be –

with – you. I do not want to be with you. The more you try to make me like you, the more I will try not to like you. And I have no idea how you could possibly want to be with me."

"But sex-" she began

"JESUS!" The man shouted to the television as he jumped out of his seat. He slapped the table, as the second foul shot was missed. "GET YOUR FUCKING HEAD IN THE GAME!" he demanded.

"Sex with you was brilliant. Besides that, I want nothing except freedom from you. I'm not capable of anything more, especially love."

"How can you say you're not capable of love?"

"Because I am not. It's all just numbers and bodies. It used to be so much more. The skin and eyes and preternatural messages radiating off of every subtle suggestion of romance-"

"So I really am just a number to you?"

"A little more. Seventy-two, though, if you must know. First virgin."

"I'm someone too, you know!" she shouted, pounding her little fist down onto the table. "Just because we're not together anymore doesn't mean I don't exist anymore, that I'm not a real living human being who has thoughts and problems and talents and flaws and shit to deal with."

"Mary," He paused, His sunken eyes blazing towards her, "it's not like we were ever *really* together."

Her eyes glistened immediately.

"What the fuck is wrong with you?" Mary hissed, rising from the table. "Why are you such a fucking asshole?" She turned around and raced towards the exit. She shot Him an unforgiving glance as the door shut out her white figure and the black evening.

A tear fell into the amber liquid, producing – for a moment - a clouded haze.

"Good," He whispered after a moment passed.

"THERE WE GO!" the old man swung triumphantly through the air.

Another tear fell. He swiped His cheeks, inhaling and exhaling deeply. He grimaced and clutched His heart with both hands.

"YEAH BABY! THAT'S HOW YOU DO IT!" The man slapped the table repeatedly. "THAT'S HOW YOU DO IT! THAT'S HOW YOUhhuhn-"

He lifted from His seat, blasted towards the bar, pulled the old man's swinging stool around, and put His face inches from his.

"IT'S JUST A FUCKING GAME!" He screamed, standing over him. "STOP FUCKING CARING! READ SOMETHING!"

The old man's eyes widened, fear and shock in his dilated pupils. He let go of the old man's seat, moved back to His table, and swigged the remaining whiskey from His glass. Silent stares scrutinized Him as He slammed the glass down on the table, rustled out two twenty-dollar bills, tossed them onto the table, and exited through the back.

He stepped into His car and turned the ignition. The screen displayed 11:33 PM. He stared at the brick wall of Hamilton's back entrance. Two voices on the radio spoke. He raised the volume.

FEMALE REPORTER
...tuned in, we have breaking news. Singer, Elizabeth 'Lizzie' Manibasse, was found dead in her New York City apartment shortly after 3:30 PM today. The official cause of death, post-biopsy, is an overdose of the narcotic heroin.

MALE REPORTER
The 27-year-old star has had a world-documented problem with alcohol and drugs. Only three weeks ago she had left her second stint in drug rehabilitation. Officials found a short note with just the words 'controlled substance' scribbled in what has been confirmed to be her handwriting.

FEMALE REPORTER
Truly a deep loss to us all. A truly talented and special young girl. An artist in more ways than one.

MALE REPORTER
This just in - more sad news, apparently…

"Lizzie Manibasse is dead," He whispered, switching the radio off.

He stared forward at the red brick-walls of Hamilton's backside. He waited in silence for a half hour, and then started the engine. He drove out of the parking lot, down Plandome Road, and eastwards on Northern Boulevard – heading towards His house. He reached into the center console and extracted a half-empty bottle of whiskey. The label was torn off the 1-liter glass. He took a swig, emptying the remains of the burning liquid down His throat. He coughed, and then tossed the bottle into the back seat.

"Lizzie Manibasse is dead," He repeated.

Less than a half-mile from His house, the white letters of Ainsworth's beamed towards Him. He turned the car sharply into the empty parking lot. He parked in a handicapped space, opened the door and wobbled out. Tears rolled down His cheeks as He stammered towards the entrance. He pressed His face against the glass, and looked inside the darkness. Chairs were upside down on top of tables. He looked around, as if tracing projections of people.

The tears were now streaming down the windows panes. The glass began vibrating as He began laughing. Restrained chuckles loudened into shrill, hysterical shrieking.

July 24th 2011
…*Lovejoy… Art… usurper?... three days… I can't wait…*

He was standing in His parents' room, staring in the mirror. He gazed down at the suit He was wearing, back up to a drop of sweat moving slowly down His forehead, and then back over His mirrored shoulder at His father moving back and forth talking with a Bluetooth in his ear.

"Okay Sanjeev, call me when you get the results," His father spoke.

He glanced down at His cellphone. There were notifications for four texts.

Bro: It's only four pages bro. You can do it in 2 seconds. If you could proofread it by tonight that would be awesome. See you soon bro. (5:16)

"Yes - yes. I'm feeling fine, Sanjeev," His father continued, running a hand over his chest. "No, no problems today. No coronary spasms, ischemic pain, vasovagal responses, nothing." His father laughed. "Feeling good for an old man!"

Art: Have a good time tonight bro! Say hi to your pop and Dr. Sanjeev (5:22)

"Low. Not too low, but low. 70-80. Manageable. The Beta-blockers are doing their job."

Alex: Wanna kick back and blaze later you big depressed homo? (5:29)

"I- yes. Oh - tell Bina I say hello as well. Give everyone my love. Of course. Of course, they'll all be there. I'll see you all tonight. I speak at 7:30. Yes. 8:00, with their expediency. Yes. Alright. Bye."

Duschey: I guess I can meet up at 8:00 if you're around. When do you get back from the city? (5:31)

"Yes. Alright. Bye."
His father removed the Bluetooth from his ear and turned to His reflection.
"You look nice, son."
"'Nice' is my least favorite word."
"Pardon my immigrant English, son," His father mused. "Why is 'nice' your least favorite word?"

"Because it shares the etymological root with the word 'ignorance', and it's generally used when a there is no meaningful compliment to provide. If I ever call anyone nice, I'm usually insulting them."

"Then-" His father considered, "-you look *fantastic*."

"That shares the same root as 'fantasy'."

His father walked towards Him, staring calculatingly at His shoulders and upper back.

"What's wrong?"

"I don't really feel comfortable."

"Is it too tight? Too loose? You've lost some weight since I last saw you."

He placed his hands on the sides of his son's body, patting up and down, and scrutinizing his eyes in the mirror.

"Everything okay?"

He stared back at His father.

"Is it alright at all if I could sit this one out?"

"Sit this one out?" His father repeated, squinting at His reflection. "Are you sick?"

"No. I just… don't feel comfortable."

"What is making you feel uncomfortable, son? Talk to me."

"I don't know. I just would rather not see everyone."

"See who? Why don't you want to see anyone? What's the big deal? You're going to be sitting down and eating a wonderful dinner and meeting a bunch of remarkable young minds and beautiful girls. Take my word for it. You're going to have a nice…" His father paused, contemplating, "…an amazing time."

"I know. I just - I rather just stay home-"

"And do what all night? Nothing? Write? Smoke marijuana? Go out and drink with your moron friends? Do you have any idea how many twenty-year-old men would kill to have the luxury to attend this dinner? To learn from these people? You can talk about the wind book you're writing. Dr. Lovejoy asks about you and your book every time we talk, and have you emailed him back since the dinner last month? No. That gives people a bad impression of you. Very bad. And his brother-in-law is the COO of Halcyon Publishing

House – the third largest in the business. If I was in your position, I would stop being arrogant, reconsider all of the luxuries I have, and beg my dad to go to an event like this."
"I'm not like you. I just-" He sighed and turned around.
His father's cell phone rang. The name Dr. Lovejoy appeared on the screen.
"Do it, at the least, to network for your book."
"I don't want to network. I don't want to do anything like that."
"YOU'RE GOING!" His father stepped out of the room and placed the Bluetooth back in his ear.
"I just-"
"PRICK! UNGRATEFUL, ARROGANT PRICK!" His father shouted as he descended the stairs.

July 25th 2011
Dr. Henry Hallward Heidelberg: *Please help me understand… what exactly is causing you to feel so miserable?*
Him: It's just so fucking obvious that I've ruined everything and let everyone down. I've done everything wrong. I've made so many mistakes. I fucking hate it. I hate making mistakes. I hate it. I didn't - I didn't become what anyone wanted. I didn't-

Piaget would say that our cognitive development is actually shaped by our mistakes, but what exactly did people want you to become?
What did they want me to become? Mandy wanted me to become her fucking human vibrator, and Selene wanted me not to have a licentious past, and Dani wanted me to replace her heroin addiction as an anxiolytic nepenthe, and Dustin wanted me to empathize with his inability to sympathize, and Art wanted me to just be a good person who can mirror his apostolicity, and Ollie wanted god knows what if it wasn't just someone with whom he could dream in interminable soundscapes, and my dad wanted me to be a business-wise science-man who makes profits, and my mom wanted me to respect her even though I was already done mourning the maternal elements of her when I was twelve, and my brother

wanted me to be his dependable inferior even though we are complete opposites, and I once wanted to be a psychiatrist like you – but now I associate psychology with wasting everyone's time and money - and then I wanted to be a writer – but now that just makes me think of Selene and misery – and now I don't know what I am or if I can even really be... anything...

I've asked you before and I'll ask you again: How could you possibly balance such contradicting expectations?
I can't. I couldn't. Not anymore. Everyone sees me now as a stupid, broken-down loser. Mandy and Selene and Dani don't even know me anymore. Everyone loathes me, and I wish I could have something to say about myself that could contradict any of it, but I don't even know who I am enough to do so. I'm just a sick, nauseous frame.

What reason do you really have to really think everyone sees you so wickedly?
The Looking Glass Self is shattered Henry, and somewhere a masked Charles Cooley weeps in a Borgesian gallery. My father thinks I'm a prick. It's the last thing he said to me before this dinner conference last night. Dani knows just as well as Mandy and Selene do that I am pathetic. Alex sees me as a basket case. Dustin is in jail because he's an idiot. And I am restlessly ensnared in a... zugzwang...

From our past conversations, you said with confidence – and I still agree – that we are often at the whims of the people around us... so, do you really think you actually destroyed anything, or that there is something else wrong?
I destroyed it all. From dropping out of BS and QS, to disobeying everything my family asked for, to lusting so strongly for the lust of others. I've done everything the wrong way, and now I am paying for it. And I'm so sick and tired of everything. I'm so tired. Yet, every night I'm restless, pacing back and forth – walking left and right, east and west, glancing at different mirrors but always seeing the same stranger. I'm waiting for something to change, but I know

I'm too gone to even see if something good was in front of me.

Are you really convinced that you're too corrupted to change and do any good, especially considering that feral imagination of yours?
First of all, I don't have an imagination. My imagination is not mine. My own emotions are barely mine. I would love to speak colloquially with you, and say I feel as if ideas just 'pop' into my head, fully-defined and justified in their complexity. But that's not it. It's not enough, and it's not what is happening. I was the amanuensis of an intermittently-active dream machine, and, as I've destroyed all of the good functioning forces around me, Dr. Heidelberg, I have become the amanuensis of an intermittently-active nightmare machine. I'm just a shell of a… barely a… misanthropic…

Don't you think it's just the explicable migraine of trying to do too much, trying to mix together too many things to possibly perform?
Do too much? Aren't you listening, Henry? I haven't *done* anything! I haven't accomplished a fucking thing. Not a single thing. I've failed everything and everyone. I've failed in any concinnity, have rendered my environment a miasma, have failed in… and… Émile Durkheim describes four types of suicide - fatalistic, anomic, altruistic and egoistic - and each one is based on the levels of imbalance between social integration and one's moral regulation. The last one - egoistic suicide - reflects a prolonged sense of not belonging, of being detached from a community, of not having something good to center yourself on. That's me. That's the unhinging of the self. I've destroyed everything. Almost.

Suicide? This suffering and this 'loss of self' you keep claiming - don't you consider, just for a second, that maybe you're just excessively punishing yourself?
Yourself. Myself. Me. I. What am I? What do you think I am? What do you see when you look at me? Am I a seven-and-a-half inch cock upon which 72 girls have sat? Am I the human dildo that that Circean nymph Mandy wanted me to be? Am I an evanescent specter semi-resurrected only by the numinous

reaction of ink, eyes, and the minds of others? Am I the outrageous narcissist who loves the teeth-gritting exothermic release of a single fucking sentence of my own disappearing writing more than I love all of my friends and all of my family combined? Depression. Sex. Addiction. Alcohol. Rage. When is any of it a real problem? My mother… she doesn't understand that her maternal elements died… she's just a woman I love… but every day she treated me like a despicable son. I fucking had to stop speaking to her the last time she made me feel worthless. It's been two-three weeks, now. What part of it is her personality and what part of it is her sickness? Where does the sickness end? When is it just an awful personality? Am I sick? Am I an awful personality? Depression: The self-loathing agony of your worst hangover stretched out boundlessly; the garish glare of fluorescent lights in a hospital waiting room; being surrounded with loved ones and feeling nothing but loneliness and guilt. I know my mother is pretty much alone in that house… especially when I am gone for a long time – and she'll – she'll – she'll – sorry – I'll stop crying no don't try to stop me, Henry, fucking god damn it! She'll text me saying something like 'Hi - how are you? Anything new? - Ma' and add one of those stupid sunglass-smiley faces in the text. After being so wretched! Can you understand how miserable that feeling really is? The pity!? The guilt!? The hatred!? The sadness!? The fakeness!? The reality? And then HA! - then HA! and then I'll wander down the fucking streets of Old Rookvale, or Manhattan, or anywhere, and I'll catch eyes with a girl, and she'll smile at me with her body and eyes and lips, and this stupid fucking cool-relaxed feeling will pass through me, and I know I am so fucking pathetic to actually feel better from a fucking smile, and I fucking know - I fucking KNOW - that I can fuck that girl who catches eyes with me. I know I can fuck her far too quickly to ever deserve fucking her, and far too quickly to ever learn how to ever begin loving her back. I fucking hate her-

Her?

No. Let's cut this one short - no. I'm good. SSNNF I'm good. I'm good...

July 26th 2011
...book in pocket... I'm already dead... especially to...

He walked down the hill His family's house stood atop, staring at His cellphone as it lit the night around Him.

    Me: Where are you going? (8:03)
    Me: We'll be out of each other's lives after tonight, I promise. (8:03)
    Duschey: I'm leaving Old Rookvale tomorrow morning and going to Montauk until late August. (8:08)
    Duschey: I'll be at the bottom of your hill at midnight. (8:11)
    Me (unsent draft): You can't just spend your days surfing at the beach and ignoring... (8:15)

He reached the bottom of the hill, turned left and Danika's car parked ahead. He walked towards the driver seat and motioned her to open the window. They made eye contact. She nodded for Him to come inside. He sighed, walked around the car and entered through the passenger seat.
    "Hey."
    "What's up?" she breathed, her eyes low and lavender-colored. "How's the writing going?"
    "Don't be mean," He responded.
    "I'm being serious. The last section you sent me was nice. I just don't have your vocab."
    He looked ahead, down the long empty road that stretched out into the darkness, and then looked leftwards – passed Danika's face – to another, equally lightless hill that led back to His house.
    "I'm sorry," He spoke. "I'd love to blame everything on me worrying about your addiction, but it was all my mistakes."

Danika turned away quickly, facing the same hill. She scratched the faded lines on her hand.

"It's my fault for pushing you to do things you don't want to do, for thinking I know better just because of one mistake you've made. You're a smart girl when you need to be – and you don't need another judgmental person around you. And-" He turned away and faced the road ahead, "-and I think laughing and eating watermelon and sitting Indian-Style with you in my room while Chet Baker was playing is a beautiful memory I could only have with someone wondrous like you."

"That was when you were playful and not dramatic all the time," she responded, her voice coarser than usual.

"That was when I didn't have to worry, but that's not the point at all." He placed His hand on the door. "The moment you were gone was the moment I began to miss you." He turned to the back seat. "I'm leaving a novel in the backseat by Gabriel Garcia Marquez." He opened the car door. "It's yours, Duschey. Read it cover to cover."

He opened the door, stepped out, closed the door, and walked over to the other side of the car without facing her. He began pacing down Village Road.

Danika's window opened.

"Wait-" She whispered loudly.

He kept walking.

"You're not even heading in the right direction."

He kept walking.

She drove next to Him at His same pace. A crestfallen melody played from her car speakers.

"Are you really providing a soundtrack to my sadness, Dani?"

"I didn't mean to!" She laughed, turning the music off. "It was already playing."

He turned to go up a different hill.

"Wait."

He kept walking.

"I have to tell you something!" she called out.

"Tell it, then," He yelled back, continuing His ascent.

"I'm not gonna just shout it, okay?"
He walked for a moment in silence.
"Text it to me."
"I might give you a kiss if you listen to what I say." His pace slowed to a stop. He sighed. He turned around and walked down the hill.
"Say it and make it quick."
"I just wanted you to know-" her periwinkle eyes moved right-upwards, and then down to Him, "-that I'm going to week-long festival out east… with Hunter…"
"Yeah, you told me," He spoke, leaning on the opened window. "Labyrinths 2011, or whatever."
"Yeah. And I am probably going to drink… and party… and smoke… okay?"
He shrugged.
"Do whatever makes you believe you're harmonious. Every part of me that cared for you belongs to you now, not me."
She smiled, leaned back in her seat, and tapped her cheek as if to receive a kiss. He looked at her lips, then her cheek, and turned around.
"Wait! One more thing!"
He began climbing the hill.
"Yoohoo!" she shouted.
He kept walking. Eventually, a motor could be heard driving away, departing with a muffled, somber melody. A motion sensor light turned on as He passed a driveway. The light beamed across His tired, low, red eyes. He entered His home, retrieved a half-consumed bottle of whiskey from the kitchen, moved into the study and sat down. He gulped down an enormous swig, wiped the glistening alcohol from His lips, pulled out a pen, reached for a stack of computer paper, and then began writing.

ALONG A WANDERING WIND

…The wind continues its flight eastward, and notices a tangled web of worries in the mind of a young girl, and searches to find her. The sun is almost setting. The sky is a deeply bruised purple which shadows over South Hampton,

Long Island. As the wind moves towards the house where music is playing, it notices a single boy in a charcoal windbreaker and plaid shorts sitting outside on the off-white wooden steps. His hand squeezes his cellphone so tightly that the phone makes creaking noises.

"Why would you say that to me?" the boy's voice comes out like a shiver. "You know that makes me miserable."

The wind wishes it had the ability to explore the boy, but it knows it cannot turn around, so it moves forward, searching the party for the girl with strange worries spiraling in her mind.

There she is, standing in the corner, holding a cup of water close to her body. The wind slows and focuses on this petite blonde with precious gray eyes. She is watching two twenty-year-old boys throwing ping-pong balls into black cups. 'Beirut Tournament' is written on the wall with a long list of names crossed out. Around the girl's wrist is an ash-hued Alcoholic Rehabilitation band with a faded date. Her free hand is shoved in her denim shorts pocket, twirling a faded-silver one-month sobriety chip. As usual, boys surround her with nervous glances and gravitating body language. As usual, she only half-notices, feeling only a vague sense of camaraderie, of appreciation and the potential of belonging.

She drinks from her water cup, stops, and places it down. She smiles whenever one of the boys makes a shot, and averts her eyes when the other swigs his drink. She sips again from her water cup, and then places the cup down again.

Her friend walks in. She runs across the room to the entrance and wraps excited arms around her. They laugh and catch up by the entrance. Things are getting better for her, and things are still going great for her friend.

"I'm soooo glad to see you, Katie. Look how hawt you look, too! I'm soooo glad your back," her friend says. "I was beginning to think you were going Karen on us."

"How is she doing?" Katie asks, one hand punched back into her denim pocket, twirling her coin. The image of a distant friend wobbling pathetically bubbles in her mind. "Don't know. Don't care." Her friend shrugs. "She's been lame for like forever now."

A muscular boy in a gray V-neck approaches and hands her friend a beer. She lifts it up to her lips, winks at Katie as she guzzles the drink, and walks away with the boy to another room with the bottle still in her mouth.

Katie returns to the table and notices that the game is almost over.

She lifts her cup up to her lips. She takes a sip. She pauses, completely frozen. A sip of alcohol has entered her mouth, just a small amount. Someone must have switched the drinks. Her expression becomes desperate. Her eyes tear. The music changes. A cheer roars throughout the room – someone must have won, someone must have lost – but she doesn't know. The voices in the room have become oceanic, like waves crashing into sand and pulling themselves back into the sea. She dives into the deepest amount of sadness she's ever felt, followed by a stomping regret, and sinks into a trembling uselessness. The wind listens to the words 'my fault – my fault – my fault' swell loudly over and over again in her mind, followed by breakneck-moving waves of rehabilitation, familial glares, encouraging quotes being crumpled, and a growing desire to drink...

She gently and pathetically spits the small amount back into the cup, and waits with clinging hope. But it is too late, and she knows it. She knows it only takes a drop to lose herself, and there are several in her mouth, on her tongue, already being swallowed and absorbed.

Her tears kamikaze down, and lend themselves entirely to the casual poison in her drink. Her fingers tremble as she crushes her coin morbidly.

With a sense of futility, the wind wishes it could help as it is pulled ever-eastwards...

EPILOGUE

...not find harmony, here.
How much is a life's worth? What is the cost of a human's life?
Pardon the ergodic structure of this lengthy epistle. In my circumscription, I seem to have vomited the opposite of a highlight reel in these departing contemplations. And yet... have I even managed to answer my questions?
I am more than these pages, dear reader. There is so much more before these words, in between these lines; sights and sounds and experiences; a rushing train and a golden-haired Danika sighing; a dangling crucifix and red wine and the prodigal father glaring distantly at his least favorite son; Mandy's doppelgänger offering to blow me for cocaine in the snow globe of a Boston mid-winter night and how it cracked the extant cracks in my heart; the microsecond daydream that sparked writing within me, the roommate that compelled me to continue, the ghost girl by the charitable Boston church that I could never locate again; that third swing swinging by Art's beach... endlessly interweaving associations and meanings... What do straws mean to me?
Friends, family, fascinations and foils...who of you is to blame? Who is to blame but me? Something else...
The sunset in front of me through this vast, pentagonal window: Smoke-like clouds drift across a grand canvas of colors. Darker clouds incoming. The ocean – the scrotumtightening sea - before me. Behind me, the earth and my sadness.
I must write something - I am back.
No one would know that that single dash represents over twenty minutes. No one would know that I called my mom just to hear her voice, and to tell her where I am for once. No one would know that I stepped outside of this car for the first time in hours and watched the lovely seagulls soaring above, and heard the sound of the waves streaming below, and that they together produced in my mind's eye the

memory of Selene first meeting Art and Dustin. No one would know that I had an erection. No one would know that I masturbated outside and ejaculated off this cliff and down into the ocean below. The thought that someone would catch me with my pants down alarmed me at first, and then I laughed. What an entangled series of emotions – fear, recklessness, excitement, lust and hope all blooming and shooting through the most intricate orgasm of my life. Perhaps this I should not have revealed, but it's too late. Mistakes, mistakes. I promised myself that I wouldn't make mistakes while writing this. I promised I would write slowly and not scribble anything out. Ollie told me it's tough to ejaculate when on LSD, so I guess it's out of my system.

    No one would know that when I stepped back into this car, I turned on the radio and heard 'Sunny, clear skies, a low of 68 degrees, and a cool westward breeze blowing at 5 miles per hour'.

    No one would know that I gulped the second pill. I've never written the word 'gulp'... is 'gulp' onamonapooetical? Yes. It is. Look how brainy I am.

    No one would know that the sound of a fluttering zephyr brought forth images of the harmony and disharmony, of love and hatred, of inebriation and sobriety, of life and death, of communication and miscommunications – a concatenation of images that permitted me to orchestrate the conclusion of Along a Wandering Wind on the back of my car's expired insurance papers while staring at the ocean beyond this cliff, and that I am almost gone from this world.

    Sirens cry warnings in the distance. I guess mother called father. Sweet girl, she is. Too late. I know I'm going to be gone soon. My life force has been decanted. This isn't the type of malady you can cure, pops. I guess I won't be turning 21, bro. I-

    Wow Instant coldness. Took it only minutes ago supposed to be longer but immediate numbness. Acid contra in dick oh god I am in and out of. I feel Reserection. I have a erection now and Selene's pink breasts Danika's larger breasts.

barely remember what Ive written but I think Im glad Ive written it. At least surface of waters. of what I need. What do I need? Appreciation. Of what? I don't know. I'm not sure what I've written
  7:58 59 rainy now have I of forgiveness mercy charity faith Body suffering magnanimity I feel so weak Selene Selene Selene write well Younophreniano no I give for you mother for you give not how much malady spilled I for giv farther artificer for hero stands the diseased strangers and I you brother for we not in the same language. you everyone Danika Selene Mandy If I could change you all or change me Id change my god I didnt expect shaking this much dont blame you a mome the mirrors fails Id change me My pen is windows and straws sipped oxy manupl and Seln? Warm whitness no focus
  I wish peopl world wer so different or that I could tried more
  I wish I was calm patient humble deter mined and good
  I wish I say I hurt instead of hurting others
  I wish I didn wanst so agrorant
  I wish I could still right write
  I wish I for gave more to
  I wish I had a name
  Most al I wish

July 27th 2011

  The phone rang just as the clock in His father's Manhattan office read 7:02 PM.
  "There's something wrong with our son," His mother spoke into the ear of His father. Hairs stood up on his arm as he placed his free hand on his chest, over his heart. "Did you do something to Him?"
  "What do you mean, honey?" His father questioned. "What did He do to give you the idea something is wrong?"
  "I don't know. He seemed different."
  "I don't have time for this, honey!" His father squeezed the phone tightly, hearing the plastic creak through

the receiver. "Is everything okay? Did He do something wrong?"

"Yes, because He never did a thing like this before, to call me and say that I'm 'nice'. Now, not to say He's wrong or anything close to that whatsoever at all - but - He never calls me – especially to say something nice. Now I know you are busy and I know He is sometimes a peculiar boy - but I just want to get to the bottom of this - you know - just to make sure everything's alright - you know? Hello? Yes?"

By the conclusion of His mother's first sentence, His father had already ran out of the office, towards the emergency stairs, bolted down eight flights and blasted through the glass-door entrance. By her concluding 'Yes?' His father was opening the driver's door of his BMW with the racing idea of being in Long Island before it was too late.

By 7:06, His father was racing eastwards on the Long Island Expressway on the phone with Mercedes who had tracked the car's exact coordinates through the GPS.

By 7:53, he was entering Montauk, knowing exactly where He was.

By 8:05, the storm was all around. The ocean waves clapped violently, white-capping and foaming towards the darkening skies. Thick sheets of rain fell and dripped off the navy-colored brims of officer caps. Between the currents of the storm, one clean-cut officer with the name Ledger on his badge stared with a most solemn-looking expression towards His father stepping out of his BMW and walking towards his son in the Mercedes SUV. There was almost nothing terribly dramatic about Him; it almost seemed typical that He would be sitting in that car with His face staring wide-eyed out of the window far away to some distant reality. But as His father approached the vehicle, the truth became tragically clear in His lifeless face.

By 8:08, the flooded corner of land shone with reds and blues of several police patrol cars and an extraneous ambulance. Pain, sadness, and confusion hung on the faces of the officers. His father shivered along a passing gust, wiped the tears and rainfall and wet hair strands from his woe-twisted face. He opened the car door, leaned in, and saw that on His lap was a black journal with sixty-five pages covered with His handwriting. He reached for the papers, and began reading. The first page began with an oddly-phrased statement that was large and neatly-written: '*I wish I had something more than words to make you understand all of this, but…*'

The last page – which was tightly packed with small, panicked letters – concluded mid-sentence, with an 'h' which dragged off the page in a rushed and fading curlicue.

Next to these eight pages was the car's expired insurance, and written upon the certificate in an almost illegible handwriting were the words:

ALONG A WANDERING WIND

…*The wind blasts forward, nearing the ocean-side cliff of Montauk Point – the eastern-most part of Long Island – and faces the brilliant sunset. A perfect spectrum has painted itself above the setting sun which rests directly atop the ocean-line. Two massive black clouds stretch towards each other on the distant horizon, and like curtains closing, come together and darken the brilliance.*

Suddenly draped in shade, the wind sprints towards the edge of the cliff and leaps off, diving towards the sands and water far below. It picks up speed, bolting passed the disgruntled sun-tanners shivering now in the shade, and passing swimmers, surfers, and sailors coming in to avoid the impending tempest. It zips through the assemblage of uniquely brooding minds, many of whom considering this gale-force gust is a harbinger of a deathly tempest. The wind accelerates and accelerates, roaring ever-eastward. Drops of rain trickle from the sky and are slapped forward powerfully by the wind's increasingly brute force.

Lightning flashes above. The wind laughs as its own crashing power muffles out the booms of thunder above. This is a speed only few winds have felt.

It laughs and laughs, saturates with rain, and spins in increasingly wet cyclones. The wind's arms and fingers sweep the air and ripple powerfully through the ocean surface. A thought flashes in the wind's consciousness: It believes that if it were human right now it might feel threads

of their nostalgia... for winds are like humans: They can experience an event, view it, learn from it, and understand it – but they can never go back to it.
   And then the wind vanishes into the dimming nothingness with an evanescent *WSHHH-*

Special Thanks to...

James Joyce's *Ulysses* and *A Portrait of the Artist as a Young Man*, **Homer's** *The Odyssey*, and **Oscar Wilde's** *The Picture of Dorian Gray* (the four texts upon which this novel is most directly grounded);

E. L. Doctorow's *Ragtime* for various naming conventions, **Allen Ginsberg's** *Howl* and **Vladimir Nabokov's** *Pale Fire* for poetical inspirations, **F. Scott Fitzgerald's** *Tender is the Night* for putting me in a psychological mood and providing me with a blank page to begin answering how much a life is worth on that near-merciless October day in 2011, **Edik Bagdassarian** (and the entire staff at *HetQ*) for helping me extinguish my Old Self, and **Zacharius Ursinus** (and the entire theological faculty at the University of Heidelberg) for authoring *The Heidelberg Catechism* (upon which the psychiatrist's dialogues with Him is grounded, though in reverse);

Émile Durkheim, Michel Foucault, Sigmund Freud, Carl Jung, Ivan Pavlov, B. F. Skinner, John Turner, Helene Deutsch, Mary Ainsworth, Charles Cooley, D. W. Winnicot, George Herbert Meade, Abraham Maslow, Urie Bronfrenbrenner, Laurence Steinberg, and **Robert Stickgold** for their contributions to our understanding of the human mind and the mind of society;

Dr. Louis Najarian, Dr. Joel Seltzer, Dr. Dalia Gefen, and **Dr. Roger Wolfsohn** for their psychological prowess; and **Dr. Nico Israel** and **Dr. Christina Alfar** for their literary knowledge;

Dr. Bassem Masri and **Christopher Yagliyan** for their medical advice; **Sarik Kumar** and **Ian Andrus** for their musical guidance; **Celine Ghazarian, Stefano Moutafidis,** and **Kalliopi Cabarcas** for their help with various translations; **Sabah Mehjabeen** at **The Tab, Mohammed Saleheen** at **NYside,** and **Fayna Pearlman** for too much to summarize;

Haig Agdere, Zachary Doe, Danielle Hacet, Sardar Singh, Sarah Singer, and **Rachel Lissandrello** for being lovely editors;

Pink Floyd for producing that sound that colors make when tightly tangled, **Chet Baker** for being the voice of blue on an autumn day, and **Lizzie Manibasse,** who will inherit this world soon.

And, most importantly, to my family, to my closest friends, and to all the other characters of my life who together forged enough light to cast shadows potential for a caricature.

Manufactured by Amazon.ca
Bolton, ON